I0591648

Secrets & Spires

DOMINIC N. ASHEN

4 Horsemen
Publications, Inc.

Secrets & Spires
Copyright © 2022 Dominic N. Ashen. All rights reserved.

4 Horsemen Publications, Inc.

4 Horsemen Publications, Inc.
1497 Main St. Suite 169
Dunedin, FL 34698
4horsemenpublications.com
info@4horsemenpublications.com

Cover by 4 Horsemen Publications, Inc.
Typeset by Autumn Skye
Edited by Tilda M. Cooke

All rights to the work within are reserved to the author and publisher. No part of this publication may be reproduced, stored in a retrieval system, or transmitted in any form or by any means, electronic, mechanical, photocopying, recording, scanning, or otherwise, except as permitted under Section 107 or 108 of the 1976 International Copyright Act, without prior written permission except in brief quotations embodied in critical articles and reviews. Please contact either the Publisher or Author to gain permission.

All characters, organizations, and events portrayed in this novel are either products of the author's imagination or are used fictitiously. All brands, quotes, and cited work respectfully belongs to the original rights holders and bear no affiliation to the authors or publisher.

Library of Congress Control Number: 2022931313

Print ISBN: 978-1-64450-508-3
Hardcover ISBN: 978-1-64450-598-4
Audio ISBN: 978-1-64450-506-9
Ebook ISBN: 978-1-64450-507-6

Table of Contents

The City of Pákannon

"Looking to the Future,
Remembering the Past"

Map Key

1. Central Bonfire
2. Sheriff's Office
3. Council House
4. Willowtree Inn
5. Tsula's Home
6. Post Office
7. General Store
8. Pákannon Mines
9. Cave to Karthani
10. Road to Onyx Spires
11. Road to Tah'lj
12. Road to Rakatune

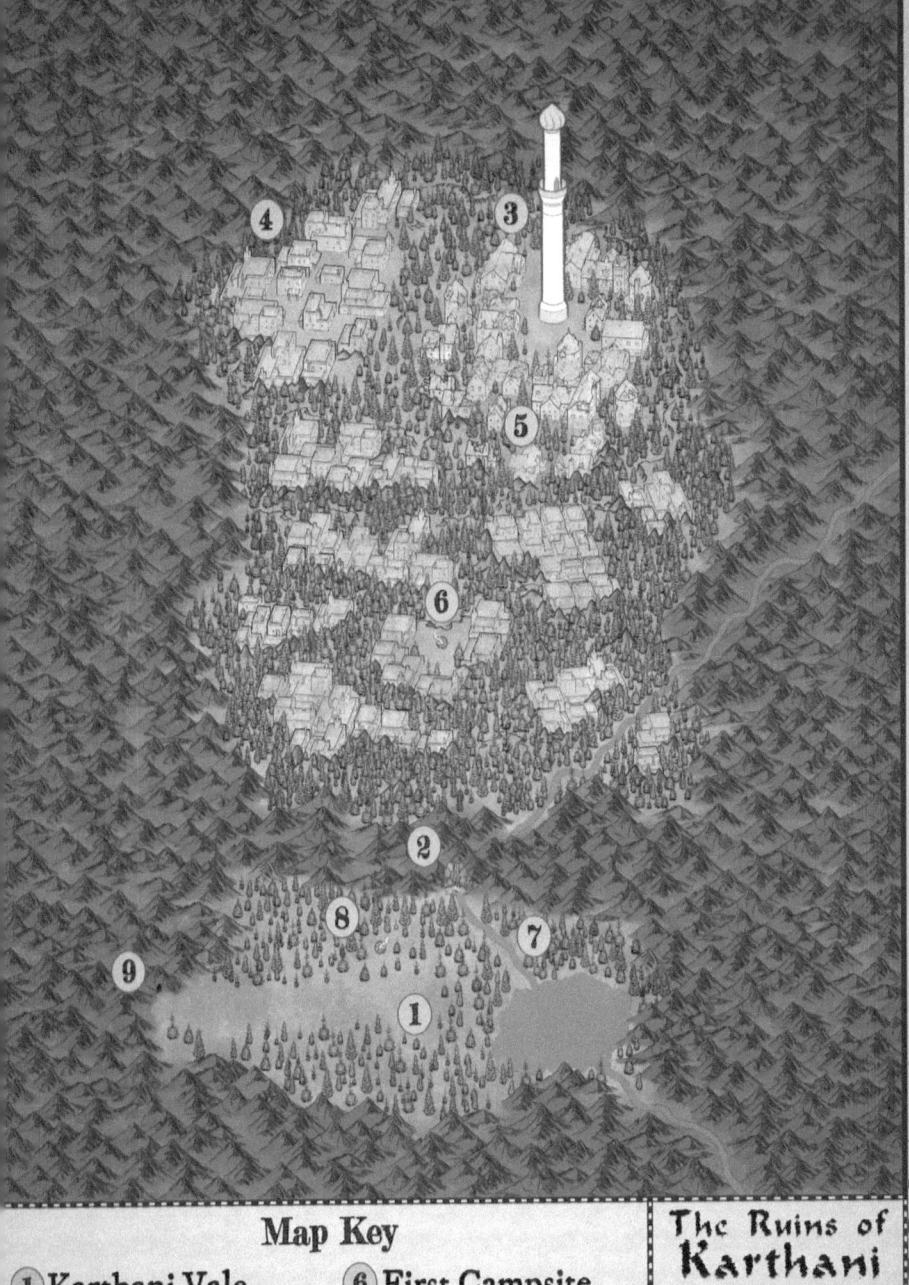

Map Key

1. Karthani Vale
2. Waterfall Entrance
3. The White Tower
4. Old Marketplace
5. Upper Class Neighborhood Ruins
6. First Campsite
7. Bathing Area
8. Second Campsite
9. Cave to Pákannon

The Ruins of Karthani

Dedication

To Jason, for always supporting and cheering me on. You really know how to make a pup feel loved.

Chapter 1

"NO!" I cry out as the sword plunges into David's chest.

He looks down in shock as the blade is removed, blood already pouring from the wound. He stumbles backward into the altar, struggling to hold himself upright, red pooling in the corners of his mouth as he tries to breathe. He collapses atop it, arm reaching out for me blindly, and I fight against my captor as the light fades from his eyes.

I cease my struggling, the fight draining out of me like the blood from David's body. Tonight, I have been shot with arrows, poisoned, and beaten, but none of that compares to the emptiness I feel at his loss. It is as though part of me died with him. As I stare numbly at his corpse, I can hear Redwish and Murbank arguing off to the side, drawing my attention.

"What do you think you are doing?!" Murbank shouts at the other man in robes. "Now the weapon and the altar are tainted! This could ruin everything!"

"So clean it up." Redwish turns his gaze to me, the crimson-stained weapon clattering to the ground when he drops it. He stalks over to me, a look of evil determination in his eyes as he sneers down, grabbing me by the hair roughly to look at him. "You are lucky you have not outlived your usefulness just yet. Otherwise, you would be joining your pet there on the altar."

I do not have a retort; I wish he had killed me. Just as I resign myself to whatever fate awaits me, the sounds of thunder crashing *outside the cavern grow louder and more frequent. Then the room, no, the entire mountain begins to shake, before an arc of lightning shoots down through the ceiling and strikes David's body. It convulses on the altar before the surge of electricity is gone as suddenly as it appeared, the entire room going silent.*

And then David moves.

"Impossible," Redwish mutters on my left.

I am unsure of what he means by that, but by the time I turn to look at him, he has already fled. Turning back to David, I watch as he pushes himself off of the altar. He looks around the room briefly before silently bending over to pick up the discarded sword. His face, passive until now, twists into something filled with rage, like a wild animal. He locks eyes with one of the cult members and leaps forward. Then the screaming starts.

I wake in our tent with a start, cursing to myself quietly as I sit up. *Spirits be damned.* That is now the *third* time I have had that dream, which is every night since leaving the city. I only have myself to blame as I continue to replay the events over in my mind every night before bed. I cannot help it. I am trying to find answers. That is the entire reason I am out here.

Well, not the *entire* reason. Turning to my right, I look over at the *real* reason I am out here: David. He is on his side, facing away from me, no longer playing the little spoon now that I am sitting up. He is still asleep, and I watch his chest rise and fall, unable to prevent myself from checking that he is still breathing. I just need to be sure.

Not quite ready to return to dreamland, I watch over my *avakesh* as he rests, smiling to myself as I tuck a shaggy lock of black hair behind his ear. I will have to see about getting him a haircut when we reach Pákannon. Some people might find it hard to believe that I gave up my entire life to follow the human currently drooling into his pillow.

I never expected to fall in love with him or that he would love me back. After everything I did to him, I am shocked he was even able to forgive me. I understand that we were both tricked, manipulated by Redwish into accepting a fight with terms and consequences that neither of us truly understood, but to think that I would be capable of forcing myself on someone like that at all... Let us just say that I have my own reasons for wanting to hunt the man down.

David *did* forgive me, though, and I will not take that forgiveness for granted. Leaving everything behind to come with him was not a difficult decision at all. My best friend, Ragnar, and his boy, Nylan, were urging me to leave before I had even made up my own mind, and Brull laughed and asked if there was anything from his store I wanted to bring with me. Even my family did not seem surprised when I rushed in to announce my immediate departure. My sister Ayla was far more shocked that I was handing her the keys to my home. *I really hope she is looking after it properly. Did I remember to tell her about the monthly butcher delivery?*

I shake the unnecessary thoughts from my head. If there is anything important I need to tell her, I can write a letter, but there is little to be done about it now. Not only is it the middle of the night, but we are still two days away from Pákannon. We have much more important things to worry about than a delivery of meat, like namely what caused David to be resurrected in the first place. Not that we seek to undo it, of course, but learning how it happened may be the only way to discover if the spell changed anything else about him as well as ensure that he will not suffer any aftereffects.

The leaders of Pákannon, as well as some of Nylan's family, should be anticipating our arrival. The former should have information for us, while the latter is more of a social call. I have not met Nylan's family aside from his mother and father, but I am sure they are as hospitable as he is. And since we have been making such good time on the road the past few days, I have been able to plan out a small surprise for David and his friends. It is just a small detour to—

A sound of distress pulls me from my thoughts, and I look down to see a frown growing on David's face with more unhappy noises following. He starts to move as though he is struggling before he finally says something coherent.

"No... Stop..." he whines as he flips onto his back, still fighting against an invisible force.

"David." I try to gently shake him awake. "David, wake up. *David.*"

A final shake to his shoulder finally gets him to open his eyes, fear and confusion flashing across his face. He stares blindly around the tent, and I curse myself for not remembering that he is unable to see in the dark like myself. I place my hand gently on his chest before continuing.

"It is only me, pup," I tell him softly. "You were having another nightmare."

"Khazak? Sir?" he asks, sounding small and afraid.

"I am right here." I lay back down and pull my distressed boy against my chest, running my hand down his back. "You are alright."

"...so much blood..." he mumbles against my skin.

I do not need to ask what the nightmare was about. David has been relieving the events of that night himself, much more viscerally, from what I can gather. Enough to wake himself with a scream two nights ago that left him unable to return to sleep at all. Given that my trauma over the events pales in comparison to his, I have neglected to tell him of my own nightmares. I do not want to give him something else to worry about.

Thankfully, David does not appear to have any issues falling asleep again tonight. About ten minutes after waking, I feel his heartbeat slow and his breathing even out as he drifts off again against my chest. I follow him not long after, holding him close in a silent plea to fend off any more bad dreams.

I wake the next morning to a finger gently tracing the tattoo on my chest, a jagged-edged sword that is the emblem of my family, Clan Ironstorm. I open my eyes, still heavy with leftover sleep, to meet David's, green and full of energy. I must admit, it has taken some getting used to having a bedmate who is more often than not awake before I am. Before David, the only person I knew to do that was my father, Orlun. If not for the fact that he has been like this since I first met him, I would be concerned it was a side-effect of the nightmares, but I have not yet noticed David ever appearing tired in the mornings. *Aside from one near-hangover.*

"Good morning." I smile, my voice rough from disuse.

"Morning." He gives me a shy smile in return, far shyer than he has any right to be, but damn if he does not look adorable.

"Any more bad dreams?" I ask, running my hand through his hair.

"No, Sir." He shakes his head. "Only been up a little while."

I relish his use of my honorific, something that is sadly more relegated to the privacy of our tent these days. As much as I miss it (and could order him to use it, should I truly desire), I understand that David is still learning to be comfortable with our relationship in front of his friends. It takes him considerable effort to work up the nerve for public displays of affection of any kind, and I can see him trying, so I feel he has more earned my patience in the "Sir" department. Besides, there are *many* ways to ensure he does not forget who is in charge here.

"Glad to hear it, pup." I bend down, kissing the top of his head. "Ready for breakfast?"

"Yessir. Gotta pee!" The human quickly wiggles out of my grasp, making me laugh as he reaches for his pants.

As silly as his antics are, I am warmed by the thought that he did not want to leave the tent—and me—until I woke up. Needing to exit for the same reasons, I reach for my own pants and sling my bag over my shoulder, following David out of the tent. A brief look around reveals no one else by the fire except for Elisabeth. She had the final watch shift last night, so she has likely been awake for the last hour.

"Good morning, Elisabeth." I wave as I head toward the forest to relieve myself.

"Good morning, Khazak." She waves back. "And I keep telling you, it's just 'Liss.'"

I nod my head with a chuckle. Between Elisabeth's request and David's own issues around his name, I cannot help but wonder if all humans are this finicky about their names. Or perhaps it is only the Lutherians. I like Elisabeth—sorry, *Liss*, so it is something I will endeavor to remember. She is strong, and from what I remember of our first meeting, more than able to handle herself in a fight. She appeared to have brown hair then, but during her time as a detainee, the original red began to show at the roots. Rather than dyeing it again, she had the remaining brown cut off. Her hair is shorter than mine or David's right now.

Out of all of David's companions, she is the quietest, though that silence belies a level of attention that some of my former colleagues would envy. I do not yet know her very well, but I have seen her reacting to sounds and motions in the trees so subtle I was sure no one but myself would notice, and she regularly scans our camp's perimeter when the group is gathered by the fire. Having spent almost a decade patrolling the forests of my hometown of V'rok'sh Tah'lj as a ranger, I understand how important it is to always be aware of your surroundings. Even when doing the most mundane of tasks, you must remain constantly vigilant—always listening for the unexpected, looking for any potential entrances or exits, ready to react at a moment's notice. It can be exhausting, which is all the more reason to be impressed with Liss. Had she been living in Tah'lj, she would have made an excellent ranger herself.

I find David behind a tree far enough from camp to garner some privacy, exhaling in relief as he empties his bladder. I find my own tree, and when we are finished tucking ourselves away, I grab him by the shoulder before he tries to head back to camp. With a grumble, he accepts one of the toothbrushes I pull from my bag, and when we are finished with those, we use my water flask to rinse. I am not sure what his dental hygiene was like before my arrival, but I am going to ensure that neither of us loses any teeth while on the road.

"Ready for breakfast?" I ask as we return to camp.

"Always, Sir." He rubs his stomach dramatically. "What are we having?"

"I believe there are still fish from yesterday's catch." *Though I am planning to do some hunting later today.* "I thought I would grill some of those with a few potatoes."

Since joining, I have done the bulk of the cooking for the group. I do not mind; between what my father Rurig taught me and having spent one week a month camping in the forest for nearly a decade, I am fairly talented when it comes to cooking outdoors. However, I always make sure someone else is assisting me, doing my best to pass along my skills to the rest of them. There are more important things for me to do on this journey than act as the group chef.

"Aww, you're not gonna pull out any of the good stuff?" David frowns while looking at my bag.

The "good stuff" he is referring to are the contents of my spacious satchel. Thanks to its magical properties, it can not only hold much more than it appears, but it also places every item inside into a form of stasis, allowing for the storage of things like meat or fresh fruit, items that would normally spoil if left out. Before I left the city, I emptied the contents of my icebox and pantry into my bag. I had only just gotten a delivery from the butcher a few days prior to leaving: beef, venison, and the item that David is most likely referring to—bacon.

Having made my decision to leave rather hastily, I knew time was of the essence, so I grabbed the meat, vegetables, spices, and anything else edible that I could find. I even brought my enchanted kettle, a pleasant surprise for everyone on our first morning together. But with my exit being so sudden, I had to spend an evening hunched over my journal with a pen, making a list of everything I brought so as not to forget what I had placed in there. I was once missing a shirt for three years all because I forgot I had put it inside my satchel and never bothered trying to retrieve it.

"I told you, pup, as I no longer have a butcher *or* regular source of income, we will be rationing all of the 'good stuff' for the time being." I made a sizable withdrawal from my savings in the Bank of V'rok'sh Tah'lj before my exit, but it is still a finite amount of money. "But if you can continue to behave the rest of the journey to Pákannon, there may be a bacon-flavored reward in your future."

"I always behave, Sir," he repeats his favorite lie, speaking low as we reenter camp.

The rest of the group has begun to wake, Adam stretching his limbs as he exits his tent. Nathaniel is sitting inside the tent he shares with Elis—Liss, watching as the woman in question tends to the fire. She appears to already be preparing it to be cooked over, concentrating all of the burning coals and embers into one location for my skillet. Corrine's tent is still closed, though I suspect she is awake and merely saying her morning prayers, as I have overheard mornings past.

David and I return to our tent to finish dressing. He strips down once we are inside, waiting for the next part of our morning ritual. It may seem silly, insignificant, or even perverted to others, but it is one I have come to treasure: selecting his underwear for the day. I choose a green jockstrap, one I originally selected due to how well it pairs with his eyes. I also just love having him wear something so revealing under his clothing and armor. I own a few pairs myself, though my undergarments are usually more along the lines of a simple loincloth, subligar, or even the occasional brief. Watching David pulling the waistband up over the swell of his ass, I am reminded of the day we bought them.

It was only his second day with me, and we still had not quite made peace with each other yet. He was mortified as he modeled each pair for me and my friend, Brull, but his slight erection told me he did not entirely hate it. His subsequent panic attack and escape attempt notwithstanding, I would like to think we still had fun on that day, but I was not the one tricked into enslavement. This is something David looks forward to now—I can tell by the way he enjoys teasing me as he slips them on—but it is hard not to feel a twinge of guilt over the ritual's origins.

Ignoring the negative parts of the memory, we finish dressing and exit the tent, ready to begin cooking. I place a cast-iron pan onto the fire to begin heating while I remove the remaining fish from my bag. With a pair of small knives at the ready, Elisabeth and I set to work cleaning them. Just as I start adding items to the skillet, Corrine emerges from her tent, and after greeting us with a cheerful "good morning!" she excuses herself to take care of her own needs. When she returns to the group a few minutes later, she sits down on a fallen log arranged not far from the fire.

"Alright David, time for your check-up!" She pats the spot next to her.

"Do we really have to keep doing this?" he complains, though when he looks to me for support and finds only a cocked eyebrow, he moves to the requested seat. "I feel fine, and besides, I was brought back to life with *magic*."

"We still don't actually know *how* you were resurrected. You were also unconscious for four days, which isn't good in any situation," she reasons with him. "Come on. We all just want to make sure you're okay. Once we get to Pákannon, we can have the healer there look you over, and once *they* give you a clean bill of health, no more morning check-ups! Promise."

"Fine," David says with a sigh, but it is the small smile he wears that gives away the contentment he feels at being looked after like this. *My pup is softer than he would have people believe.*

Corrine quickly runs through a few basic tests—pulse, eyesight, and hearing—before moving on to a quick scan of his body for any lingering magical effects. David's body glows as her spell passes through him, and when it is finished, she smiles. "All clear!"

I appreciate her taking her duty as team healer so seriously as David requires a firm hand. Though I have yet to see how the blonde handles herself in combat, Corrine has proven to be quite capable at healing, both with and without magic. She is the second quietest member of the group after Elisabeth, though it seems to be more out of politeness than any stoicism. She is also the most religious of the group, though other than the necklace she keeps tucked into her robe, overheard prayers, and the blessing she says to herself before meals, I have not noticed many outward expressions of her beliefs at all.

It is a pleasant surprise. My past experiences with Lutherian colonists, especially the religious ones, have not been all that positive. Truth be told, those experiences combined with the fact that our first meeting was an all-out brawl made me very nervous to set out with not one but *five* Lutherians. So far though, everything has gone smoothly.

After David is released from his medical exam, it is only a few more minutes before breakfast is done. Corrine cheerfully assists me and Elisabeth in passing out breakfast using the bowls and outdoor cutlery I packed, an amenity the group had not previously considered. Honestly, I have no idea how these humans managed to survive this long on their own.

After we have finished breakfast, it is time to pack up camp and begin our journey for the day. Corrine volunteers herself and Nathaniel to clean our dishes and utensils in the nearby river while the rest of us work to break down the tents. The one I share with David is the largest, brought from my own home. Thanks to my satchel, it is also technically the lightest, though it does not leave me with room to carry much else. It is not as nice or spacious as the tent I used when I was captain of the rangers, but it suits our needs just fine.

The three other tents are practically identical, only differing in the amount of wear their occupants have inflicted on them. Corrine has a tent to herself, her personal items already packed and laid to the side. Elisabeth shares her tent with Nathaniel, though she appears to take most of the responsibility in its construction and transportation. Adam occupies the final tent on his own, though prior to my arrival, he had been sharing with David. I doubt he minds having the extra space to himself, and I do not think David minds his new bedmate either. I certainly do not.

Adam is the team's leader. Tall, muscular, blonde—I would be lying if I said the man was not attractive. He is also confident, charismatic, and mature—that last bit is especially important, seeing as he is *eight* years my junior. The entire group is. I was not ecstatic about agreeing to follow the leadership of someone so much younger than myself, but thus far he has proven to be more than competent.

There is also the matter of him being David's best friend, so though I would not admit it out loud, part of me also just wants the man to like me. Shortly after I joined, David shared with me that some of Adam's interests may align more closely with ours than I thought, something I am curious to learn more about for myself as we travel together. I am always on the lookout for new ways I can tease and torment my puppy.

The campfire extinguished and the tents broken down quickly, everyone is collecting their personal items and preparing for the day's journey when Corrine and Nathaniel return. Corrine moves to gather her things while Nathaniel brings the stack of bowls and forks to me.

Nathaniel is an interesting fellow, and the last member of our group. With his shaggy and unkempt brown hair, unevenly stubbled face, and a general lack of concern about his appearance, I can assure you I do not share the same feelings of attraction I have for Adam. Although I do understand how difficult it is to maintain a beard while on the road.

The man is an arcane mage, a wizard in his own words, though I do not have an exact read on his skill level yet. He was sufficiently powerful enough to have sent several of the rangers serving under me to the healers, but we have not yet fought a battle on the same side. He is polite enough, and I cannot say I fully understand the level of disdain David seems to hold for the man.

"Here you go." The mage hands the stack of bowls to me.

"Thank you, Nathaniel." I return the bowls to my bag.

"David, what the hell kind of underwear are you wearing?" I look up abruptly at the sound of Nathaniel's mocking tone.

His eyes are on David, who is bent over packing up one of the tents. His shirt is riding up, and the green strap of his jock is visible just above the top of his pants. His form freezes at the man's comment, rising to his feet a second later and turning around. If he felt embarrassed, it is gone now, looking more annoyed than anything.

"I don't know, Nate. Why are you staring my ass?" he asks while wearing an annoyed smirk.

"I'm not—! I wasn't—!" the mage sputters. *Alright, perhaps I understand David's feelings a little.*

"Nate, stop staring at David's ass and finish packing so we can leave," Liss orders her beau without missing a beat, the man moving to help her with a grumble.

Once we have everything together, bags are loaded onto backs, and we begin the day's journey. We are walking a well-traveled road, so there is little chance of actual danger, but we still travel two by two in a defensive formation. Adam and Elisabeth are in front, followed by the two spellcasters, with David and me bringing up the rear. I am quite happy with our positioning, as with Liss in front and myself in the back, our scouting needs are covered. I am also happy because since we are behind everyone else, I get to walk with David with a small amount of privacy.

"David, I wanted to talk to you about your nightmares," I speak low, knowing he will not want the rest of the group to hear.

"What about them?" he answers tersely, his posture stiffening as he walks.

"You have been having them every night since you left the city." *We both have.* "We have not spoken about them, or even what happened that night, since you woke up."

"What's there to talk about?" He is looking straight ahead as he speaks, hands clenching.

I do not know: the fear, the trauma, the way you cannot so much as look at the sword you carry on your back without flinching? Of course, I do not actually say any of that. "I just think that talking about it might help. It is—"

"I told you, I'm *fine*, Khazak," he snaps, loud enough for Corrine to turn her head around toward us in question.

I give her an apologetic look, mentally sighing at David's refusal to discuss what is bothering him. I also add ten to his spanking demerits for the day, something I will tell him about later when he is feeling a little less raw. It has been difficult getting him to talk about what happened: being kidnapped, tortured, and having some of your friends and colleagues die while barely saving another. Then being killed himself, and the bloodbath that came after he was resurrected. He is not the only one who needs to talk about things. I may need to consider a different tactic.

I understand his feelings, quite well in fact. When I was younger, my parents made the very ill-advised decision to leave me home alone with my siblings during a very dangerous time. They thought I was mature enough to handle the responsibility, but it took quite a bit of counseling before I was able to really process my feelings about what happened. David is much older than I was then, but I believe dealing with feelings like those he is experiencing is uncharted territory for him.

Not that it excuses him for snapping at me. Nightmares or not, I am still his *kavan*, his owner, and he knows I expect at least a *modicum* of respect when being spoken to. He is lucky he is only getting is ten; any worse and that promised reward of bacon would be off the table as well. It is not even ten-o-clock yet. *Getting started early today.*

I have a few hours to contemplate the best time to dish out said punishment before we stop for lunch. We do not bother with a full camp, only a small fire to cook the last of our fish. While they grill over the fire, we pass the time with a little sparring. The group has not seen any combat yet, and that will hopefully continue, but you can never be too prepared. Some members of the group need it more than others; I have a distinct memory of a certain blonde-haired priestess doing more running than fighting the last time I saw her in battle.

Adam and Elisabeth have paired up, both trained sword fighters. Adam fights with a one-handed broadsword and shield in a style not unlike my own: defensive, studying his opponent for any weaknesses before striking. We fought once before in the Temple of Zeus ruins, which led to his team's arrest. Considering how outnumbered they were, he did a very good job holding his own. Elisabeth wields a two-handed longsword, which is the same weapon I favor, though her fighting style is much more aggressive. The two are an even match for each other, though they have also clearly fought together for years.

David is also a warrior, having attended the same "knight academy" as Adam and Elisabeth. I am still not entirely sure I understand what being a "knight" entails, but I can say they do not lack in combat training. David tells me he used to fight with a sword and shield like Adam but now prefers to wield a sword in each hand. The style suits him since he possesses both the speed and reflexes to deflect blows as quickly as he can strike with his own. He has actually been carrying three swords on his back for the last few days, but he only uses two of them to fight. The third is the same sword that ended his life and is linked to his subsequent resurrection, a fact which I suspect is the reason he has yet to wield it. *Something else he will not talk about.*

The remaining members of our group, Corrine and Nathaniel, have little-to-no practical combat experience. They both wield large walking staffs, which they could do considerable damage with when used correctly, so I have taken it upon myself to impart some basic lessons in fighting and self-defense. David is assisting, having paired off with Corrine while I teach Nathaniel.

"No, you need to grip it lower; otherwise, there will not be enough force behind your blows." It is going...alright.

"Like this?" The mage comes at me again.

"Better," I tell him. "Once more. Do not be afraid to hit me. I am more than capable of defending myself."

To my left, David is faring much better with Corrine. She is in the middle of using her staff to deflect David's strikes when a loud *snap* followed by an animal's cry has the entire group freezing.

"What was that?" Adam asks.

"A wolf from the sound of it." I pause, hearing faint whimpers of pain coming from the forest. "Injured, though I am not sure by what."

"I think I hear it, too." David squints into the forest. *That is curious.* The only reason I can hear it is my orc biology granting me larger ears and enhanced hearing.

"Should we check it out?" Elisabeth asks, already reaching for her weapon.

"Just to be safe." Adam does the same as he turns to me. "Khazak, will you lead the way?"

I nod and arm myself, the group entering the forest in reverse order with David and me in front. We make it around twenty meters before the animal's cries are loud enough for the rest of the group to hear, and another thirty before we find the source among the trees: a young, black-furred wolf with its front paw caught in the jaws of a large metal trap. Sensing our approach, it turns to face us as best it can, whimpers of pain morphing into growls. The group pauses, fanning out and stowing our weapons but still leaving distance between us and the wolf.

"That's not one of the wolves from before, is it?" David asks immediately upon seeing the color of its fur, thinking back to the three wolves that attacked the two of us over a month ago when we were patrolling the forest. Due to an ill-timed tumble into a patch full of paralytic flowers, we nearly did not survive, but thanks to David's stubbornness, he managed to protect us both.

"No, this one is much younger." Only one of those wolves survived to get away.

"Is that a bear trap?" Adam asks, looking at its caught paw.

"It would appear so." The trap is made of two half circles, the inner edges jagged like two rows of sharp teeth, a bloody grin clamped on the poor animal's leg.

"Where did it come from?" David asks next.

"Well, seeing as these did not exist on our shores prior to the Lutherian settlements being built..." I turn to give David and the other humans an unimpressed look.

"...Oh." David scratches his head sheepishly. "Sorry."

"What do we do?" Adam moves past the awkwardness. "Do we...let nature take its course?"

"I don't think a bear trap counts as nature," Nathaniel snarks.

"So what, we put it out of its misery?" Elisabeth asks with some measure of hesitation.

"I do not think it needs to come to that." *That was rather fast to reach the 'put out of its misery' stage of things, but at least they mean well.* "I would normally agree with you Adam, but Nathaniel is correct. This hardly counts as natural." I turn to our healer. "Corrine, do you think you could try putting it to sleep?"

"Hmm. It might be too scared or in too much pain, but I can try." She looks at the wolf, nodding.

"I may be able to help with that." I step toward the wolf, motioning for Corrine to follow while the rest of the group stays back to watch. The wolf's growls grow louder as we approach, wide amber eyes nervously flicking back and forth between me and the cleric.

"I am going to try to calm it," I tell Corrine as I drop to one knee once we are close enough. "Then, if you are able to put it to sleep, we should be able to free it."

Corrine nods, and I take a moment to clear my mind before locking eyes with the wolf. Tentatively, I push out with my magic, reaching for the animal's aura with mine. There's a moment of recognition when they finally touch, the creature's fight or flight instinct flashing from its mind to mine. The longer we stay connected, the longer I can feel its emotions: its anger and pain, its hunger, its loneliness. Eyes still locked, I try to match my breathing to the wolf's, projecting feelings of peace. It takes a few minutes, but eventually the wolf begins to calm, its back legs dropping to lay flat.

With my part done, it is now Corrine's turn. Copying me and dropping to her knee, she reaches into the collar of her robes to free the necklace around her neck. It is her spell focus, a symbol of her god that she uses to channel her magic, in this instance a golden dove. Holding the chain out in front of her, she allows the focus to dangle between her fingers and begins to sway it back and forth. As the wolf turns its eyes to this new movement, Corrine hums what I can only assume is a lullaby. Both the focus and the wolf's eyes start to glow an almost unearthly white. The wolf's eyes begin to drop, and it sinks to the ground as it succumbs to the spell and falls asleep.

"Wonderful work, Corrine." I stand, dusting off my knee and helping Corrine to do the same.

"Thank you, Khazak, you as well." She offers me a small curtsy.

With the wolf unconscious, it is safe to move in close, where I can see she is a young female. Very thin too. I think back to the wolves I last saw with David. They were also hungry and far from their normal hunting grounds. *Could they be from the same pack?* Black wolves are not the most common sight, so to come across four in such a short period of time leads me to believe something is wrong.

"Alright, I am going to hold open the trap." I kneel down again, finding the best way to get a hold of the trap's jaws. "While I do that, can you free its paw?"

"Got it." Corrine nods, moving into position and putting one hand on the wolf's upper leg.

Making sure my fingers are free of any jagged points, I pry apart the metal mandibles. It is not impossible, but it does take some strength, and from this angle, I am not able to open it all the way. As soon as the space is wide enough, Corrine pulls the wolf free. With the trap still in my hand, I stand, taking a few steps away before quickly and carefully releasing the trap in front of me, watching it slam shut as it falls to the ground.

"I cannot stand things like this," I say aloud to no one in particular, kicking the closed trap with my foot. "Aside from the fact that *anyone* could have stumbled on it and gotten hurt, it is also an incredibly cowardly way to hunt. If you refuse to give your kill a fighting chance, at least have the courage to look it in the eye."

"At least it was the wolf and not us," David adds, sounding like he may be resentful of the entire species.

"I don't think anything's broken; I should be able to heal him just fine." I turn to see Corrine is still kneeling by the unconscious wolf, inspecting her injured leg.

"Her, actually." I look down and the poor injured pup. "She is young, too young to be on her own. She should not be in this area either; she belongs farther north. Something must have happened to her pack to drive her down here."

"You said the same thing about the other wolves," David remembers as well. "Think it's related?"

"Perhaps." I kneel down to look over the wolf as Corrine works her magic, hands glowing as they are placed over the injured leg. When she pulls away, the only indication of an injury is the small amount of dried blood stuck to the wolf's fur.

"Good as new!" She stands cheerily.

"Great job, both of you." Adam steps forward, not able to do anything but watch with the rest of the team. "Should we do anything else? Leave her some food or something?"

"Food might attract other predators while she sleeps." I stand and look around us for a good spot with cover, hiding the wolf's sleeping form under the brush. "She should be safe there until she wakes up."

"What do we do with the trap?" Nathaniel points his staff at the damned thing.

"Sell it to the blacksmith in Pákannon for scrap." I pick up the trap and squeeze it through the mouth of my satchel. "At the very least they can destroy it. I am not going to leave it out here."

"I agree with you there." Adam nods before turning to lead the group out of the forest. "Alright, let's eat and then get back on the road."

"I guess that was pretty cool, rescuing the wolf," David begrudgingly admits to me after lunch, when we are once more on the road. "Kinda hot watching you step up and take charge like that, too. Even if the last time we saw one of those things, it and its two friends tried to eat us."

I laugh at his comment. *Still resentful of the wolves, then.* "I was only doing what was right, David. Just like those wolves were only doing what their instincts told them."

"I get that, but maybe their instincts could include trying to bite fewer chunks outta my ass," he grumbles.

"Can you blame them? It is a lovely ass." I smack the rump in question, making David squawk indignantly. The combined noises cause Corrine and Nathaniel to turn and look, and I cannot help but laugh as I watch David fight the urge to rub away the sting. I reach over and pull him closer, offering a silent apology, already looking forward to the rest of our day.

Chapter 2

"**Dammit, should I have brought my bag?**" I hold in a sigh when Nathaniel speaks aloud *again*.

"I don't know, I don't *care*, but I told you that if you were going to come with us then you had to *be quiet*," Elisabeth hisses at her...lover? I am not entirely sure I understand their relationship.

"*Excuse me.* Sorry." There does not seem to be much affection.

We have finished traveling for the day, finding a good spot not far from the road to set up camp. The sun is starting to set, which means larger animals will be preparing for sleep while smaller creatures will just be waking up: a perfect time for hunting. Before I left, I extended an open invitation to anyone who wanted to join me, eager to pass along my skills to anyone willing, just as with my cooking.

David and Elisabeth I expected, but Nathaniel I did not, and I am starting to regret the invitation being so open. Adam and Corrine are working to gather wood to start the campfire before we return; perhaps Nathaniel would be better suited assisting there. In fact, I am willing to bet that he is only tagging along to get out of helping to set up camp at all, which I truly do not care about, so long as he *remains quiet*.

Pushing the frustration from my mind, I focus my senses on the forest, listening for potential prey. We are only a day out from Pákannon, so I would prefer smaller game. I do not have room in my satchel to transport anything too large and would rather not see it go to waste. With my eyes closed, I try to filter through the sounds. *There.* West by northwest, I hear something headed in our direction.

"Follow me," I whisper, leading our group closer, an area with good cover but still far enough away that we won't be noticed. The three humans are silent as we move, crouching in the brush and waiting. I have my bow out, as do David and Elisabeth, and while I doubt this is his intention, I suppose Nathaniel could *technically* use his magic.

We are waiting for a few minutes and thankfully no one has had any questions or complaints. I can still hear the animal moving closer, though it seems to be larger than I first thought. Still, may as well see what we are dealing with. It is not until I catch a glint of reflected light in the distance that I realize what the creature is.

"Is that another—" David starts as male deer with crystalline antlers, a crystal hart, passes into view.

"*Cervus crystallus,*" Nathaniel cuts him off in a breathless whisper, causing all three of us to turn to look at him. *Is that its taxonomic name?* "What?"

"You know what that is?" Elisabeth asks, voice still low.

"Yeah. I've studied all kinds of magical creatures." He turns back to the unsuspecting animal. "Never thought I'd see one of these up close, though. I should be taking notes. I *knew* I should have brought my bag."

"Wait, you actually know something *useful?*" David snarks, and I'm tempted to add another five to his demerit tally.

"I know it's considered bad luck to kill them, so maybe put down the bow, Robin Hood," Nathaniel says with a roll of his eyes. *These two are incorrigible.*

I clear my throat loudly, turning all heads in my direction and spooking the deer enough to send it jumping into the woods, nicking one of its antlers on the side of a tree.

"If you two are finished, we still need to find dinner," I say at a normal volume, standing up straight.

"Aww, you scared it away." Nathaniel pouts.

"You just got done saying we weren't supposed to eat it." Elisabeth is ever the pragmatist.

"Hey look," David calls out, already moving ahead of us. He bends down, picking up a piece of antler that must have been chipped off when the deer scraped the tree.

"Two sightings *and* a souvenir?" I comment, staring at the prism in his palm. "That is a lot of good luck."

"Yeah, considering everything that happened after we saw the last one, I'm not so sure I believe that." He frowns slightly.

"I would say at least a few things worked out pretty well." I smile and tip his chin up, getting him to do the same.

It is Elisabeth's turn to clear her throat. "If you two are done making googly-eyes at each other, I believe we were looking for dinner?"

I chuckle while David blushes, then start listening for our next target.

"This way." I can hear what I think are rabbits just north of us.

"You know, seeing as you can't actually use magic, there's not really any point in you keeping that antler piece," Nathaniel tries convincing David to part with his prize.

"Well that sucks for you, spell-boy." David pockets the crystal gleefully. "Finders keepers."

I was right about the rabbits, which were perfect in size for eating but also much harder to catch, especially when one of your hunting partners is suddenly too reluctant to hurt the "fuzzy little bunnies." David did not strike me as an animal lover, but I suppose I have not yet seen him around very many. Elisabeth and I told him and Nathaniel to wait back while we took care of things, returning with two large rabbits as our prizes.

It was requested that I take care of the cleaning and butchering just outside of the camp, so that, to quote Elisabeth, I do not "scar Corrine with a bloody rabbit corpse." I do not mind; I brought my tools to do just such a thing. I just need to remember to clean these when we reach the city tomorrow. By the time I reenter camp, it is with a pot full of unrecognizable meat that I set on the fire.

"You're just jealous because I'm a better hunter than you." I come upon Elisabeth and David in a decidedly un-heated argument while setting up the tents.

"And *you're* just jealous cause I'm the one who gets to share a tent with a himbo," David retorts with a word I am unfamiliar with.

"What is a 'himbo?'" My question makes David jump and Elisabeth laugh.

"Oh, hey Khazak." David turns around sheepishly. "It's... uh..."

"Yeah, David, what's a 'himbo?'" Elisabeth taunts, crossing her arms.

"Am I not going to like this?" *What is he saying about me?*

"No! It just means a guy who's really strong, and nice..." *Okay, sounds good so far.* "...and kinda dumb."

"*Dumb?*" I raise an eyebrow as Elisabeth laughs louder in the background.

"Nono! Not like, *dumb* dumb!" He tries to backtrack. "I just mean that their intelligence isn't the first thing you think of."

My eyebrow goes even higher, and Elisabeth laughs even louder.

"Nope, wait, that's not what I mean either, because we both know you are *way* smarter than me." *At least now he is trying to suck up.* "I just mean someone who's not studying all the time, or doing experiments, or talking about math and junk."

"Who sits around talking about math?" Nathaniel chimes in.

"Shut up! You know what I'm trying to say!" He turns back to me. "It just means that you're not a nerd. Like..." He quickly looks around the camp before pointing at our blonde team leader setting up his own tent. "Adam. Adam's a himbo."

"I heard that," the blonde replies, his back to us, "and thank you."

"See? It's a compliment." I am not *entirely* convinced, but I do not think he is lying to me.

"So, strong, kind, and dumb... Would that not make you a himbo?" I cannot help the smirk when I ask, my question making Elisabeth laugh the loudest.

David glares at her before answering my question. "I think I'm a little too grumpy and opinionated to qualify."

"I see. Well, you are *my* himbo." I lean in to give him a kiss before whispering low enough that no one else can hear. "But I am still adding twenty for insulting my intelligence. See? Plenty of people talk about math."

When I pull away, David's face is a mixture of shocked and amused. I do love when I can turn his words around on him like that. Doubly so when I know I will get to spank him later for them.

Dinner is rabbit stew with some bread that has not yet gone stale thanks to my satchel. I am starting to feel a little like a walking icebox. I suppose I asked for it as I did offer to do additional hunting and cooking when I requested to join the group. That was partially to ingratiate me with David's friends but also because of differing nutritional needs: both mine and David's. Orcs requires more protein and iron than most other species, leading to a largely meat-based diet. Combined with my size, that means extra hunting is needed.

David's diet is still that of a human; his issue is more with quantity. He is only about a head shorter than me, but I weigh a good eighty pounds more than he does. Despite our size difference, he eats almost as much as I do, which is nearly twice that of his companions. Given that he was rather scrawny when I met him, it was surprising. What has been more surprising is how quickly he has put the weight back on. He has not reached the muscled heights of Adam or Elisabeth, but to grow so much in only two months seems almost unnatural. But I am willing to do whatever is needed to keep my pup healthy.

After dinner we have a couple of hours before bed: the perfect time to take care of someone's spanking demerits. I come up with a flimsy excuse for David to follow me into the woods—that I saw something strange on the perimeter when I was cleaning the rabbits—and he does his best not to stammer when he agrees to come with me. We are fooling absolutely no one, but I am not going to tell him that.

Once we are far enough away from human ears (at least for David's normal sex-volume), I find us a sturdy tree with a thick trunk—large enough for two bodies to somewhat hide behind. Then I put the tree between us and the camp and turn to David.

"Time for your punishment, puppy." I point to the tree. "Assume the position."

"Yes, Sir." He moves without complaint, hands already moving to unbutton his pants.

He's frowning, but there's a hint of a smile. He likes being corrected like this as much as I like correcting him, at least when it comes to minor infractions like today's. He braces both his forearms against the tree of the trunk, pushing his butt out toward me. I step up behind his bent over form, running my hands over his jock-clad rump. This green one is easily my favorite. With a quick squeeze to both cheeks, I step back, ready to begin.

"How many did you earn today?" I always keep track, but he knows that if he lies to me, I will double it.

"Twenty, Sir." He sighs.

"Correct. I am also adding ten for the way you snapped at me this morning when I tried to discuss your nightmares."

"What!? I did *not* snap at—" He cuts himself off when he looks back at my face, seeing there is no room for argument. "...Yessir."

"You do not need to count." I rub his back soothingly.

He gives a stiff nod, wanting to make as little noise as possible. And then we begin. I watch his left cheek shake after delivering the first strike. He already had a nice ass when we first met, but the recent weight gain has really done him some favors back here. There are days where I think about adding to his tally just so I have a reason to spank him.

I keep count in my head, alternating sides as I go. We make it to ten before the whimpering starts. If this were something more serious, I would be giving him a lecture right now. The nightmare issue would normally qualify, but I do not think he would respond well to that at the moment. So for now, I will keep this a simple spanking, and wait for a better opportunity to talk about the rest. Hopefully in Pákannon.

I take a break at the halfway point, allowing David a few moments to breathe and prepare for the remaining fifteen. Rubbing my hands lightly over his ass, I feel the heat rising from his inflamed skin. I reach up to clasp him gently on the back of his neck, stroking my thumb just under his ear and feeling him relax into my touch. He is beautiful when he submits. *Alright, time to finish.*

David's breath hitches when I resume the spanking, quickly delivering four alternating strikes. He fights against the urge to pull away, and I watch his flesh ripple with each blow. A small grunt accompanies each strike past twenty, and by the time we reach thirty, his fists are clenched tightly above his head. His shoulders rise and fall in time with his breath, and a small sheen of sweat has broken out on his lower back.

I stroke my hands up and down David's sides as he composes himself. When he is ready, he pushes himself off of the tree to stand. I take the opportunity to wrap my arms around him, pulling him back against my chest. He whines as his sore rump comes into contact with my pants but voices no complaints when I grind my erection against him, turning his head to the side so that my mouth can capture his in a hungry kiss. We both know we came out here for more than just a spanking.

I reach into my pocket to retrieve one of the items I brought out for this portion of the evening. It is a small, flat, round stone. Granite, I believe. It appears perfectly innocuous, but it is enchanted with a spell that aids in, well, anal intercourse. I hold the stone against David's lower stomach, which activates as we continue to kiss. The spell cast cleans out the lower end of his gastrointestinal tract, while also adding some lubricant. Overall, a very handy charm, and one whose usage I had not been keeping track of until the day after leaving, when I realized we had no idea how many charges it still held. I am hoping to find a location in Pákannon that may be able to recharge it if not sell us a new one, lest we be forced to wait even longer. Most healers should be capable but finding one who knows the spell and is willing may be difficult. Hopefully there are enough charges to last before we become desperate. I think David might have an aneurysm if I tried to ask Corrine.

Back to the matter at hand, I replace the charm in my pocket. Pausing for just a moment, I grab David's ass in both hands, squeezing roughly and pulling whimpers from my pup's throat. Removing only one hand, I retrieve the other item I brought with me: a vial of olive oil. As useful as the charm is, you really cannot ever use enough lubricant. It is another resource we will need to conserve, and one that will be up to me to look for when we stop, as David will be far too shy.

I uncork the vial, dribbling a small amount onto my fingers and pressing them into the cleft of his ass. He moans into my mouth as they seek their target, pushing back when they rub over his hole. I press them inside, as quickly and gently as I can. I would not say we are in a rush, but the longer we are away from camp, the longer David has to panic about someone knowing what we are doing. *Even though they already do.*

It takes only a moment for David's body to accept my fingers. We have not actually done *this* since my first night with the group, but as we have been fucking regularly for two months now, I do not have to work very hard to open him up. I work my fingers in past the second knuckle, spreading and twisting gently to stretch him. He finally breaks our kiss, biting back a moan when he leans forward again to brace himself against the tree. I slowly pump them in and out as he presses back against me for more.

I use a little more lubricant to slick myself up before returning it to my pocket. With my dry hand on David's hip, I grip myself and move into position. When he feels my wet cockhead brushing against his ass, he pushes back, legs spreading even wider to help me find my target. I slip between his cheeks, teasing his hole for just a moment before pressing inside.

David goes still as I enter him, focused on adjusting to the stretch while I enjoy the feeling of his inner heat enveloping me. Even after all this time, despite how easily his body accepts me, he is still so *tight*. I am not trying to brag about the size of my endowment (a respectable 24 centimeters), but in the past, I have run into issues with men who are unable to adjust to my size in a way that makes the experience as pleasurable as intended. I have even met some who, without *extensive* preparation, I am unable to enter altogether. For someone who was a virgin when I met him, David has become accustomed to getting fucked like he has been doing it for years.

I relish the feeling of his warmth wrapped around me for a few more moments before we *really* begin. With both hands on his hips, I hold David in place while I pull the out first few centimeters of my cock. I watch him carefully for any signs of discomfort, pleased when all I notice is a muffled moan as I slide back into place. Holding him more confidently, I work my length in and out as his hole works to grip me tightly.

Before long, David's back drops down even lower as he holds himself up with only one hand, bringing the other to his mouth in an attempt to bite back more noises. His muffled groans join the soft slapping of our flesh meeting in the forest air around us. Each time I pull back, the tight ring of his hole drags along my cock, driving me to slam it back in and repeat the process. Then, once we have set a steady rhythm, I feel his hole start to spasm, a tell-tale sign of an oncoming orgasm.

Words cannot express just how awe-inspiring it is to see someone adapt to sex like this so quickly. Some people try for *years* to experience an anal orgasm, and David had his first within fifteen minutes of losing his virginity. And to be the person to cause that? My cock grows harder just thinking about it. If I did not have such a personal penchant for topping and dominating, I might even be jealous. As it is, I get to enjoy the feeling of his muscles squeezing me each time he has one.

David's hole continues to tremble as I spear it steadily, pressure building until it finally crescendos. His body goes still as it washes over him, his hole bearing down as if trying to expel an intruder. That is another reason the charm is so useful, as your typical anal orgasm leaves your body with no choice but to try and push *everything* out. If I did not know what was going on, I might be insulted. Instead, I fuck him through it, his ass no match for my rock-hard length. Each tremble of his muscles only pushes me closer to my own orgasm, and this is only the first of many.

Unlike a regular orgasm, an anal orgasm comes with zero refractory period. This is because there typically is no actual ejaculation accompanying one. Many people cannot even retain an erection while getting fucked, let alone cum from it. I have been known to require partners with a lot of stamina in order to keep up with me, so David's propensity for being on the receiving end of things suits our purposes perfectly. The fact that I get to take him apart over and over again during it only serves to turn me on more.

As tonight will *not* be one of our longer sessions, I use that to my advantage. I close my eyes, savoring the feeling of his warm, wet hole squeezing me as I fuck into him. I use my hands to feel along his muscles and ass, listen to the sounds of his breath and cut-off moans, even smell the musk from the sweat he has worked up. When I feel him starting to cum again, I know I will not be far behind.

"You know, you guys really gotta move farther away from camp for this, or you're gonna start making some of us jealous." Adam's voice nearly makes me jump right out of David.

We freeze, both of us completely thrown by his sudden appearance. I cannot actually see him, but I can hear him coming from the other side of the tree, several meters away. David looks back at me over his shoulder, half-terrified and seeking guidance for something I do not have experience with. It is not something I am particularly worried about, nor do I think David should be; we have done this in front of entire crowds of strangers before. While this might be a little embarrassing, sex is nothing his friend is not familiar with.

I try to convey this to David with my eyes, but the look I get back only changes from scared to annoyed. I am unsure as to who that is directed at, but seeing as I do not know what he expects *me* to do, it had better be Adam. While this happens, I hear the sound of the blonde relieving himself against a tree (likely his reason for coming out here), and I realize that the silent conversation we are having has gone on far too long. Sensing what I am about to do, David frantically shakes his head no.

"Apologies, Adam," I call out, causing David to freeze once more.

The man laughs in response. "Sorry, I couldn't help myself." I hear his stream slow to a trickle, and the rustle of clothes shifting as he puts himself away. "I'll see you guys back at camp. Tell David to stop freaking out."

I chuckle as David turns to silently glare at me, his body red as a berry. I listen for Adam's footsteps to leave before letting myself laugh again, bending forward to wrap both arms around David's chest. I nuzzle his neck, the absurdity of what just occurred making me smile, though I can sense that he may not share my feelings.

"I *cannot* believe you did that," he grumbles while I kiss his shoulders.

"What was I *supposed* to do?" I nibble on his skin, waiting for an answer.

"I don't know, but 'talk to him while you're still *inside of me*' was not on the list!" he hisses, still whispering.

"He already caught us. Should I have pretended we were exercising?" I make a point to pump my still half-hard erection in his ass. "Do you want to stop?"

"...No," he mumbles into my forearm.

"Good." I take his face in my hand and turn him to claim his mouth again.

I love kissing him. Swiping my tongue along his, I slowly stretch his walls as my cock expands once more. David whines when he feels me growing inside of him, and I release him to brace against the tree. I am no longer looking to take my time; we have already been out here longer than I originally anticipated. As he relaxes and I begin to pump my hips, I cannot help but think more about our interaction with Adam.

While he had a perfectly normal reason to be out here, he also could have picked any other direction from camp to go besides the one the two of us *very* obviously took to have sex. Combined with what he told David about his attraction to men, it makes me suspect that his coming upon us like that was no accident. I do not get the sense that Adam thinks of David as anything more than a friend, but I *do* think the many months of traveling with only his hand for companionship makes this more than just a case of morbid curiosity. And gives me more ideas for later.

I am not a man who gets jealous easily. Which is a good thing because I suspect David's feelings for Adam may extend a little further than friendship. Nothing more than a schoolyard crush, one I am not sure David is even aware he has. There is something about the way he looks at the blonde man, seeks his approval, that feels familiar. I actually find it rather endearing; as I said, I do not get jealous easily. Despite our shaky start, I am more than confident in my relationship with David and his feelings for me. And it is not as though I have never seen him have sex with anyone else.

I snap my hips faster at the memory. Several of them. Where I come from, people have fairly liberal ideas when it comes to sex, and sharing your partner or bringing another into your bed is not uncommon. It is something David and I engaged in when we were still there, and just as when he submits, he is beautiful in action. I look down as I fuck him, watching the way his hole swallows me over and over, pink skin dragging over green. The way he moans, the way his body shivers—it almost seems selfish not to share that.

No matter what happens, at the end of the day he is still *mine*. He still wears my collar, still calls me his owner, still cries out my name when he is being fucked out of his mind. The wave of possession surges through me, my hands gripping him almost bruisingly tight as I pound into his ass. Any concerns about keeping the noise down are gone, the sound of our skin slapping together audible to anyone close enough to hear. Even David seems to have stopped caring, barely remembering to stifle a groan as he cums again.

That is all it takes to finally push me over my own edge. I crush us together, growling low as let loose the first shot of cum deep within my pup's hole. I continue to hump forward in small, jerky movements with each volley that follows, still holding my groin tightly to his ass. When I finish, I exhale with a happy sigh, pulling David up and holding him to my chest while still remaining firmly lodged inside of him.

After we have both settled, I carefully pull out, taking in the sight of David's wet and pink hole. Unfortunately, there is not much to be done for cleaning up, so I tuck myself away as best I can and help David with his pants. There are some rags in my bag for just this sort of thing, and we should be passing near a river tomorrow morning where we can take the opportunity for a more thorough washing.

"Ready to head back?" I finish, straightening out the rest of my clothes and turning to him.

"...Do we have to?" He frowns, looking in the direction of camp.

"David, even if Adam *did* say something to the rest of the group—which I am sure he did not—what are you worried about?" I tip his chin up at me. "Everyone with *maybe* the exception of Corrine is well-versed on the subject of sexual relations. I have even overheard Elisabeth and Nathaniel in their tent together, more than once." *Having above-average hearing is not always a blessing.*

"Yeah, but that's different. That's..." He frowns and looks down as he frowns. "You know."

"What?" I squeeze his shoulder.

"Normal!" he snaps, body turning red again. "Not two men."

Ah, *there* is the rub. When we first met, to say that David struggled with his sexuality would be an understatement. But over time, he has been able to relax and come to terms with his feelings, things he had pushed down or locked away and refused to think about. Being in a place where no one knew him, or had any way of contacting people who did, he grew more comfortable with that side of himself, almost as though he was able to live a second life. But now that we are with his friends, people he has history with, he is falling back into old habits, concerned about appearances. Even though he struggles, he still tries with small gestures like holding my hand or kissing me in front of others. Hell, even the "himbo" discussion earlier counts in my book. Things get a little easier each day, and I just hope this event has not set us back.

"There is nothing *abnormal* about what we do together." *At least not the two men part of it.*

"You know what I mean." *Stubborn as always.*

"They know who we are to each other, puppy." I am trying to appeal to logic but that does not always work with him. "They know we are together, and they know what people who are together do at night. They are also *your friends—*"

"Except Nate."

"Except Nate." I roll my eyes with a chuckle at his interruption. "But even he, like the rest of them, has not used this as a weapon against either of us. Perhaps it is only because I am intimidating them into silence, but rest assured that if anyone *did*, they will be dealt with."

David cracks a smile at that. "My protector, huh?"

"That is what I signed up for." I crowd into his space, reaching into his shirt to pull out the collar he wears around his neck. I swipe my thumb over the lock, its face engraved with the same image as my tattoo, the symbol of Clan Ironstorm. I hold the key on a silver chain around my own neck, not that I have any plans to remove it.

"Okay. I'm ready, Sir," he says after a big sigh.

We start the walk back hand in hand, David reluctantly letting go once we are close. We re-enter camp to find everyone around the fire, almost ready to turn in. I silently nod to Adam as I take my seat while David cannot seem to look away from the fire to meet anyone's eyes. No one seems to particularly notice, but it is not until Nathaniel begins to tell the group random facts about the crystal hart we saw earlier that he finally relaxes.

Much later, when everyone is asleep and I am on watch duty by the campfire, I contemplate what has happened over the past week. I fell in love with a man I met barely two months ago, and after nearly trying to kill me, he instead wound up as my property. Then he was killed and brought back to life through an unknown, ancient ritual, and I decided to leave behind everyone and everything I know to follow him and his friends on a journey to *hopefully* discover the truth behind his resurrection.

When I think of it all together like that, I wonder if I might be going insane.

Sounds behind me have me turning to see our tent flap opening, a bleary-eyed David stumbling out. Seeing me by the fire, he sits down next to me, and I throw my arm over his shoulder to pull him closer. He unleashes a massive yawn as he leans against me, head on my shoulder.

"Is everything alright?" Even for David, this is early, and his watch shift is not for another forty minutes.

" 's weird sleeping without you," he mumbles, nuzzling closer.

"Did you have another nightmare?" I suspect that may be the reason for his early waking.

"...Maybe a small one," he whispers.

Small is good; small hopefully means they are becoming less severe. I smile, kissing the top of his head while he cuddles into me, already starting to nod off again. I will be sure to wake him in time for his shift, but for now I am content to hold him by the fire. I know that if I chose not to chase after him, I would have regretted it for the rest of my life. Whatever awaits us in the future, we will face it together.

But first, we are going to work on getting him more comfortable with sex because I am really getting tired of all the standing up when we have a perfectly fine bedroll right there in our tent.

Chapter 3

We are up early the next morning, foregoing a large breakfast in favor of a simple one of bread and jerky. Today will be our longest day of travel, but the hope is that if we make good time, we will reach Pákannon early enough to enjoy a nice, hot dinner. One that none of us had to hunt for or cook ourselves. Once the tents are packed and bags loaded up, we start walking, eating as we go.

It is around three hours later that we come near the river. Though we'll be able to bathe in the city (with hot water, even), when you have spent several days in the forest, you take every opportunity you can to get cleaned up. David should remember washing in the cold river water during our weeks patrolling the forest.

We bathe in shifts, one group keeping watch over our belongings while the other moves farther downstream. The group on shore also takes the opportunity to eat lunch as we are not planning on stopping again until we reach the city. Elisabeth and Corrine go first, and I am just finishing off the last of my jerky when they rejoin us, fully clothed but with their hair still wet. Now it is the men's turn.

Once we reach the river, the four of us strip down, adjusting to the cold temperature as we enter the water. We stay relatively close but still leave enough space for everyone to have a modicum of privacy. It is nothing I am worried about, but from what I have gathered group nudity, let alone bathing, is not common where they are from. So, as I scrub myself with my bar of soap, I take care not to let my eyes wander, at least not obviously.

Of course, with my back turned to the others, I have no problem ogling my puppy. I amusingly watch his attempts to stealthily clean his backside after last night's activities, paranoid that someone might notice even that. I also catch him sparing Adam the occasional glance when the blonde is not looking, and then notice Adam doing the same to him *and* myself a moment later. It could just be simple curiosity, but my other recent observations say otherwise. Nathaniel does not notice any of this and is also the first one to finish.

After drying off and redressing, we regroup with Corrine and Elisabeth who are already prepared to leave. We pull on our packs and continue our journey, feeling refreshed from our late morning dip. That feeling lasts for a few hours before we work up a sweat as the midday sun hangs high in the sky. Wiping my brow, I reach into my satchel for a waterskin, taking a long pull before handing it to David.

"Thanks," he tells me before taking a drink himself and handing it back. Ahead of us, Nathaniel is chatting Corrine's ear off about yesterday's deer encounter, and farther up from them I can hear Adam and Elisabeth discussing what food they hope to find in Pákannon—a conversation that is making me hungry.

"So, I am curious," I start as I put away the water, keeping my voice low enough for only David to hear. "How long do you think you have been attracted to Adam?"

David's head quickly swivels around to face me. "I'm not—" He cuts himself off, then looks forward to the man in question, then back to me before his eyes land on the ground in front of him, growing wider as he contemplates what exactly I just said. Finally, he meets my gaze, a hint of fear in his eyes. "I'm sorry. I swear I didn't—"

"David, it is alright." I only meant to tease, not cause an existential crisis. "I was only having a little fun with you."

"You're not mad?" He sounds afraid to ask.

"Why would I be mad?" *That* was not a question I was expecting.

"Because he's my best friend, and we're going to be spending every day together?" He looks ahead, nervously making sure our conversation is still going unheard.

"David, you slept with *my* best friend, who we worked alongside constantly." Not to mention Nylan, who is practically the man's husband.

"You're not worried?" Now he sounds hopeful, if not confused.

"Should I be? It is not as though I have not seen you interested in other people." *More than just interested.* "I have no problem admitting that the man is attractive, and I certainly would not blame him for thinking the same of you."

He goes quiet after that, mulling over my words. It is sometimes easy to forget that this is not just his first relationship with a man, but his first real relationship at all. Our age gap already speaks to the differing amount of romantic experience we have, and when you combine that with the more "unique" aspects of our relationship, things can get even more muddled for my younger partner. Not to mention the cultural differences...

"Where I come from, things don't usually work that way," he finally answers, apparently thinking of the same subject. "You're with the person you're with, and that's it. If you catch them looking at someone else like that, you're supposed to get jealous and fight about it."

"Does it bother you that I am not jealous?" I would understand if it did. It is an emotion I am not unfamiliar with, just one that I have had many years to consider in relation to my romantic pursuits. "Would you rather our relationship was more closed off to others?"

"I dunno. I mean, the idea sounds kind of nice. Two people, only with each other." *Monogamy certainly has its appeal.* "But I've also seen people who are *miserable* together. Couples who stay together because they think they have to, who seem like they're never going to be happy, let alone do anything fun. So... Yeah. I dunno. I think this has been working out pretty well so far." He smiles sheepishly. "Sorry I'm not better at this."

"It is not something you need to apologize for. I am happy you are open to discussing it. I guarantee you half the problem with all of those miserable couples is that they do not." I reach over to take his hand, smiling when he does not pull away. "And for your own information, there are plenty of things that would make me jealous. This is just not one of them."

"Oh yeah? Like what." He looks over, eager to be indulged.

"If I were to find out you were sneaking around, calling some other man 'Sir' behind my back, you would not be able to sit for a week," I tease, squeezing his hand. "Or if someone were to touch you without my permission, let alone try to take you from me... I am not sure they would leave with all of their limbs intact."

"My big strong Sir." He grins, squeezing my hand in return.

"Aaahh!" I hear Adam's sudden shout of surprise ahead of us when an arrow flies in front of his face, landing in the trunk of a tree on our right with a *thunk.*

We all stop and draw our weapons, turning to the left as four figures emerge from the forest clad in leather armor and hoods. They are either human or elf; three of them have their bows drawn and aimed at us, while the fourth appears unarmed. *Bandits.*

"What the hell do you want?" Adam speaks for the group.

"Your money and all your possessions," the unarmed man answers simply. He is speaking Common, but if his tan skin were not already a giveaway, his accent is, at least to me. They are local, possibly even from Pákannon.

"Why would we do that?" Adam asks.

"Because if you do not, my friends here will lodge an arrow in your skulls." He says it like the most normal thing in the world.

"You realize we outnumber you, right?" David cannot help but speak up next.

"Are you sure about that?" Once the man is done speaking, he holds his arm outstretched, chanting an incantation his eyes start to glow. Four spouts of water bubble up on the ground in front of him, rapidly growing in size. Once they are almost a meter high, they lose their amorphous shapes as four limbs and a head mold into place. *Elementals.* This man is a summoner.

"Into the forest, now!" Adam shouts, holding his shield in front of himself.

The archers let loose their arrows as soon as Adam shouts the order, one missing entirely and another flying just past my head, with the third landing in Adam's shield with another *thunk.* That is all the team needs to get moving, all six of us tearing into the trees behind us before the water creatures can finish forming. A good strategy—the trees might make fighting a little more difficult but will also provide cover from the arrows and maybe even a place to hide.

"What the hell were those things?" Elisabeth asks as we run.

"Water elementals," Nathaniel answers, "and they are *not* easy to take out, at least not with regular weapons."

"So how do we—OWW, FUCK!" David cries out on my right, and I turn to see an arrow lodged in the back of his upper arm, just as another flies only centimeters above my head.

"David!" I call out.

"I'm fine! Keep moving," he growls, hissing in pain. He is right. There is no time to deal with it now. We continue running, putting more distance between our groups.

"Get behind something," Adam tells us after gaining enough of a lead.

"What do we do?" Elisabeth asks after ducking behind a tree, knowing we only have seconds before they are on us.

"David, can you still fight?" Adam asks my injured pup, who is examining the arrow sticking out near his shoulder.

"Yeah, just, maybe only one handed." He reaches to touch the arrow shaft protruding from his arm, and I smack his hand away.

"We can take the archers out if we get close enough, but then we still have the elementals," Adam answers. "Nate, Cory, do you have anything to deal with them?"

"If the summoner is unconscious, it'll disrupt the spirit's connection to the material plane and they won't be able to maintain their physical form," Corrine answers. "But getting close enough to do that might be hard with four of them."

"I *might* have something that could work, but—" Nathaniel starts.

"They're coming," I announce when I hear their footsteps approaching.

"It'll have to do. There's no time," Adam tells the wizard as he pushes up from the tree. "We need to split up so they can't concentrate their fire. Nate, David, Khazak, you head that way, and Liss and Cory, you're with me. Try and separate the archers from the rest if you can, then focus on knocking out the mage." I note that Adam uses 'knock out' instead of kill, and I like the man even more.

Our orders given, we take off in two different directions, the three of us going left with the bandit group visible just through the trees on our right. When they see us, the archers reach for fresh arrows, eyes trained on our movements. I hear the sound of an arrow ricocheting off a tree trunk, but only one, which hopefully means Adam's plan worked and the other archers are off chasing them.

Once we have put more distance between us, we take cover again so we can formulate the next part of our plan. While the two humans catch their breath, I peer around the tree in front of me, looking for signs of our pursuers. At this distance, I can see four figures: the archer, the summoner, and two water elementals. Which means taking down the summoner falls to our group.

"We need to separate them further or at least draw the archer away." She is faster and can cover more distance than the other three. "Otherwise, she will make it impossible to get close enough to do anything about the summoner or his minions."

"I can do that," David volunteers, doing his best not to move his injured arm.

"Are you certain?" I look at the arrow still sticking out of his arm. Corrine will be able to take care of the injury when we are safe, and I know firsthand that he is a capable fighter, but I am still worried.

"I'll be fine. It's only one person, and I'm expecting her this time. I got this." He smiles confidently. "Worry more about how you're going to deal with those two walking puddles playing gatekeeper with the asshole summoner."

David peers around the tree, getting the archer in his sights before he takes off, running away from us and back toward the road. He whistles loudly as he runs, taunting the bandits and provoking the archer into firing another arrow, which thankfully misses. Then, just as we hoped, the archer breaks away from the other three, chasing after David as she notches another arrow.

"Alright, you said that you had a way to fight the elementals. A spell of some sort?" I turn back to Nathaniel, trusting David to take care of himself.

"Err... Kinda?" He nervously fiddles with his staff. "I know of a spell that that would freeze them, and once they're frozen, it wouldn't take much to shatter them. Destroy their physical form, and they're sent back to the astral plane."

"That is perfect." We may have a chance at this.

"*Except* I don't have the right components. I was trying to tell Adam before you interrupted me." The mage sighs, fixing me with an annoyed gaze. "I need something frozen, which I obviously don't have. None of us do."

Dammit. Where are we supposed to find something frozen right now? I have not seen anything *remotely* cold since emptying my icebox back at... Spirits be damned, I may actually have something for this. "Would meat work? Frozen meat?"

"What?" He looks at me, confused. "I mean, I guess?"

"Perfect." Reaching for the satchel attached to my pack, reaching inside quickly to retrieve an ice-cold slab of steak. Because of the way the satchel stores the objects, it also preserves the item's original temperature. I hold up the frozen beef after tearing it out of the parchment wrapping. "Will this do?"

"Yeah, that'll work." He looks torn between relief and more confusion, but he takes the steak from me nonetheless.

Holding it flat in the palm of one hand, his other hand hovers over it as he prepares to cast. As he chants to himself, I watch as the steak starts to glow a dim, blue colored light. He curls the hand above the steak as if clutching something, and the light begins to flow up from the steak into his hand. A small ball of energy grows in his palm, and then the steak loses not just its glow but its shape as well, flopping over the edges of Nathaniel's hand like it's been defrosted. When he hands it back to me, it feels room temperature.

"Damn, that was cold." The mage shakes out the hand that held the frozen steak, then holds it up to his nose. "And now my hand smells like meat. You probably could've left that in the wrapping."

"Back to the task at hand?" I roll my eyes as I return the steak to my satchel.

"Right. So now all we have to do is hit one of those things with this." He holds up the hand still clutching the glowing orb. "And it will freeze solid. Then you just give it a good whack with that big sword of yours and it'll be in pieces!"

"And you can do this again?" Removing one of them may not be enough,

"I'll need another piece of meat, but yeah." He shrugs. "The spell won't last very long though; you'll only have a minute or two before it wears off."

"That is all I will need. We just need to get close enough to do that." I look around the tree again, seeing the summoner has moved closer, still searching for us. "Stay right behind me and move when I move. Understand?"

"Got it." He nods before examining the spell energy in his hand. "Really hope I don't miss with this."

I am going to pretend I did not hear that. Both of us ready, I take off, running for a nearby tree with Nathaniel on my tail. The bandit calls out when he sees us, no doubt directing his creatures to give chase. We run for another tree, moving just a little closer, barely making it to our cover when something blasts against the other side of the tree, spraying water and wood into the forest air. On our next run, I can see the elementals aiming at us, both arms melded together like some sort of water cannon.

We repeat this run-and-cover strategy a few more times, each time moving a little closer, but also giving us less time to get out of harm's way. Behind us, the trees have been stripped of bark from the water hitting their trunks. Once we are about as near to them as we can get without being smashed against a tree, I turn to Nathaniel.

"Are you ready?" *They are only ten or so meters away; surely he can hit them from that distance.*

"...Yes?" *That is not supposed to be a question.*

"Okay. I am going to make this next run alone." I see his eyes go wide. "When they fire at me, you are going to go around the *other* side of the tree and throw your spell at the nearest elemental. Can you do that?"

"I think?" I glower at his answer. "I mean yes! I can do it."

"Okay. Prepare yourself." I eye my next running target, say a small prayer to the Three, and take off. I just *barely* make it, a powerful jet of water hitting the side of my pack and almost throwing me off balance. Then I hear what sounds like glass cracking.

"I DID IT! I GOT HIM!" Nathaniel cheers as I peer around the tree to see one of the elementals frozen in place, the summoner staring at it in shock. The other elemental, however, is still looking for me, and I almost don't pull my head back behind the tree in time. I can hear my teammate cursing under his breath as he remembers to get back behind cover himself.

That still leaves one of them. I should have given Nathaniel another steak before we split. Where did he go? I will have to look while I destroy the frozen elemental. We cannot risk it thawing out. I would like to use my bow, but I do not think it is strong enough to break something that large. Perhaps I should have listened to Ragnar's ideas about explosive-tipped arrows... *I am wasting too much time!*

I start to run again, trying to draw the elemental away from his frozen compatriot as I inch closer. It takes me a few attempts, but once I am finally in position, I see Nathaniel's hiding spot. *Perfect.* I can destroy the elemental, then double back to him to repeat the process for the second one.

Sword in hand, I run, stopping to duck behind a single tree between me and the frozen elemental. The *second* I hear the water hit the tree, I run toward my target, cleaving the disturbing looking ice sculpture at the waist. I continue to run past as the upper half topples to the ground, shattering into icy crystals along the forest floor. As I duck into cover with the unfrozen elemental behind me, I am struck in the side by a bolt of force shaped like a glowing arrow, slamming me against the tree.

Damn. I forgot about the summoner, and also that he is not limited to *only* summoning spells; he just specializes in them. I stand up straight, searching for where the magic came from, the spellcaster in question looking all too pleased with himself—the same caster stupid enough to let me get between him and his aquatic bodyguard.

I drop my sword to the ground as I charge the man, his eyes going wide in fear. As he turns to run, I throw myself at him, slamming his smaller body into the ground underneath me. Before he has a chance to cast anything further, I slam my fist against the side of his head, one, two, *three* times, until the man's eyes flutter shut as he loses consciousness. I hear a heavy splash of water behind me as the remaining elemental spirit is banished and take a deep breath now that we are safe.

"Holy shit." I turn my head and see Nate approaching, looking down at the unconscious bandit underneath me. "That was brutal."

"He will be fine. The important thing is that we are—Wait, where is David?" I stand in sudden panic.

"I'm right here," a familiar voice calls out, "and I brought a friend."

From my left comes David, marching the bandit archer he distracted in front of him. The woman looks none too happy, though I would not be either if I were being walked with my hands in the air, a sword pointed at my back. She glares down at the summoner's body, then back up at me.

"Whoa, nice job," David comments, looking at the same unconscious spellcaster. "What about the others?"

"We need to find them and hope they did not have any problems with their group." I step around behind the woman, pulling some rope from my satchel to tie her arms behind her back.

"What about this guy?" Nathaniel kicks his foot against the man's thigh.

"I have him." I reach down and hoist the man's body over my shoulder. "We will need to tie him before he wakes up."

"*If* he wakes up." ...I understand David's feelings toward Nathaniel more and more each day.

We march through the forest with our captives in tow, searching for the rest of our team. Just as I start to worry, I hear footsteps and look up to see them walking toward us in the distance. They have captured both bandits, one walking in front of Adam and the other in front of Elisabeth, while Corrine is at their side. The one in front of Adam has his hands tied behind his back, but the other is holding a single arm in the air while the other dangles limply at her side. When they get closer, I can see that Adam and Elisabeth are soaked from head to toe, and all three of them look exhausted. The bandits all share looks of exasperation among themselves, but otherwise remain silent.

"How did it go?" I ask the obviously beleaguered group.

"Wow, Liss." I can see David biting one side of his lip, trying to hold in a terrible joke. "If you really wanted to take another bath, it probably would have been easier just to double back to the river." *There it is.*

"You ever wonder what it feels like to almost drown on dry land?" Liss asks dryly. "C'mere and let me show you."

"We got one of the archers, but the elementals caged us in." Adam pushes past whatever was brewing between those too. "I think Corrine was trying to remember how to do mouth-to-mouth resuscitation before you guys knocked the summoner out and they turned into puddles of mud. What about you?"

"Once David pulled the archer away, Nathaniel was able to freeze one of the elementals, and I was able to attack the summoner." I lift the unconscious man on my shoulder for emphasis.

"Great job." Adam smiles, before his look turns slightly concerned. "...Is he alright?"

"If he's alive, he has a concussion," Nathaniel answers for me.

"He is *fine*," I roll my eyes, but press my fingers to the back of the man's knee to feel for a pulse, just to be sure. *Phew.* Then I look to Corrine. "But yes, he almost certainly has a concussion."

"Let's get back to the road first." Adam turns to the direction we first entered from. "We can take care of everyone's injuries and make sure these guys are tied up before we start walking again."

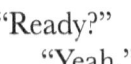

"Ready?"
"Yeah."

"Alright. One... two... *three*." I grip the arrow shaft tightly in my hand, pulling it as cleanly as I can from David's arm.

"*Fuck!*" he cries out, blood already starting to ooze up.

"Got it." Corrine quickly moves in, holding a bandage in both hands and pressing it to the open wound. "*Caroconsuo.*"

The cleric's hands glow, and I watch David's grimace of pain slowly morph into something more tolerable. By the time she moves her hands away, it is like there was never a wound to begin with. Wadding up the bloody bandage, Corrine stands, walking over to the four bandits.

David's injury was by far the worst of our group, the rest of us making it out with minor nicks and bruises and perhaps a little water in the ear. The bandits, however, are doing much worse. In addition to the one I pummeled into unconsciousness, another has a broken arm, and a third has a large, almost too-deep slash across his chest. After ensuring their bonds were secure (including the uncon-scious one), we tied their legs together with barely enough room between them to move and sat them on the floor while we took care of our injuries. Now it is their turn.

Corrine starts with the one currently in Dreamland, first straightening out the nose that I *may* have broken when sub-duing him. Then she places both hands on the man's head, healing not just his face but also his brain, taking care of any potential swelling that could lead to other complica-tions. The man still does not wake up, but when he does, he should be fine. The man with the bleeding chest is next, but when Corrine reaches the final bandit, the woman with the broken arm, she frowns, feeling her arm carefully.

"This needs to be set before I can heal it." The woman hisses in pain as her arm is touched.

"Can you do that?" Adam asks, standing guard over the two

"Yes." She pauses, looking up at the bandit. "But it's going to hurt."

Before her patient can react, the cleric quickly snaps the bone back into place, the bandit howling in pain.

"*Bitch!*" she snarls. "You did that on purpose!"

"Oh shut up." Corrine stands and dusts off her robes. "You tried to *rob us*. You're lucky I even did that much." *Remind me to not get on her bad side.*

After the bandit's arm is healed, Elisabeth steps in to tie her hands together like the others. "Unless you three want to carry your friend there back to town, you better start waking him up," she tells them.

"You good, Liss?" Adam hooks a thumb over his shoulder at the forest behind us. "I want to check out where they've been hiding out here before we leave."

"Yeah, I got it." She stands over the kneeling bandits, trying to nudge their unconscious companion awake, sword at her side.

"Cool. David, Khazak, with me." He nods over his shoulder at us to follow.

The three of us walk into the woods on the opposite side of the road, cautiously making our way through the trees. Not far in, we find a small camp, two tents around smoldering embers that used to be a fire. We carefully search through the tents and are unsurprised when we find a bag of coins, jewelry, and other valuable items alongside their supplies.

"I do not think they have been out here for very long," I comment, inspecting the wear on the tents. "Maybe only a few weeks."

"Long enough for them to rob plenty of people though." David whistles as he looks in the bag containing the valuables.

"Hopefully, the authorities in Pákannon will be able to return some of this." Adam takes the bag from David.

"Oooo, maybe there's a reward!" David grins at the two of us.

We rejoin the others, all of the bandits now awake and standing. The summoner's mouth has been gagged, likely to make spellcasting difficult.

"Alright, you four in front!" Liss barks at them. "Start marching!"

Now a group of ten, we continue our journey. Judging from the sun in the sky, it is nearly four in the afternoon. And we still have a lot of distance to cover before we reach Pákannon.

"How much longer do we have to go?" David asks as we trudge along.

"Like... five hours," Adam answers with a sigh, and a collective groan goes out among the group. Even the bandits.

Chapter 4

Night has fallen by the time we wearily approach the outer gates of Pákannon. After five days of travel, the lights of the city in the distance are a welcome sight. Our captives did not make the rest of our journey any smoother. After a sloppy escape attempt in which they all managed to trip over themselves, we were forced to alter our formation to keep them trudging along to their inevitable arrest. Honestly, what did they think they were going to do?

Since then, they have mostly been silent, but every now and then I hear them talking among themselves in their native dialect, Pákagi. The language shares some similarities with my own, Atasi, and I have a rudimentary understanding cobbled together from things I picked up as a child. Nylan made sure to teach me all the curses, several of which have been uttered by the bandits, but for the sake of keeping things moving, I have kept that to myself. For now.

"Is it just me, or are those lights coming from the mountain?" David squints his eyes.

"I think they're coming from the trees," Elisabeth replies from my right.

"You are correct." I smile, not realizing this detail was unknown to the group. "The city extends into the forest behind it, literally. There are homes built among the treetops with an entire system of interconnected walkways leading into the mountains to the west."

"Really?" Corrine looks over to me for confirmation, face brightening when I nod. "That sounds amazing."

I can feel the collective spirits of the group rise as the torches outside the gate become visible. The walls surrounding Pákannon are large, though not as large as the one that protects V'rok'sh Tah'lj. It is made up of thick, horizontal logs with a walkway along the top allowing for guards to patrol its length. It extends through the forest right into the base of the mountain, doubling as both a boundary marker and line of defense. Thankfully, the cities along the eastern coast have not seen war for quite some time.

Two guards are posted on either side of the open gate, one elf and one human. Both have black hair, the humans coming down to his ears while the elf's sinks past his shoulders. They look nervous as we approach, the human's hands both moving to grip his spear. We did not consider the way a group this large marching in at such a late hour would appear. Especially when you consider that almost half the group is restrained, and most of the half that is not are very obviously not from around here. *Better get ahead of this.*

"Adam, I do not want to overstep, but perhaps it would be best if I—"

"Go for it." Adam flashes me a thumbs up. "You do the talking for now, big guy."

I nod my head before turning to the two nervous guards. "<Hail!>" I raise my hand and call out in Pákagi.

"<Who approaches?>" the elf responds warily.

"A tired group of travelers." I am unprepared for a full conversation, so I switch into Common, hoping that at least the elf will understand me. "We ran into a group of bandits about thirty kilometers up the road."

"Wait right there." The elf approaches, hand finally moving to his weapon. He walks around us before inspecting the four bound humans in front more closely. "We have been getting reports of bandit attacks along the road for a few weeks now but the information was never consistent enough to locate them. I think they match their description."

"I took care of most of their injuries," Corrine nervously speaks up. "A broken arm and a possible concussion were the worst of it. I did what I could, but after all the fighting and traveling you may still want to call for a more professional healer to look over—"

"It is alright, ma'am. We will take care of it." The elf puts his hand up to calm her before turning to the human guard and saying something I do not catch. "Please, come with me. I'll take you to the peace office, where I can put these bandits in a cell and call for a healer."

"Thank you very much, Mister..." None of us have exchanged names yet.

"Atohi, Atohi Craydark." He reaches out to shake my hand. "Pleasure to meet you all. Please, follow me."

After some light shoving to get the bandits moving, Atohi leads us through the gate and into the city of Pákannon. I hear more than one sharp intake of breath as we enter, the city in the trees returning to view. While much of the town is built along a flat plain, the northwestern quarter of the city is blanketed in a thick forest leading into the Emerald Hill Mountains. It is an impressive sight on its own, but I like it even more at night, when the lights of the torches above flicker like twinkling stars. Nathaniel nearly trips, too distracted by what is over his head to notice a dip in the road. I can see Atohi smiling ahead of us, no doubt used to new visitors to the city being in such awe.

Pákannon is roughly the same size as V'rok'sh Tah'lj, though with only half the population. Originally founded by humans, the citizenry is far more diverse in the present-day. Still approximately half human, the other half is split three ways between elves, gnomes, and dwarfs. The elves are known as the *Nuñnehi*, and their ancestors originally lived in cities deep in the mountains while those of the gnomes—the *Yunwi Tsunsdi*—came from the forests. The dwarfs call themselves the *Nimerigar* with most having originally immigrated from the mountain city of Kiz'Urngor in the west. The Emerald Hills are rich with valuable minerals, and the city has a trade deal with the dwarfs in exchange for their assistance in mining.

Ahead of us is the town square, and at its center is a large bonfire, one that is kept constantly burning day and night. I am already familiar with the building Atohi is leading us to, having visited the peace office and jail previously. Only in an official capacity, of course. As Captain, I met with Pákannon's Marshal and her officers several times. With Pákannon being the closest major city to V'rok'sh Tah'lj, circumstances would occasionally arise that required cooperation between our law enforcement departments. It did not happen often, but when a suspect or fugitive would manage to evade us and escape the city, Pákannon would almost always be their destination. There simply are not many other places to run.

The building itself is square and only a single story high, roughly two-thirds the size of one of our ranger stations. Its walls are made of a combination of earth and clay that has been plastered over stacks of stripped wooden logs with a low-angled roof shingled with wood and tree bark. Two lit torches hang over two small windows on either side of the wooden double doors that make up the entrance, which barely goes over my head—an issue with non-orc cities I had forgotten about. Humans and elves aside, a third of the city's population barely reaches a meter in height.

Atohi leads us inside, having our group take a seat near some desks while he calls over some other peace officers to help him move the bandits to a cell. One of them takes the bag of stolen goods from us, both as evidence and so they can hopefully be given back to their rightful owners. The other officers march the bandits to the cell room, leaving us unattended.

While waiting to give the officers the information they still need, I overhear two voices, both familiar, one more than the other. My curiosity gets the better of me, and I look for the source, finding it in an office not far from us. After poking my head in, two faces turn to greet me in confusion: one dwarf, and one half-elf, half-gnome.

"Captain Ironstorm?" Ranger Kignun Hazatin, a black-haired dwarf, asks me with a salute.

One of my last acts as Captain was to send out a small contingent of rangers to search for any escaped members of the former Councilman Murbank's cult, the Order of Zeus. It took Ragnar and I days to vet through all of our remaining officers, unsure of how deep the cult's reach had dug. In the end, we decided to send Ranger Kignun Hazatin, another survivor of the attack that night. The dwarf left with two other officers only days before we did, not long after David woke up—meaning he is unaware of my resignation.

"Not anymore," I respond, but I cannot help but return his salute. "I am afraid I tendered my resignation several days ago."

"Ay?" the dwarf asks, confusion coloring his face. "Why did you do—Ah."

Something behind me catches his eye, and I turn to see David coming into view, followed by the rest of the group. When I turn back, the dwarf is giving me a knowing look, and I wonder if my sudden departure was a surprise to *anyone* back home. The woman standing next to him, still wearing a confused look, is Marshal Verona Yelxina. Due to her mixed background, her height just about matches Hazatin's at one-and-a-quarter meters, or four feet, as David would say. Her long black hair falls down to her waist, tied together with a simple brown cord.

"Captain, or I suppose just *Khazak* Ironstorm." She smiles, still looking a little unsure. "I trust your resignation was not for anything *untoward*?"

"No, nothing like that Marshal Yelxina." I shake my head.

"I think you've known me long enough to call me Verona." She smiles before looking over the group behind. "What is it that brings you here?"

"It is actually related to what Ranger Hazatin was sent to investigate." As I speak, Verona leads us out into the open room rather than attempt to cram more people into her office. "Though the reason we are here *tonight* is to hand over a group of bandits that attacked us on the road."

"The same bandits that have been giving my officers trouble for weeks?" She looks over the group, impressed if not surprised. "I am glad to see that you made it here in one piece. Now who do I have to thank for helping to keep our roads safe?"

"This is Adam Bauer," I start the introductions but stutter, becoming self-conscious mid-sentence, "...the team's leader."

"Nice to meet you, ma'am." The man reaches forward to shake Verona's hand.

"Likewise." She seems to consider the human differently after my revelation.

"And this is Elisabeth Taylor, Corrine Jones, Nathaniel Smith, and David Cerano," I finish with the rest of the group, having remembered everyone's names from their arrest paperwork. "As I said, the main reason we are here are the events that took place last week."

"Yes, Ranger Hazatin arrived four days ago and informed me and the city's leadership of the situation." A sudden look of realization crosses the woman's face, and she turns to Kignun. "You said that we could expect a visit from the victim and his friends—this must be them." From the corner of my eye, I see David bristle slightly at her use of the word victim.

"That would be David." Kignun gestures in his direction.

"Very sorry to hear what happened to you, son," the marshal offers her condolences. "The mayor's office is expecting you, so I would head there first thing tomorrow morning. I am also happy to be able to tell you we apprehended two of the alleged cult members. They're sitting in a cell right now."

"Really? Do you think we could speak to them?" I try not to sound too eager. It is small, but there is a chance they could know something.

"I would be fine with that." Verona nods after considering my request. "We were just discussing the possibility of finding the rest of their ilk."

"Ay, we believe there is a chance some may have passed through town and continued north," Kignun adds. "We caught these two trying to escape up the mountains to the west."

"Come with me." Verona motions for us all to follow. "They weren't terribly chatty with any of us, but seeing you might pull something out of them."

We are led down a hallway to the section of the building with the cells. Inside, I can see Atohi and another officer have placed the bandits in their own cell and are working on processing them. He gives us a questioning look as we are brought in front of the cell containing the arrested orcs, two older men in simple tunics and pants issued by the jail. I do not recognize either of them, but they seem to recognize me, looking surprised as I approach. That surprise morphs to fear when they see David enter behind me.

"Here they are." The marshal crosses her arms. "Good luck getting them to talk. <They have been nothing but shameful cowards since being arrested.>" The arrestees actually look at the marshal when she finishes her sentence in Atasi, meaning it is safe to assume they do not speak Common, and I should do the same.

"<Alright, what do you—>"

"<We will tell you everything we know!>" The first man does not even let me finish.

"<Just please do not let him hurt us!>" The second's eyes fly to David.

"What are they saying?" Elisabeth asks from behind me.

"I think I got the gist," grumbles David on my left.

I do not bother confirming David's assumption. "<What do you know about the ritual that was performed that night? What did Murbank think was going to happen?>"

"<Only that we were to sacrifice the elf, and then the gods would gift us their power,>" the first man answers.

"<What sort of power?>" This entire time, I have not heard a single member of this "order" explain what exactly they were hoping to receive.

"<I do not know.>" He shakes his head. "<Strength? Magic?>"

"<We did not expect them to return the dead to us as a demon!>" the second man nearly yells, eyes still locked on David.

"I think I'm going to wait outside," David grits out.

With a sigh, I watch him stomp away, and I turn to the remaining group. "They do not seem to know anything about the ritual at all. I do not think Murbank was very forthcoming with his lackeys."

"Ask them about Redwish," Adam suggests. "Maybe they'll know where he went."

"<What do you know about Naruk Redwish?>" Both men seem calmer without David's presence.

"<Brother Redwish?>" the second man confirms. "<He joined us shortly after he moved to V'rok'sh Tah'lj, but not as an initiate. Brother Murbank introduced him as his second.>"

"<Not that he ever took orders from him.>" I can almost hear the first man's eye-roll in his tone.

"<What do you mean?>" I noticed that the two did not get along, but this seems like something else. "<Why was Redwish's membership different?>"

"<Brother Redwish brought certain *resources* to the group,>" the first man continues. "<Before then, our numbers were much smaller, and we only met on rare occasions. After he joined, Brother Murbank was able to begin funding the plans we had spent decades only discussing, but Redwish...>"

"<What?>" Both orcs suddenly go silent, sharing a look of fear. Fear that is not due to me or David, so I growl out my next words to redirect it. "<If you do not tell me, I will bring the *demon* back in here and lock him in that cell with you.>"

"<We do not think the money came from Redwish!>" the second orc blurts out.

"<Brother Redwish seemingly took orders from someone else, someone Brother Murbank did not deal with directly,>" the first tells me more calmly.

"<Who?>" Murbank has always been wealthy, but it never crossed my mind that some of that wealth might have come from an outside source.

"<We do not know.>" He shakes his head. "<But that is where we believe the funds came from.>"

"<Do not lie to me!>" I bang on the bars of their cell with my fists.

"<We are not! I swear!>" He cowers. "<That is everything we know.>"

"<If I find out you are not telling me something, I can assure you that you will live to regret it.>" I finish my threat and straighten my posture. "I trust you caught all of that, Ranger?"

"Ay, every word. You know, I always suspected Murbank's wealth was ill gotten," the dwarf answers. "I will be sure to include the information in the report I send back to Tah'lj with these two."

"Excellent, please—" I have to stop myself from giving him an order. "—tell Captain Rockfang I said hello."

"Happy to, Khazak." *Oof,* hearing my former subordinate say my name is stranger than I anticipated. "Thank you for the assistance in getting them to speak."

"With the Summer Solstice only days away, we cannot get them out fast enough," Marshal Verona adds as we exit the cell room. *That is right; the beginning of summer is almost here.*

"The officers I rode with will be transporting them home tomorrow while I continue north," Hazatin concludes. "Perhaps I will see you all again soon."

"Perhaps you will, Kignun." The dwarf and I clasp each other's right wrists, pulling the other in for a hug. "Safe travels."

"Yes, it is late, and I am sure you are all eager to rest after your journey." The marshal seems ready to wrap her night up, and I do not blame her.

"With a demon outside waiting for you," the dwarf adds with a chuckle.

"Thank you again for dealing with the bandits," the marshal tells us as she leads us to the front. "You should know that you are free to carry your weapons while within Pákannon's walls, but drawing them in public is a fineable offense my officers are trained to respond to."

"Thank you for the info, ma'am. We aren't looking to cause any trouble," Adam assures her.

"Actually, your guard mentioned something about a reward for catching the bandits? *Oww*." Nathaniel rubs his side after being elbowed by Elisabeth.

"You are correct, one that comes to roughly a hundred gold," the marshal responds with a laugh. "If you don't mind coming back, I can have it ready for you first thing in the morning."

"That would be fine, ma'am. Thank you very much," Adam tells her with a small bow, then turns to me. "Khazak, do you know where to find us a good inn?"

"I should." I look to the marshal. "Is the Sleeping Willow still open?"

"Yes it is, and they should have more than enough room for your group." She nods. "Thank you again for your assistance with the prisoners *and* bandits. I will see you all in the morning."

"Happy to help, ma'am. See you then," Adam speaks for the group before leading us toward the exit. "Can you catch us up on what the guys in the cell were saying?"

"Of course, let us gather David and then—"

"Is it true?" The question catches me off guard, and I turn to see Atohi. "What they were saying about that human—is it true? That he was killed and brought back?"

"I... Yes, it is." I watch him questioningly. A look of shock, or maybe awe crosses his face at my answer, but he says nothing else, and after a beat of awkward silence, we finally leave.

" 'Bout time." David pushes himself off the wall to the left of the double doors. "You guys ready to eat something and crash?"

"First, we need to talk about what we just learned in there." I give him a look of confusion.

"Do we have to?" I resist the urge to sigh. Seems my pup is feeling bratty tonight.

"Seeing as it's the *entire reason* we're here? Yeah, David, we do." *Adam might make a half-decent brat tamer himself.*

Happy when there is no response, I lead us toward the inn.

"While they did not have any more info on the ritual, they were able to shed some more light on Murbank and Redwish's working relationship." Adam and Elisabeth move to walk on either side of me. "Namely that while Redwish was not working for Murbank, he was answering to someone. Someone who provided Murbank the funding to enact his plans for the cult."

"Ragnar said he couldn't have been that rich without doing something fucked up," David grumbles from behind me, where I am sure he is still pouting. "Didn't think it would be something *that* fucked up."

"I suspect that this person, as well as Redwish, knew more about the ritual than Murbank was aware." I think back to Redwish's muttered "impossible" as he ran from the temple. "They could even know more than he did."

"Did they know where he went?" Adam asks from my right.

"No, he was the first one to flee." I shake my head. "Given his tenuous ties to the Order, I doubt he told anyone anything about where he was headed."

"And we're sure they aren't lying?" Elisabeth asks on my left.

"I do not think so." I meant every word of my threat if they were. "But the ranger did say they suspect someone else may have already passed through. He's continuing north to track them."

"Perfect, we're headed in that direction next." Adam nods to himself. "We can spend tomorrow meeting with the mayor, resting, and restocking, then leave the day after."

"I think that sounds like an excellent plan." I ignore the groaning behind us, happy to return some control to Adam.

We reach the Sleeping Willow Inn a short walk later. It is a large two-story building, made of the same stacked wooden logs as many of the homes here are. The bottom floor's walls are covered in the same tan clay as the peace office, while the top leaves the logs bare. The windows on the top floor are dark, most patrons having already gone to bed, but the bottom is lit so hopefully the kitchen is still open.

We have no problem securing four rooms. We even get a slight discount as the owner remembers me from my previous stay. I believe she thinks I am still a captain, and I do not bother correcting her. We manage to catch the cook *just* before he closes up, though all he has left is venison stew and bread. It is better than nothing, and I am happy for the break in preparing our food.

The six of us eat in relative silence, the events of the day having finally caught up with us. One by one (or two, in the case of a couple), we finish and make our way upstairs to our rooms. They are fairly simple with a bed large enough for two, a desk and chair in one corner, and a small bathroom. Most of the inn's furniture is made from carved wood, simple but sturdy. David greets our bed by flopping onto it face first before turning his head and eyeing the bathroom.

"Is that a shower?" David asks me, leaning up on his hands as I light one of the room's lanterns. "And a toilet?"

"Yes, though it does not function the same as in my home." I nod, placing my bags and weapons near his.

"Is there hot water?" he asks as he enters the bathroom.

"In a way. There is no indoor plumbing, so we must get the water ourselves." He looks at me, confused. "See those buckets against the wall? Hand me two and grab two for yourself." I point to a stack of wooden buckets stacked in one corner of the bathroom.

After some minor complaining and a couple of swats to the ass, the two of us are heading downstairs with a bucket in each hand. I lead us out the inn's back door to the nearby water pump, where we fill all four buckets and trudge back upstairs. The shower is made up of a large wooden tub against one wall with a second, smaller tub hanging above it. I place my two buckets against the bottom tub, and David does the same.

"So, if you have not already guessed, the shower is enchanted," I say as I lift and empty one of the buckets into the higher "shower" tub. Then I repeat this with my other bucket. "After you fill the tub, you turn this knob, and the water is heated as it moves through the pipes and sprays down. As neither of us wants to go back down for more water, you will want to get wet, turn it off as you lather and wash, and then use the remaining water to rinse. You may go first, but those," I point to the two remaining buckets David carried up, "are mine, so use your water wisely."

"Yessir!" David answers as he eagerly begins disrobing.

I do the same, gathering up both of our clothes and draping them over the back of the chair. I have a seat on the bed while David showers, not at all complaining about the view of his wet and soapy body I get while I wait. As nice as it is when he is trying to show off for me, I love getting to see him candid like this.

"So how does the toilet work?" David asks as he turns the water off after getting wet.

"That is much simpler. Just do your business and then close the lid." I actually assumed this one was a bit more self-explanatory. "The waste will be magicked away."

"Just like that?" David sounds surprised.

"Just like that." I see a frown growing on his face. "What's wrong?"

"I'm annoyed we don't have stuff like this back home." David has mentioned the lack of certain luxuries in his family home before. "The academy had working toilets, but most of the day-to-day citizens still pull all their water from a well."

"You could always do what Councilman Murbank's father did and make your money by inventing your own plumbing system," I joke about the source of our enemy's original fortune.

"You mean *I* could be the next Magical Toilet King of Lutheria?" David asks in sarcastic wonder before bending over to lather up his legs. "I was wondering. Didn't we see Hazatin, like, two days before we left? How did he get here so fast?"

"Well, I imagine it is due to the horse he was riding," I point out what I thought was obvious.

"You mean those giant monsters you like to *pretend* are horses?" he responds over his shoulder. "Why didn't we get to use any of those?"

"Because I no longer work for the city?" Not to mention I am not sure how I would have gotten them to the group after they had already left.

"Oh, right. Sorry," he mumbles as he finishes rinsing.

"Nothing to apologize for. It was my decision to leave." It was not a very difficult choice to make, and not just because of David, either.

"All yours, Sir." David exits the bathroom with a towel around his waist. "Even filled it up for you."

"Thank you, pup." I kiss him on the forehead as I pass him to take my own shower.

Due to my height, I am forced to crouch for the water to get over my head and shoulders. It also means I need to be more economical with its usage as I have more area to cover when I rinse off. As I scrub the soap along my body, David's words echo in my head.

David *is* the main reason for me to come on this journey, but as I said, it was not the only one. Even had David not been a factor, I was still planning to resign. With everything that happened, it is easy for some people to forget that it all happened on *my watch*. I was Captain: it was my force that was infiltrated and compromised; those were my rangers attacking the city and people they were sworn to protect. How could anyone still want or trust me to be in charge after all that?

These people were not just colleagues or employees; some of them were my *friends*. People I worked with for the better part of a decade, some who started even before I did. Morgal Keenguard, my former deputy, went to the same school as me, Ragnar, and Nylan. We celebrated her father's birthday with her family last year! That she or any of the others could do something so heinous... I am not sure who I would be able to trust anymore. I am not sure I have much faith left in the system at all.

Stepping down was what was best for everyone.

Once I finish rinsing and drying, I leave the bathroom to find David on the bed, lightly dozing on his stomach. His butt is raised to the air, the flesh parting ever so slightly to reveal a peak of the tightly furled hole within. Approaching the bed and carefully lowering myself to my knees in front of it, I cup his cheeks gently before spreading them and leaning forward to swipe my tongue along his freshly washed crack.

I hear a squeak of surprise followed by a moan as David relaxes into my touch. I even feel his hole relax when my tongue passes over it, enticing me to press inside—an invitation I take, pushing my tongue in deep as my hands spread him even further. Moaning again, David pushes back against my mouth, wordlessly asking for more.

With a growl, I rip myself away from him for just a moment, grabbing both of his legs and flipping him onto his back. Pulling him to the edge of the bed, I bend his legs back and dive back in, resuming my tongue work. I can see his cock, angry and leaking against his stomach. My own cock throbs in the air, hanging heavily between my spread thighs.

I release my grip on the back of his legs, allowing them to fall to my shoulders. Taking myself in one hand and him in the other, I slowly stroke the both of us. A bead of precum sits on his head, and I am sure that if I am not already leaking onto the floor, I will be soon. Without another word, I swallow David down to the hilt.

"*Oh fuck.*" I see his hands scrabbling for purchase on the bedsheet in my peripheral vision.

I hum to myself as I bob up and down on his length, enjoying not just his taste, but the weight of him on my tongue. I stroke myself in time with the movement of my mouth, working us both closer to our respective releases. I do not think David will take very long; it has been several days since he has cum this way. I can already feel him twitching.

"Touch yourself." I push his legs back once more. "And tell me when you are close."

"Yessir." David eagerly takes himself in hand and begins stroking.

As I once again feast on his ass, I grab David's empty hand and move it to hold back his own leg. With one of my hands now free, I return to stroking myself as I tongue-fuck him slow and deep, pushing as far into his wet and open hole as I can. The hand I have on his thigh is gripping him tight enough to leave a bruise, the thought of which only makes me hungrier.

"Sir, I-I'm getting close," David tells me, his hand never slowing.

I release his leg and bat his hand out of the way, replacing his fingers with my lips. Grabbing the base of his cock, I stroke him in time with my bobbing, moving up and down as I seek to rapidly push him over the edge. With a groan, I feel the first shot hit the roof of my mouth, and I happily swallow as I continue to nurse him through the remaining four or five volleys of cum, all while still steadily working my own cock.

"Turn around with your head over the edge of the bed," I order gruffly as I stand, still stroking myself. "I will not be long."

David flips around, still on his back with his head hanging just off the bed. I quickly push myself into his mouth, gripping him lightly by the neck to hold him steady. While I pump myself in and out of his throat, I increase the pressure slightly, just letting him know I am there. As if the cock rapidly knocking against his tonsils was not enough.

"Unless you want to get more water for washing, you better make sure you swallow everything," I grit out as I tip over the edge.

I unload, still fucking in and out of his mouth with small, shallow thrusts. I feel his Adam's apple moving under my thumb as he swallows me down, not stopping until I finally pull out of his mouth with a wet *pop*. Looking down, I see his red and swollen lips and watery eyes, the telltale signs of someone who has just had their face fucked. It makes my deflating cock twitch in the air.

Helping him to sit up, I retrieve a water flask to rinse with as well as using David's discarded towel to wipe up whatever we missed. I toss it over the chair when we are finished, too tired to care about decorum. With David yawning beside me, I blow out the lantern and climb into the bed, eager for sleep to take us.

Chapter 5

"...and the butcher arrives on the morning of the first Solisday of the month." I shut the lid on my icebox after emptying its contents into my satchel. *"The order usually runs about twenty-five gral, but you are free to change however you would like or cancel it altogether."*

I turn to look at my sister, Ayla, who is still staring at the key I placed in her hand, dumbfounded. Keys... That reminds me. I pass her, walking toward the small table I keep near the front door. I open its drawer and fish out a small chain—the same I gave to David as a temporary collar when he was no longer wearing mine. His neck is once again bare, and the custom-made metal is now a heavy weight in my pocket. I shake the thoughts from my head—I am going to remedy that problem shortly. I fish out the key to said collar and thread the chain through it, wearing it around my own neck.

"Khazak, I swear I'm not trying to talk you out of anything, but I feel like I have to ask. You've worked so hard for all of this." My sister gestures to the house, but I know she is also referring to my career, my friends—everything I will be leaving behind. "Are you sure this is what you want to do?"

"I do not think I have ever been surer of anything in my life," I reply without hesitation.

Across the table, I watch as David hungrily stuffs more bread into his mouth, pausing mid-chew when he notices my gaze.

"Wha?" he asks, some bread hanging out of his mouth.

"Nothing." I shake my head with a chuckle. "Just thinking about decisions I do not regret making."

He gives my answer an odd look but says nothing as he continues eating. It is just after 9 a.m. on Aquaday, Geminus 26th, and we are downstairs in the dining hall of the Sleeping Willow Inn. The rest of the team is here, looking refreshed after a night of sleeping in decent accommodations. David and I have trimmed our beards and Adam's face is cleanly shaven, though Nate still has his perpetual stubble, all of us eating a hearty breakfast before getting started with the day's activities.

Finished with my food, I find myself doing something that is an old habit of mine: people watching. Without staring around the room, I take note of its occupants, not expecting anything out of the ordinary. It is a room full of hungry travelers, some still waking up, all except two men in a booth in the corner. They are both dressed in almost all black, but strange fashion choice aside, what catches my attention is that neither man is eating. Perhaps they are just getting off a late work shift and are not hungry? Is it a shame because today's breakfast consists of some hominy with onions, venison sausage, and a type of bread that is really more of a dumpling.

"What with this bread?" David asks as if reading my mind. "It's not bad, just different. Are those beans?"

"They are." I nod, putting down one of the extra sausages I grabbed for myself. "I could not tell you all the ingredients, but I know it is a mixture of cornmeal, wheat flour, and cooked beans."

"Huh." He looks at the bread in his hand thoughtfully before shrugging and taking another bite.

"Alright, after we're all done here, the first stop is the marshal's, and then the mayor's," Adam begins to plan after wiping his mouth. "Then we're supposed to meet up with the family of that friend of yours. Nylan, right? He gave me the address."

"Oh, that's good, because I, uh, definitely forgot to write it down when he told me," David answers after wiping his mouth. I am not surprised to find that Adam is the one on top of the planning, even though it is something for *David's* benefit.

"Correct," I tell Adam, ignoring David's lack of preparation for the time being. "They should be expecting us, though I am not sure when."

"Should be simple enough to drop by," he reasons.

"What are we doing after that?" Elisabeth asks, speaking for I think the first time this morning.

"I guess we can check the city out?" Adam shrugs. "We probably need to do some laundry and restock anything we're low on. I've got to get my shield repaired, but we don't have to leave until tomorrow."

"David still needs to get checked out by the healer at some point," Corrine adds.

"I know we are all a little tired of walking, but if the group would not be opposed, there is a place just over the mountains I think you all would enjoy visiting." After all of David's talk of wanting to see the world, I started thinking of locations I could take him myself. "It would only be a few hours there and back."

"What kind of place?" Corrine asks next.

"It is a bit hard to describe..." Especially as I am trying to leave it a surprise. "It is a landmark of sorts. You really need to see it for yourselves. It is visible from the top of the mountain, so if you all decided it was not worth continuing, we could turn around there."

"I'm in," David agrees with a smile, kicking a foot out under the table to scuff his shoe lightly against mine. "Sounds like fun."

The rest of the group looks between each other, considering my offer before coming to a consensus.

"Sure, why not?" Adam speaks for the rest of them.

We finish with breakfast and exit into the morning air, the sun rising into the clear sky. Remembering our path from last night, Adam leads the group away toward the peace office. The city is much easier to see in the daylight, the group taking in the sights as we walk. Most of the buildings follow the same architecture as the peace office and inn, walls made of packed clay over wood. Most of the homes have large open windows, allowing the air to flow through during hot summer days. Some have a second, smaller dwelling attached, a round domed room with thick walls that is partially sunken into the ground, used in the winter when it gets too cold.

Many of the homes are decorated, their outside walls painted in different colors, but the real eye-catch is in the northwestern corner of the city, or more specifically what lies above it. In the light of day, one can look up and see dozens of homes built in and around the treetops, and the spiderweb of wooden walkways and bridges connecting them. The trees that have been built onto are all large, their size and durability enhanced through magic. Some possess spiral staircases wrapping around their trunks to meet the ground while others use wooden lifts with long rope pulleys attached to a hand crank. Several of the trees have homes built against their base, though there are fewer as the forest begins to grow up the uneven terrain of the mountainside.

It is quite the sight to look upon, and I can feel the group's excitement as we draw closer, eager to climb up and begin exploring. I wish I shared their feelings. But there will be time to deal with that later. For now, we have business with the marshal's office. When we enter, it only takes a brief explanation to the officer at the front counter before he disappears into the back and returns with Marshal Yelxina, who has either just come in or was working all night. I am familiar with the hours.

"I wanted to thank you all again personally," she tells us while handing a small pouch to Adam containing our reward. "I've sent a message ahead to the mayor's office. They should be expecting you this morning at the Council House. Just take a right when you leave here, then another right when you pass the central bonfire. It will be at the base of a large tree at the end of the road. You can't miss it."

"Thank you, ma'am." Adam pockets the pouch. In addition to being the leader, he also handles the "group" finances, something I trust him with enough to not worry about. Then as we leave, the blonde leans toward me. "You know how to get there if we get lost, right?"

"I do," I answer with a laugh. The marshal was not incorrect; the Pákannon Council House will be very obvious once it is in sight.

Continuing through the city in our instructed direction, we pass through an area largely filled businesses and other administration buildings. We pass the bonfire on our left, and as we turn the corner, I glance inside a nearby general store. Though it is early, there are already plenty of citizens out and about. Humans, elves, dwarfs, gnomes, even the occasional halfling or orc—likely expatriates from V'rok'sh Tah'lj, or at least descended from them.

Regardless of species, many of the people of the city share some common physical features, namely their naturally tanned skin (for the non-orcs), dark hair, and brown eyes. Long hair seems to be in fashion, particularly among the elf and gnome population, though I also note many of the men opted to shave the sides of their heads, not too dissimilar to Nylan's hairstyle. As the temperature gets warmed, clothing choices favor looser fitting items made of thin leathers or cotton. Things like skirts and shorts paired with short-sleeved shirts and blouses, if they opt for any top at all.

Ahead of us, at the end of the street, sits the Pákannon Council House. Though you cannot count them from this angle, it is a seven-sided building built around the large tree at its center. A pathway around the tree leads up from the middle of the building to additional offices in the trees above, though hopefully all of our business can be conducted on the ground floor. In addition to housing the mayor's and many of the city's other official offices, the town also uses the building to host events and celebrations.

The guards posted outside the building's entrance watch us carefully as we climb the short staircase, but otherwise remain silent. We enter a warmly lit room, the wooden walls decorated with paintings and tapestries showcasing moments of the city's history. The walls to our right and left are angled such that the room is shaped almost like a slice of pie, one whose center had already been removed. To our sides and behind us are a number of chairs and couches, some of them occupied, while ahead of us is a desk with an older human woman sitting behind it, streaks of grey visible in her long black hair.

"<Good morning. How may I help you?>" the woman greets us as we approach.

"Good morning," Adam starts, confidently assuming what the woman was saying. "Sorry to bother you, but I believe we have a meeting with the mayor?"

"We are the group from the Shad'rok Logging Camp," I interject, using the alias used to identify V'rok'sh Tah'lj to outsiders. Those in the know, especially city officials, will know exactly what I am talking about.

"Oh yes, we have been expecting you," she answers with realization. "Let me just make sure he is ready for you; I will be right back."

"Thank you," Adam tells her as she stands and enters a door on the wall behind her, leaving our group of six at the desk.

"Logging camp?" David questions.

"That is the name we use when referencing the city in public," I tell him lowly—the others would have been briefed on this after their incarceration.

"E-excuse me?" a soft-spoken voice asks from behind me.

We all turn around to see a shy-looking elf girl. I would estimate she is no more than 160cm tall and weighs approximately 55 kilograms. She is wearing a light-blue dress that comes down to just below her knees, cinched at the waist with a simple red sash. A pair of round glasses adorn her face, and her long black hair is woven into a single braid that lays over her left shoulder.

...I mentally shake my head and sigh. Quickly profiling someone like that is a holdover from my years as a ranger.

"A-Are any of you Khazak and David?" She manages to find her voice after watching us all turn to face her, one hand fiddling nervously with her braid.

"Uh..." David raises his hand. "David." Then he points to me. "Khazak. Who're you?"

"Oh thank goodness." She looks relieved, then offers us a small bow. "My name is Tsula, Tsula Erlaxim. I'm Nylan's older cousin."

"It is wonderful to meet you, Tsula." I have heard Nylan say her name in passing a few times, though not many specifics. I turn to David on my right. "Hers is the family we are supposed to be meeting."

"Did you say *older* cousin?" David of course focuses on something completely inane. "How old are you?"

"*David*," I chastise because that is a rude question to ask *anyone*.

"No, it's alright," she answers with a giggle. "I'm 40."

David looks like she just slapped him. I want to laugh at his reaction, shocked that she is older than Nylan but possibly looks even younger. Unlike her cousin, whose father is a human, I believe that both of Tsula's parents are elves, resulting in an even longer life-span and delayed aging process—one that also seems to affect emotional maturity, if Nylan is anything to go by.

"How did you know to meet us here?" I move the conversation forward.

"The mayor is good friends with my family. When he learned of your arrival this morning, he sent us a message letting us know as well." She continues to toy with her braid as she speaks, then points upwards. "We live in the Upper Boughs and if you don't know where you're going it can be *really* confusing, so I thought it would be easier to just meet you here."

"Excuse me, Mayor Elajor is ready to see you." The woman watching the front desk returns through the same door, holding it open for us.

"Oh, I can wait here until you all are done," Tsula offers, turning to one of the empty seats.

"Nah, you might as well come along." David swings his arm for her to join the group as we round the desk to the door. "I'm sure Ny already told you all the gory details."

"...Maybe a few," the elf girl squeaks out before quickly following.

We are led through the door into a large circular room. At the center of the room is the tree around which this building is built, a staircase rising up past the ceiling as it circles around the trunk. There are desks set up at various points around us, many with people seated at them and working. No one pays us any mind as we are guided past them and through one of the many doors lining the walls of the room.

"Sir, I have them here for you," the woman announces as we enter what appears to be the mayor's office.

"Thank you, Leotie. Come in, please." A middle-aged elf gentleman stands and walks around his desk as we file in, his short black hair greying at the edges of his slightly receded hairline. "I am Mayor Austenaco Elajor. I hope you are feeling well rested after your long journey to our fine city."

"Yes sir, thank you for asking. Everyone has been very accommodating," Adam greets the man. "My name is Adam, and this is Elisabeth, David, Khazak, Corrine, and Nathaniel. Thank you for taking the time to meet with—"

"*Yes*, let's get right to business." The man leans back against his desk. "Forgive me for being blunt, but which of you is the one who was resurrected?"

"That would be me." David holds his hand up as he hesitantly moves to the front of the group. On instinct, I move to stand behind him.

"Well, you certainly are alive, aren't you?" David forces a laugh at the man's "joke." "And you have the sword from the temple? Oh no, that won't be necessary." He stops

David before he can slide the scabbard from his back. "I was curious though... Could I see the scar?"

"I... Sure, okay." David nods then begins to unbutton the top of his shirt. I can sense how uncomfortable he is, and it is taking all of my willpower not to say something on his behalf. I cannot tell if the man is ignoring David's discomfort, or if he is truly that oblivious, but as he is the head of the city and we need his help, I bite my tongue.

"Fascinating," the mayor comments, drawing his face closer to David's exposed skin. He does not try to touch him, which is good because if he did, I might be tempted to smack that curious smile right off his face. "Thank you. As you already know, the temple ruins were investigated by an archaeological team from this city. Unfortunately, two of the six members of that team have since passed, and the other four no longer call Pákannon home."

"You can still help us though, right?" David asks as he rebuttons his shirt.

"Yes. Not to worry because we have the full report the team made during their investigation. I had a copy made just for you." I can see David visibly relax at his words. "I have looked over them myself, and they are very detailed. The team took extensive notes. I understand you will be visiting one of the expedition members next, correct?"

"That is the plan. He is the father of a close personal friend," I speak to the man for the first time.

"You mean Uncle Atsadi?" Tsula voice squeaks from behind me, reminding me that she is here. I suppose Nylan's father would be her uncle.

"Tsula, is that you?" The mayor peers around Adam to spot the woman in question. "You're so quiet I didn't even notice you came in with them. I am glad to see your mother got my message. How is she?"

"She's doing well, sir," she says more confidently. "She and my father both say hello."

"Excellent, please tell them the same for me." I cannot help but sense a lack of sincerity in this conversation. "When was the last time I had your family over for dinner? We really should—"

"Sorry, sir, but you were talking about the notes?" Adam attempts to redirect the conversation.

"Of course, of course, I am sure you all are very busy. I understand you have even assisted the marshal and her officers in keeping our roads safe." The man is nothing if not charismatic, I will give him that. "Our records office is just upstairs. Leotie here will be able to show your group there and get you sorted out."

Did he say upstairs?

"Thank you, sir." Adam shakes the man's hand.

"Yes, thank you." David does as well.

"You are very welcome," Mayor Elajor tells us as we begin exiting. "Read over the report and let me know if there is anything else we can do to assist you."

"Please follow me," the woman, Leotie, tells us as she leads us back to the central room.

She walks us around the tree until we reach the staircase, climbing up with our group following her, one by one. Adam, Elisabeth, Corrine, Nathaniel, Tsula, David, and then... I hesitate. David makes it a few steps before realizing I am not behind him and stops to turn around.

"Everything okay?" He steps back down, face growing concerned when he takes in my state.

"I am fine," I lie, still standing at the bottom of the stairs.

My left hand is gripping the handrail tightly, despite the fact that I am still on solid ground. I have had no problem walking up flights of stairs in the past, including at the inn this morning, but none of those were leading me nearly a thousand meters into the sky where I will surely plummet to my death. I cannot bring myself to step forward and start climbing; just looking at the bottom step fills me with anxiety. Though I know I should not, I cannot help myself and take a step backward, peering up through the gap in the ceiling to see how the staircase wraps around the tree over and over as it climbs higher and higher and higher... *Spirits, I think I am going to be sick.*

"What's wrong?" David is suddenly standing next to me, hand on my shoulder. He looks me over, then looks at the stairway that has surely led to multiple deaths. "Are you scared of heights?"

My skin goes cold at the casual mention of my phobia, confirming what I was afraid of, that he now knows. The last thing I wanted was to become fodder in his or someone else's jokes. *Haha, the big orc man is afraid of heights.* I can already feel myself getting defensive, opening my mouth to argue. "Just because I may be afraid of heights does not—"

"Hey, hey, no." David's hand on my shoulder moves to my hand. "I didn't mean it like that. I was really just asking."

"...You are not going to make a joke?" I wince at how small my voice sounds.

"It's not funny if it's something that *actually* upsets you." He squeezes my hand.

"Hey David!" We both step back from the stairs to look up once more and see Adam's face poking over the railing three "floors" up. "Everything alright?"

"Yeah, we'll catch up!" David shouts back before turning to me. "Do you want to go back to the inn? I could walk you, or maybe they could just bring the report back down to us."

The genuine concern he is showing warms me, and I lean forward to capture his lips in a quick kiss. "Thank you, but no. We do not need to delay things any further. I will be fine." I leave out the injury my pride will feel at being the only one of us not able to handle climbing some stairs.

"Alright, if you're sure." He steps between me and the staircase, still holding my hand. "I've got one hand. You keep the other one on the rail and we'll take this one step at a time."

"Easier said than done," I try to grumble, but his smile makes it difficult.

"Just focus on something else." He takes the first step and waits for me. "Tell me a story."

"What story?" I ask, confused and anxious as I join him on the first step.

"Tell me about Khazak Steelrun," he requests, and we take another step together.

"You already know that one." *We saw an entire play about it.*

"So what?" He shrugs and we take another step. "Pretend I don't and tell me again. Give me all the details."

"Alright," I laugh with a huff. *Another step.*

So, I tell him the story of Khazak Steelrun and Vakesh Gorecrash, the first true *kavan* and *avakesh* pairing in my city's history, and my ancestors. I talk about how they met after Vakesh led a failed attack on Khazak's camp, how Khazak claimed Vakesh as his own, how they were attacked by a bear, how they fell in love. Throughout my tale, David asks me questions or makes comments, all serving to distract me. Before I even realize it, we are at the top of the staircase.

The stairs empty out onto a room much like the one we began in, if not a little smaller, which helps me to trick myself into believing we are still on the ground. Already looking around for our friends, we spot Corrine sitting in a chair outside of one of the doors, and she stands eagerly as we approach. I am worried she may ask about the holdup, but instead she just leads us through the door into an office.

The rest of our group is gathered around a table, two stacks of paper at the center.

"Hey guys," Adam greets us from the opposite end of the table, eyes going to the papers. "We have the copy of the report, but there's a problem."

"What is it?" I ask as I approach the table, looking down to read the top of the report myself.

Only I cannot because it is written in Elvish.

As far as I am aware, elves are the only species with languages spoken by nearly their entire global population, and Elvish—more properly known as New Elvish—is one of those languages. The use of the term "new" is relative as it is the language that was developed after the great cataclysm that befell the ancient elven empire. Prior to that, the primary language they spoke was Old Elvish, which was *previously* known as Elvish. After much of their population was wiped out, taking most of the speakers of with them, a new language began to form. It contained similarities to Old Elvish but also amalgamated words and phrases from dozens, if not hundreds, of other languages.

"*Dammit,*" I curse aloud.

"Our thoughts exactly," Elisabeth adds before turning to Leotie. "Any way we could get this translated into Common?"

"I am certain you could find someone in town capable, but it would cost you a good amount of time and money," she tells us honestly.

"I was afraid of that." David huffs as he steps up to the table.

"I could take a look at it if you'd like?" Tsula speaks up from a corner she has been hiding in. "I mean, unless I'd be getting in the way..."

"You would not mind?" I ask if she is sure.

"Not at all!" she tells us cheerfully. "My parents were actually hoping you would all join us for lunch. Since we're already up here, we could go over there now, and I can start reading. I can at least get some of the basic information translated for you."

"That would be wonderful, Tsula. Thank you." I ignore the part of her statement where she mentioned already being "up here."

Most elves speak multiple languages, so I am not surprised that Tsula speaks both Common and Elvish. As a result of their increased longevity, and subsequent longer adolescence, it is extremely common for elves to be polyglots. I believe most elves speak at least three languages on average: the language local to their homes, Common, and Elvish. I know that was the case for Nylan, and Tsula may even know one or two others.

"Thank you for your help, ma'am," Adam thanks Leotie as we gather up the report papers and prepare to exit.

"I hope you all enjoy the rest of your stay in the city!" She waves us off as we follow Tsula out of the office and then the building.

We exit onto a large wooden deck, the edges of which are all protected by thick guard rails. Still, even being able to see the edge from this distance raises my heart rate, and I have to look away toward the center to stop myself from thinking about how high up we are. I grab for David's hand on instinct, happy when he does not flinch or pull away. Tsula is already walking toward her home with the group right behind her, David and I bringing up the rear.

The view from up here is so different. I do not mean the view of the ground—I do not think I could look over the edge without having a heart attack—I am referring to the view in front of us. The green leaves of the trees that fill our vision, marked by the occasional patch of blue where the sky leaks through. The branches sway in the breeze, and if

I were not worried about the fact that we are on some of those branches, it might seem gentle.

We cross from deck to deck, sometimes on bridges tied with rope that swing in the air, and other times on more solid wooden ramps and walkways. I definitely prefer the latter. We pass more buildings on each of the decks, houses and the occasional business, none reaching the size of the mayor's offices. After more walking than I care to recount, Tsula finally comes to a stop in front of her home. We are deep in the forest, the mountainside clearly visible in the distance.

Opening the door, Tsula leads us inside, calling out, "Ama, Ada, I'm back! I brought Nylan's friends!"

The home we enter is nice, if not cozy for the amount of people. I have to duck to clear the doorway. Colored rugs line the floor of the main living area, where two elves are seated at a couch next to a short table. There is a second couch to our right and stuffed bookshelves line the walls. You can tell that all the furniture is old but well maintained. I suppose when you have a long life ahead of you, furniture upkeep is more of a priority.

"It is so wonderful to meet you!" the woman tells us as they both stand to excitedly greet us each with a hug. "Please call me Inola."

"And I am Mohe," the man adds. "We are happy you were able to make it. Please, sit, relax, make yourselves at home."

"Oh, I need to get started on lunch!" Inola excitedly stands as the rest of us take our seats, exiting presumably to the kitchen.

"Should I go help her?" Tsula asks her father.

"No, she's been preparing for this for days," he tells her, looking in the direction his wife left, then turning to us.

"Alright, let me just grab some paper and a pen, and I can start reading over the report with you," she tells the rest of the group with a smile before exiting the room.

"You have a lovely home, sir," Corrine compliments the man.

"Yes, thank you for having us," Adam adds. "Though really, we only ate about an hour ago, your wife doesn't need to go to the trouble of making lunch for us."

"Nonsense, she loves an excuse to cook for people." *She shares that with my father.*

"Well, I love an excuse to eat what people cook for me." David also looks in the direction Inola left.

"You must be David," Mohe guesses correctly and then turns to me. "And you must be Khazak. Nylan has told us about you before. You are Ragnar's friend, correct?"

"Correct. The three of us all went to school together." I nod at the man. "Nylan is a very dear friend."

"He's a good kid. His mother was my sister." The man looks sad for a moment. "After what happened, we expected Nylan and his father to move back here, but that man is nothing if not stubborn. I am happy to see what a fine young man Nylan has become."

"I knew your sister only briefly, but from what I remember, she was a very kind and warm woman." I clasp the man's shoulder in solidarity. "She raised a wonderful son."

"That she did." The man nods, retaking his seat. "Why don't the two of you sit down and tell me about how he's doing while you wait for Tsula?"

I am more than happy to do just that.

Chapter 6

"I think this entire section covers just the composition of the materials used in the temple's construction," Tsula says with a sigh.

"Better than the one that detailed the dimensions of the cave and *all* of its contents," I reply wearily.

"At least they were thorough?" Corrine offers, not entirely sounding like she believes herself.

The three of us have been seated together for over an hour as we comb through the archaeological report on the Temple of Zeus, Tsula translating while Corrine and I take notes. David is also sitting with us, but he has added little, mostly looking bored while the rest of us talk over the papers. Saying it is a dry piece of reading is an understatement. The writers left no stone unturned, literally, recording every last detail they could think of. And because of the seriousness of the situation, I am unwilling to skim over anything lest we miss something important.

Over on the couches, Adam, Elisabeth, and Nathaniel are speaking with Mohe. Adam is doing most of the actual talking, with Elisabeth adding the occasional word or grunt, while Nathaniel has for the most part remained silent and uninterested. From the bits of conversation I pick up, they have been discussing pieces of the town's history before moving on to the upcoming Summer Solstice celebrations. It seems that aside from the standard revelry that accompanies the holiday, Pákannon hosts an annual feast. It is a shame we are not going to be in the city by then.

"Is there anything I can get you all?" Inola comes by the table and refills the waters she gave us. "Lunch should be ready in about twenty minutes."

"No, ma'am. Thank you," I tell her before she does the same with the group on the couches.

"Sorry about her," Tsula tells us once she is out of earshot.

"She is a very kind and attentive woman." Though after growing up with my father Rurig, I do understand what she is apologizing for. I am still trying to think of the politest way of telling her I am not yet hungry.

"You should see how she gets when my nieces and nephews come to visit," she jokes.

"I have yet to see what my fathers will be like when it comes to grandchildren." I cannot say they have ever pressured me or my siblings to provide them, though it may only be a matter of time.

"Lucky you," David comments dryly before drinking more water. "I need to use the bathroom. Can you—"

"I'll show you where it is," Corrine offers, having used it herself not long ago, and the two leave the table together.

"Thank you again for your help, Tsula," I tell her as she turns to the next page. "I am sure you have much better things to do than this."

"Not really. Information on rocks aside, this is actually a little exciting. Not a whole lot happens around here." She pauses to adjust her glasses. "What about all of you? Were you going to do anything else today?"

"I did have a bit of a surprise planned." I lean in and speak a little lower. "I was going to take everyone over the mountains to see the Onyx Spires. I do not think they even know about their existence."

"That's a great idea!" she congratulates me in a whisper. "They'll love it."

"Thank you." I pause to look at a clock. "But with lunch, I am not sure we will have enough time. I do not want it to be too late by the time we get back."

"Hmm... Give me a minute." She pushes out her chair and leaves the room in the direction her mother left.

Corrine returns to the table just as she leaves, and David comes back a minute later, before Tsula rejoins us.

"Is everything alright?" I ask as she takes her seat.

"Yes, I just told my mother about your plans, and she thought it was a great idea too," she tells me with a smile. "So now she's packing up lunch for you to take with you instead."

"Thank you very much, Tsula." I cover one of her hands with mine. "That is very thoughtful of both you and your mother."

"This the thing you're dragging us over the mountain for?" David asks with a smirk.

"No one is dragging anyone over anything, but yes." *At least he is feeling well enough to tease.* "Tsula, you should come with us."

"Oh, thank you, but I wouldn't want to intrude," she politely attempts to decline, shaking her head. "Besides while you are all gone, I can read over more of the report for you."

"Oh no, I am not going to be the reason that someone is stuck inside doing *homework*," David tells her pointedly. "Come on, come with us."

"I d-don't know..." She worries her braid.

"I am afraid I agree with David. Join us—I insist." I nod, looking over the report. "Perhaps some fresh air and sun- light will make this a more interesting read."

"Doubt it," David snarks, and I lift my hand to show him my palm, all fingers extended. *That's five.*

"Well, if you all are sure..." Tsula nods to herself, releasing her hold on her braid. "Okay. Thank you for inviting me."

"Yay!" Corrine cheers lightly from her spot. "We're going to have a picnic."

⟷

We leave the Erlaxim household about thirty minutes later carrying a large sack which Inola has packed with our lunch. After saying goodbye to both of her parents, Tsula leads us through the treetops, and I am once again clutching onto David's hand like a terrified child would their parent on a busy street. We take a different path this time, using a walkway that leads about halfway down into the mountains and will shave a good forty minutes off of our climb. I am glad that all the climbing we have already done will not go to waste, though getting back down is even harder. Unlike when we were going up the stairs, I am forced to look down as we descend, the ground seeming so close yet so far, and for all the wrong reasons.

I cannot explain the relief I feel once we reach the bottom. I could kiss the ground if I were not trying so hard to hide my fears from my teammates. After I gather my wits, we begin start to head up the rest of the mountain path. I make it a point not to look behind me—climbing a mountain might be less nerve wracking than a city in the trees, but I am still well aware we are going up, and I have no desire to tempt fate.

The forested mountains we are climbing are known as the Emerald Hills. The range starts approximately 500 kilometers southwest of V'rok'sh Tah'lj and stretches over 3000 kilometers north-by-northeast, creating a barrier between the eastern coastline and the western plains. The mountains are well traveled with a number of paths and trails cutting across and through them.

The road we are walking is wide and not terribly steep, cutting a diagonal path up the mountainside before leveling off and turning in the other direction. Wheel grooves are visible in the dirt below us from carts transporting goods to and from the mine. Though the main mine entrance is at the mountain's base, other entrances are peppered throughout the hills. After climbing a little higher, we find a number of pickaxe-wielding dwarfs in helmets milling around an entrance to the mines. I know not all the miners are dwarfs, but with their increased lung capacity and natural durability, it is a profession many flock to.

Farther up our path, we find another cave, this one with two guards posted out front, a human and a gnome, both dressed in the same uniform as the guards watching the city's gate. Whatever they are guarding does not seem to be terribly important as they are both seated on the ground playing a card game. They pay us no mind, only looking over at us briefly as we pass by.

After a few more minutes of walking, we finally reach the top, where we see two more guards on the road, both elves. These two are actually seem to be paying much more attention to their posts than the last two, nodding as we approach. Passing through the rocky outcropping as we cross the mountain's peak, I see the members of our group ahead of me give pause once they are able to look down the mountainside and see my "surprise" in the distance.

"Whoa," David comments once he is able to see for himself. "Is that where you're taking us?"

"Yes," I nod before taking a moment to look for myself. "The Onyx Spires."

The Onyx Spires is the informal name used for the landmark that has caught everyone's eye, called that because no one knows what its original name or purpose was. A black stone platform sits in a clearing at the base of the mountain with four large black pillars—one posted in each corner—stretching high into the sky. The pillars all curve inward as if aiming at the same point in the air. After confirming its location, I finish staring at the base of the mountain, and the ground that is so, so far away.

"What is it?" Adam asks next.

"Yeah, and what does it do?" Nathaniel adds.

"I could not tell you. I only know that it is ancient, magical, and mysterious." All three of which fall squarely into this group's interests. "Shall we continue down and look for ourselves?"

"Hell yeah!" cheers David.

"I think we're all in," Adam speaks for the group.

We waste no more time, working quickly to descend the mountain. We are moving a little faster than I would like, my teammate's eagerness causing them to rush, but less than a half-hour later, we all make it down safely in one piece. From there, it is just another twenty minutes along the road through the forest. The trees overhead block the sky, giving away once we reach the clearing as the first of the pillars comes into view, towering over us.

The platform is roughly a twenty-meter square, and each pillar stretches at least three or four stories into the air, both made of the same black stone material. Up close, it is possible to see that the stone is not actually solid black but contains veins of gold, or at least a gold-colored substance. It shines in the daylight, unnaturally smooth for something that has sat out in the open air for thousands of years.

"Whoa," David repeats himself. "So much bigger up close."

"Thank you for stating the obvious," Nathaniel snarks, and I have the sudden urge to smack the back of his head. "So, what is it for?"

"Its actual purpose is still unknown, and I am afraid I do not have much more information than that." We are not exactly next door to V'rok'sh Tah'lj, so learning about this was outside our usual purview.

"That's correct," Tsula confirms. I had nearly forgotten she was with us. She would know more about this than I. "It's been studied for centuries, but no one has ever been able to determine what it does or was used for."

"Who built it?" Adam asks next.

"Yeah, an' 'ow?" David asks, mouth already filled with a sandwich he has dug out of the bag. He moves to take another bite but pauses. "Wait, I'm not being rude or anything by eating here, right?"

"No, you're fine," Tsula answers with a laugh and gestures for him to set the bag down.

The platform of the monument is raised, and David sets the food down at the edge, passing out its contents with Corrine's assistance. For lunch, Tsula's mother Inola packed sandwiches (*more venison... hooray...*) and roasted ears of corn covered in spices. It is not that I want to complain about the choice of meat—deer are what is most common to the area—I just became accustomed to more of a variety back home with access to livestock and a butcher. *Perhaps I am going soft...*

"We know it was built by ancestors of the elves in Pákannon. My ancestors," Tsula begins to explain after swallowing her own mouthful. "The architecture, the details carved into the stone, all match up with other structures built during that era."

"But you don't know what it does?" Elisabeth speaks for the first time since leaving the city, following David onto the platform.

"Nope." Tsula shakes her head. "There are a lot of theories, but none have been proven."

"Could it be religious?" Corrine asks next as she and the rest of us join David and Elisabeth in taking a closer look.

"It's possible." Tsula takes another bite as she thinks for a moment. "Are you all familiar with the concept of leylines?"

There is a mixture of heads nodding and shaking among the group, mostly split between who is a spellcaster and who is not, with the exception of Adam.

"Think of them as pathways of magical energy that run across the surface of planet," she explains to David and Elisabeth. "Magical energy concentrates in places where they cross, forming what is basically a well of magic. The walls between our world and the astral plane are thinner, and the connections between the two stronger."

"The Spires are built on top of one of those wells," she continues explaining, gesturing around to the structure. "The stone it's made of isn't real onyx, it's called *astral* onyx, and it can only be found at places where leylines meet. It's what most elven monuments are carved from, and it reacts to magical energy in strange ways, absorbing or amplifying certain spells, while rendering others completely inert. There are even some enchantments on the stone that are still active. They've monitored the monument on all sorts of holidays, during specific sun, moon, *and* star positions; there once was a team of people assigned to watch it every day for *five years*. Not once has anything ever happened."

"No one's ever been able to figure out anything about what it's for?" Nathaniel sounds more than a little skeptical. "That doesn't make sense. They should be able to learn *something*. Even the mages in the orc city were able to figure out things like the basin in the temple being a conduit." He has a point, but I am not sure I like his use of the word "even."

"I know it seems really far-fetched," she concedes. "There were able to decipher some of the monument's enchantments but not its origin or what it actually does. It's designed to act as a receiver or transmitter for some sort of magic, not unlike a conduit I guess."

At the second mention of the word conduit, David and I share a look. *Could they be related?*

"Actually, if you look closely, you can see the Old Elvish runes carved into the stone," Tsula points out. "Some of the enchantments are in place to keep the structure from falling apart. It's almost five-thousand years old." That explains why it still looks so pristine.

"I think I see what you're talking about," David says with his mouth half-full, leaning in close to one of the towers and brushing his hand along the stone.

Everyone jumps when the ground begins to rumble. No, not the ground, the monument. All around us, the runes carved across the shiny black surface begin to glow, including those David just ran his hand over. The group watches, bewildered as the glow spreads to the rock underneath, starting at the base and moving toward the tip of each spire. *Something is happening.*

"Everyone off of the platform!" I shout, waking everyone from their stupor as we all rush off in a panic. David even drops his sandwich.

We make it without a moment to spare because the second the glow reaches the peak of each tower, a beam of multi-colored light is fired into the air from the tip. They meet at a single point in the center where the energy seems to swell only briefly before shooting straight down at the platform, like one end of a volatile rainbow. With a loud *boom*, a bubble forms, the force of its sudden appearance pushing back the air violently. Several of us stumble, while David's discarded sandwich goes flying overhead.

The flow of energy from the monument begins to lessen as it fills the bubble, expanding rapidly to its edges. Once it is full, the pillars continue to glow as the energy takes shape, splitting into three amorphous forms, then condensing further into...bodies, all made of the same rapidly churning multi-colored energy. Until suddenly they are not, and I am staring at what looks like three flesh-and-blood people standing in a circle at the center. Then, even quicker than it came, the bubble "pops," shrinking back into nothingness and sucking the air back in with it. The stones lose their glow as the remaining energy dissipates, and all we are left with are the three figures on the platform.

They appear to be two men and a woman, either human or elf based on their heights. They are dressed in fairly heavy robes, far more than you would expect to see on a warm and sunny day like today. All three of them have a bag thrown over one shoulder, and one of the men is holding a wooden staff while the other has one strapped to his back. After being still for only a moment, they begin to look around at each other, before taking one another by the hand and jumping around excitedly in a circle. *What is happening?*

"Did... Did I do that?" David asks worriedly.

"I don't think so?" Tsula offers, sounding entirely unsure.

"Wait, David." Adam squints as he points toward the three people on the platform. "Is that—?"

"Michael?" David finishes, already stepping toward them. *Michael, as in his twin brother?!* "Mikey?" he calls louder.

One of the men dancing comes to a sudden stop when he hears David's voice, releasing his companions and turning to him.

"David?" The man with lightly curled brown hair steps toward us. He looks to be roughly David's height, perhaps slightly shorter, and with a little more weight on his frame as well. Even from here, I can see the same bright green eyes as my David's. "D? Is that really you?"

From the back of David's head, I can only see him nod before he quickly closes the distance between them, jumping onto the platform as the two embrace in a tight hug.

"How are you here?" David asks his brother as the two groups begin to slowly converge on one another. "And since when do you have a mustache?"

"You really one to talk, beard-bro? Did you get skinnier? And how are *you* here? Where have you even *been*?" The man—Michael—pauses to look up at the sky. "Wait, why is the sun out?" *It would seem that obliviousness runs in the family.*

"Because that's what the sun usually does at three in the afternoon?" David answers in confusion.

"It's not three in the afternoon—" He cuts himself off and finally takes in the rest of his surroundings. "Where are we?"

"Where do you *think* you are?" David asks skeptically.

"We should be outside Neherama..." He turns around to face his two companions. "Did we get something wrong?"

"I don't think so," the other man, a red-head with shaggy hair and equally shaggy beard, answers in a thick accent I am unfamiliar with. "The two o' ya triple checked all the maths. Maybe we—"

"Boys, *focus*," the woman tells both men in an accent I can place as Albionian. She has dark skin, and medium length, tightly curled black hair that is parted on the left. "Wherever we are, it is clearly *not* Neherama. Judging by the lack of a desert, I'd say we aren't even anywhere near Kemet. So where are we?"

"Right, sorry." Michael turns back to his brother. "Where are we?"

"Uhhhh..." I can hear the panic in David's voice, having the sudden realization that the family he's been hiding from has found him. Though I am not sure what he thinks he can do about it now; his brother is already here.

"Nova Mundus," Adam answers for him, using the name for the continent that most of those present would know. "About five-hundred miles northwest of Holbrooke."

"Adam?" Michael looks around David's torso to take in the other man. "What are you doing—" It's Michael's turn for a moment of realization, looking back at his brother and then shoving him on the shoulders with both hands. "*This* is where you've been for the last five months? What the hell?! Mom's been freaking out! Everyone has! Do you have any idea how pissed off Dad is? He's going to *kill* you when he finds—"

"Hold the fuck on!" David shouts, poking an angry finger into his twin's chest. "Dad isn't going to find out anything because how do I know you're even my real brother and not some illusion, or shapeshifting monster, or fever-induced hallucination? Prove it."

"When we were little, you used to pretend you were a puppy and got caught crawling inside through the doggie-door," Michael replies without missing a beat.

"...That was *one* time," David says after a pause. *Well, now I have to know more about that story...*

"*Twice.*" Michael crosses his arms.

David's eyes narrow. "*Fine*, you're my brother." He pokes his brother in the chest again. "But Dad *still* isn't going to find out anything because you're not going to tell him anything."

"David, you know everyone's been really worried, right? Mom, Dad, Kira, Joseph..." Michael's face softens as he tries to reason with his twin, even bring up their other two siblings.

"I still don't understand how you're even standing here," David changes the subject. "There were these lights and like a bubble and then an explosion and now you're just... here. What the hell?"

"Oh. Well, we teleported." He looks back at his companions for confirmation.

I think I can hear the collective eyebrow of everyone in the group go up.

"No, really," Michael defends against our skepticism.

"Bullshit!" Nathaniel exclaims what several of us are thinking. "It's not possible."

"I mean, it *is*, it's just unbelievably complicated," Michael tries to reason. "The spell has so many moving parts and variables, and it took us forever to get the correct calculations for the energy-to-mass conversions, and *then* we had to figure out which locations would actually work for—Wait. You said we're in Nova? Near Holbrooke?" He looks up and around at the structure we are all standing on. "Are these the Onyx Spires?!" He looks back at his companions in excitement. "We were right! They're all connected!"

"I told Professor Kraylop!" the woman shouts back triumphantly. "But I thought you said that one of us would need to have some sort of attunement with our destination. I've never set foot here, have either of you?" Both men shake their heads. "Then the only connection we have here is Michael's..." She trails off, looking at David.

"Oh! Sorry." Michael shakes his head. "Riley, Piper, this is my twin brother, David. I also know Adam." He points at the blonde man. "But everyone else is new. David, Piper is a student at the institute with me, and Riley is visiting from his druid circle."

"You already know Adam, and this is Liss, Khazak, Corrine, Nate, and Tsula." David points each of us out. "Wait, you teleported here all the way from your school?" I am as shocked as David is. The Elven Institute for Arcane Studies is considered the preeminent training school for wizards and other arcane spellcasters and is located halfway around the world. "I still don't... How? You can just...do that? Could you go back if you wanted to, too?"

"I mean, yeah." Michael shrugs. "We already figured out all the hard stuff. We might need a few minutes to recharge, but we've got more than enough 'fuel.'" He pats the bag thrown over his shoulder, and a puff of smoke flies out. No, not smoke, soot. Michael looks down in shock. "Uh-oh."

"Michael..." The anxiety is clear on Piper's face as she watches the man open the bag, releasing another cloud of soot into the air.

"Oh no." Michael begins to sift through his bag, which appears to be filled with some sort of black and grey powder. "Nononononononono." He pulls his hand out, a large pile of soot in his palm. "The spell burned through all of it."

"Must be the added distance, aye?" Riley, the red-head guesses.

"How are we supposed to get home?" Piper appears livid.

"What is that stuff?" David nods toward the powder-filled bag.

"It *was* reponiam—a special kind of crystal that can store magical energy." He sifts his hand through the powder. "But only once, and then after it's been used, it turns into ash."

"How are we supposed to get home, Michael?" Piper repeats her question with significantly more worry.

"I don't know!" he half-shouts in frustration, throwing his hands in the air. "Let me think..."

"We just need to get you more of that repo... Whatever it is, right?" David shrugs.

"It's not that easy, David." Michael shakes his head.

"Why, is it rare or something?" He gestures to the bag.

"Sort of?" Michael worries his lip. "It's not hard to get if you know where to find it, but it only grows in specific caves—"

"Well, there's like a dozen caves right over—"

"Located at least three miles below sea level, directly underneath a leywell," Michael quickly finishes his thought. "We're able to make as much as we want, but there are only six known caves like that in the world right now."

"Five," Piper corrects. "One was sealed by an earthquake a few months ago."

"See?" Michael nods his head in her direction with a sigh.

"So then what do we do?" David's question is genuine as if there are not at least a hundred others worth asking right now.

"I guess we're stuck here until we find more. At least we have you and your—" Michael's posture stiffens as his own eyes narrow. "Hold the fuck on. We skipped the part where you explain what the fuck you've been doing for the last five fucking months! We're almost four-fucking-thousand miles from home! I couldn't even find you with fucking magic! Mom's worried you might be *dead*! Who the fuck even are these people?!" He pauses and peers around his twin at the rest of us. "No offense."

If I had any lingering doubts that they were siblings, the six "fucks" in a row just took care of them.

"Uhhhh…" David steps backward slowly in a panic, eyes going wide. Then he holds his hands in front of his chest in the shape of the letter T. "Timeout!"

"David, you can't just call a timeout in real li—"

"Can and did, nerd!" David continues to step backward, turning around and squeezing between Adam and Corrine before raising his hand to the air and circling a finger around. "Huddle up, team!"

I watch as, with a sigh, the rest of the team all turn to follow David, grouping together with their arms thrown over each other's shoulders and forming a half circle. Then they look at myself and Tsula, David gesturing expectantly with his head for us to join them. *Oh.* This bizarre human ritual seems to confuse Tsula as much as myself, and she points at herself to make sure they mean her as well. With a shared shrug, the two of us crouch down to squeeze together with the others and close the circle, all while the three still on the platform look on in a mixture of confusion and exasperation, the latter emotion mostly coming from Michael.

"So, I know this seems pretty insane," David understates, "but apparently my brother and his friends are going to be stuck with us for a little while."

"I still don't believe that they actually teleported here," Nathaniel gripes.

"We *literally* saw it happen," Elisabeth gripes more.

"Regardless, they're here, and the right thing to do is to help them," Adam settles. "And there are certain things that happened in the last few months that we probably need to leave out of the story we're about to tell them."

"Like getting arrested and spending two months in jail," Corrine says sheepishly.

"Among other things," David adds.

"You mean like your new tent buddy?" Nathaniel snarks.

"No, asshole, I mean like *being murdered and then coming back to life*," David corrects him angrily. "I don't see a point in freaking him out over something we still don't really know anything about."

"But David, he might be able to help," Adam offers.

"No. I don't want him or anyone else in my family to know. Period." David shakes his head. "But...we probably need to keep quiet about some of the other things, too." I feel the hand on my back squeeze my shoulder as David's head turns to me. "Sorry."

"It is okay," I lie as I watch him ensure his collar is tucked into his shirt. "I understand." Which I do, but that does not mean it stings any less to hear.

"So, when we talk to these guys, we need to leave out... just about everything from the last two months," Adam concludes with a sigh.

"I would also like to point out that not speaking about the *secret city in the forest* was one of the conditions for your release," I remind the four humans who are not David.

"What do we say we were doing instead?" Corrine asks.

"Just more of what we spent that first month doing," David suggests. "Stupid errands and deliveries up and down the coast."

"I guess that works," Elisabeth agrees.

"So, when we talk about anything that happened after Holbrooke until we left V'rok'sh Tah'lj, we—" Adam pauses his clarification. "Wait, what do we say we're doing *now*?"

"Uhhh..." David thinks. "Sightseeing?"

Adam stares at David for a beat before shaking his head with a sigh. "You know what? Sure. We left Holbrooke after finishing a delivery to do some sightseeing. We don't talk about Tah'lj, or getting arrested, or David dying, or any other sensitive topics. Everyone clear?" As we all murmur our assent and nod our heads, Adam turns to Tsula. "Sorry, I'm sure this all seems pretty crazy."

"...Just happy to be included?" She makes the statement sound like a question.

"Was that everything?" Adam asks, wrapping up our talk.

"I missed team huddles," Elisabeth says from David's right.

"Aww." David bumps his head into hers lightly.

The "huddle" breaks after that with David again taking the lead as we move back onto the platform with his brother.

"Okay!" David tells his brother with a thumbs up.

"Okay?" Michael asks, still irritated by the entire display. "Okay *what?*"

"Oh, sorry." David shakes his head. "Okay, you and your friends can travel with us." He gives another thumbs up, this one with his signature grin.

Which does not seem to impress his twin in the slightest. Michael stares at him, half-dumbfounded and half-annoyed. I must admit, it is a *lot* more fun being on this side of David's antics. I am not sure what his plan here is though. Does he honestly expect to keep *everything* from his brother?

"*David.*" It is *strange* hearing that name said in that tone coming from someone else.

"What?" David asks his brother innocently.

"*WHAT THE HELL IS GOING ON!?*" Michael screams in his brother's face.

His brother who is...trying and failing to hold in a laugh.

"I hate you so fucking much," Michael whines as he wipes both his hands down his face in frustration. I get the feeling that is not the first time he has said that.

"Okay, okay, sorry." David's smile and apology are sincere. "Just come with us. It's over an hour's walk to get back into town. I'll fill you in on what's been happening on the way, okay?"

That seems to calm Michael, rage vanishing from his still slightly reddened face. "Okay. Thank you."

"What is the nearest city?" Piper asks as the group begins to walk off the platform.

"Pákannon," Corrine answers her.

"Hopefully we'll be able to find some way to contact the institute." Piper tells Michael.

"Yeah, we can probably—" Michael stops when the ground gives another shake.

"What was that?" Elisabeth asks, turning to face the platform. "Is it turning on again?"

"No, that was somethin' else," Riley answers, eyes scanning the ground in front of us as the rumbling continues. "There!"

The druid points at a spot in the dirt, where a crack in the earth has formed, and without warning a writing mass of vines bursts forth to the surface. Then at least ten more appear and do the same. With a sigh, I draw my sword, the rest of my team reaching for their own weapons. So much for that picnic.

Chapter 7

"**What the hell are those things?**" **Elisabeth asks as more** vines burst up through the ground and some sort of creatures slither out. They look to be made of vines. leaves, and other vegetation, and there are over a dozen of them now, slowly shambling towards us as our group draws our weapons.

"*Vitaceae Ambulatis,*" Nathaniel answers quickly. "Living vines. A magical plant creature."

"They live underground, attracted to leylines," Riley, the druid, fills in. "They're normally a peaceful bunch, but I'm guessin' activatin' the Spires woke 'em up and they're none too happy about it."

"Look out!" I hear Tsula shout, rushing forward in front of Corrine as a creature extends one of its "limbs," firing off more vines which wrap around her arm.

Before anyone else can react, David slices through them with his sword. The plants around Tsula's wrist immediately go slack and fall loosely to the ground while the creature makes a strange chittering noise as it draws back what is left of its appendage, now leaking a green sap-like substance.

"Mike, you and your friends get behind—" David cuts himself off when he looks up to see his brother already in the middle of the action.

Michael has stepped forward, calling out something I do not catch as he holds out his left hand and a thin column of green light begins to form in it, like he is holding a pole upright. He pulls his other arm back as if drawing back a bowstring, the pole bending into shape as an arrow of light forms on its notching point. He releases the "string" and the arrow goes flying, striking one of the creatures and sending it tumbling to the ground.

To his right, Piper has summoned her own magical weapon, a purple-colored whip extending from a wand held tightly in her grip. It crackles with energy as she swings it in a circle overhead, striking out at another living vine. The violet tendril growing brighter as it wraps around the creature, overcharging it with an arcane current. Next to her, Riley has also joined the fight, using his druid magic to cause another of the creatures to wither. Its body turns brown as it dries out, and he uses his staff to knock it to the ground in a shower of vegetation.

For a split second, a few members of our group stare at the trio of attacking mages dumbfounded—namely David and Adam. I do not fully understand why, but there is no time to ask. With three new allies, the rest of us quickly jump into the fray. We may be outnumbered, but I still see these things as little more than walking foliage.

I rush forward, swinging wide to cleave my longsword through one of them. My attack connects, and I watch as the top half of the living vine falls to the floor, the bottom half tumbling with it. And then they...continue moving. I watch bewildered as they writhe on the ground before one of the halves begins to crawl toward me, its vines reaching for me and making me jump back. As I lift my sword to strike at the undead plant, more vines wrap around my forearm from the right as another of the creatures moves in on me. *Damn!*

"Got him!" My forearm is not trapped for long, David rushing in to free me the same as he did to Tsula.

"Thank you." I offer David a quick smile before returning to my previous target and David turns to his new one.

"How do we stop these things since they don't exactly seem to die?" David calls out his question for anyone to answer.

"Just keep hackin' away!" Riley replies. "They can't really be killed, short of destroying every last bit, but ya hurt 'em enough and they'll go dormant."

I use my sword to cut into the creature over and over until it does just that, its writhing coming to a stop and allowing me to join David in finishing off his own enemy. All around me the rest of the group is doing the same, the mages with their magic while Adam and Elisabeth use their weapons. I even see Corrine repeatedly striking one with her staff that Tsula is holding in place with a conjured snare—and I wasn't even aware she was a spellcaster. I am just glad that Nathaniel has not decided to attempt any fire spells in the middle of a forest.

I try to stay somewhat near David as we fight, who in turn tries to stay near his brother. It looks as though he is trying to guard him as if he is unsure that his brother is capable of defending himself. Which is strange because I have not seen the man break even a drop of sweat as he slings his spells. He and his two friends have been taking down vines left and right. By the time the final shrub stops wriggling, those of us using our swords are exhausted.

"Is that all of them?" Adam asks, panting.

"I think so." Elisabeth nods, then waves her hand in the direction of the mountains. "But maybe we should start walking back to the city before something else wakes up."

"There's something I want to test out first," Adam says then turns to David. "David, go touch the spire again, the same one you did right before your brother teleported in. I want to see if anything happens."

"You were touching the monument right before we teleported?" Michael asks his brother to confirm.

"I brushed my hand over part of it." David steps onto the platform. "Do you think that's what made you all show up here instead of where you were aiming for?"

"I mean, no, because it makes absolutely no sense," Michael says honestly. "But we might as well see. Crazier stuff has happened." *You have no idea.*

David walks up to the black and gold column, looking for the spot with the runes he touched before. After sparing the rest of us a brief glance, he swipes his hand across the stone. We all hold our collective breaths as we wait for a reaction. When none comes, we relax, and David climbs off the platform and rejoins.

"Yeah, see?" Michael comments as his brother rejoins us. "Couldn't have been that"

After gathering up our abandoned picnic, we start the journey back with our new additions. Our formation is looser, Adam and Elisabeth still in front, but Tsula has joined me at the rear while everyone else is jumbled up in the middle. David is just ahead of me, next to his brother.

"Where did you learn how to fight like that?" David asks his twin.

"What do you mean? The institute," Michael responds, slightly confused. "Did you think we just sit around reading books all day?"

"I mean yeah, kinda." David shrugs.

"*Casting* spells is actually a pretty important part of the curriculum," Michael responds flatly. "So is practicing how to use them in self-defense and combat. We have magical duels all the time."

"Wait, really? That actually sounds cool." I can hear the interest rise in David's voice. "How many have *you* won?"

"I, uh..." *Apparently the stammering is genetic as well.* "A few? Not that many."

"He's lying," Piper's voice rings out from up ahead. "He's the current record holder for most wins in a single semester. He won the Merlin Cup last year!"

"Dude!" David looks to his brother in surprise and joy and smacks him in the arm with the back of his hand. "That's awesome. What's the Merlin Cup?"

"It's just this silly unofficial tournament the students put together." He rubs his arm as he continues to try to downplay his accomplishments. *Is he always this humble?* "It's nothing, really."

"I dunno, man. Seems like you might be kind of a big deal over there." David nudges his brother in the side with his elbow. "You also just teleported halfway across the world."

"I actually have a *lot* of questions about that still." Nathaniel turns around as he speaks, walking backwards.

"Me too," David says with his hand raised. "Like namely, *how?*"

"I'm not sure I know where to start." I hear the young wizard blow out on an exhale before continuing. "It's something I've been working on for over a year. Well, the actual teleportation spell took a year. We spent at least six months before that researching monuments like the Onyx Spires."

"So, there are other places you could have teleported to?" Corrine asks next. "Why did you end up here?"

"I still don't get how that happened," David agrees.

"I don't either." Michael shakes his head. "We only meant to travel about thousand miles from the Institute and back. I'll have to check through all my notes once we get to Pákannon and see what might have gone wrong." He pats the bag his notes are presumably kept in, more soot escaping. "Right after I clean everything off," he finishes with a sigh. "We shouldn't have even been able to get here."

"What do you mean?" David asks next.

"Well, the spell calls for something familiar to this place and the monument. Like a rock, or a plant, or even just a strong memory or personal connection." Michael half shrugs. "None of us have anything like that. You're the only odd variable I can think of."

"How did you determine that the monuments could be used for teleportation?" Tsula asks from my left.

"Well, it was still mostly a hypothesis until we actually tried it, but it had been my working theory for a while," Michael answers after turning his head back in our direction. "I'm not the first person to suspect it or anything. There are old documents and reports that mention the monuments and bright lights, loud noises, people appearing from nowhere. But nothing from the elves themselves."

"Aye, and some druid circles hold writings datin' back almost as long, speakin' about people who can 'move through the earth,'" Riley turns to add. "An' almost all of 'em are near a monument."

"I met Riley last year when he was passing through the institute on his pilgrimage," Michael explains to his brother.

That would explain what a druid was doing at a school traditionally for *arcane* magic users. As they grow in skill, it is common for druids to make "pilgrimages" to other druid circles and continue their training. New teachers bring new knowledge, and the changes in the terrain and weather force them to examine their magic and how to apply it differently. This is a common practice for many natural spellcasters, but druid circles have a semi-formal system in place.

"When I found out what he was workin' on, I was happy to share my own thoughts," the red head explains. "Never been the best with numbers, but I had ideas about what ya could do with the connections between leylines with the right spells."

"He helped me to stop thinking about the problem from a solely arcane standpoint," Michael continues. "I was kinda getting lost in the weeds, looking for more complicated solutions instead of simpler ones."

"That all sounds absolutely *lovely*," Nathaniel's sarcasm cuts through the air, "but it does not change the fact that it is *impossible* to convert a living creature into energy and back again."

"Huh?" David looks around at the spellcasters surrounding him, confused.

"You're not wrong," Michael tells Nathaniel, ignoring his confused twin. "But part of thinking of things differently was looking into alternate ways to make that conversion. Piper was a big help with that."

"Yes, where would you be without me?" Piper responds from ahead, a hint of teasing cockiness in her voice.

"You mean besides four-thousand miles from home?" Riley adds with a teasing nudge.

"I didn't contribute *that* much," Piper continues, ignoring the red-head. "I just helped figure out the correct parameters to work within. We limited spells to only what would be available to both arcane and natural spellcasters since those were the two branches of magic with evidence of this even being possible."

"The basic concept of teleportation is to transform a person's body into magical energy, which moves at the speed of light—very, very fast—and then reform them at another location," Michael explains, mostly to his twin, who continues to look confused. "I kept thinking about the energy traveling through the air, but Riley got me to start thinking, what if it moved through the earth?"

"That still doesn't solve the problem with converting something *living* into energy and back," Nathaniel reminds.

"Getting to that," Michael assures him. "So, since we were already re-examining the similarities between natural and arcane magic, we started looking at other things the monuments had in common. And Riley's ideas of moving through the earth got me thinking about caves."

"Caves?" David asks.

"It's more about what grows in them," Piper responds. "The reponiam. Four of the six cave systems it can be grown in are under elven monuments. Given its properties, we gathered that there might be more than just a tenuous link."

"Reponiam has a lot of uses, but the main one is storing spells," Michael continues. "You can sort of save the spell inside the crystal, before it's actually cast. Then later, you or someone else can activate and release it. But what if you could store something—or someone—who has been transformed into energy instead?"

"You're hardly the first to wonder that, and you would have run into the same issues as everyone else, namely that *you can't transform the living.*" Nathaniel seems awfully defensive about something that is in no way an attack on him. "People have used reponiam to store objects for…ever, but it doesn't work the same with something that's alive."

"Again, you're not wrong. There are two reasons a person dies because of the transformation," Michael continues explaining, remaining calm and collected despite the hostility. "The first is that the body no longer makes electrical impulses on its own after being reconstituted. Your heart is stopped. That can actually be reversed, though it is still *super* dangerous, and entirely pointless because of the second reason: when a person, animal, or even plant is transformed into energy, their astral form loses the connection with their body, and there's no way to reconnect the two. Even if you managed to revive someone, they would just be an empty shell."

"So how'd you figure out a way to fix that?" David asks, and I feel like I have to credit him for being able to follow along so far as even I am having a hard time understanding some of this.

"Research. A *lot* of research," Piper answers with a sigh. "We probably spent the better part of last year looking into everything we could about astral forms and ways to affect them."

"Aye, I remember the two of ya sendin' me on my way with *homework*," Riley complains. "All I asked fer was a faster way to travel!"

"After a couple of months of looking, Piper came across the notes of an old gnome wizard. He had developed a way to use his magic to attack his enemy's astral forms and defend his own," Michael continues. "All of his spells used reponiam as a component, so we started to experiment with the formulas."

"He had a few interesting techniques to shield or reflect psychic and astral attacks," Piper adds. "But nothing to actually protect the connection between the astral form and its host on the physical plane."

"While I was away, I came across old druid texts describin' a way to cast spells from a distance by sendin' the energy through the earth along the path of a leyline," Riley explains his own research findings. "It also used reponiam as a spell reagent."

"When Riley shared that info with us, we had another piece of the puzzle," Michael continues, and I cannot help but notice this is starting to feel less like an explanation and more like a story. *Are all the Ceranos this theatrical?* "But we were still missing something, and there was one last component that we still hadn't looked too closely at: the monuments."

Piper elicits a groan of disapproval at Michael's mention of monuments. "*Please* do not make it sound more interesting than it actually was. We spent nearly *four months* scouring the surface of that bloody thing. I can still see it when I close my eyes. It haunts me."

"So, right outside the Institute is our own elven monument," Michael says with a small laugh at his friend's outburst. "Nguzo Umoja, The Pillars of Unity. It's about as big as the Onyx Spires on a triangular platform with a pillar in each corner that meet diagonally over the center of the platform."

"It, and every other ancient elven monument, are covered in Old Elvish runes," Piper says with a sigh. "Not in any particularly easy to read order or even at a consistent height. No, they are dotted all over the surface, like a terrible case of chickenpox. And we recorded every. Last. One. *Then* we had to translate them."

"Right, we had almost another month of just translating whatever we could, which wasn't a lot," Michael matches Piper's sigh. "But of what we *could* translate, we saw a lot of similarity to the spellwork we had been researching. Even bits and pieces of the astral protection. As if the monuments were prepared for the exact thing we were saying they were. So, we came up with a plan."

"They were the ones comin' up with plans. I was just taggin' along at that point." Riley shakes his head. "Maths are nothing but a pain in the arse."

"Okay, so Piper and I came up with a plan," Michael concedes. "Taking what we knew about the monument's runes, we built a spell that we hoped would take us from one monument to the other."

"You 'built a spell' just like that?" Now David is sounding skeptical.

"Well no, not 'just' like that. It's an extremely compli-cated process." I catch Michael rolling his eyes as he turns to the side. "We had to figure out a dozen different spells, all stacked on top of each other and cast in a very specific order in a very specific location. We had to determine the mass-to-energy conversions, work out how much additional power would be needed to propel us along the leyline to our target, calculate the distance to that target and how much reponiam would be needed for the journey..." Michael trails off when he notices the blank look on David's face. "Like I said, it was complicated. Not to mention the guess-work required for the astral connection parts, and since we couldn't test it, we made sure to go over the details with a fine-toothed comb, multiple times."

"Why couldn't you test it?" David quirks his head in confusion.

"Because of the way the spell works, the person casting it has to be part of what's being teleported," Michael rea-sons. "Since we couldn't translate *everything*, there was no way of knowing if what we were doing would work until we actually did it."

"Wait, so that was the first time you've ever done *anything* like that?" David points his thumb behind us in the direc-tion of the Onyx Spires. When his brother only nods his head, he reaches over and shoves him on the hard shoulder. "What the hell!? You could have fucking died! Or a million other things could have gone wrong! What if you screwed up something important? What were you thinking?!"

"Uh, 'don't screw up,' I guess?" Michael rubs his shoulder, glaring at his brother. "I wasn't really that worried. I knew we had figured it out. Or at least I was pretty sure."

David can only stare at his brother in shock, mouth hanging open. I take more than a little joy in seeing how David feels when someone he cares about does something reckless and ill thought out. I cannot help the snort of laughter that escapes me, causing both men to turn and look at its source.

"Apologies." I wave to both of them, doing my best to hide my smile.

"I can't believe your school would let you do something like that." David shakes his head, continuing the conversation. "Shit, there's gotta be like a whole group of people that saw you disappear, right? They must be freaking out that you haven't come back yet."

"Actually, we didn't have anyone watching. It was really late and stuff..." Michael trails off, his posture growing stiffer as he looks ahead instead of at his brother.

"Hold on." David's voice turns suspicious. "It's like the middle of the night over there now, isn't it? Why were you up so late doing this alone?"

"It just seemed like the best time. We didn't want to disturb anyone or distract from classes, you know..." Michael is still not meeting his twin's eyes, and his friends have gone silent as well.

"Holy shit." David looks at his brother in realization. "You weren't supposed to do this at all, were you?"

There's a beat of silence before Michael finally growls in frustration. "The professors all thought it was too dangerous! Even after presenting them with *two years* of research, not *one* of them would allow us to make an attempt. I just needed a chance to prove to them that it would work!"

"Breaking rules and disobeying teachers? Who are you and what did you do with my brother?" There's a pause before David gasps dramatically and leans in toward his twin. "Is it the mustache? Did it make you evil?" David's post-bad-joke grin is a sight I am all too familiar with, and the annoyed look Michael gives him in return is one I have worn myself. "Blink twice if you need me to get you a razor."

"*Anyways*, like I said, I was sure it would work, and it did," Michael returns to his story. "When we were working to translate the runes etched into the monument, we figured out that some of them were spell fragments. Spells that we would only need to cast the missing parts of to activate. If it worked the way we suspected, it would be like feeding the monument information about who was traveling and where they wanted to go."

"But you still didn't solve the astral connection issue." Nathaniel is beginning to sound less skeptical. "Not to mention reviving the body."

"Actually, one of the spells we *were* able to almost fully translate was in place to revive a person's body with an electrical charge. Which meant there were enchantments in place for both sending and receiving. Since we knew there was at least *something* in place related to astral forms, we really just needed to figure out how to activate it. But just to be safe, we still spent another two weeks working on the spell theory to prove it would work."

"Using the old wizard's astral magic as a base, we devised a spell that would create a 'bubble' around a person's physical and astral forms." Piper seems to have found her voice. "When reponiam itself is converted from matter into energy, it still maintains its 'magical storage' properties. You can store a spell in a reponiam crystal, transform it into energy and back, and it will still be holding the original spell. At least in theory, that should also extend onto the astral plane. If we could use the reponiam to protect not just our corporeal bodies on this plane, but also our astral spirits, it should preserve the link between them."

"Bubble? There was a giant bubble that formed on the platform right before you guys appeared. Is that what that was?" David sounds eager to have made a connection.

"Er, no." Michael shakes his head. "The kind of bubble she's talking about you wouldn't be able to see. It wouldn't even really be bubble-shaped. The 'bubble' you saw was actually a vacuum. There was *nothing* in it, not even air. It's like an anti-bubble."

"*Oooohhhhh*," David responds as though the invented word has cleared everything up. "Was it to like, make sure there was room for you guys when you came in?"

"Actually yeah, that's *exactly* what it's for." Michael is the one to hit David's shoulder for once, though much lighter and with a bright smile at his twin for understanding him. "When our bodies reform, it's to make sure that our matter isn't occupying the same space as any other matter. If so much as a molecule got in the way of even a single strand of hair, it would cause an explosion large enough to level this entire area," Michael finishes his description of absolute destruction as though it were a funny anecdote.

David, myself, and several others stare at his brother in abject horror, his eyes going wide before quickly narrowing, and he reaches out to give the man another forceful shove. "What the *hell* is wrong with you?! You, me, and every other fucking person around us nearly died just so you could prove your teachers wrong?! Are you fucking insane!? What would mom and dad say?!"

"Are *you* seriously going to lecture me about what mom and dad would say right now?" Michael bites back after regaining his balance, rubbing his arm.

"I—"

"Not to cut things short, guys, but we have company," Adam cuts David off with his announcement, bringing us all to a halt.

We are almost to the base of the mountain, when just ahead of us, I can see the guards previously stationed at the top of the mountain pass coming down toward us. Both are wearing looks of determination and worry, and it is not hard to figure out why. The Onyx Spires activating was no doubt quite the spectacle from their vantage point.

"What happened at the Spires?" One of the guards asks, her spear already aimed in our direction. "We saw bright lights and felt the ground shake. Who are these other people with you now?"

"We can explain everything," Adam tells the guard with his hands up in front of him to show we mean no harm.

"Then *start*." Both guards are jumpy, eyes flitting between all the members of our large group.

"It was us." The group spreads as Michael begins to talk, gesturing to his two friends. "We used the Spires to teleport here."

"*Teleport?*" The explanation does little to calm either guard.

"Yes." Michael nods. "From the Arcane Institute in Kirinyaga."

Both guards turn to each other and begin conversing in what sounds like Elvish, so I do not catch what they are saying. They do not seem convinced, but I am not entirely sure what else they could think happened. I am also not sure what options they really have even if we *were* lying.

"They're telling the truth," Tsula's normally small voice rings out from her spot at my side, silencing both guards. She steps forward as she continues to speak. "Just take us to speak with Mayor Elajor. They can explain everything there."

With a final shared look, the guards nod and lead our group back up the mountain. While the rest of the group falls into a tense silence, David seems almost happy for the reprieve in talking to his brother. I hope he does not expect that to last very long.

"And you've been studying this for almost two years now?" Mayor Elajor asks, bent over an open notebook. "Fascinating."

"Yes sir, thank you." Michael bows his head slightly as he speaks. "We're of course happy to share our notes."

It was late afternoon by the time we arrived back at the Council House. After a very brief explanation of what happened, Mayor Elajor moved quickly to set up a more formal inquiry, sending off for note takers as well as three individuals known as the Karthani Elders. It seems to be a largely ceremonial position, a set of elf advisers for the city's head office for things pertaining to local elven matters. Though from the way Elajor sounded when he sent for them, I do not think he finds their advice all that valuable.

"I am not so sure I like the idea of humans using our relics and artifacts as test subjects," one of the elders, an older elf woman with long grey hair complains after Michael and Piper have finished their explanation.

"They're humans studying at one of *our* schools, Elune," another elder, a man with receding hairline, defends.

"Ah yes, the Institute!" Elajor clasps his hands together, returning attention to him. "They must be ecstatic at your success. When are they expecting your return?"

"Err, well you see—" A snort of laughter interrupts Michael, and he turns to glare at David before continuing. "We're not exactly sure how we'll be able to get home yet. We didn't actually intend to travel this far, and when we did, it burned through all of our fuel. Reponiam. Is there any place in town we could get a hold of more?"

"I suppose that would depend on how much you needed." The mayor frowns. "You may be able to find some at one of the specialty shops but not much."

"I was afraid of that." Michael looks crestfallen. "Do you know where the nearest place we might find enough for our needs is?"

"North. Manamequohi most likely." Elajor crosses his arms as he thinks. "It is the only city big enough and with a large enough of a spellcaster presence that might have a stockpile the size you seek. But you are looking at quite a journey."

"*Fuck,*" Michael mutters to himself while a groan passes between the other two teleportees. "Then we also need to contact the Institute and let them know what happened."

"Of course. No doubt they will be worried when you do not reappear in Kirinyaga as expected." Elajor nods to himself.

Michael takes a breath before continuing. "The school is not actually aware of our journey. Not just here but at all."

The mayor's eyes go wide, but a smile slowly creeps across his face. "A little bit of after hours studying, then?"

"I swear, we meant no disrespect. We only wanted to prove—"

"No need to explain yourself to me." Elajor holds out a hand and shakes his head. "I understand. Sometimes you must bend the rules in the name of progress. I would say your results showed that the risk more than paid off."

"Thank you, sir," Michael responds hesitantly. I am not sure he agrees entirely with the mayor's sentiment, and neither do I.

"Speak for yourself, Elajor," Elune states loudly. "I cannot believe they would—"

"This is an amazing accomplishment," the third elder, another woman, younger than the other two finally speaks.

"These three figured what no one else has been able to for thousands of years. This is something to celebrate."

Elune says nothing in return, though I can feel the heat from her glowering from here.

"So about contacting the institute." Michael seems slightly rattled. "Is there a spell-o-gram office in town?"

"I am so sorry to tell you that our last spell-o-gram operator retired just last month." The mayor looks genuinely unhappy to report this to us. "We've contacted the guild and hired a replacement, but he is not due to arrive for another two weeks."

"So that means the only option is—" Michael starts.

"An actual letter," Piper finishes. "Which will take almost a month to arrive."

"They're not even going to know what happened for at least two weeks." Michael's voice sounds grave. "If not longer."

"Think about all the time and resources they're going to waste trying to find us." Piper's voice joins Michael's.

"They're probably freaking out right now." Oh dear. "They probably think we're *dead*."

"We'll be expelled for sure." Both wizards appear to be spiraling.

"Wait, don't they have one of the last—" Michael appears to have remembered something.

"We can't just—"

"We can at least *ask*." Michael turns from Piper to Mayor Elajor. "Sir, correct me if I'm wrong, but isn't Pákannon one of the few cities to have a working prismatic transmitter?"

All four elves are taken aback at Michael's mention of this transmitter.

"I am impressed you are even aware of such a thing." The mayor looks between both humans thoughtfully. "You are correct: we do possess a functioning prismatic transmitter. Unfortunately, it is not in working order at the moment."

"I'm not sure I understand." Michael tilts his head, confused. "You said it was functioning?"

"It *would* be functioning, had one of the conduit crystals not met an untimely end several months ago when *someone* took it upon themselves to dust the artifact collection." The mayor's eyes drift to his right, his posture going stiff.

"...Sorry..." One of the note takers mumbles sheepishly.

"We have not had a chance to retrieve a replacement yet," Elajor finishes.

"Sorry to sound stupid, but what's a 'prismatic transmitter?'" Adam asks what I think most of us are wondering.

"An ancient piece of elven technology," the mayor begins explaining. "They are able to communicate with each other at great distances, sending pictures and sound instantaneously. But only a few remain working in the world."

"They use a similar method to our teleportation spell, moving energy along leylines," Piper adds. "It's partially what we based our theories on."

"How difficult would it be to get one of these crystals?" David jumps in, eager to assist.

"It is not exactly that it would be difficult." The mayor looks as though he is thinking. "The only nearby place one could be found would be the Ruins of Karthani."

"What's to stop us from going there and getting one?" David asks next, apparently volunteering the rest of us.

"David, they're ancient elven ruins," Michael corrects his twin. "Meaning off-limits to non-elves."

"Speaking of ruins, is this not the group here because of the—" the male Elder begins to ask.

"Believe it or not, sir, this is completely unconnected to our original reasons for visiting," I find myself saying before he has a chance to finish. There are a few confused looks, especially from Michael, but David mouths a silent "thank you" in my direction.

"Right." The mayor is one of the people to look at me questioningly. "But Michael is correct, typically only those of elven heritage are permitted to venture onto those lands."

"Th-that's not *entirely* true," Tsula's voice rings out from the back of the room.

"Tsula! How did I miss you for a second time today?" The mayor smiles at her sudden appearance.

"Hello, sir." Tsula offers the man a small bow after moving toward the front of our group.

"What were you about to say?" I elbow David for his bluntness.

"In the past, we've allowed non-elves to travel the ruins with an escort." She mostly looks at the mayor while she speaks. "For research or even emergencies. I can remember when little Yansa went missing a few years ago; her search party had a lot more than just elves, and no one questioned when they trailed her all the way to the outskirts of Karthani."

"You make a very good point, Tsula." Elajor appears to be mulling over her words thoughtfully. "You are not the only one to think so. The marshal sang this group's praises in regard to turning in those bandits. You might even be able to find some reponiam there, though I am not sure if it will be enough for everything you need. The ruins are full of all sorts of magical artifacts that were left behind."

"If we had enough to send back even one person, we could easily get more and return for the rest," Michael sounds hopeful. "Would you really let us do that, sir?"

"I've only known them for a short while, but from what I've seen, they are a very capable group of people," Tsula bolsters the group's chances.

"You cannot honestly be considering—" Elune starts to complain again.

"That is *enough*, Elune." Mayor Elajor turns to give the woman his direct attention. "Since you seem so keen to focus on our differences, I would like to remind you that this is not in fact *our* city. *Our* city lies in ruins in the mountains, and the only reason any of our families are able to call this place home is because the good people of Pákannon took in the survivors and gave them *all* a chance to rebuild. The descendants of those good people have elected me to be their mayor for the next four years, so if you will *kindly* stop trying to undermine me for the sake of your pride, I would like to be able to do my job and help these people!"

The mayor receives no response to his outburst, though Elune looks suitably chastised and I cannot help but notice the smirks the other two elders are wearing.

"Now then." Mayor Elajor turns around to fully face us once again. "I am granting your request to journey to the Karthani Ruins and retrieve a conduit crystal as well as any reponiam you may find."

"That's wonderful!" Tsula cheers, though I am struggling to remember when exactly we made that request. I suppose it at least helps David's brother, even if it also adds a few extra days to our travel schedule.

"—On the condition that Tsula acts as your escort," Elajor apparently finishes.

"W-what?" The young elf's voice squeaks.

"In fact, if you would not mind retrieving several crystals, we can hopefully avoid this problem should any future *accidents* occur," the mayor adds, looking over to the same note taker, who is decidedly not looking at anything but the table in front of him.

"You guys really don't mind doing this for us?" Michael asks Adam. "I know you have to have better things to do."

"Hey, we're friends, man. I'm not just gonna leave you all hanging out to dry." He clasps his friend's shoulder. "I don't think David would let me."

"Damn right," David adds.

"We'd be more than happy to retrieve the crystals for you, sir." Adam steps forward to accept for the group, not wanting to give him the chance to change his mind. "Would you be able to provide us with some directions? I'd also like to know anything else we can do to ensure we are as respectful as possible while there."

"Of course, if you and Tsula will come with me, my assistants and I will be able to get you a map and some information on the ruins." The mayor smiles at Adam and Tsula, then turns to the three elves seated behind. "Elders, I would like to thank you for your council today. This meeting is adjourned."

"We'll meet back up with you at the inn once I get all the details," Adam tells us as he and a very nervous-looking Tsula exit the room with the mayor and his aides, the three Elders leaving soon after.

"Alright, while they're doing that, who wants to get some food?" David asks as soon as we are alone, patting his stomach. "You guys kinda interrupted our lunch with all the teleporting stuff."

Before anyone has a chance to answer, Michael moves to stand right in front of his twin, a serious look on his face.

"...Not hungry?" David dares to ask.

Without another word, Michael grabs David by the shirt collar and drags him sputtering from the room. It seems my pup's time on avoiding that conversation has finally run out.

Chapter 8

With Adam and Tsula working out our travel details with Mayor Elajor, and David and Michael occupied with their familial discussion, Corrine, Elisabeth, and I take it upon ourselves to bring Piper and Riley to the inn and get the rooming situation for the night sorted out. Our visiting mages did not exactly bring their wallets, so in order to not go broke on lodging, some of us may need to double up.

"You can share my room!" Corrine cheerfully offers Piper.

"As long as everyone is alright with sharing, I believe we will only require one additional room," I tell the others as I work out the details with the innkeeper.

"Khazak, Liss, thank you very much for helping us with our accommodations," Piper thanks us both.

"Yeah, Adam'll be totally fine with you bunking together, Riley," Liss is quick to offer for our absent leader.

"Why would he not room with—" She gives me a subtle look that jogs my memory, and I try to quickly correct myself. "Of course, Michael will no doubt want to stay with his brother. Who up until now has roomed with Adam. Which means my room is also available to share, should Adam not be okay with it." *Spirits, have I always been this awkward?*

"Well thank ya Khazak, but assumin' there's no complaints, I think I'll stick with Adam." He leans in to give me a small wink. "Yer both beefy boys, but I imagine I'll get a little more leg room with the blonde."

"Of course." I am happy to concede that battle to Adam.

"Come on. You can store your stuff in Mike and David's room while we wait for Adam to get back," Liss tells Riley after paying the innkeeper for an additional room and picking up the key.

"I'll bring you up to my room so you can do the same," Corrine tells Piper. "There's even a shower if you'd like."

"That sounds *wonderful*," the dark-skinned mage practically purrs. I hope she realizes she will be responsible for getting her own water.

With that taken care of, the rest of the group turns toward the staircase leading to our rooms. Even Nathaniel, who up until now has been content to sit back silently while the three of us figured out logistics, is following after Liss, though I also see his eyes landing squarely on Piper's ass for more than a brief glance. Sensing an opportunity to do some of the "shopping" David and I previously discussed, I make a polite exit.

"I am actually going to take care of a few things around town," I tell the group as they begin to walk away. "Shall we meet back here for dinner in a few hours?"

"Sounds good," Liss confirms with a nod. "We'll need to pick up extra supplies and stuff for the next few days, too. See you back here later."

Stepping out into the open air and away from the group, I feel my body relax, releasing a tension I had not realized I was holding. The past few hours have been stressful to say the least. Not only was Michael's appearance an extremely volatile surprise (both physically and emotionally), but we now have three additional people to consider *and* an entire side mission that will be adding several days onto our journey.

To top it all off, I am unable to turn to my pup for any comfort because he is too afraid of what his brother might think. I understand his concern, but I am still not looking forward to sleeping alone in bed tonight. At least it is only for a few... I freeze in my tracks. Surely, he would not expect us to do this for a nearly full month... What am I saying? If I am only just coming to this realization, then I know damn well David has not thought about any of this.

I am considerably less relaxed as I make my way to the general store, feet stomping with each step. It takes me a few minutes of searching the shelves to locate the oil, and by the time I do, I no longer want to bother with it. What is the point if it will just sit unused in my bag for the next four weeks? Frustrated, I growl to myself and manage to frighten a small woman to my right who is only trying to do her own shopping.

That helps to shake me from my bad mood. I sigh, grabbing the bottle of oil to pay for at the front counter. I know more than anything right now, David needs my support and understanding, and perhaps I am making a few too many assumptions. I just need to talk to him, and we will be able to figure it out.

Or else I will spank him until we do.

After the lubricant is taken care of, the next item on my list proves to be much more difficult to track down: recharging David's cleansing charm. I am not even sure where to start. It is not as though I am aware of any sex shops in the city. I should have thought to ask Brull before I left V'rok'sh Tah'lj. The man is like an older brother to me, and he runs such a shop himself. I should have asked him for a fresh charm before I left. Oil too.

"<You are leaving right now?>" Brull asks with a laugh as soon as I finish telling him. "<Is there anything you want to take from the store?>"

"<I am already worried they may be too far ahead to catch up with before nightfall.>" I shake my head. "<There are still so many things to do before I can leave.>"

"<You two really do not like making things easy.>" His generous belly shakes as he laughs again. "<Damn, and I started on something you would like, too. Just needs a few more days.>"

"<What is it?>" I am always curious to learn of Brull's new inventions, and not just because most of them are to be used in the bedroom.

"<You remember that Yehasuri girl I used to date?>" he asks, then gestures to the top of his bald head. "<The one who used to change her hair color a lot? The enchanter.>"

"<I do. She moved back to Yasurdi, did she not?>" The Yehasuri are a tribe of halflings, and their main city, Yasurdi, is located to the south of ours.

"<Well she moved back, and she learned some new tricks.">" He gives me a lecherous grin. "<Been getting together here and there, and between her magic and my crafting, we have come up with some very interesting toy ideas.>"

"<Really? Do tell.>" Even though I have absolutely no time for this.

"<I do not want to ruin the surprise, but I just know you are gonna love the new toy we have been working on—and David will think it is downright evil.>" He grins again before stopping to think. "<I still need to work out the issues with the prototype though. Hmmm...>"

"<Friend, as much as I would love to hear more—>"

"<Tell you what.>" He holds out his hand to stop me. "<I know you are not going to be there long, but if I can finish it in the next few days, I will mail it up to Pákannon on horseback. I will tell them to hold it there for three days, and if you have already left, I will have them send it on to Maname. Sound good?>"

"<*Sounds wonderful, my brother.*>" I reach for the inside of his wrist, pulling him into a hug. "<*I am afraid I really must go now though. I will miss you.*>"

"<*Of course. I will miss you too, Khazak,*>" he tells me as we release each other. "<*Now, go get your boy.*>"

Remembering that I may have some new toy to torture my pup with helps brighten my day. After stopping to ask directions, I make my way toward the city's post office, electing to worry about recharging the charm later. I find it not far from the Council House, a large and fairly nondescript building. Inside are a number of counters, the employees behind them attending to a small line of people in front.

Off to the right I see a similar-looking-but-still-different counter, the sign above spelling out "Spell-o-gram Office" as well as "Temporarily Closed" in several different languages. I do not know exactly how spell-o-grams work, only that it takes quite a bit of training before a guild member can be assigned to an office. Sending information over long distances from one person to another requires a lot of energy and concentration, and you also need to take into account the actual physical location of the people communicating. That is the main reason we do not have an office in V'rok'sh Tah'lj.

There are many options for using magic to send messages and information. The Magical Communications Guild, which runs and maintains the spell-o-gram network, often works hand-in-hand with local post offices to supplement their city's ability to communicate over distances with magic. There are teams of creatures large and small that are trained to make deliveries, boats and airships utilizing magic to move through the seas and air more quickly, and even enchanted vellum, an extremely expensive form of magical parchment that when written on, copies the same message onto its twin instantly.

But I am not here for any magical purposes. I only need to see if I have a package waiting for me, so I step into the back of the line and wait my turn. One by one, each person in front of me gets called to one the counters and helped until fifteen minutes later it is finally mine.

"<Good afternoon!>" The man working the counter, a human, tells me in Pákagi before finishing with what I assume is some variant of "<How can I help you?>"

"Good afternoon," I repeat back in Common. "I am checking to see if a package has been delivered for Khazak Uzi'gor. It may also be under Khazak Ironstorm." I drop my voice and lean forward slightly for the next part. "It would have come from the Shad'rok Logging Camp from a Brull Lugdum or Flamemaul."

"Yes, we did get a few things in this morning," the man tells me with a nod. "Let me just step in the back and check for you."

I am only alone for a few minutes before he returns with a small square package wrapped in brown paper and tied with twine.

"Here you are, sir!" The man cheerfully hands over the package. "Is there anything else I can help you with?"

"No, that was everything. Thank you very much." With a small bow of my head, I take the package and exit.

Outside, I cannot help myself and lift the box to my head, jostling it slightly to see if I can hear anything about its contents. Alas, the man seems to have packed it well. I will just have to wait until I am back in my room. Given who it is from and what it is to be used for, opening it in public could be dangerous.

I only have two final stops to make. The first is to the town blacksmith to get rid of the bear trap we picked up on the road. The man does not look pleased to see it, at least not until I tell him it is scrap. Then I find a public water pump and take the time to scrub the various cooking implements and utensils we have been using the past few days. As I am drying and returning them to my bag, I catch something moving in the bushes in the corner of my eye, something black, but when I look over, I find nothing there. *Hmm...*

With those chores finished, the afternoon is almost over, and after managing to only eat half of a sandwich before the craziness of the day took over, I am famished. Time for dinner. I begin my walk back to the inn, crossing through the town square once again. Just as I pass by the bonfire, I notice Tsula staring at it from a nearby bench, deep in thought. Catching her eye, I wave as I walk over, taking a seat next to her.

"Khazak, it's good to see you again," she tells me with a smile, though I can see the stress behind her eyes.

"You as well, Tsula." I think back to her reaction to the mayor's decision in the Council earlier. "I hope I am not interrupting anything."

"Oh no. I just like to come here to think sometimes." She looks toward the fire once again. "And pray a little too, I guess."

"Do you pray often?" I never got the feeling from Nylan that his family was overly religious.

"Not as much as I probably should," she jokes. "My mother likes to tell me to trust in the Great Spirit's guidance, but I'm not sure I can even hear it."

"I understand what you mean," I commiserate, thinking of my own record of sporadic prayer to the Three. "I wanted to apologize. It seems as though you may have been dragged into our group's mess against your wishes." It is likely the reason she is praying.

"Oh, no. It's alright, really," she lies, playing with her braid. "I-I'm sure everything will be fine."

"I can tell this is something outside of your comfort zone." I really do not like the idea of forcing this poor girl to help us. "Perhaps we could try to speak with the mayor again before we leave in the morning and ask about getting a different guide."

"I am pretty sure the only reason Mayor Elajor is allowing you all to enter at all is because I'm going with you." She did refer to him as a "good friend" of her family earlier. "He's always been more willing to bend the rules when me or my mother are involved."

"Yes, I got the sense that there was some history there." A *lot* of history. "Was he recently elected?"

"His term started when the new year did." Tsula nods. "This isn't his first time as mayor though; it's his fourth or fifth term. His last one was about twelve years ago."

"I see. Is he always so combative with the Elven Council?" There seemed to be a lot of tension, at least between Elune and...everyone else.

"I think it can depend?" she offers honestly. "The council doesn't have any real power, especially when the mayor is also an elf. They're mostly in place for when a non-elf is in charge, for when there are concerns over elven lands and artifacts, like now." She hesitates before adding, "It mostly just seems like an excuse for the older people to throw their weight around."

"I am very familiar with that type of person," I tell her with a chuckle. I look up at the sky to gauge the time. "I do not mean to keep you. Are your parents expecting you home for dinner? If not, I was just about to get some myself and would love to hear more if you would like to join me."

"Dinner sounds wonderful. Thank you," she accepts. We stand and walk toward the inn together. "The truth is, Mayor Elajor is more than just a family friend. He is also my mother's ex-boyfriend, and even though they dated over a hundred years ago—literally—he's still carrying a torch for her."

"Oh my." Being his ex's child certainly seems like an awkward relationship to have with someone. "Has that caused him to treat you negatively at all?"

"The exact opposite actually. He's always been amazing to me and my mother." She shrugs. "He thinks of himself as my father's rival, but the man couldn't care less. Barely even pays him attention. But when it comes to Ama and me, he's the nicest guy I've ever met."

"So then, if I may ask, what was the reason for your strong reaction earlier?" I ask her next, remembering her nervous stutter. "When the mayor said you would act as our chaperone."

"Well, I-I've just never really done anything like this before. Like the things you and your friends do." She looks down as she speaks "The trip to the Spires today was the farthest I've been away from home in probably ten years? And even then I was always with my family. I can't fight. What if something happens?"

"You seemed to handle yourself well against the living vines this afternoon." I watched her leap in to defend Corrine and take at least one of them down with her magic.

"Sure, I was fine against a mostly-mindless plant creature with nine other people around me in case something went wrong." She shakes her head. "It was dumb luck."

"You would be surprised how much dumb luck comes into play when fighting," I assure her as we turn onto the road containing the inn. "There is nothing wrong with having a team of people around to back you up. That is why they are formed in the first place. And with the addition of Michael and his friends, we have even more backup."

"I know you are right. Everything will be fine," she repeats herself and takes a deep breath, not sounding as convinced as I think she would like. "Now I have a question: I understand why you want to keep things like David's death and your group's...criminal issues a secret, but why hide your relationship?"

"Ah, that." I take a deep breath myself, trying to stop the negative emotions from returning. "Most of them are from Lutheria, and in that part of the world, two men or two women being in a relationship is not considered publicly acceptable. Many people have negative reactions when seeing one, sometimes even violent ones. Though he has not actually stated as much, I believe David is afraid of that happening with his brother."

"Really? I didn't get the impression that Michael would be like that at all." Tsula looks almost more confused by my explanation.

"I agree with you, but unfortunately, it is not something I can force David into believing." I reach for the handle as we approach the inn's front door, holding it open for my companion. "I am just trying to be understanding and supportive for now."

"Well, that's very sweet of you. I hope he appreciates that," she responds after entering.

"I do as well." Letting the door close behind me, I lead us toward the dining room.

A quick scan reveals some of our group seated together at one of the long tables, specifically Adam, David, and Elisabeth—with our new "recruits" nowhere to be seen. I also note the strange men from this morning in the same seats and wearing the same outfits, though this time they at least each have a plate of food in front of them. After putting in our dinner order, Tsula and I join them. I sit next to David and am happy when he leans over to kiss me without prompting or looking around nervously.

"Where is everyone else?" I ask the rest of the table.

"After I finished talking to Mike, more people wanted to pick his brain about teleporting," David explains, spearing a piece of meat on his plate with a fork. "I came back to see if Piper or Riley would go back to help him out."

"Nate went with them, too. I think he still is having a hard time believing them," Elisabeth speaks next, though I am not so sure he did not go just to stare at Piper's ass some more. "Corrine finished eating and wanted to get some bible-study in early since she has a roommate now."

"On our way back, David and I stopped and picked up another tent and some extra rations and supplies for the next few days. Got my shield repaired too," Adam tells me next, ending with a sigh. "It feels like we've barely had a chance to rest."

"Shit, you know what we forgot?" David half-asks the rest of us. "To see the healer. And we're not going to be able to do any morning check-ups with everyone else around."

"Yes, you seem very upset about that." I fix David with a look. "You *will* see the healer before we leave the city permanently."

"Yes, Sir," David responds, chastised.

"How did the planning go?" I ask Adam, realizing I did not question Tsula for details earlier.

"Good. We have a map to get us to and from Karthani, and another of the city itself marking the places we will hopefully find the crystals we need." Adam nods. "We still have to tell the others, but we'll be meeting Tsula and one of the town's guards at the bonfire at 8 a.m. tomorrow, then we climb up the mountain and start our journey." Adam leans forward so he can look around Elisabeth to Tsula. "Still sound good?"

"Y-yes." Tsula nods much less confidently. "Looking forward to it!" I offer the girl a small smile, hoping her first "mission" goes as smoothly as I've assured her it will.

"What did you end up telling your brother?" I ask David next.

"Exactly what we talked about." David nods confidently. "A very condensed version of what happened in the past few months—with a lot left out."

"Did he believe you?" Elisabeth requests confirmation.

"I don't know." David shakes his head. "He didn't really have a chance to ask any follow-up questions, and I got out of there as fast as I could."

"We'll have to hope it's enough for now," Adam comments with a sigh. "Did you guys have a chance to go over any more of that report?" he asks me, David, and Tsula.

"Oh no! I completely forgot!" The poor girl brings her hands up to cover her face in shame. "I am *so* sorry."

"Hey, it's really not that big of a deal," David reassures her. "It's been a crazy day, and you've already done a lot for us. You don't even have to worry about it, really."

"No, I'll make sure to get through a lot of it tonight." She actually does sound more confident now. "I'll be able to tell you about it tomorrow."

"We will just have to wait for a moment where we can get away from the others." Which might prove difficult. "Thank you, Tsula."

"Don't stay up too late," Elisabeth warns. "I have a feeling tomorrow is going to be a *long* day."

Tsula's and my food is brought out not long after, and a few minutes later, our four missing mages enter the dining room, looking for their own meals. After sharing our plans and schedule for the morning, everyone eats quickly and silently. Our three visitors look exhausted, no doubt from not having slept for almost a full twenty-four hours. One by one, people retire to their rooms as they finish eating, and I say goodnight to David at the table after Tsula leaves for home.

Closing my door behind me, I notice David's things are already gone, leaving me in the room alone. I push down the growing melancholy, setting my bag on the table and placing Brull's package on the center of the mattress. Pulling out my pocketknife, I make quick work of the twine, tearing off the paper to reveal a small wooden box underneath. Lifting the top off of that reveals the inside is stuffed with more paper, and a small note is stuck to the inside of the lid.

I empty the contents of the box, pulling out the crumbled paper stuffing to reveal a very familiar sight, and one I should not be surprised came from Brull: a butt plug. It shines in the light of my room's lantern, made of dark, polished wood, a common material for Brull to work with. It is a decent size, but otherwise appears to be nothing special. The other object in the box confuses me more: a square stone with rounded edges, made of marble. *Is this supposed to go inside of David, too?* Hopefully the note will explain. Pulling it from the inside of the box's lid, I unfold the paper to find Brull's scratchy handwriting within.

<*Khazak,*>

<*I hope this package finds you well. You left in such a hurry and there were so many things I did not get to say to you. I am not going to write them here, so you will just have to come back to Tah'lj and hear them for yourself.*>

<*Now onto your gift! I know, it looks like just a plain old plug, right? Well, I want you to pick it up and tap your finger against the base three times.*>

I set the note down to do as asked, examining the plug in my left hand closely before bringing my other hand in and tapping it three times in quick succession. Immediately, the plug springs to life, vibrating intensely and causing me to drop it onto the mattress with a laugh. *Brull, you evil genius. I could kiss you.* Picking up the vibrating plug, I return to the note.

<Crazy, right? Now, try rotating your finger around the base counterclockwise, and then do the opposite.>

Moving my finger around the base as instructed, I feel the vibrations on the plug start to slow down, then speed back up when I begin to move clockwise instead. Spirits, this is *amazing*. I cannot *wait* to use this with David.

<You tap three times again to turn it off. You can thank Celuma. We came up with the idea together, but it is her magic doing the work. And that is not all! Try doing the same finger gestures on the square stone we packed in there, too.>

Celuma is the Yehasuri girl Brull resumed seeing, and I will need to remember to write a thank you note to both of them. This is not the first of Celuma's work I have seen— she and Brull are also responsible for the creation of our friend Arik's magical harness-attached cock, which allows him to experience all of the sensations of topping when he wears it. She is also the reason for the eclectic underwear selection in Brull's shop, connecting Brull to her equally-kinky tailor friend.

I pick up the stone and repeat what I did with the plug, expecting it to react the same way. Nothing happens at first, at least not that I immediately pick up on. Then I notice the plug has turned back on, and as I continue to make gestures on the stone, I realize I am controlling it from a distance.

I am going to owe them so much more than a thank you note for this.

<We have not tested the exact distance, but Celuma says it should be good for at least a hundred meters. I expect lots of stories of what

you do to David with this when you come back! Give the pup my love. And a load or two. >

<*You are missed, brother,* >

<*Brull* >

Finishing the note brings light tears to my eyes, and after wiping them and playing with the plug a little longer, I put both away in my bag and get ready for bed. After a quick trip downstairs for water and one shower later, I am curled up with a book. It is an old favorite of mine, one of the first I ever read, filled with pirates and adventure. When I finish, I tuck the book back into my bag, and just as I am about to reach over and turn out the lantern, there is a soft knock at my door. *Who could it be at this hour?*

Reaching for my pants, I slide them on as I walk to the door, opening it a crack to peer outside. *David?*

"Hey," he says softly before worrying his bottom lip with his teeth. "Can I come in?"

I nod, too surprised at his appearance to say anything else, and step back, opening the door so he can enter. "What are you doing here?"

"What do you mean?" He steps up to me after closing the door, rubbing his hands along my upper arms. "I wanted to see you."

"What about your brother?" He is going to wonder why David is sleeping in my room instead of his.

"Mike's always been a heavy sleeper." David shrugs. "As long as I'm back in the room before he wakes up, he'll never know the difference."

I want to point out the many flaws in his plan, like what would happen if his brother were to get up for the bathroom or any number of reasons in the middle of the night, but for once, I am feeling selfish enough to use David's obliviousness to my own advantage. I am not going to turn down the opportunity to sleep in the same bed when I am not sure when we will have another chance any time soon.

"Alright, let me set my alarm." With a smile, I retrieve the small stone I placed on the room's table, adjusting the sundial-like knob on top to the needed time. "Does six in the morning sound acceptable?"

"Perfect." I set the alarm back down and turn to find David already stripped down to his underwear, cheeks on display in his red thong. "I believe I am owed a few spankings, Sir."

"Much as I would like to, I think it best to not risk waking someone with all the noise you will undoubtedly make." I step over and run my hand along his ass. Even though he has only earned five today, we both know I would make them count. "Besides, think of how much more fun it will be to let them build up until I can punish you properly."

"Yes, Sir." I can hear David swallow nervously at that revelation. I cannot wait to surprise him with the plug.

"However, since I have you for the night, I am certain I can still find a few uses for you." I grasp his ass in both hands, kneading his flesh roughly. "We just need to find ways of keeping that mouth of yours occupied. Turn around."

David does as told, coming face to face with my stomach and groin. I can feel his eyes on me as my hands work to unbutton my pants, sliding them down my hips to free my cock from its confines. My pup eyes it hungrily, licking his lips as it hangs in the air before him.

I place one hand on the back of his head, pulling him toward me and closing the gap between my cock and his mouth. I growl low when I feel it wrap around me, thrusting forward to quickly bury another quarter of the way into his oral orifice. I close my eyes, savoring the wet heat of his mouth as he attempts to take more of me in.

Eyes open, I bend over his form, forcing more of my cock into him as I reach for his ass. I palm both of his cheeks before giving each a light smack, pleased with the small jiggle they give in return. David whimpers as he arches his back, wordlessly begging for more. It is a pity we must be careful of the noise because right now I want nothing more than to match the color of his ass to the fabric of his underwear.

For now, I will have to make do with this. I grab the back of David's head and spend a few minutes fucking his face, enjoying the feeling of throat spasming around my length. Once I am satisfied with his efforts, I release my hold on his head, allowing him to kneel up on the mattress while I turn to grab the charm and lubricant from my bag.

"Turn around." I twirl my fingers in the air when I step back to the bed, items in hand.

David complies, biting his lip as he presents his ass to me. He lowers his chest to the mattress without being told, his body automatically spreading itself to give me access to his most sensitive areas. I follow the thin red line of his thong down from the top of his ass, barely concealing the dusty hole at the center as it moves down to the red pouch straining with his erection. After pressing the charm up against his stomach, I toss it to the side, ready to focus where my attention is needed.

I slip one of my thumbs under the strap of his thong, sliding it to the side and revealing my prize. I lick my other thumb, bringing it down to gently rub over his hole, watching the muscle twitch and flex as David releases a full-body shudder. After a few more teasing strokes, I reach for the oil, uncorking it with my teeth and dribbling some down his crack. Then comes the awkward dance of trying to recork it without letting go of his thong with my other hand.

Discarding the resealed oil on the bed, I use my thumb to spread the slippery liquid down his crack. I press the pad of my thumb against his hole, watching the tight ring of muscle give way as it swallows the digit. I push in all the way down to my knuckle, feeling David twitch and shudder as I open him. This is really more to help slick my way in than stretch him, but I still cannot help but tease and play with his hole.

Satisfied, I give my boy a light smack on the rump and push him to move farther up the bed. I finish pulling off my own pants, kicking them into the corner but hanging onto my underwear, a simple pair of cloth briefs. Climbing onto the bed behind David, I grab the discarded vial of oil and use it to quickly slick myself up as I shuffle forward on my knees. Once the head of my hard cock begins to poke between his cheeks, I pull the thong strap to the side once more and take aim at my target.

As soon as our skin meets, David is arching and pushing back against me, trying to get the head of my cock to slip inside. I chuckle, sliding my shaft up and down his cleft before taking myself in hand and smacking it across his hole. Before he has the chance to start begging, I reach around and shove my balled-up briefs into his mouth, crotch first. Then, while he is torn between confusion and the intoxicating smell of his owner, I grip myself tightly, take aim, and push inside.

David's low groan of pleasure is muffled by my underwear, his legs spreading farther automatically. I stare down, mesmerized by the sight of my thick green length disappearing into his body, centimeter by centimeter. When his ass is finally touching my thighs, I squeeze him tightly around my shaft, pumping in and out a few times slowly.

Being in an actual bed is so much better than in our tent or up against a tree, but I still have to be careful, lest we wake up one of our neighbors, or worse, Michael. With that in mind, I start to fuck David at a steady pace, slow enough to prevent the bed from creaking while also keeping the sounds of flesh smacking against flesh low enough to not escape the room. David uses a pillow to help further deaden all the involuntary sounds he is prone to making, clutching it to his chest.

As is typical, David is the first to get close, his hole starting to twitch and spasm around my shaft. A few more thrusts and his body goes tense as the orgasm is forced from his hole, his ring trying in vain to push me out. David's only voluntary movement is to clutch the pillow tighter, the soft *squeak* of a high-pitched moan barely escaping the musk-filled fabric still stuffed in his mouth.

After his body relaxes once more, I start to fuck him in earnest, still taking care to keep down our volume. One thing I will say about David's ability to cum dry: it never leaves you wondering if he is enjoying himself. Unless I am punishing him or feeling particularly selfish, I always feel the urge to ensure he gets off first, proving the point that I control his pleasure. Once that is done with, I have no problem taking the reins and diverting that focus back where it belongs: on me, his kavan and Dominant.

His hole grips me tightly as I thrust in and out of his ass. The skin of my cock is shiny, slick with oil to ease my way as I fuck him open. The flesh of his ass shakes each time it strikes my groin, rippling like a stone in a pond. The room is warm from all of our physical activity, the air thick with the smell of sex. Sweat drips down my chest and lands on David's back, his own skin glowing in the lantern light.

Fuck, I am going to cum.

I nearly bite off my tongue to keep from growling as I pull David back and bury my cock deep. I continue to pump with short, strong thrusts as I fill him with cum for the first time in several days. I can feel myself twitch with each shot, no doubt painting David's inner walls white. I bend my body over his, laying atop him while we both catch our breaths.

When I am finally finished, I reluctantly climb off of his warm body, making my way to the bathroom to retrieve a damp towel to clean our bodies with. After wiping down his ass, my cock, and the worst of our sweat, I rejoin David on the bed, pulling him to lay across my chest. Another long day behind us and several more in our future, I know neither of us will be fighting off sleep for long.

"You may want to be very careful about your underwear choices for the time being." I think back to Nathniel's comments on his underwear the other morning and can only imagine what his brother would do if he woke up and saw David sleeping in nothing but a bright red thong. "At least as long as you are sharing a bed and bathroom with your brother."

"Good idea. Thank you, Sir." David nods against my shoulder.

"You know, you have not talked about how you are feeling after everything that happened today." I decide to try and use our post-coital stupor to see if I can get David to open up.

"What do you mean?" David traces his finger over my tattoo as he asks.

"David, you have avoided even *thinking* about your family since before I even met you, and today your twin brother *literally* appeared out of thin air." Is he really going to play dumb with me, too? "I know you must be feeling something."

"...I don't know. Confused at how it happened. Worried about what means for the rest of my family. Maybe even a little scared?" Though he will not actually say what it is he is scared of, I can venture a guess. "But... When I saw him? I just *knew* it was him. And the first thing I felt was *happy*. I missed him so much, Khaz." I can hear the happiness, twinged with just a hint of regret, in his voice. "Like I said, confused."

"Your brother seems like a good man, David." For all his complaints about their father, the man seems to have raised decent children. "I do not think you have anything to be afraid of. You just need to talk to him."

"I know you're right," David says even though we both also know he is still going to worry regardless. "I'm sorry for ignoring you today."

"You did not ignore me, exactly." I kiss the top of his head. "But thank you. I appreciate that."

"It was hard having you so close but not being able to touch or even really talk to you." He stops tracing to wrap his arm around my chest and squeeze.

"It was hard for me, too." I squeeze him back.

"I promise I'll figure something out soon." I know he will. Part of me is just worried that we have very different ideas of what "something" should be.

Chapter 9

I wake up the next morning alone, barely an hour and half after the last time I was awake. David has already returned to his brother's room, though it was not my alarm that woke us but another nightmare. I wanted to ask about what he would do if he has one while rooming with Michael, but as I held his shivering form in the early morning hours, I could not find my voice. Once 6 o'clock rolled around, I released him reluctantly so he could redress and sneak back across the hall.

After laying in the dark for a few more minutes, I pull myself out of bed and get ready for the day, pulling on my clothes after taking care of things in the bathroom. Once I'm finished, I look around the room to make sure I've packed away all of my things; as we are going to be gone on this crystal hunt for the next few days, we did not want to pay for rooms that would go unused. We reserved another five rooms two nights from now when we expect to return. Just in time too as with the upcoming holiday, the city is experiencing an influx of visitors.

I meet Adam, Riley, Corrine, and Piper in the dining room with David, Michael, Nathaniel, and Elisabeth joining soon after. Breakfast is the same as yesterday, and we eat quickly in silence. A glance around the room reveals nothing out of the ordinary, though I do notice the two strange men in their seats by the door again. *Perhaps they are here for the Solstice.*

"Hey, I meant to ask," Michael says to his brother as the last of us finishes eating. "I got up last night to pee and you were gone. What happened?"

"Oh, uh..." David's posture stiffens unnaturally. *I knew I should have said something.* "I had some trouble sleeping so I went for a run."

"In the middle of the night?" Michael questions. "You still do that?"

"Yep!" David agrees eagerly.

"That must be what all the noise I heard last night was," Liss comments slyly, and I cannot hold back the small snicker of laughter that escapes me—her and Nathaniel's room was right next to ours. I regret it immediately when I receive an odd look from Michael, while Liss earns a glare from David.

Stomachs fueled for the first part of our journey, our group of nine stands and files out of the inn. There are more than a few eyes on us given our size, but we cannot be the first group of adventurers to walk the halls of the Sleeping Willow Inn. *Is that what I am now? An adventurer?*

As we approach the town square and bonfire, I see Tsula standing next to an elf in a guard's uniform, likely our guide up the mountain. The poor girl looks nervous, staring down at her feet while her left hand plays with her braid, but when she looks up and notices our approach, she seems to relax.

"Good morning, everyone!" she tells us cheerfully. "I hope you all slept alright."

"Good morning, Tsula," Adam responds for the group. "I think we are all feeling pretty good. What about you?"

"I think so." She nods. "This is Degoto. He will be taking us to the entrance of the cave that will lead to Karthani."

"Nice to meet you, Degoto." Adam holds out his hand for a handshake, which the man takes after a moment of hesitation.

"If you are all ready, I can take you up now." He looks over our group of (mostly) humans with a hint of nervousness.

"Lead the way." Adam takes a step back from the man, turning toward the mountain.

We begin our ascent from the mountain's base, passing the network of mining tunnels on our way up. We came down this way when we returned yesterday, but there must have just been a recent shift change as I see far more miners this time around. Some of them give our group a strange look as we pass by, but most pay us no mind. We are not walking in anything resembling our normal formation, with Adam and Tsula in front to handle the guard.

"So, what's with the orc?" I hear Michael ask his brother quietly just ahead of me. *What?*

"What do you mean?" David answers in a loud whisper. "Also, even if he wasn't *right* behind us, he can totally hear you."

"Sorry," he turns to apologize to me sheepishly. "You're sort of the odd man out, and I was curious how you all ended up getting together."

I see David tense slightly at the words "getting together," so I press forward with an explanation, despite my annoyance at the accusatory tone of the question.

"My home is farther to the south," I start, trying to keep my answers vague in case I contradict something David has already told him, remembering his sightseeing suggestion from yesterday. "I work as a guide for travelers in the area, and this group hired me to take them to see the Onyx Spires."

"Okay. So, no offense, but why are you coming with us now?" Michael poses an entirely reasonable question, and I am realizing this plan may have already backfired.

"Ah, well, you see..." *Spirits, I have always been this awkward.* "I am still to guide them back, and my time is paid for until then regardless."

"Yeah, just making sure we're getting what we paid for," David adds.

"Oh. Well, thanks," Michael accepts my explanation and David and I both relax. "I'm sure you have much better things to do then to help us clean up our mess."

"It is no trouble. A job is a job, after all." *That sounds like something Khazak the Guide would say.*

There are no more strange questions for the rest of our climb, and by the time we reach the top, I can already feel my legs getting tired. We are making our way toward the cave near the peak of the mountain, the one with the guards posted outside playing cards. Today they have moved on to a dice rolling game, placing small bets with copper coins. They do not notice our approach until Degoto clears his throat, causing them both to scramble in an attempt to hide what we have already seen.

"This group has permission from Mayor Elajor to venture through the cave to Karthani." He sounds none too impressed as he hands a piece of paper to one of his slacking compatriots. "Tsula Erlaxim will be acting as their chaperone."

"Yes, sir," one of the guards, the female, responds as she takes the paper. "I apologize. We were only—"

"I honestly don't care," our guide-guard cuts off her explanation. "Just make sure no one except this group goes in or out."

"Yes, sir," the other guard, the male, responds, both of them giving our guard a salute, which he seems to ignore in favor of turning to us.

"Safe travels to you all," Degoto tells us before pausing to consider his next words. "Please respect the lands you are about to explore, and above all, *be careful*. Though the area has long been abandoned, there is no telling what sort of creatures may have taken up residence in the time since."

"We will, sir," Adam tells the man with a bow of his head. "Thank you."

With a final glance to his co-workers, Degoto turns and begins walking back down the mountain. The two guards at the top watch him leave, then look at us for a moment before stepping to the side of the cave's entrance. Adam acknowledges them with a somewhat awkward nod before facing the cave and pulling out a folded-up map.

"What did that guy mean by 'creatures?'" David asks, hooking his thumb over his shoulder behind him. "Is there something we need to be on the lookout for?"

"The mayor and his aides didn't mention anything in particular." Adam looks to Tsula for confirmation, who shakes her head. "We're going through a lot of caves and valleys. Who knows what could have burrowed in to make a home for themselves since the last time anyone came this way?"

"Alright, but caves mean darkness and darkness means torches," Elisabeth adds next. "Do we have enough to get there and back?"

"I might have a more economical solution to that issue," Piper speaks up, raising her hand and walking toward Adam. "Could you please hold out your shield for me?"

"Sure." Adam removes the piece of armor from his back, raising it on his forearm toward Piper, who places her hand over the shield boss at its center.

"*Illuminos!*" she calls out, and the metal under her finders begins to glow a bright white.

"Whoa." Adam tests the light out by aiming it at the cave, illuminating it far more than a torch would. "Thank you."

"No trouble at all," she tells him with a short curtsy. "That should last the rest of the day, but I can always recast if needed."

"I coulda done that..." I hear Nathaniel grumble quietly to my left.

"I would also like to point out that myself and Tsula are both able to see in the dark somewhat." Tsula more so.

"Aye, and I could extend that ability to others, if ya want?" Riley adds.

"Good to know but no. Not yet, at least." Adam shakes his head. "Our group has basically doubled, which makes you our secondary healer. Save your magic for emergencies."

"Will do." Riley gives a two fingered salute from his forehead.

"Alright, anything else?" Adam asks, looking over his map once more. When no one responds, he continues. "Okay, usual formation. Liss, you're in front with me, David in back with Khazak, and mages in the middle. Let's move."

We enter the cave two by two, the guards outside watching us leave with a hint of nervousness. With the way everyone has acted, I am starting to wonder if I should be more concerned. I am also wondering how long it has been since anyone has traveled these roads. Though no one has exactly seemed eager for us to do this, they seemed even less willing to do it themselves.

The cave is, as many caves are, damp, dark, and cramped. Adam's lit shield helps with the darkness, though it has its own issues. The shadows the various rock formations cast are disturbing in their own right, but far worse is the way the light upsets the local fauna. It has mostly been things like lizards or bugs skittering away, but deeper inside, we manage to wake an entire colony of bats. The chaos from the resulting aerial stampede causes several of our number to shriek loudly as we crouch on the ground for cover—namely Piper, Tsula, and Michael. I can see David itching to tease his brother, but he manages to hold back.

The farther we delve, the closer the walls start to grow, and eventually we are forced to walk single file with Adam in the lead and me in the rear. It has been nearly an hour, and everyone has grown somewhat comfortable with the darkness, but I can feel the tension start to rise again as people's vision is relegated to the back of the head of the person in front of them, especially those of us farthest from the light. When we are finally near the end, seeing the literal light at the end of the tunnel is quite the relief.

We exit the cave into a forested valley, the crisp air blowing through the tree-covered mountain peaks that surround us. The ground is uneven with no visible path in the grass ahead of us. However, given the lack of traversable terrain, there is really only one direction to go. We continue forward, at least until we reach a fork in the road. We pause while Adam pulls out a compass and checks the sun's position as he consults the map. It takes a moment, but he figures it out, leading us to the right and onward.

Our path winds deeper into the mountains, where we reach another fork a short while later, and then a third ten minutes after that. Each time we stop, Adam has looked more confused and has taken more time to determine the correct direction, which is not inspiring confidence. When we reach a *fourth* fork, the man's frustrated grunts finally have some of us speaking up.

"Are you sure we're going the right way?" Liss asks while looking at the map over his shoulder.

"Yes, I think," Adam replies, holding the paper out in front of him and turning it to the side. "We've got a bunch more of these forks coming up, and the next part of the map has a lot of annotations. I'm just not sure I'm reading them correctly."

"Please, allow me to take a look," I finally say, unable to contain myself any longer. Were it not for the fact that I am supposed to only be a temporary hire for the group, I would have said something sooner. I am a ranger; tracking is in my blood. It is something I did for ten years, and something my father did for nearly twenty.

"Sure." Adam turns the map to me, pointing at one section with his finger. "We should be right here. See where the path gets a little...erratic?"

"Yes, I see." Adam is correct, the path on the map is rather difficult to discern, and because of the length of our journey, is not laid out in a clear line. "The annotations are actually directions in shorthand. Honestly, it will be easier to ignore the map altogether for this section and just follow those. I can lead if you do not mind?"

"Sounds good to me," he agrees. "Thanks, Khazak."

"Of course. That is what you hired me for, after all," I reply, calling back to my excuse from earlier in the morning.

I continue to use this excuse as justification for taking over the navigation duties, swapping positions with Elisabeth next to Adam and leading the group through the winding mountain paths. It is a good thing too because with the number of times the road splits, all of the stopping would have added an extra hour to our travel time. I have to wonder if all the splits in the path are even natural; perhaps they were carved out to make it more difficult for anyone to find the city.

It feels good to take the lead again, even if it is only for a limited reason. I am not ashamed to admit that I enjoy being in charge, and I would like to think that other than a certain black-haired, green-eyed exception, I have done a good job of not abusing the power that comes with it. I was captain to a force that was two-hundred strong. *Not that I will ever lead a group that large again after resigning in shame when a quarter of those people betrayed the city, and myself.*

Using navigation to distract myself, I lead the group for another two hours. By then, the sun is high in the sky, and the first questions about lunch are tossed around. Coming across the closest thing to a clearing we will find on this densely packed mountain, we stop for a short break to eat. No cooking, just trail rations, which should get us through until we stop to camp for the night and have dinner. Most everyone is sitting on the ground, giving our feet a moment to rest before we resume our hike.

"Hey David, I was wondering," Michael starts after swallowing a mouthful of trail mix. "What's with the three swords you're carrying around? You learn how to fight with one between your teeth or something?"

"Oh, uh..." David freezes while he thinks. "It's a delivery." *I need to remember to talk to David about thinking up some of these excuses beforehand. They will at least sound more believable that way.*

"I thought you said you were sightseeing?" Michael pokes another hole in David's story. *What is with all the damn questions?*

"We were. Are." David sticks to his story. "It's not a rush job. We decided to take a detour."

"Oh. Where are you supposed to deliver it to, then?" Michael looks exactly like someone who know he is being lied to.

"Uh, it's up north..." David answers quickly. "It starts with an M? Mana-mak... something."

"Manamequohi?" David looks annoyed as the name rolls off of his twin's tongue. "You're gonna walk all the way up there?"

"That was their main reason for hiring me," I decide to corroborate. "I am helping them find the fastest route north."

"Yeah, and like I said, there's no rush, so we're doing some sightseeing on the way." David takes a confident bite of his jerky.

"Well, I guess if we don't find any reponiam here, at least you were already headed in that direction." Michael shrugs and seems to accept our version of the truth, eating another handful of trail mix.

"Yeah... Lucky." David has been very unsure of where he exactly stands with regard to luck lately.

"Don't even *joke* about that," Piper calls out, rubbing the sore foot she has removed from her shoe. "We *have* to find some reponiam here. Can you imagine having to travel like this for nearly a month?" She pauses to consider her audience for a moment. "Of course, I am sure you all look so wonderful when *you* do it."

"Thank you, Piper." I manage not to roll my eyes. *If there is one thing we are concerned about, it is staying fashionable while on the road.* "We will need to get moving soon. We are still only about halfway there."

"You heard the man. Wrap it up!" Adam tells the chorus of groans.

After finishing lunch, about half a kilometer up the road, I run into *my* first issue on our journey—the path we are following curves out onto a very narrow walkway on the mountainside, right above an extremely steep drop. My breath hitches when I first see the empty sky ahead of us, but I manage not to hesitate until we reach the actual edge. I pause, trying to focus solely on the road ahead of us and not the steep drop just to its left.

"Do you want me to scout ahead and make sure it's safe?" David's voice has me turning, the concerned look on his face helping me to focus.

"No, I think it is alright," I decline with a smile. "Everyone just be careful and move slowly."

I move slower than I care to admit, but I *do* make it across. That thankfully seems to be the only instance in which my acrophobia comes to play as the rest of our journey is through more shallow valleys and caves. An hour later, when we approach the second cave exactly where it should be, according to the map. This one looks to be almost twice as long as the last, but by the time we emerge, we will be just outside the outskirts of the Ruins of Karthani.

Even while outside, Adam's shield shines brightly, and I take advantage of the light to read the map as I lead the group into the cave. Despite the light, I still hear some slight whimpers behind me as we go deeper. Considering what I had to go through just to walk across the mountainside, I am in no position to judge.

This cave is much narrower than the last, and I am forced to crouch down so as not to hit my head on the roof. We also seem to be going downward slightly, which I am sure is a worrying development to some of those behind me. As we continue down into the mountain, the path winds slightly until it opens into a large cavern. There are openings to several other tunnels ahead of and around us, and the entire group pauses after entering. I immediately look at the map to determine which is our way out. It is marked easily enough, but the other tunnels have notes that I cannot quite make out.

"Are you sure you know where we're going?" The tone of Michael's question makes me wince.

"Yes," I struggle not to grit out. "The print on this section is just particularly small." *And appears to have been written by a four-year-old.*

"Maybe you should let me take a look. I'm pretty good with this stuff." Michael holds his hand out expectantly.

"I have it fine, Michael." I point at the tunnel to my left. "This is the correct path to take. I am just trying to decipher what it says about some of these other—"

A low growl interrupts me, and Adam turns his shield toward the source to reveal a—

"BEAR!" Elisabeth shouts, just before the screaming begins.

The animal roars as it charges forward, forcing everyone to scatter around the too-small room. The flashing of Adam's shield-light is disorienting, but thankfully that applies as much to the bear as it does us. It skids into the wall, picking itself up from the ground with a roar before coming at us again.

"*Gheasainmhi!*" I barely have time to register Riley's red hair when the short man leaps into the animal's path, a bright light emanating from his extended palm. The bear comes to an immediate stop, standing still and staring into the empty air ahead of it.

"We need ta move fast. That won't hold long." The druid nods at the dazed creature.

"Right. This way." I immediately walk toward our exit, setting a brisk pace for everyone behind me.

Before long, the tunnel we are in begins to climb back up, a good sign that we are hopefully nearing the end of this cave. I do not know how long Riley's spell will last, but I hope it is long enough for us to finish our escape. I have never tried to fight a bear in a cave before, and I do not wish to do so now. I do not even understand what one is doing in a cave this deep in the mountains.

We reach another cavern, this one smaller but also splitting into multiple paths. Three to be exact. Stepping in front of Adam's shield, I quickly assess the map, searching for which of the tunnels is our exit, only to find that it is entirely illegible.

"I cannot read it." I squint, holding the paper right next to Adam's beacon of a shield. "The text is smudged."

"What? They used magic to copy it. Give it here." Michael snatches the map from my hands before I can react. "Let me... Shit, it really is smudged."

"Who could have thought?" I am done hiding my annoyance with this man. "The original must be smudged as well."

"What do we do?" Corrine asks, voice laced with worry.

"Split up?" offers Elisabeth.

"No." Adam and I declare in unison.

"I just need everyone to be quiet for a moment," I request. *At least I hope that is all I need.*

"What we *need* is to get moving." Michael gets in my face, or as close to as his height allows. "You're the guide. Which way are we supposed to go?"

"If you would *shut up* for a moment, I might be able to tell you!" I snap, causing him to jerk back. "I understand you are very talented, but contrary to what you believe, I *do* actually know what I am doing here!"

His face pulls tight, but he says nothing, nor does anyone else, though if it is because of my request or my outburst I am not sure. There will be time to worry about that later when there is not a bear waiting to maul us. I move to stand between all three entrances, closing my eyes and focusing my hearing. It takes a moment to filter through the ambient noise—people breathing, water dripping from the cave ceiling, a skittering bug—but then I hear it.

"There." I point to the right tunnel.

"Ah!" Riley exclaims, smacking himself on the forehead, a look of realization on his face. Standing next to me, he uses his magic to transform his body into that of a shaggy-furred dog, lifting one of his ears as he listens for the same thing I did—I should have thought to ask him sooner, honestly. He gives a single bark at the same exit I chose, tail wagging.

"Good boy?" *Am I supposed to pet him now?*

After a small huff of annoyance, the dog takes off with another bark up the tunnel to freedom.

"This way," I call to everyone else.

"What just happened?" Elisabeth asks from behind.

"I hear it now, too." I hear David from all the way in the back. "Running water."

A roar of anger bellows through the tunnel behind us as the bear returns to its senses.

"Let us hope the bear does not." *And also that it is slow.* "Quickly, everyone."

I am not sure how long we run for—and we do run—but as we come upon the exit, I can see the bright light of the sun shining down into the tunnel. This close I can hear more than just running water. I can hear the mountain air blowing through trees and birds chirping on their branches. I have to close my eyes as I exit the cave, needing a moment to adjust to the light while the sun warms my skin.

After catching our breaths, we are finally able to take in the wonder around us. This valley is much more open than the last, with fields of wildflowers stretching across the grass. Trees dot the landscape, and there is a small waterfall in the distance. The resulting stream runs along the valley on one side before disappearing over the mountainside. Simply put, it is beautiful.

"Wow, what is this place?" David asks me, staring off toward the waterfall. "Are we there?"

"Almost," I reply, confirming on the map. "I believe this is the Karthani Vale. The entrance is not far."

"Not to detract from how pretty all this is," Elisabeth starts, "but if we could please get our asses as far away from this cave as possible, I would rather not end up as some bear's dinner."

"That goes double for me," Riley comments. "Not sure that trick'll work a second time. Not even sure what a bear is doin' in a damned cave like that to begin with."

"What do you mean?" Corrine asks as we put some distance between us and the exit.

"Bears are not known for venturing very deep into caves," I explain. "They generally live near the entrances, and only temporarily in the spring and summer. It is far too early for it to be hibernating."

"Maybe it was lost?" the blonde woman offers.

"Maybe." *But I doubt it.* That is the fourth animal outside of its usual habitat I have seen in as many months. Looking around, other than the occasional bird or rodent, I do not see much in the way of wildlife. Certainly nothing a bear could survive on. Corrine may not be entirely wrong about it being lost. It could have been searching for food, followed something into the cave, and not been able to find its way out. It had to have come from somewhere else.

"How is there a waterfall this high?" Nathaniel asks as we approach.

"Underwater springs," Tsula replies. "There are a few along the mountain range. Tracking their source was actually what helped people rediscover the Karthani Ruins after being abandoned for so long."

"Wait, waterfall," Adam comments, snapping his fingers. "Check the map. I'm pretty sure the entrance is—"

"Behind it, yes." I try not to look too annoyed as I hold my hand out to Michael, who mumbles an apology as he returns the map.

We walk through the grass and flowers toward the waterfall. It seems larger as we approach it, though otherwise appears completely ordinary. It is only when we move closer to its side that a gap between the water and the stone behind becomes visible. As we draw closer, we can see more clearly what looks like a dark cave just beyond the cascading water. Adam takes point, the first one inside, hugging the wall and using his shield to deflect as the water passes over him.

Once inside, he illuminates the darkness for the rest of us, and one by one, we enter after him. Try as we might, none of us are able to stay completely dry, each of us a varying degree of wetness. I get it the worst by far; thanks to my larger size, the water pours directly over my shoulders, soaking the front and back of my shirt. While everyone else attempts to dry off, Adam and I examine the back of the cave.

The walls are covered in markings, some of them runes and others more decorative. At the very back of the cave is what looks like a large, circular entrance, complete with a round door made of solid stone. At the center of this "door" are more markings, focused around what appears to be the imprint of a hand at the center. Within the handprint are numerous colored gems, each glittering in the light of Adam's shield.

"I think I understand why we needed an elven chaperone," I say out loud, looking at the handprint. "Tsula, could you come here, please?"

Timidly, the mousy elf girl approaches the back of the cave as Adam and I step to the side of the entrance. "D-do I just...?"

"Yes, just place your hand in the recess there I believe." I point with a small smile.

"Alright," she says with a nod and a look of determination.

Stepping forward, Tsula places her hand into the hand-shaped imprint on the door. Around us, the cave grows brighter as the various markings and runes begin to glow. Light emanates from underneath Tsula's hand before the door suddenly pulls away from her, sinking back before it rolls into the side of the doorway, opening to us what has been locked away for years.

Dark green plants fill the entryway, and we must hack our way through in order to even exit the waterfall cave. As I push some branches to the side and hold others out of the way for the rest of the group, my breath is taken away by the landscape that stretches out before us. If the last location was beautiful, this one is nothing short of otherworldly.

We are standing on the ridge of a deep, lush, valley. But despite all the green and vegetation, this is not a forest; it is a city. One even larger than V'rok'sh Tah'lj. Streets and buildings stretch out ahead of us with many built directly into the mountainside, lining the valley's walls. Trees grow in at odd angles and in places they should not, and on the opposite end of the city sits a large, white tower, stretching high into the mountain tops.

Welcome to the Ruins of Karthani.

Chapter 10

"It's breathtaking."

"It kinda reminds me of Old Man Winters' backyard after he died."

Michael gives his brother an exasperated look as the group stands on the ridge overlooking the Karthani Ruins.

"Remember?" David continues, undeterred. "The place was already falling apart, but after he died, the brick fence in the backyard fell over, and a few months later, they were all covered in grass and moss. We used to take those toy knights grandpa carved us and pretend it was a city."

"Oh yeah," Michael responds, surprised. "I haven't thought about that in years."

Behind us, there is a rumble as the circular stone door we entered through rolls back into place, a similar hand-shaped recess on this side, which means Tsula will be our only way in and out.

"Alright, we have a couple more hours of daylight left, but I want to find a good place to set up camp before the sun starts to go down," Adam announces, taking point. "I'm not expecting to run into any trouble, but I still want to keep our base camp close to the exit just in case."

"There, a ridge less than a tenth of a mile down." Elisabeth points into the valley with her sword. "It looks like a courtyard between a few different buildings. Only two ways in or out, and we can look over the rest of the city."

"Good eye, Liss. Let's move." Adam gestures with his hand to follow as he walks toward the scouted location.

It is hard to tell that the road we are walking on is even a road at all as it is as overgrown as the rest of the city. Each of the buildings we pass seem to be built into sides of the valley, placing all of them at least partially underground. Solid stone walls extend out from the mountainside, either carved out or molded into place with magic. Those that have not crumbled, at least. I could not tell you much about how the outsides were decorated, as whatever is not covered by ivy or other greenery has long since faded away. The windowpanes are all empty, the glass no doubt shattered and worn down in the thousands of years since. Almost all of the roofs are flat with several acting as a terrace for the building above it.

The courtyard we enter is one such roof, one of the corners having collapsed into the building below. Riley uses his magic to sense where the ground is most sturdy before giving us the all clear to set up camp. The majority of it is covered in a rough patch of grass, but there is the occasional grouping of square stones in the ground indicating that there used to be some sort of tile or stonework. There are several buildings to the west and north, lined in a row with their side walls shared. If I were to guess from their size, they look like single occupancy homes, but given their close grouping and placement on the outskirts of the city, it is far more likely these were used by poorer families.

We build a campfire in the center of the courtyard and then set up our five tents in a circle around it. We have as many tents as we did rooms, but the addition of Tsula requires some minor adjustments to our sleeping arrangements. Liss has elected to share with her, leaving Nathaniel to instead share with me—

"Khazak, do you mind if I share your tent tonight instead of Nate?" Adam interrupts my thought as I finish tying the leather to the frame. "I want to go over the map and make sure our exit goes a little smoother than our entrance."

"Certainly. No trouble at all." I get the feeling this is not actually about the map, but I will have to wait until later to ask.

"Thanks." He pats my shoulder before heading back to the campfire to tell Nate about the change in plans.

Once everyone has finished with their tent setup, we take in our surroundings. This place is unlike any I have ever seen, and the same is undoubtedly true for my younger companions. Even I can feel the energy, the urge to explore, rippling through us.

"Alright, let's use the last of this daylight to scout the surrounding area." He gestures to the houses around and below us. "We might find something useful."

"Doubt it," Liss states flatly.

"Why do you say that?" Michael asks her.

"Look at this place and look at where we are compared to the rest of the city." She gestures to the area below us. "Even the elves had slums."

"Still worth looking around." Adam remains firm. "I don't usually like to split us up, but there's ten of us, and no one is going very far, so..." He points to the group of homes in the west, the closest that are also the largest. "Riley, Nate, Liss, and Piper, you search those. Khazak, David, and Tsula, you take the ones to the north, and Mike and Cory, you're with me checking the ones under our feet." *This must be his plan to get the three of us alone to talk. I will have to thank him later.* "Everyone needs to be careful—if the place looks like it's about to collapse, don't go in."

After some mumbling of agreement, our groups split up for our respective assignments. I move to the front, leading David and Tsula into the first home, which has a large hole in the middle of its roof, but otherwise looks sturdy. After some cursory looking around, we drop the pretense and gather in the back, away from any potential prying ears or eyes.

"So, were you able to learn anything from the report?" David asks, sounding cautiously hopeful.

"*Yes* actually!" Tsula tells us with an excited little jump. "I've still got a lot left to read. I only made it through that first section on the physical makeup of everything."

"Aww," David sounds disappointed. "I figured you were going to skip the rest of that."

"No, it's a good thing I didn't," Tsula corrects him. "Toward the end, it covers the sword and the sacrificial altar."

"Really? What did it say?" Mention of the sword has my interest piqued, having known that it and the basin were made from the same unknown metal.

"First, I want to say that a lot of this stuff is speculation on the part of the report's writers," she starts explaining. "I'll start with saying they both appear to be made from the same metal, and that they were unable to determine exactly how either was forged. They suspected that the scabbard and the leather around the sword's handle aren't the original because the way those are marked and constructed can be linked to early leatherworking techniques of the era, but they can't match any of the methods used to forge the sword."

"So, they don't know where the sword came from?" David asks next.

"They don't even know how old it is," Tsula continues. "They couldn't test it; it was impervious to all their attempts to break or scrape off even the tiniest fraction of metal.

Because of that, and because of where it was found, they believe the sword to be made out of *adamantine*."

"What's that?" David looks confused.

"A legendary type of metal, believed to be indestructible," I answer for Tsula, having heard the name in tales and fables I was told as a child.

"It's said to be harder than a diamond, unbreakable, and that a weapon forged from it can cut through anything," Tsula confirms my assumption. "More than just that... You know how the walls of the temple were covered in retellings of Olympian myths?"

"I am familiar with some of them, but David is not." Having protected the area for so long, I could not help but look into it.

"Well, several of those myths feature a long, curved adamantine sword." *Is she saying what I think she is?* "The archaeologists weren't positive it was always the same sword, but with all of the other evidence surrounding it, they believed the sword to be the mythical Olympian weapon known as the—"

"Harpe," David finishes for her, causing both of our heads to swivel in his direction. "It's called the Harpe."

"Yes, exactly." Tsula sounds as surprised as I am.

"How did you know that?" I know I have underestimated his knowledge in the past, but this feels different.

"When... When I came back, I just knew." David's eyes cast down as he remembers. "I knew it was the Harpe and that it...belonged to me."

This information is new to me, and I am unsure of how to process it. There is so much David still has not told me about that night.

"It makes sense. In the myths, it's always wielded by the hero," Tsula tries to lift his mood. "Perseus used it to behead the gorgon, Medusa, and slay the sea monster, Cetus, and Heracles wielded it when he fought the Lernaean Hydra—"

"Wait, I know that one!" David says excitedly. "Whenever he cut off one of its heads, two more would grow back in its place, so he had his nephew seal the wounds with a torch. Io... Io-something."

"Iolaus," I finish, once again impressed by David's knowledge, and knowing about his upbringing, I cannot help but add what I do next. "You know, he is believed to be one of Heracles' many male lovers."

"He had male lovers? Really?" From the intrigued look on David's face, I assume whoever passed along the story may have left out that part. "Hold on a minute, his *nephew*?"

"Oh, Olympian myths are full of all kinds of weird stuff like that," Tsula assures him. "In another, a titan named Cronus used the Harpe to cut off his dad's..." Her face suddenly goes red. "Nevermind."

"Uh-uh, you don't start a sentence like that and not finish it." David fixes her with a firm look.

"It is said that Cronus wielded such a weapon when he castrated his father, Uranus," I finish her tale with a smirk.

"*What!?*" David's voice goes high pitched as his hands move to cover his crotch.

"Were you able to learn anything else?" I try to get us back on topic after my testicular removal revelation.

"There's an Ancient Olympian inscription around the edge of the basin," she tells us next. "Translated it reads: 'Only blood spilled in sacrifice can restore the strength of the gods.'"

"That sounds like what the cult was attempting to do." I was not aware there was an inscription, but the basin was always covered with a box before that night. "I suppose it worked."

"So happy I could help them out," David grumbles.

"The sword is also resistant to magic, meaning it can't be enchanted." Tsula jumps in with another subject change. "The basin was as well, but they weren't sure if it was because of an already existing enchantment, or if it's just a property of the metal. Same for its ability to absorb lightning."

"It can do that?" That sounds fascinating.

"Yes."

"*Yes.*"

Though they both answer in unison, David's is much gruffer, and I remember how the fight with Murbank ended.

"Was there anything else?" I suddenly want another subject change.

"That was it for that section." She shakes her head. "I moved onto the next, which covers the myths and writings on the wall. A much, *much* more interesting read, but it's still a lot of information. I brought it with me so I can go over more of it tonight."

"Thank you so much, Tsula," I tell her with a small bow of the head. "Your help on this has been invaluable."

"Yeah, thank you. Seriously." David manages to sound sincere despite the way his mood has vacillated.

"I'm happy to be able to help Nylan's friends," she downplays with a shy smile.

"We should get to our search so we can return to the rest of the group." I take a look around the home we are in, the furniture so dilapidated it is impossible to tell what was what.

"Yeah, and since this place is so small, I'm gonna get started next door." David turns and heads toward the front.

"Be careful," I warn as he exits.

"Yes, Si—Khazak. Yes, Khazak." David pauses but does not turn around when he catches himself, so he thankfully does not catch my chuckle either.

"He knows I'm aware of that part of your relationship, right?" Tsula asks after he's gone. "My parents don't exactly 'get it,' but I've heard Nylan call Ragnar 'sir' plenty of times."

"Honestly, between his friends and his brother, I am not sure he is aware of who knows what anymore." I try not to sound exhausted as I describe the situation.

"I'm sure he'll figure it out." *That makes one of us.*

We finish searching the home after a few minutes, finding little more than moldy wood and torn scraps of cloth. We spot David in the next home through the open window and elect to skip on to the final building to finish faster. We once again turn up nothing, this home not appearing to *have* any furniture. When we're done, I tell Tsula she can head back to camp while I will collect David from next door. Just as I walk back to the middle home's entrance, I hear someone talking inside.

"Find anything interesting?" *That is not David's voice.*

"Piper? What are you doing here?" I peer in through the empty window to see David as surprised as I am to find the woman walking toward him.

"My group already finished; empty handed at that." She doesn't sound too disappointed. "The rest are back at camp, but I thought I might come over and see if I you could use any assistance."

"Oh, well. Thanks." David's posture relaxes.

"Though if I'm being honest, my intentions are not *entirely* altruistic." She walks around the room a little as she talks, looking at nothing in particular, but her posture gives her away. *She is flirting with him. Or at least attempting to.*

"You don't say, heh." David has picked up on the same thing and is less relaxed as he determines how to respond.

"Your brother has told me a lot about you over the years." Her gaze returns to my pup. "*Mostly* good things. He said you were very popular in school, but he never mentioned just how cute you are."

"Sounds like a good thing. I'm not sure I'd want my brother going around talking about how 'cute' I am." David is trying to remain cool, but I can tell this is throwing him off.

It is safe to say he did not consider what might happen in this scenario. *I really should step in there and save him.* I start to walk inside but pause when I realize I am unsure of how to proceed without revealing our relationship. Even if I did interrupt, it would only delay things until she got him alone again. Now fully in his line of sight, I catch David's eye, and I think he realizes the same dilemma.

"I suppose that's true." Piper gives a small laugh as she closes the distance between them. "Seeing as the two of us will be spending at least the next few days together, I was wondering if you might be interested in a—"

"I'm with him!" David calls out in a panic, his arm raised and pointing at me in the doorway.

She wheels around in surprise, looking at me with wide, confused eyes, then back at David, who is still pointing. "I'm...sorry? I'm not sure I understand."

I enter the home fully, though remain silent to give David the opportunity to correct himself.

"I'm *with* him," he repeats with a small exhale, dropping his arm. "Like, we're together."

Piper looks between the two of us again, still baffled until a look of realization passes over her face. "Oh. *Oh.* Okay, I understand now." She turns to address David fully. "I am so sorry. I had no idea you were—"

"*Mike doesn't know*," he quickly blurts out before she can finish. "Please don't tell him."

"Oh, love, no. I would never." She pauses, deciding on her next words carefully. "I have a cousin in a similar situation. Your secret is safe with me." She touches him gently on the arm.

"Thank you, Piper." I move to stand beside David. "Your discretion is appreciated."

"So, the two of you, huh?" She looks back and forth between us a few times, bringing her thumb up to her mouth and biting into the tip. "Yes, I think that will work nicely. Alright, thank you boys! See you at dinner." With a practiced curtsy, she leaves the two of us in the building.

"What just happened?" David asks once we are alone.

"Well, Piper was flirting with you, which caused you to reveal your sexuality and relationship with me in a panic." I place my hand on the small of his back as I explain. "Then I think she may have begun imagining the two of us having sex."

"So, we just became her spank bank material?" He gestures toward the exit with his thumb. "Is it weird that that makes me feel a little proud?"

"Assuming 'spank bank' means what I think it does, no." *It is clearly related to masturbatory fantasies, but how does one keep spanks in a bank? And why would you?* "She would not be the first."

"That's true." David smiles, thinking back to some of our times together in V'rok'sh Tah'lj. "Kinda makes you miss all the public sex."

"Some of us are beginning to miss sex altogether," I complain, even though we fucked just last night.

"I'm working on it, I promise." He turns around to face me. "...I'm sorry for how he's been acting."

"Yes, I would not say he and I are becoming overly fond of each other." I do my best not to glower.

"I'd say he's not usually like this, but that would be a lie," he begrudgingly admits. "He's always been kind of a know-it-all; I'm just used to dealing with his shit. Just ignore him."

"I am not sure if it is that or if he has a problem with me, personally." Aside from Adam, the rest of our group are all new faces to Michael, and it is not hard to see what separates me from the rest of them. I remember David's own preconceived notions about what my species is like. "Perhaps he has a problem with orcs."

"I dunno, I don't think it's that. He's just acting like one of those yappy little guard dogs old ladies seem to love so much. Loud and annoying but ultimately harmless." David steps closer, stroking his hands along my shoulders. "He just needs to spend a few days with you, and he'll see what a smart, kind, strong, sexy guy you are, and he'll love you like I do."

"You think your brother is going to find me sexy?" I choose to focus on the least-plausible portion of his statement.

"Has anyone ever told you that you're bad at flirting, Sir?" He wears a half-annoyed smirk as he lifts himself up on his toes for a kiss, which I happily return.

"Well as much as I would like to stay and improve my skills, we need to get back to camp." I tuck a short lock of hair behind his ear. *Haircuts when we are back in town, for the both of us.*

David grumbles unintelligibly as he knocks his forehead against the top of my chest. "Yes, Sir." As he pulls away, he gives me a hopeful look. "I'll talk to Adam about putting our watch shifts together."

"That would be nice." I offer him a small smile. A few groggy hours in the middle of the night are better than nothing, I suppose.

After another kiss (that I selfishly allow to go on for too long), we exit the dilapidated home and return to camp. The rest of the group has already returned, several of them gathered around the fire and chatting happily. Piper gives us a knowing look as we approach, and I spot Michael deep in conversation with Tsula, both talking animatedly. It will be dark soon, the sun almost finished setting.

Dinner tonight is cured fish the others purchased in Pákannon yesterday when shopping for supplies. While the area probably has decent game for hunting, the terrain being so foreign and full of any number of unknown dangers takes that option off the table this late. The river we crossed on our way in might have some fish, though the higher up the mountain we are, the less likely that is. I should speak with Riley in the morning and see what he thinks; his abilities will make things much easier.

After grilling and passing out the food, I take a seat with Adam, Elisabeth, and David to go over the map of the city and determine where we will begin our search in the morning. Not long after, I notice Michael approaching, seeking to pull his twin aside for a private conversation. One I cannot help but eavesdrop on. *What? It could be about me.*

"So, what do you know about Tsula?" Michael asks quietly.

"What do you mean?" David asks in return, looking toward the oblivious elf woman absentmindedly eating trail-mix as she reads.

"How well do you know her?" Michael looks in her direction as well.

"She's a friend of a friend. A friend's cousin, technically," David admits. "I haven't known her that much longer than you, but she's been really nice and helpful since we met. Her cousin, my friend Nylan, is a really great guy."

"...Is she single?" His voice goes even lower as he asks.

"Look at you, asking out girls." I chuckle silently at David's surprised tone. "I mean, I think so. Why not ask her yourself?"

"Just trying to do some research first," Michael defends.

"Nerd," David retorts.

"Whatever." I can hear Michael's eyes roll. "I also wanted to tell *you* that Piper was asking me about you earlier today. She's interested and wanted to make sure anything happening between her and my brother would be cool." I struggle to hold in another laugh and can see David's skin flushing red from here. "Full disclosure, we almost had a thing a while back, like two years ago. It was just a couple of dates, and we realized we liked each other as more as friends before anything actually happened. So, it's cool with me. I swear it won't make anything weird. We've been friends for years. She's an awesome girl."

"Thanks, yeah. Piper seems nice." David does his best to sound convincing, seemingly satisfying his brother, who allows him to return to planning with us. I say nothing—just give him a look. The next few days are going to be long.

After dinner, the group insists on a tradition from their part of the world in honor of our new human companions' first night outside—telling ghost stories around a campfire. It is more than a little amusing to watch them each dramatically tell their tale, even if few are actually all that frightening. Many of the stories are already familiar to most of the group with them doing more laughing than being afraid. It even has me starting to think of a few of my own.

David has just finished a story about a young couple who spent the evening canoodling in a horse carriage together on the same night that a deranged man with a hook for a hand has escaped from a local asylum. The tale ends with the couple hearing a strange scraping noise and then finding a mysterious hook hanging from the handle of their carriage's door, but the way David exaggerates both of their frightened voices has me snorting in laughter. *If the couple could hear the scraping, how did the carriage's horses not get spooked?*

"Alright, who's next?" Adam asks, the skies dark, the sun having long since set.

"I-I have one," Tsula surprises everyone by speaking up. "I-it actually takes place here, in these ruins."

"Really? That sounds so interesting," Michael is quick to respond. "We'd love to hear it." *Very subtle.*

"It takes place a long, long time ago, before they had really been explored or mapped out. Back then, it was a popular spot for scavengers who would sneak past the guards and enter intent on looting the ruins," Tsula begins. "It was a very lucrative business at the time, but one that could only be conducted during the day. No one wanted to enter the ruins at night. They were all far too frightened by the noises."

"What noises?" Corrine asks from the other side of the fire.

"The wails of the Woman in White." As if on cue, wind blows through the trees around us, rustling the leaves and sending a shiver down our collective spines. "Every night, after the sun would fall behind the mountains, her moans would echo through the valley, searching for something she'd lost."

"What did she lose?" Adam asks next.

"Not what. Who. A child, her family, a lover; no one knew for sure," Tsula answers mysteriously. "No one was willing to stay and find out. But sometimes, just as the sun would set and people were leaving, they would speak of seeing a ghostly figure in the distance." She pauses for dramatic effect before continuing. "Not everyone was convinced. Other people said that the rumors were fake, that the noises were nothing more than the wind howling through the city's alleys. One night, two scavengers who thought exactly that ventured into the city late into the evening. The way they saw it, being the only two inside meant not having to worry about any rivals. They would be free to pick through things at their leisure."

"But it didn't work out that way, did it?" Elisabeth comments with a knowing grin.

"Things were fine, at first. Just after sunset, the two men searched through building after building to their heart's content, filling their bags with all the treasures they could find. But then the wailing started." Tsula looks around the group as she pauses again. "They ignored it at first, sure that it was nothing more than a trick of the wind. But it grew louder, and with each home they picked through, it only seemed to grow louder still. Finally, when the first man had had enough, when the wails had nearly driven him to his breaking point, he asked his companion if he was ready to leave. His companion turned to answer, but froze when over his friend's shoulder, off in the distance, he saw her."

"The Woman in White," I find myself answering, as transfixed by the story as everyone else. The ruins are still around us as the wood cracks in the fire.

"A ghostly figure floated through the air, a billowing white dress attached to an almost painfully thin body." Tsula looks at me in confirmation. "Her skin was pale and sickly with long, silvery hair that shone brightly in the moonlight. Her eyes were orbs of solid white, glowing like two full moons, and her mouth hung agape as her cries filled the air."

"The second man screamed, making the first man turn and do the same," she continues. "And as his friend shrieked in terror, he ran deeper into the city, desperate for a place to hide. But no matter where he turned, the wails only seemed to follow him until he finally managed to escape. He ran all the way out of Karthani, all the way down the mountain, until he collapsed at the city gates. When they found him in the next morning, he was hysterical."

"What happened to his friend?" It is Nathaniel's turn to chime in.

"He tried to explain what had happened, what he saw, but no one quite believed him. Like him, most of the citizens thought of the whole thing as nothing more than a scary story to tell children. Still, they searched the ruins high and low for his companion." Tsula straightens her posture as she looks around the group once more. "But neither he, nor the Woman in White, were ever heard from again. No one knows for sure what happened that night, but afterward, the ruins were silent. Some people believe that the woman found what she was looking for and was finally able to rest, but others say that sometimes, on nights just like this, you can still hear the woman's wails echoing down the mountain, searching for those she lost."

A sudden gust of wind howls through the trees, strong enough to nearly put out the campfire and causing Corrine, Piper, and Michael to scream, and everyone else jump, including Tsula. Everyone except Riley, who is bent over laughing into his knees.

"Sorry! Sorry. That was me." The druid holds up his hand as he wipes a tear from his eye. "Couldn't help myself. That was a great story, and you, Tsula, have *perfect* timing. Just had to add a little wind for dramatic effect."

"Warn a guy next time," David gripes. "Now I gotta take a leak. That story was creepy as hell, Tsula." He gives her a thumbs up as he stands.

Both confessions put the group at ease as the fire returns to its full strength. As David steps off to relieve himself, I watch as Michael moves in to compliment Tsula on her storytelling abilities. Between him, Piper, and our other new additions, I wonder if David and I will be the only ones *not* having sex on this journey.

Chapter 11

"It's so peaceful here."

David is standing with me on a grassy hill overlooking the Shad'rok Springs. A cool breeze filters through the trees as sun shines in the sky. The waters below are a clear blue, rippling as a family of ducks float across the surface.

"It is one of my favorite places to be." I look over to my favorite person to be with.

"Thanks for sharing it with me." David smiles as he shyly reaches a hand toward mine.

I look down at our intertwined fingers, running my thumb across his, when his grip suddenly tightens and jerks. I look up, staring in shock at the blade protruding out of David's chest, thick red blood already flowing from the wound. David looks down in confusion and then back up at me.

"Khazak?"

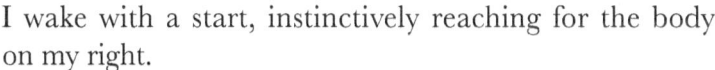

I wake with a start, instinctively reaching for the body on my right.

"Whoa! Hey, everything okay?" Adam's voice rings out as I make contact with his stomach.

I pull my hand back as if burned, only remembering about David's absence after hearing Adam speak. The light outside seems brighter than usual. Perhaps the ghost stories got to my companions after all, and they decided to keep the campfire well fueled. After that nightmare, they may have even gotten to me. In the dim light, I am able to see Adam fairly clearly, and I imagine he can see me as well.

"Sorry about that." *This is embarrassing.*

"It's okay," he assures me. "What happened?"

"Just a nightmare," I tell him with a groan.

"Do you have those a lot?" He sits up slightly.

"No." I sigh, laying back. "They only began shortly after David's...incident."

"*Ah*, and I'm guessing that's what it was about?" He turns to his side as he asks.

"Correct." I nod to myself. "I apologize again for grabbing you. It is something of an instinct to check on David."

"Sorry man," he consoles. "You...want a hug?"

"Thank you, but that is not exactly what I meant." I chuckle at his offer. "Typically if I am having a nightmare, then David is not far behind."

"Aww, well it's nice that you guys have each other," he reasons. "Usually."

"That is true, though David is not exactly aware of my own nightmares. Yet," I reveal.

"What? Why not?" He sounds confused.

"Because he refuses to talk about his own." I know I must sound bitter. "As his seem to be *exponentially* worse, forcing him to talk to me about mine feels rather…trivial."

"David has never been great at talking about how he's feeling." As his best friend, Adam would certainly be familiar with his behavior. "Other people though—that he's pretty good with. You should try talking to him about your nightmares, see if you can use that to get him to open up about his."

"Thank you for the advice." I am only now noticing that he does not sound tired at all. "Have you been awake long?"

"Yeah, having some trouble falling asleep," he admits.

"I hope it is not because of anything I am doing." This *is* our first time sharing a tent.

"Oh, no, this just happens to me sometimes." He waves off my concern. "There's something I usually do to help me get back to sleep, but it's uh, not something you do when sharing a tent, if you know what I mean."

Is he talking about... "Masturbation?"

He quietly snorts a laugh. "Yeah, that is the incredibly formal term for it."

I have to laugh myself. "I...suppose I could turn around and give you some privacy?"

"No, no. It's fine." Adam shakes his head. "I don't even know why I'm telling you."

"Just as I am sure you do not know why you wandered so close to me and David having sex in the woods the other night." I know. I can be *very* direct.

"I guess I'm not very good at being subtle, am I?" Adam asks bashfully.

"Your approach has its charms," I admit with a small smile. "Has it been a while since you have spent an evening with someone else?"

"Not that long. Usually when we stop in a town, I can find some nice girl in a tavern or maybe a guy in a dark room looking to exchange a little relief." He shrugs. "Even when we were locked up, it wasn't too hard to find someone who wanted to 'help each other out.'"

"And now that you know where David's proclivities lie, you thought we might all 'help each other out?'" I wonder if

David had any idea who Adam was spending his time with these past months. At least I know I will not be his first orc.

"I swear, I wasn't trying to make things weird," he starts to explain. "I had just heard about some of the things that happened with you and David and wanted to...test the waters, I guess."

"Consider them tested." I am happy to see that my instincts were not off. "Unfortunately, with David in another tent, I'm afraid I'm in the same boat as you at the moment."

"Yeah, sorry about that." He grimaces slightly.

"It is nothing I cannot endure." My eyes move down his bare chest to a small tent poking up from under his bedroll. "But I see no reason for you to not sleep."

I pull back the top of my bedroll, exposing my cock, which has grown considerably during our conversation. After raking his eyes down my body toward my groin, he follows suit, pulling away his own bedding to reveal an equally erect member. For a moment, we just lay there, taking in each other's bodies in silence.

As I saw before at the river, the man has a nice form with broad, muscled shoulders framing an equally broad chest. A patch of golden-colored hair covers its center, trailing down over his soft but muscled stomach to his crotch, which is just as golden. His cock is nicely sized, just a smidge larger than David's I would wager, and I am suddenly curious to know if they have ever compared.

Adam is looking at my body in the same way, his right hand moving from his side to palm his erection. He squeezes as he strokes down, pulling back his foreskin to reveal the glistening pink head underneath. I find myself mirroring his movements, taking myself in my left hand.

"Nice dick," Adam says with the confidence of someone who has said that before. "David can actually...handle that thing?"

"Thank you," I reply with a chuckle. "You have nothing to be ashamed of yourself. And yes, David is surprisingly something of a natural."

"I think I'd like to see that." He begins to slowly stroke himself as he talks, eyes locked on my crotch.

"Hopefully we can arrange something sooner than next month," I grumble with no real bite.

Adam's hand picks up speed as it moves up and down his cock, the thick muscles of his thighs growing tense. While usually covering most of his length, he occasionally spends a few seconds making small, quick strokes just under the crown of his head. He alternates back and forth between these, his erection giving the occasional twitch when a new burst of stickiness leaks from the head.

My own technique is not too dissimilar, my thick hand grabbing the top half of my member and steadily stroking enough to draw back the foreskin. The sounds of skin sliding over skin fill the tent, alongside the heaviness of our breaths. The air is hot, thick with the scent of our bodies, our sweat, even precum. If anyone outside were to enter, they'd certainly think people had been having sex in here.

I know I have been saying I have been working on plans involving Adam, but this is not exactly what I had in mind. Mutual masturbation can certainly be fun; it is just not something I have engaged in since I was much younger. However, given the current situation around my relationship with David, it feels appropriate. We have not exactly discussed it, but I have the feeling that having sex with someone else while he is forced to be celibate will only leave me dealing with a grumpy puppy, despite that celibacy being his own fault.

I continue to stroke my cock faster and faster, imagining us in another time, two young rangers on patrol, turning to each other in the middle of the night. I can also picture some of the things we might do in the future. David on his knees swallowing him down. The two of us taking turns at either of his ends. Coming to our tent at night and asking for permission to use his ass. I would not mind getting a look at his own, for that matter. I wonder if he has the same golden fuzz there as he does on his front.

I'm the first to cum, the mental image of Adam sandwiched between David and me being the one to send me over the edge. I grit my teeth to hold in my growl as I paint my stomach, my arm flexing furiously as I wring out every last drop. Seeing me is enough to trigger Adam, who cums with a silent shout, his eyes scrunched as he coats himself the same way. Each shot hits him progressively lower until the last bit dribbles out over his pubic hair.

We both lay back in silence, panting as our body temperatures return to normal. Aside from my own spend, I am covered in a sheen of sweat, as is Adam. Once my limbs no longer feel as loose as a snapped bowstring, I force myself to sit up, reaching for my satchel and removing a towel and my waterskin. Wetting it slightly, I wipe down my chest, stomach, and cock before tossing them to Adam to do the same.

"Thanks," he tells me as he cleans off his chest. "I needed that."

"Pleasure was all mine." That will be a fun story to tell David later. When he has earned it.

"Are you left-handed?" he asks, handing back the towel when he's finished.

"Ah, only when I masturbate, actually," I reply, somewhat surprised that he noticed.

"Why's that?" I suppose there is no harm in telling him.

"Well... I used to enjoy reading what I think you would call *trashy* romance novels," I start to explain. "The kind with very descriptive erotic scenes. It was easier for me to hold the book and turn the pages with my right hand, so that my left hand would be free to..." I gesture down to my deflating member.

"Huh." Adam considers my explanation with a small smile. "I wonder if I do anything weirdly specific like that."

"I will be happy to keep my eyes open and report back," I joke as we both settle back on our bedrolls. "So, tell me, is this what you had in mind when you asked me to switch tents this evening?"

"Oh, that? No, that was because sometimes Nate snores *really* loudly, and I didn't want to share a tent with him if I could help it." Adam shakes his head. "Seriously, I don't know how Liss deals with it."

Morning comes sooner rather than later. With our new additions, we have more than enough people to cover watch shifts, but given that all of them are very inexperienced in that area, we have elected to continue with just the six of us rotating every hour and a half. I had the second to last shift, just after David, who stayed up an extra half hour to sit with me. We did not do any real talking, but I will not deny his presence was comforting.

Adam had the watch shift after me, and after tossing and turning in my bedroll for a half hour, I elect to get up and sit by the fire with him and watch the sun come up. The rest of our group begins to slowly wake up after that with some of our more inexperienced campers taking a little longer to get moving than the others. Thankfully, Riley is not one of them.

"Riley," I call for his attention once he has exited his tent, while I hold two fishing poles. "Would you care to join me in catching some breakfast?" With his talents, he will be able to locate animals much faster than my tracking.

"Be happy to, Khazak," he answers with a stretch. "Lemme just take care o' some things first."

Once he has finished his morning ablutions, Riley and I walk a short distance from camp to a small stream, one that appears to come from the same source as the waterfall we passed under on our way in. The waters are clear, though they are not teeming with fish, but using his druidic magic, Riley is able to locate a spot with more than enough to satisfy our needs. I hand one of the poles to my human companion as we both take a seat along the bank.

"So, how long have you been on your druidic pilgrimage now?" I ask as we wait for something to bite.

"Goin' on year *four* now," he answers with a scratch of his chin.

"That is quite a long journey." I believe most druids only go for around two. "Is there a particular reason you are continuing?"

"You mean besides getting to sit on my arse in beautiful lookin' places like this?" he answers with a smile. "There's just a lot out there. So much to learn, so many people. If I hadn't kept goin', I never woulda met Piper or Mike, and I wouldn't have been a part of figurin' out the 'great mystery of teleportation.' Wouldn't have met the rest of ya either."

His answer makes me think of David, who said something similar, and it makes me consider my own motivations for leaving or at least what they might be without David. Would I have been content to spend the rest of my days within V'rok'sh Tah'lj's walls? I do not have long to contemplate as our lines finally catch something with several more fish following quickly after that. By the time we return an hour later, the rest of the group is up and milling around camp, and while Riley cleans the fish, I prepare to grill them.

"Alright, there are basically three sections of the city for us to search," Adam begins after everyone has started eating. He walks to the ledge overlooking the ruins, pointing down toward the center. "In the center of the city was an 'upper class' neighborhood with houses it would be worth searching through." Next, Adam points to the northwestern side of the valley. "Then there was a marketplace that specialized in magical goods along that part of the mountainside." Adam moves his finger one last, this time aiming toward the large white tower in the distance. "And finally, we have the big, ominous tower. The seat of the city's government. That's where we'll find the conduit crystals, and also where they likely kept some of the more powerful magical artifacts."

"So, where do we go first?" Elisabeth asks after crumbling the parchment that held her fish.

"Wanna just skip the first two and head straight for the huge, obvious one?" David suggests. "I mean we *know* that's where the conduit crystals are."

"No, actually." Adam shakes his head. "Even if we find what we're looking for right away, I still want to check out all three. I mean, we're the first non-elves to be allowed in here in decades, maybe even longer. I kinda want to see what it's all about. We aren't going to get another chance."

"Good point," David concedes.

"Then I believe the order you named would be the most direct route to reach all three," I add after looking down over the city and taking in the layout of the roads.

"Great. We'll get started as soon as everyone's finished with breakfast," Adam confirms with a nod.

Our stomachs filled, we put out the campfire and descend farther into the valley. Confirming Elisabeth's suspicions about our camp's location, the buildings we pass start to look nicer, though no less ruined. They are larger and more spread apart, instead of being stacked on top of each other. Some even have yards. There are small birds in the trees, the occasional squirrel skittering across the branches, and I even see a butterfly fluttering over a patch of flowers. There's an eerie beauty to it, the ruins of civilization being retaken by nature.

Once we reach the bottom of the valley, I start to notice things that remind me of city living: the crisscrossing roads and alleyways, the buildings stretching up on either side of you. The deeper in we go, the taller they seem to grow, some to three or four stories tall. Ivy stretches high up along their walls, and the roads are overgrown with grass.

"Tsula, I was curious," Corrine's voice breaks through the silence to ask a question. "I know the elves disappeared thousands of years ago, but does anyone know anything about what happened? I learned a little about the cataclysm in school, but I guess I expected more chaos. This place looks so well preserved. It's almost like the people here vanished."

"N-no one is really sure what happened, not exactly." I can hear the uncertainty in Tsula's voice. "Every elven homeland was affected at the same time. The people just… disappeared. Bodies were never found. No one is sure if it was an attack, or an accident, or something else entirely."

"Scholars call it the Great Rending," Michael speaks up, having likely studied this event at the institute. "Elf lands were the only ones physically altered, but the rest of the world still had to deal with the aftereffects. Whatever it was, it affected the world's connection with the astral plane. For centuries afterwards, it was next to impossible to use magic, and those that could found the spells they cast would be wild and unpredictable. People still aren't sure if things are back to the way they were before the Rending."

"Did the people in Pákannon notice anything?" Elisabeth asks Tsula next. "It was originally a human city, right?"

"That was thousands of years ago, I'm not sure I would have called it a city then. More like a settlement," Tsula points out. "I'm not an expert, but I know that before then, there wasn't a lot of contact between the elves and anyone else. The Nuññehi—my ancestors, the elves from Karthani—were not social by any means, but they occasionally showed themselves to others. There are legends of them helping lost travelers find their way or providing shelter in the winters. They were called 'the people who live anywhere' because they could be heard all over the mountains, but their location never discovered. Then, after the Rending… There's talk of a loud explosion, bright lights, and a slow trickle of survivors coming to Pákannon—those who weren't in Karthani proper when it happened. There's not a ton of documentation after that, but they eventually called it home, and the city became what it is today."

"There are similar stories found in other cultures that were in close proximity to an elven city," Michael adds. After he spent so long researching their monuments, I would expect him to have some knowledge on the subjects. "Still very little information on what happened, but it is interesting to see that it seems to have happened around the world at the same time. Karthani is actually in better condition than most other elven ruins and a lot safer, too. Like look over here."

The group pauses as Michael leads us slightly off the path toward a field of grass surrounded by what remains of a stone fence. It's overgrown, all except one area, a corner of the "yard" that has a patch that appears dried and brown. Stranger still is the shape of the patch or more specifically its edges. The shape itself is an amorphous blob, one that almost appears to have tendrils, but there is such a clean line between it and the healthy grass surrounding it, it does not seem natural.

"What is it?" David, as usual, is the first to voice a question. When he attempts to get an even closer look, his brother's arm shoots out to grab him before he can step on it.

"Don't. It's not safe," Michael explains, pulling him back. "It's a deadzone. A place that's been stripped of any connection to the astral plane, where spells won't work, and it feels like your energy is being drained right out of you. Most elven ruins have areas like this, usually a lot more, and they're much, much bigger. The places where they're really concentrated attract all sorts of monsters, the kind that like to feed on energy themselves."

"Is there anything you can do to fix it?" Liss asks, staring at the brown patch of grass that is much deadlier than it appears.

"Not really." Michael shakes his head. "Some spots have improved over time, but most locations are still completed covered in them. Mostly, you're just supposed to avoid them. That's the main reason most of the ruins are off-limits to outsiders. It's too dangerous."

With his explanation complete, the group returns to our original path. It is hard to say when exactly we reach our destination, but when we see a large, ruined fountain in the distance, complete with worn-down statues in the center, we come to a stop.

"Alright, we'll split into three groups like we did yesterday," Adam tells us as we gather into a circle, counting off what he says next on three fingers. "Everyone stays nearby, you check that the building is safe before you go in, and no one enters a new one without telling the others first."

Everyone agrees to those ground rules, and we split into groups. I can see Tsula about to make her way over to join me and David, when Michael calls out to her.

"Tsula," he looks almost bashful as he starts. "Would you want to group with me? I'd love to hear more about your theories on some of the elven monuments other potential capabilities."

There's a moment of hesitation, where she looks at me with a look of regret, not able to (and perhaps not wanting to) decline the invitation. I try to shrug nonchalantly so as to not draw anymore of the brown-haired mage's ire.

"I'd be happy to," she tells him with a smile.

I push David to go with them as well, figuring that if she learned anything more since yesterday, at least one of us will find out. Instead, I pair up with Elisabeth and Nathaniel. The homes we search are larger than the last ones, but the insides more of the same, crumbling walls and decrepit bits of wood that were once furniture. We spend at least two hours of the morning searching different houses on the block but mostly come up empty handed.

The most interesting thing we find are these pieces of clothing and furniture that are in shockingly good condition. I really do mean pieces: I come across what looks to be a shirt sleeve that, other than missing the shirt it should be attached to, doesn't have a scratch on it. I see the upper part of a leather boot, half of an empty picture frame, and even find an entire table leg that looks to be in near-pristine condition but *only* the leg. It is all very odd.

"Are you seeing this?" I hold up the wooden post to my companions.

"Yeah, I've found a couple of weird things like that." Elisabeth holds up what looks like a skirt panel.

"What about you, Nathaniel?" I look over to see the man not paying attention, instead peering into his bag. I've caught him doing that several times this morning, but this time he looks distressed. "Is everything alright?"

"Huh?" The mage looks up at my question, confused. "Oh, yeah. Just...looking for my water." He quickly rummages through and pulls out the item in question, taking a suspiciously long drink. *Hmmm...*

"Well, I do not think we are going to find anything else here." I sigh, returning to the task at hand. "I think we should rejoin the others and see if they have had better luck."

"Sounds good to me," Elisabeth agrees.

We step back outside, standing in the street as we wait for our companions to exit the

buildings next to ours. We are not left waiting long, and from the lack of excitement on anyone's face, I would say their searches have been just as fruitful. We return to our circle formation with Adam taking the lead.

"Anyone find anything?" he asks, looking around.

"Not much," David reports for his group. "Some weird stuff, I guess. Like, I'm pretty sure this is half of a spoon." He holds up the partial utensil.

"Our group found items like that as well." I pull the table leg from my satchel. "I assume it is due to some sort of magical protection, but I cannot for the life of me figure out why only parts of these objects survived."

"May I see that for a moment?" Piper asks from my left.

"Certainly." I hand the wood over to her, knowing she may be able to learn more from it than I can.

She holds it in her hand, examining it closely, before I see her eyes flash purple. "That is *very* old magic. Fascinating."

"What did you just do?" David asks the woman.

"What do you mean?" Piper looks back confused. "I'm a sorcerer." *Ah, that explains it.* Sorcerers are a specific type of arcane caster, similar to a wizard but with certain abilities not found in other spellcasters."

"Yeah, you're gonna have to explain what that means to him," Michael informs her.

"I'm innately gifted when it comes to certain feats of magic," she starts to explain. "I can detect magic a little easier than others out in the world or determine roughly how old a spell is or the type of magic that was used to cast it. It's also easier for me to do things like increase the size of a spell, or its range, or add little flourishes."

"Normal people add flourishes. *You* make your fireballs pink and heart shaped," Michael teases his friend.

"Just because we are in school to learn does not mean we cannot have style while doing it," Piper replies without a ruffled feather. "The spell on this table leg is at least four-*thousand* years old. A protection spell, as Khazak guessed. Arcane in nature, no doubt cast by an enchanter. A powerful one, for the spell to have lasted this long."

"But why only that piece?" Elisabeth asks next.

"This is pure conjecture, but I think it is likely related to the attack that destroyed this place." Piper hands me back the table leg, which I nearly put back in my satchel instead of tossing it to the side, as it is just a table leg. "It stripped away most, but not all, of the enchantments, and very unevenly, leaving us with pieces like this."

"Kinda bleak, but it makes sense," Adam admits. "Alright, I don't think we're going to find anything here. Let's move onto the market before we grab a late lunch."

The rest of the group agrees, exiting this section of the city in our fighters-mages-fighters formation with David in back next to me as we head to the old market.

"Was Tsula able to learn anything more from the report?" I ask quietly as we walk.

"Dunno, never had a chance to ask," he replies quietly. "Every time I looked over, they were nervously trying to flirt with each other. Was almost cute since neither of them know what they're doing."

That is unfortunate, but we still have some time before returning to the city and losing Tsula as a resource. We start to climb up again slightly as we leave the city's center, the surrounding buildings starting to match those we camped outside of. They are not quite as cramped, but as we climb the valley's walls, they start to make use of the vertical space in the same ways, sharing roofs and terraces.

It is easy to tell once we have reached the market, the roads growing wider, no doubt because they once held all manner of stands and carts. But the farther we walk in, the more I cannot shake the feeling that something is wrong. We come to a stop in a large open area between several buildings.

"Something about this location seems off," I announce as I take in our surroundings.

"What do you mean?" Adam asks me.

"I am not sure. Call it instinct." I think about how to describe my feelings. "It is too quiet."

"Doesn't that make sense?" Elisabeth asks. "We're the only ones here."

"No, he's right. We should be able to hear somethin'. Birds or other animals skitterin' about." Riley shakes his head. "I'm gettin' bad vibes from this place."

Several members of the group share looks between each other.

"Alright. Everyone on guard, and no splitting up this time," Adam announces before we begin our search.

Things go slower than they did the last time, but I would rather spend a little more time here than risk...whatever is making the hairs on the back of my neck stand up. The buildings themselves do not turn up much, though we do find a few useful things, like a preserved jar of dried heartmoss and what appears to be a pouch of drake's teeth. But other than that, it is more empty buildings, only with most of us standing around and watching this time.

"I'm starting to think David might have been right about skipping straight to the tower," Liss says with a sigh after exiting another building empty handed.

"It hasn't been a total bust," Adam replies, referring to our meager findings. "Let's check out a few more, then we can move on to the tower."

We move on to another tucked-away corner of the market. The first two buildings are more of the same, but there's something about the third that seems...wrong. To start with, the entrance is damaged, the wall above the doorway having crumbled, making it even taller. I'm also able to hear the sound of wind bellowing through it.

"There is a strange draft coming from that building." I point ahead at the building in question.

"There's somethin' else in there, too," Riley adds, squinting suspiciously.

"Let's check it out," Adam decides as we cautiously approach.

It is not hard to see what is causing the draft once we are inside. The entire back wall of the building has been destroyed, instead emptying into a large cavern. There is some rustling to my left and then a few soft clicks as Adam lights a torch to illuminate the large room for the rest of the group. As the flame flickers, the light catches on something in the very back of the cavern, something shiny.

I am only just able to make out what looks like some sort of a gem when the part of the wall it is sitting in *moves*, sliding away to reveal the face of a serpent. *That is no wall.* The full picture of what I'm looking at clicks into place, and I realize we are looking at a giant coiled snake, the shiny object in question a scale on the center of its forehead. It is massive, almost as wide around as a tree trunk with two large, curved horns rising from either side of the top of its head. It's hard to make out its coloring or markings from here, and thankfully, it seems to still be sleeping.

"*U-uktena,*" Tsula whispers fearfully.

"We need to leave *right now,*" Nathaniel speaks low and quickly.

None of us need be told twice, everyone turning or backing up to leave. Of course, with ten people in the building it is a little difficult to make a quick *and* quiet exit. In the panic to get out, Corrine trips over her robe, a split second before reaching out to grab ahold of an old set of shelves. She manages to right herself, but they fracture under her weight and crash to the ground.

A low hiss echoes from the back of the cavern.

Chapter 12

"**RUN!**" I shout as everyone clambers toward the exit.

Back outside, the ten of us scatter in different directions, some into buildings and others down alleyways. I turn left and then quickly duck into an alley myself, peering my head around the corner to watch the snake slithering out, its horns scraping against the top of the crumbled doorway. In the light, I can see that its scales are bright red, almost glowing as if they had been lit ablaze, the solid color broken by a number of dark bands along the rest of its body.

"Khazak!" I hear David's whispered voice above me and look up to see him peering down over a balcony with Tsula and Nathaniel. "Up here!"

I sprint around the corner into the same building, rushing up the stairs to the roof to find the others.

"What the hell is that thing?" David asks no one in particular.

"An *uktena*," Tsula repeats herself. "A-a great horned serpent."

"*Lampropeltis cornigigantus*," Nathaniel continues with a scientific moniker. "An incredibly deadly and resilient serpent."

"What's it doing?" David asks from his perch, watching as it flicks its tongue into the air.

"Scenting," I tell him, before turning to the two mages. "How do we stop it?"

"Yeah, what are its strengths and weaknesses?" David asks next.

"You mean aside from being a *giant snake*?" Nathaniel snarks before losing the attitude. "Its hide is incredibly tough. Normal weapons can't break through its scales."

"Except on its belly!" Tsula excitedly corrects. "They're softer there. You also have to be careful of the gem on its forehead. You *cannot* look at it."

"It's a specialized translucent scale," Nathaniel continues the explanation. "The snake can channel energy through it to create a bright burst of light, capable of stunning someone."

"A-and its breath is *incredibly* noxious." It is Tsula's turn to add to our horror. "Inhaling it could kill a person."

"Great, so we're fighting a giant, invincible snake that we can't get close to, look at, or breathe around," David summarizes our predicament, unimpressed.

"Where is your other sword?" I ask, noticing he only has two. "You know, the one allegedly able to *cut through anything*?"

"I left it back at camp." He rolls his eyes at my exasperated expression. "Forgive me for not realizing we would be fighting a *giant fucking snake* today!"

"That's *ten*," I warn, but before I can say more, the ground shakes as something crashes nearby.

"Aaaaahhh!" *That's Corrine!*

Looking down, I see the snake is attempting to burrow its way into another building, no doubt where Corrine and some of the others are hiding. Thankfully, its large horns are getting in the way, crashing against the entrance. But each time it rears back and tries again, more cracks form in the stone above it.

"Hey!" Michael comes running out of a different building, calling out to the snake. "Over here, asshole!" He fires off a magical light arrow, the snake hissing in pain as it bursts against its skin.

"We have to get down there and help them," I decide immediately. "They have no idea what they're dealing with."

"Let's go." David is already moving toward the stairs, Nathaniel and Tsula right behind him.

We rush outside, but the snake has already turned toward its new target. It hisses threateningly at Michael, forgetting about its prey in the other building. Before it slithers any closer, its head starts to glow.

"Cover your eyes!" I shout to David and anyone else who can hear.

I hear a bursting sound followed by a bright flash of light behind my eyelids, and when I open them again, I see Michael still standing in front of the serpent, arms limp at his side, stunned. David and I start running to him, but the snake is already rearing its head back. We are not going to make it to him in time.

A blur of black flies in from the alley on the left, landing on one of the snake's horns. *What in the spirits' name?* Hissing in surprise, it shakes its head, frantically trying to dislodge whatever has latched on. As David and I grab Michael to pull him off the street, I can see that the black shape is distinctly canine shaped: a wolf. At first, I assume it must be Riley in animal form, but then I see the redhead tumbling out of a shop on our right with Elisabeth to assist us.

With a final shake, the wolf loses its grip and is sent sliding across the dirt road. It is up in a heartbeat, dropping into an attack stance and giving the serpent a bark of challenge before turning down another street. No longer paying us any attention, the snake follows its new target away from us. I pick up Michael myself as the others usher

Corrine, Adam, and Piper from their crumbling building to their slightly safer hiding spot.

"What the hell was that?" David asks once we are safely inside.

"A wolf, I think," I answer bewilderedly, laying Michael down gently, his expression dazed and unfocused. Corrine is already next to me, kneeling down as she inspects his features.

"A black one?" He cannot believe it either. "You don't think it's the same—"

"Whatever it was, it bought us some time," Adam refocuses us. "We need to either stop that snake or figure out how to get away."

"We have to be careful," I tell the man. "Its breath is deadly to inhale, and as Michael has demonstrated, gazing at the bright flash it releases will leave you completely stupefied."

"How long will it last?" David asks either Tsula or Nathaniel.

"A few minutes?" Nathaniel guesses. "Most people don't survive after an encounter, so there's not a whole lot of research on the subject."

"Do you know if there are any other side effects?" Corrine asks, trying and failing to get Michael to follow her moving finger.

"I don't think so." Tsula shakes her head, kneeling down with Corrine. "At least none that I've heard of."

"We need to find a way to get underneath it. That is its only weak point." I sigh, racking my brain for ideas.

"*Where* on its underbelly is it the weakest?" David asks our two snake experts. "Like, is there a specific location?"

Both mages look like they are trying to think of something, but Tsula is the first to change her expression.

"Oh! The seventh ring. The seventh black ring on its body," she clarifies. "That's where its heart should be, right underneath."

"Okay, that's good." David nods his head, then stares up at the ceiling. Now *he* looks like he is thinking of something.

"What are you planning?" I ask somewhat reluctantly.

"I think I'm gonna get the snake to chase me off the roof," he answers, still looking upward.

"*What?*" I look up now myself.

"The roof is level with the street behind us," he starts to explain. "If I can get the snake to chase me up and onto the roof, then I can jump off right over that doorway." He points to the entrance to the building. "When it follows me down, *you* will be waiting right here with the biggest fucking arrows you have to plant in its heart. What do you think?"

"I will not say I *like* it, but it could work." *At least he is asking for my opinion, I suppose.* "Does it have to be you who does the running?"

"I'm the fastest person in the group," he replies without a hint of cockiness.

"Short of Riley turning into an animal," Elisabeth points out, all eyes turning to the druid.

"I, er, suppose I could give it a go?" he replies anxiously.

"It's alright," David assures him. "It needs to be me."

"I don't like it either, but I don't think we have any other options," Adam interjects.

I hear barks of distress in the distance, and they are growing louder. "The snake is headed back this way," I announce. *I hope our lupine friend survives long enough for us to thank them.*

"We should move," Adam agrees.

"Okay, get in position and get ready." David tries not to sound nervous as he moves to the exit. "Once that thing starts chasing me, I am not looking back until it's dead."

"Wait, I can at least help make ya a little faster," Riley places his hands on David's shoulders. "*Mactire'luas.*" His hands and David's body glow a light blue as he casts his spell.

"Thanks." David tests his new abilities with a few small jumps in place. Then he turns to me. "Wish me luck."

"Please be careful," I plead.

"Hey, I'll be fine. Promise." He looks down at his brother's still dazed form, then quickly pulls me in for a kiss before rushing out.

I am wearing a surprised smile for a moment, but then remember what David did not: Riley is not aware of our relationship or need for secrecy. I quickly make a request of the redhead: "If you could please not tell Michael about that kiss..."

He looks at me understandably confused but nods his head. "Consider it forgotten."

Satisfied for now, I move to the entrance to watch David as he rushes forward toward a crossroad. I can still hear the snake and the wolf getting closer. Once he's in the intersection, he stops, turning to the left before shouting.

"OVER HERE, YOU DUMB SCALEY MOTHERFUCKER!" He jumps, waving his arms in the air. "COME AND GET ME!"

He stops only seconds after he started, and after a brief look of worry, turns and runs in the opposite direction. The ground shakes violently as the snake slithers past, its massive body indiscriminately knocking into buildings as it hunts its new prey. A moment later, the black wolf ambles onto our street, panting as it plops down against the wall, tired. It locks eyes with me for a moment, lowering its head as it takes a moment to rest. *Thank you, friend.*

Another rumble from above us draws me back to the task at hand. Pulling my bow from my back, I move to kneel down in the entryway. Notching two arrows on my bowstring, I aim them upward, watching the skies. From this angle, I can just make out the lip of the roof, and the spot where David should drop from. It is only a single story high, but I am still worried. After some movement on my right, I notice Liss with her own bow taking the same position as me, and then on either side of us are the mages, preparing spells to launch through the open windows.

"The seventh black stripe," I remind Liss, still looking up. "We only have one shot, so we have to make it count."

"Ready," is all she replies.

The rumbling grows stronger until the walls of the room are shaking, and a few seconds later, I see David leaping from the rooftop. He lands on the street in front of us with a roll, quickly jumping to his feet and running forward. A second after that, the snake throws itself from the building, landing with a heavy *thud* to continue the chase. I quickly count the stripes as the rest of its body follows it off. *One, two, three, four, five, six, NOW!*

We let our arrows fly, all three connecting with our target and landing in the dark, soft, underscales of the snake's body. If that were not enough, a combination of fire and lightning strike it on either side. The reaction is immediate, the serpent crying out in pain as scales are singed and its body punctured. Judging by the speed and volume its blood is being pumped out, there's no doubt we pierced the heart. It writhes in pain, coiling in on itself and twisting unnaturally as it tries to dislodge the arrows.

This causes more blood to spray, much of it flying right into our hiding spot and covering Liss, myself, and several others. It continues to lurch slowly before finally coming to a stop, the remaining portion of its body falling from the roof above us with a *crash*. Though we are messy, a cheer goes up as we realize our victory. We step outside, giving the serpent's corpse a wide berth.

"We did it!" David shouts cheerfully as he rejoins us. "My plan worked!"

"It certainly did." I breathe a sigh of relief at seeing him unscathed. "I am glad you are alright."

"Told you I'd be fine," he replies cheekily. "Thanks for the boost, Riley."

"Anytime," the druid answers. "Now, what's with the wolf? Friend o' yers?" He points his thumb in the animal's direction, which stands once it realizes we are paying attention to it again.

"Isn't that the same wolf you and Cory helped?" Adam asks, looking at the canine in question.

"I think it might be," I answer, walking toward it. "It must have followed us here. Somehow." *Those guards must have moved on to something even more distracting.*

"What does it want?" David asks next.

"I do not know." I slowly approach the wolf, who seems unbothered by my presence, but eyes my companions cautiously. "What brings you here, little one?"

<*Help friend.*> The wolf "replies" to me, barking happily. I immediately notice the lack of effort needed on my part to translate the body language or noises. That only means one thing.

"I think we may have bonded," I announce, still looking at the wolf.

"What does that mean?" David questions.

"It's a thing natural spellcasters can do," Riley answers for me. "Forming magical bonds with other creatures. Witches and shamans have familiars and totemic spirits, but for the rest of us, we have regular animals like this little lass. I used to have a sweet little hedgehog, myself."

"It must have happened when I used my magic to calm her." Though there is no definitive way to form a bond, casting a spell that linked our auras and emotions would make sense. Suddenly, I am reminded the blur of black I saw when washing things in the city two days ago. "I think I saw her in Pákannon as well. She must have followed us all the way here."

"What do we do with her? What does she want?" David is starting to sound accusatory.

"Let me find out." I sink down so I can be closer to the wolf's level and attempt to communicate. The magic of the bond should make things a little easier. "Thank you, friend. Where is your home? Where is your pack?"

The wolf makes a sad whine. *<Home gone. Pack gone.>*

"She's alone," I tell the group. "I told you she was too young to be on her own. Something happened to her pack. Where did they go, little one?"

<Others. Not-friends. Looked like friend's friends. Smelled funny.> The wolf looks sadly at my companions then back at me. I sigh. Of course.

"I think she is wary of humans because humans were the ones to... I assume hunt the rest of her pack." I shake my head at the thought.

"Fuck, we just keep screwing things up over here, don't we?" Adam says aloud.

"I have not had a...*friend* in a long time." Not since my childhood dog, Nalki, passed when I was twenty-three. "Do you want to stay with me?" I ask the wolf, curious if the fact that I am surrounded by humans will affect her decision.

<Yes! Stay with friend. Help friend.> The wolf barks happily, tail wagging as she stands on all fours.

"Khazak." I point at myself and say my name.

<Khazak friend.> The wolf barks happily.

"It seems we have a new four-legged team member," I tell the group as I lean forward, cautiously seeing if the wolf will allow me to touch her and scratching her behind the ears when she allows it. "I suppose I will have to think of a good name for you."

"So, you're keeping her?" David asks for confirmation, not exactly sounding happy.

"It would appear so." I catch his eyes and can see the inner turmoil about his feelings on black wolves.

"Well, congrats on the new wolf Khazak, but," Elisabeth starts, pointing at the giant dead snake behind us, "what do we do about this? Do we *need* to do anything about it?"

"That glitter scale on its forehead is a pretty powerful magical focus and would also sell for a lot," Nathaniel assures her as we walk around to the dead snake's head. "... But is anyone actually willing to pull it out?"

"I got it," Liss replies with cool anger, pulling a knife from her pocket and walking up to the snake. Its head is turned on its side at an angle, so she only needs to stretch her arms up to reach. She sticks the knife underneath the scale, blood seeping out as she attempts to pry it free.

"What the hell happened?" We all turn to see Michael stumbling out of the shop we had been hiding in.

"Mikey, you're alright!" David cheers at his brother's appearance. "Look, we killed the giant snake."

"Yeah, I noticed that." The wizard pats his hand against the snake's corpse. "What happened to me, though?"

"Oh, it has this magical scale thing that flashes this bright light that kinda...knocked you out," David explains, pointing to the serpent's head. "Liss is trying to remove it now, actually."

"Hey, this blood isn't dangerous, is it?" Liss asks, perhaps a little too late. "Because a bunch of us are covered in it."

"I mean we probably want to get cleaned up, but it's not supposed to be poisonous or anything," Nathaniel assures her and the rest of us.

"Yeah, that thing really sprayed you guys bad, huh?" David laughs at our misfortune.

"I guess that's one good thing about being knocked out." Michael compares his relatively clean attire to ours.

"Got it!" Liss announces triumphantly, finally wresting the scale from the snake's body—and releasing a torrent of blood, one that manages to hit David and Michael directly on their backs and shoulders. They stand there, dejected, annoyed, and looking like they're contemplating more than a few curses.

"Come on. We should get cleaned up," I tell David and my other dirty comrades. "Maybe the cold river water will help you cool down."

"Ugh, I feel so gross," Nathaniel complains, looking at the red splatter on the front of his robe.

"*You* feel gross?" David counters, having been painted with more snake blood than even Elisabeth or myself.

We are back at camp, at least the six men are. The nearby stream isn't really large enough to decently wash in, so the women have gone to the river outside of the ruins to clean up first. We mill about as we wait for their return, each of us covered in varying amounts of blood. My skin itches as it dries, not to mention the smell. I am seated near my tent with my new wolf friend, trying to think of a name. Wild animals do not typically have them.

"So, you just have a pet wolf now?" David asks after coming to stand next to me.

"More or less." I am not sure if that is what the wolf would call herself.

"I'm still not sure I understand exactly how that works." He looks down at the wolf skeptically.

"Some people believe it is a fated thing." *I am not really one of those people.* "But what is *actually* happening, is that... Remember when we talked about people who cannot cast spells, but still have latent magical potential?" David nods, being one of those people himself. "Most animals cannot cast spells either, but some of them have that same latent potential. Sometimes, when a spellcaster and one of those animals meet, and the conditions are right, a connection forms." I reach out and give the wolf a scratch behind her ears.

David looks down and watches, considering the wolf and this new information.

"Hey, they're coming back," Michael announces, standing as he sees the four women returning, washed clothing in hand.

"It's all yours, boys," Liss tells us once they are near enough.

"Thanks, Liss," Adam replies as he stands, turning to the rest of us. "Let's go. If we're fast enough, we might still be able to check out the tower before dark."

"E-excuse me," Tsula holds her hand up from the back of the returning group. "How are you all going to get back in? Do you...n-need me to come with you?" The "and potentially see you all bathe" goes unspoken, but judging from her crimson complexion, she is thinking it.

"I might have a solution for that," Michael tells her as he approaches. "When we're finished, I'll signal you with this."

He holds up his right hand, pointing his index finger straight into the air. It glows briefly before a small beam of light shoots from the tip high into the air, bursting with a soft *pop*. I am not sure what that was, but the fact that he cast it without any sort of verbal incantation is impressive, even for what appears to be a small spell.

"What do you think?" Michael asks her when he's finished.

"I think it's great," Tsula tells him with a smile that says she is talking about more than the spell.

As the men start to leave, I crouch down to speak to my new furry companion. "Stay here and guard the camp."

<*Guard camp.*> She huffs into the air before laying down on her paws.

Tsula walks with us back up the path to unlock the gate, watching the six of us enter the cave before the door rolls back into place. We get wet as we pass back under the water-fall but move farther downstream before finding a place to actually wash. Everyone cautiously avoids letting their gaze wander to anyone else—all except Riley, who after making eye contact, wiggles his eyebrows at me. *Something else to note for later...*

Given our altitude, the water feels close to freezing when we first wade in, but our need to be clean is so great that it is not long before we are all in the river. Before we got back to camp, Riley and Corrine used their magic to make sure the uktena's blood would be safe to wash off in the river without contaminating anything. I watch the water around me turn red as the dried blood is rinsed from my skin, then look up into the sky. *What a day it has been.*

"Gods, this feels good," David says with a happy sigh, fully submerged up to his neck, then going completely under and running his hands through his hair before standing. "*So* much better."

"I don't think I've ever been covered in this much bloo—" Michael stops mid-sentence, eyes locked on his brother. "David, what the hell is on your chest?"

My eyes go wide. *The scar,* shit.

"Oh, that?" David tries to act nonchalant while also turning around. "It's nothing—just a weird scratch I got the other day."

"And the matching one on your back?" The brown-haired mage is now wading closer to his brother. "That looks like a scar. Why is it…yellow?"

"I told you—it's nothing." David tries to cover the scar with his hand as his brother forces him to turn and face him.

"It's on the center of your fucking torso," Michael states as he tries to pry the hand away. Then his eyes lock onto his collar, his hands grabbing the lock. "And what the fuck is locked around your neck?" *Oh no.*

"Do you actually want me to answer any of these, or do you want to ask another million fucking questions first?" David deflects while pulling the collar from his brother's hand. The four of us on the sidelines can only watch awkwardly as the brothers argue, which is only made more awkward by the fact that they are doing it while we are all naked in the river.

"I've been *trying* to get you to answer my questions for two fucking days now!" Michael shouts angrily. "So, what is it David? You can start with the scar."

"I-I…" David hesitates.

Michael growls in frustration and throws his hands into the air in frustration, wading a few steps away from his brother. "Do you have any idea what the past few months have been like?"

"Look, I know everyone's been worried about me, but—"

"*I THOUGHT YOU WERE FUCKING DEAD!*" Michael yells as he turns back around. "Mom and Dad didn't even tell me you were missing for a month! I only found out because *Kira* finally wrote me a letter. As soon as I got it, the *first* thing I did was try to find you with magic, but the scrying spell came up empty."

"Mike, I—"

"I tried every night for a month, and it was always the same thing. That only happens if..." Michael's voice grows quieter. "I kept telling myself that the magic had to be wrong, that I was screwing up the spell somehow. You couldn't be dead. We're twins. I would *know* if something happened to you. But after an entire fucking month..." His voice finally cracks. "I've been freaking out over how I was going to tell Mom and Dad, but now that I've actually found you, alive, four fucking months later, you still won't tell me anything!"

"It's not that I don't want to tell you!" David takes a step toward his brother. "It's just...*complicated.*"

"So uncomplicate it!" Michael closes more of the distance.

"It's not that easy." I can sense David is at the end of his rope.

"Why the hell not?" Michael is not backing down.

"Because I did fucking die! Okay?" I wince at David's words. *There were certainly better ways to tell him that.*

"What are you talking about?" Michael is understandably thrown off.

"Exactly what you've been asking for. This scar?" David points to the gold marking on his chest. "I got it when a guy ran me through with a sword, right before I bled to death. Then I came back."

"What do you mean you 'came back?'" Michael takes a step backward. "This isn't funny, David."

"Does it look like I'm fucking joking?" David asks angrily.

"Why... Why didn't you tell me?" Michael is looking at his brother's scar as he speaks.

"Because I'm still trying to figure out what happened!" I do not know if it is intentional, but I can see David using his anger in an attempt to turn this around on his brother.

"Michael, we have been trying to do everything we can to determine what exactly took place that night." I cannot help myself and attempt to diffuse the situation.

"What the hell would you know about it?" Michael turns his anger on me. "I thought you were just escorting them on a delivery."

Shit! My voice is caught in my throat as I try to frantically think of an excuse.

"Guys, maybe we can all just cool off for a second?" Adam tries his own hand at calming things.

"*You* fucking knew about this too, didn't you?" Michael is still on the attack, this time with Adam. "Why didn't you fucking tell me about my *brother* getting stabbed to death? Why does this asshole know about it?" He points at me.

"I... Khazak..." It is apparently Adam's turn to fumble over his words, looking to both me and David in desperation.

"Un*fucking*believable." Michael throws his hands in the air, growling in frustration as he exits the river.

"Mike, will you just hold on a second?" David starts to follow his brother, who is angrily pulling his pants on over his still-wet legs.

"Why, so you can feed me more bullshit?" he sneers as he buttons his pants.

"I'm not feeding you bullshit!" David pleads.

"Oh yeah?" Michael takes this as a challenge, looking between David and myself. "Fine. Then tell me why that thing around your neck has the same symbol that's tattooed on his chest?"

Simultaneously and without thinking, we both reach our hands up to cover the symbols in question.

"Exactly what I fucking thought." Michael shakes his head in anger, pulling his tunic over his head and grabbing his dirty clothes before stomping off.

"Mikey..." David calls after his brother while attempting to pull on his own clothes.

"Fuck you, D." Michael does not look back. I am not sure where he is going, but it is not to camp.

Seeing that he is going to follow his brother, I start to exit the river as well. "David, hold on, I will go with—"

"Look, I get that you think you're helping or whatever, but all you've done is make everything fucking worse!" he snaps at me while tightening the laces on his boots before standing. "So do you think you could just back the fuck off and let me handle this?"

I am physically taken aback by David's words. "Consider it done," I manage to grit out.

Not actually bothering to wait for my answer, David chases after his brother, his own dirty clothes left forgotten by the riverside. The forest suddenly seems deathly silent, and I can feel Adam, Nathaniel, and Riley's eyes on my back. Turning around, I do my best not to betray any emotion on my face, to middling results.

"...Should we go after 'em?" Riley asks after a beat of silence.

"You heard the man." Even I can hear that my voice sounds unnaturally calm, my face pulled tight in anger as I bore my eyes into a stone on the opposite riverbank. "He wants to handle it himself."

The rest of our washing excursion passes quickly in silence. When we are finished and redressing, it is so extremely tempting to just leave the twins' belongings here, but I help Adam gather them with a sigh before we leave. As we approach the waterfall cave with no sign of David or Michael, Riley speaks up once more.

"Are you sure we should leave 'em out here alone?" Riley looks around worried.

"They're big boys," Adam tells him, frustrated. "They can handle themselves. We'll give it an hour; if we don't hear from them by then, we'll go looking." He then looks to Nathaniel. "Nate, could you signal Tsula for us?"

"Huh?" He seems confused for a moment. "Oh, sure." He holds one hand aloft before thrusting it out, palm up. "*IGNI!*"

A fireball bursts from his palm and into the air, where it explodes into embers which float to the forest floor. I watch them in slight horror, as does Riley, wanting to make sure they are all out before they touch the ground and potentially start a fire. Adam looks up in shock, then at Nate in anger.

"Dude!" He throws both hands up, as if asking "what the hell?"

"What?" Nathaniel seems confused by our reactions. "I don't know his weird little light spell."

Despite its flamboyant display, Nathaniel's spell does not in fact start any forest fires, and a few minutes later, the cave door opens and Tsula lets us back in to the ruins. She is confused at David and Michael's disappearance but accepts the explanation that they are talking alone. I overhear Adam telling the girls a brief summary of the afternoon's events, but I aim straight for my tent, needing to get my emotions under control.

When I exit a little while later, multiple eyes are on me, but no one says anything or approaches. Even the wolf can tell that something is wrong, content to lay quietly by my feet when I take a seat by the fire. I am feeling calmer but not any less hurt or upset by David's actions.

About twenty minutes before we are due to look for them, we see Michael's signal in the sky and Tsula leaves camp for the third time to allow the two brothers back in. Both are fine, though neither is talking to the other. Michael stands off to the side while David speaks with Riley, concluding with both men going to their respective tents.

I wonder what they talked about out there. Did David finally come clean, or just make up more excuses? Judging from the way they are silent, the latter seems more likely. When exactly is he going to tell his brother about me? Is he ever going to, or has his plan this entire time really been to keep me his dirty little secret? What if he—

The wolf whines, sensing my growing distress, and I have to stop and take a deep breath before I let my thoughts spiral out of control. Given the hour and the group's overall low morale, I think it is safe to say we will not be venturing to the tower tonight. I will also not be doing any cooking, so I retrieve my pack to pull out my own set of rations for a late lunch/early dinner.

"I wish my other pup made as much sense as you did," I say offhandedly to the wolf, tossing her a small chunk of my venison jerky.

She quickly snaps up the treat, chewing while tilting her head in confusion at my statement.

"Do not worry about it," I say with a chuckle and shake of my head. "Are you hungry?"

<Food!> She gives a small happy bark.

"Go hunt," I tell her with a smile. "Do not wander too far and be back before it is too late."

<Food!> She repeats as she runs off into the wild to catch her own dinner.

"This group just keeps getting bigger and bigger," Adam makes the comment as he comes to stand next to me. As he does, Riley and David both emerge from tents with their arms full, walking toward each other and then...ah. They are switching places. "Shit, the conversation must have gone *really* badly if David would rather bunk with Nate."

"I wouldn't know," I deadpan, pulling out more of my jerky. "I was specifically asked to 'back the fuck off.'"

"Yeah, that was...not great." Adam takes a seat on my left.

"You have known them both a long time. Tell me," I decide to take the opportunity to ask a question, "have they always been so..." I am trying to think of a polite way of saying this.

"Self-absorbed?" *Never mind. It appears I do not need to.* "Yeah, kinda. At least when it comes to their own shit."

"How did you deal with it?" I have not even been around them for three full days—I cannot imagine a lifetime.

"Usually by ignoring them until they've figured it out and calmed down." He shrugs with a smile. "Unfortunately, this time, we're all stuck here together and the stuff they need to figure out involves some of the rest of us." He looks over at me when he says the last part of his sentence.

"I wish I had a good answer for you," he continues. "I've known them my entire life, and they've been my best friends almost as long. As wrapped up in themselves as they can get, they've always been there when I needed them. Like after my parents died."

"I am sorry to hear that, Adam." I remember David mentioning something in passing months ago.

"Thanks. It was a fire, almost two years ago," he tells me somberly. "They still don't know what really happened, how it started. I just know that in the middle of the night, the house was ablaze. I didn't find out about it until the next morning. It was just the two of them inside. No survivors."

"...I am so sorry, Adam," I repeat myself, unsure of what else to say. "Do you have any siblings? Extended relatives?"

"Nope." Adam shakes his head. "I am an only child of only children. After I was born, my mom wasn't able to have any more kids, so I was their everything. When they died, I think I saw David almost every day, always making sure I was okay or if I needed anything. When he wasn't with me, he was covering my guard shifts, or getting me food, or even copying notes from class for me. And I think I got a care package from Mike every other week for three months before I had to ask him to stop."

"That was very kind of them." I wince at my tone. *That sounded more bitter than I intended.*

"It's not like anything they did was going to bring my parents back, but it helped," he presses forward despite my shitty attitude. "It took a while after they passed, but I started to realize that I was doing a lot of things in my life because I thought it was what *they* wanted me to do. So, I spent the next year thinking about what *I* wanted to do. What would make *me* feel proud? I didn't really have an answer, but I knew I didn't want to stay at the academy. I was terrified of leaving by myself, so late one night, after a particularly bad day for us as knights-in-training, I talked to David. I think you know the rest of the story."

"I do," I admit. "I am again very sorry to hear about your parents, and I am very happy that David and Michael were able to help you through such a difficult time, but..." I pause, worried that what I say next may come off rude. "Is there a point to this story, Adam?"

"I dunno," he replies with a half-smile. "I guess I'm just trying to stick up for my best friend when I know he's acting like an idiot and going to regret it."

"That is very noble of you." I offer a half-smile in return.

"You know, I see the way he looks at you. When he doesn't think anyone else is paying attention," he tells me, looking over at the man-in-question's tent. "Like you're... special. *Important.* I don't think I've ever seen him look at anyone like that before. I know he's done a lot to piss you off, and you have every right to be, but I don't think this is that easy on him either. Just something to think about, maybe?"

"Thank you." I am at a loss for what else to say. As much as Adam's words warm me, they do not fix any of my and David's current issues.

"No problem," he replies with a nod of his head, standing. "Alright, I'm going to make sure things are at least civil between everyone before we turn in for the night. Hopefully we can tackle that tower in the morning and get out of here."

With a final silent nod, Adam leaves me to my thoughts, and as the sky begins to darken and the flames grow brighter, I am once again contemplating what the future might hold.

Chapter 13

*"<*That boy is infuriating!*>" I growl as soon as I enter.*

"<*Uh-oh,*>" *Nylan responds, closing the door to the home he shares with Ragnar behind me. "<I assume you are talking about the boy who has been keeping you busy the last few days?>"*

"<*Yes. He has been giving me trouble since losing the ritual, but tonight he*—>" *I pause, anger rising as I relive the events. "<He drugged me with sleeping grass, stole my keys to the station, and attempted to break his friends out of their cell! Ragnar is the one who caught him.>"*

"<*Oh, that is...not good.*>" *Nylan comes to sit next to me on the couch. "<Are you alright? Where is he now?>"*

"<*I am fine.*>" *I take a breath and calm down. "<Right now, he is bound and locked in my spare bedroom.>"*

"<*Well at least he is not going anywhere else tonight.*>" *Nylan offers me a wry smile.*

"<*I just do not understand why he would do something like this.*>" *I shake my head, looking down at my hands.*

"<*Really?*>" *I turn to look at Nylan and his questioning tone.* "<*I am not saying that drugging you like that was right, but I can understand why a guy being kept in a place he does not want to be would try and escape.*>"

"<*It is not as though he or his friends have anywhere to go.*>" *I feel the need to point out the ridiculousness of his attempt. "<Even if*

they made it out of the city, they have no supplies. He did not think his plan through at all.>"

"<So, he is impatient and not thinking logically.>" Nylan shrugs. "<Still makes sense to me. How long does he have to go, anyway?>"

"<Two months.>" The next part of my sentence gives me pause. "<...Though I have not actually told him that yet.>"

"<What?>" Nylan pulls back, confused. "<Why not?>"

"<I was only intending on keeping him with me for the duration of his friends' sentences. We only just learned about them this morning.>" I start to defend myself. "<...But I suppose I could have said something sooner. It is just... We have been making such good progress the past few days. Getting along so well.>"

"<Oh, sweetheart.>" Nylan hugs me again, which has me confused. "<What?>" I ask the elf as he pulls away.

"<Well, do not spank the messenger, but I find myself wondering...>" Nylan starts. "<Are you more upset that he drugged and stole from you, or because he does not want to stay with you?>"

"Hey, everyone should finally be set to go soon." Adam's voice pulls me from my memory.

"Hmm?" I look up at the blonde man, remembering what it is we are doing. "Right. I am ready when the rest of you are."

"Great. See you in a sec." He gives me a thumbs up as he goes to speak with some of the others.

It is the day after our afternoon of snake slaying and sibling arguments. Lunaday, if I am not mistaken. It is later in the morning than we would normally get started—some of our group had a rough night and seem to be having trouble getting started now. I slept alright myself. No nightmares, but I did have a little trouble letting go of David's final words to me. Which I suppose may be why I am reliving the events of the last real time we fought like this, back before we were even... *sigh*, whatever it is we are now.

The two of us have not spoken since yesterday, and I do not think he has with Michael either. In fact, no one seems to be doing much talking at all right now. Despite that, there is the hope that today we will be able to put whatever differences aside and accomplish our goals. As beautiful as this place is, I think we would all rather not spend any more nights out here than we have to. We already risk losing the rooms we reserved at the inn.

Once everyone has gotten their equipment together, we gather up and head out. The group is still quiet, though it feels more stoic than out of any lingering awkwardness. I hope that after the unexpected *giant snake battle* yesterday, none of us are taking any chances. I stand at the back alongside my wolf. I am not sure she will be of much use in climbing the tower, but she can still guard the area. Maybe I will finally think of her name today.

The white tower looms ahead like a beacon, its pointed, circular roof almost reaching the highest mountains of the valley around it. From a distance it appears smooth, almost bleached by the sun, but as we get closer, the many green vines growing up the sides come into view, as do the various balconies and walkways adorning the outside walls. Unlike the other buildings that appeared to be made of a single solid stone, the tower is clearly made up of more traditional brickwork. I also realize its true size, coming to over sixty meters wide while being exponentially taller.

"So according to the mayor, the upper half of the tower has a room where we should be able to find plenty of conduit crystals," Adam says as we approach the tower's base. "Then, toward the top is supposed to be a magical storeroom, where components and artifacts were kept. That's where we'll find the reponiam, if there's any here. We just have to figure out how to get inside."

"Why can't we just use the front—" Nathaniel stops as we turn a corner and the front of the tower comes into view, where a large open door sits—completely filled with rubble. "Oh."

"Shit." Adam brings the group to a halt just outside of the tower. "I didn't realize that was what he meant."

"A little inconvenient but won't be a problem for us at all," Riley assuages. "Not with as many mages as we got."

"Yeah, we can have this cleared in no time." Michael steps up, cracking both sets of knuckles as he walks toward the base. He holds his hands out to begin an incantation, then stops. "Oh *fuck*."

"What is it?" Piper steps forward to ask.

"I think it's—" He holds his hands out again as if trying to cast. "Yeah, shit. It's an anti-magic field."

"What?" The dark-skinned woman walks toward her fellow institute attendee to test herself. Then she pouts. "Damn."

The rest of the spellcasters, myself included, walk into the field to verify for ourselves, feeling our magical abilities drain away once we cross the threshold.

"Is it like the deadzone we saw yesterday?" Elisabeth asks, scratching her head.

"No, they're much simpler and safer," Michael tells her. "They cut off a person's magic in the same way—by disrupting the connection to the astral plane—but it only affects people and animals, and it doesn't damage or decay them or anything else in the surrounding area. It's actually a spell in its own right, one that has to be attached to a source object, so we should be able to turn it off."

"It does, however, mean we will have to find a way inside that will not require the use of any magic," I add with a sigh.

"What about you?" I see David turning to Riley. "Couldn't you turn into an animal or something?"

"Same principle." Riley shakes his head. "Soon as I crossed the threshold, I'd be forced back into human form."

"Although if you went high enough..." Michael seems to be thinking out loud, walking away from the tower. "First let's see if we can figure out how big the field actually is. *Illuminos.*"

Michael casts the same light spell Piper used on Adam's shield, this time on the end of his staff. He holds it out vertically as it glows, walking back toward the tower slowly. As he draws near, he reaches a point where the light flickers out, and he stops. He sticks the other end of his staff into the ground, using the light to test where the threshold lies. Then he walks forward, drawing a line in the dirt as he drags the staff with him, tracing the boundaries of the field.

We follow him a quarter of the way around the building before it becomes apparent that the field is at the center of the tower extending outward. It is not exact, but it is almost equidistant all the way around. In addition to the bits of random vegetation, the base of the tower is also surrounded by rubble, much of it from above us where certain walls have collapsed or caved in. We see a few crumbled balconies, some windows and doorways, but none low enough for us to climb to.

"So, what do we do?" Tsula asks once we've finished.

"Well, Riley could fly up higher than the field extends and look for a way in that way," Michael offers.

"Aye, about how high do ya think the field goes?" Riley asks, looking up.

"Assuming the source is on ground level?" Michael looks up with him. "At least a hundred feet. Thirty meters."

"Alright, wish me luck!" Riley says, taking a step back and turning into a bird—a crow, specifically.

Taking off, he flies in wide circles around the tower, making sure to avoid the field as he ascends. Once he is at a safe enough height, he flies back in to the tower, circling until he finds an opening to perch on, before entering and disappearing altogether. The nine of us still on the ground are left squinting into the sky for at least ten minutes before I manage to spot him descending.

"Here he comes." I point up at the ball of black exiting the same opening.

"Sorry to say, I've not got good news," the druid tells us after shedding his feathers. "I was able to get in, but farther down, on the inside of the field, is a broken bridge. I can't cross without magic, an' I doubt anyone else here can either."

"Dammit. Thanks anyway for trying," Adam tells him with an understanding look. "I think our best bet is going to be to use one of these openings on the second or third floors. We just have to figure out a way to get up there."

"Told you I should've gotten that grappling hook," Liss tells the man.

"Ugh, I guess if we have to, we can go back to the city for supplies, but I really don't want to waste that much time." Adam shakes his head before turning around and looking back up at the tower. "Maybe we can build some sort of ladder?"

"I think I can get up there," David announces from off to our right, staring at a section of the tower just to the side of the entrance.

"What are you talking about?" Michael asks his brother, now looking at the same part of the tower.

"That window there, right above that balcony with the blocked door." David points at least two stories up to an empty window. "I'm pretty sure I can climb up there."

"Bullshit," Nate calls out immediately.

"Afraid I might have to agree with Nate, man." Adam looks at the window skeptically.

"I would not be so certain about that," I tell him, remembering the way David managed to break into the ranger station's yard using only his acrobatic skills. *We had to enchant all the walls with alarms after that...*

"How sure are you?" Michael asks, not paying our conversation any attention.

"Like... 80/20?" David holds out his hand and wiggles it side to side. Then he bends down to pick up a stone, throwing it up at one end of a broken walkway he was no doubt planning to use. The stonework immediately crumbles. "...Okay, maybe 70/30."

"Seriously?" Elisabeth asks skeptically.

"Yeah." David nods. "I'm gonna need some help though." Then he turns and points to me and Adam.

Oh, now you want my help? is what I would really, really love to say, but it is not the time. "What is it you need?"

"Adam, do you remember when you, me, and Patrick McMahon snuck into the officer's tournament last summer?" David checks his friend's memory.

"When we helped you climb the fence?" Adam verifies.

"Yeah, and then I went around and unlocked one of the back gates to let the two of you in," David confirms, then turns to me. "Have you ever boosted someone with your hands?" He demonstrates by clasping his fingers together like a basket and half-kneeling.

"Yes, I am familiar." I nod my head, a questioning tone in my voice.

"Great. Now you guys are gonna do that together, except... you're gonna throw me." He says it with a straight face.

"*What?*" I look between David and the window. "Throw you?"

"Not *all* the way up!" He rolls his eyes.

"David, are you *sure* you can make that?" Adam looks between him and the target.

"Like, I said, 70/30." We both scowl. "I'll be *fine*. Come on. Over here."

He leads us toward the tower wall, standing underneath the remains of a balcony extending outward from the tower, the door behind it completely buried in more rubble. Just above it is a partial walkway, the missing center making up most of the crumbled rubble around us. There are doorways at either end, though they are both sealed off with more rubble the same as the others.

"Stand right...here." David swaps places with us, centering us how he wants. "Okay, on the count of three, I'm going to step into your hands, and at the same time that I jump, you're both going to throw me straight up as hard as you can. That should get me high enough to grab the edge."

"David, this seems unsafe." I look up, remembering the stonework crumbling only seconds ago.

"So was searching those old buildings yesterday. We gotta do what we gotta do." He shrugs, then turns to the rest of the group. "How much rope do we have?"

"I've got twenty feet," Adam says with his hand raised.

"Ditto." That is Elisabeth.

"I have fifty in my bag." I pull my spacious satchel off my shoulder to retrieve it.

"Fifty should do," David replies as I hand it to him, pulling it far up his arm and shoulder to hold it in place. "Alright, ready?" David asks me after taking a step backward.

"I suppose," I answer honestly, kneeling down.

"For the record, I'm with Khazak in thinking this isn't safe." Adam joins our hands.

With a nod of his head, David steps into our grip. Just as I feel the full weight of his boot in my hand, I heave my body and arms upward with all the strength I can muster.

I watch as David's body shoots into the air, jerking when he grabs onto the edge of the walkway as planned, and allowing me to release the breath I have been holding once I see it does not collapse under his weight.

A few of our group clap at the display, and I step away from the wall so I can watch David more carefully. Though not entirely—I want to be here in the event that he falls. He swings himself back and forth slightly until he is able to flip himself up, climbing the rest of the way onto the walkway. I hold my breath again as he looks upward and to the right at his next target.

Stepping back as much as he can, he leaps with his hands outstretched, grabbing onto the ledge of an open room at the peak of his jump. As soon as he does, the stone under his left hand gives away, and he has to quickly replace it before he loses his grip entirely. My stomach sinks faster than the loose rocks falling to the ground as I watch him dangling in the air, and I can hear a collective sigh of relief from the group when he finally manages to pull himself up.

"Be careful, David," Michael calls to his brother.

"Really? Cause I was up here throwing caution to the fuckin' wind," he replies sarcastically.

"You don't have to be *more* of an ass, you know," Michael complains, and for once I agree with him.

David ignores his brother's statement, walking farther into the room to assess his next move. I have to step back more to see him from this angle, rejoining the rest of the group. From what I can see, the far wall is covered in rubble with no way to exit into the tower proper. At the height he is now, he is halfway to the window, but there is still a considerable distance, and he is only going higher.

To the left of the room David is in, on the outside of the wall, is a balcony holding another blocked doorway. Higher above that doorway is the open window that is our target.

While I am curious as to how David is planning to reach the window, I am more concerned with the balcony, seeing as this is the end that crumbled after he threw a stone at it, not to mention that it is on the *outside* of the wall while David is on the inside.

Backing up into the far-right corner, David runs and jumps from the room at an angle, his hands catching on the corner edge of the balcony. The momentum has the rest of his body swinging to the left, and I hear Tsula gasp loudly as he dangles from just below his elbows. More loose stones fall to the ground, but none cause him to lose his grip. A collective cheer goes through the group as he pulls himself up.

"Now what?" Elisabeth shouts up through her cupped hands, seeing that David appears to be at a dead end.

"Gimme a minute," David shouts back, examining the wall in front of him.

The blocked doorway ahead is large, taking up a full third of the wall, and it is at least twice as high, its decorative frame extending outward. The door itself is filled with debris, and the rest of the wall is plain aside from the open window farther up. Some of the stones look to have been worn away with large bricks poking out at odd lengths.

David walks around the doorway, examining it and the wall above. Nodding to himself, he starts to climb the rubble, testing his footholds carefully. He makes it more than halfway up, slowly climbing toward the top of the doorframe. When he can go no higher, he steadies himself as best he can, and with a final jump, reaches out both hands out to grab a hold of the edge of the doorframe.

"Holy shit," Adam mutters on my left as David starts to pull himself up.

The frame is not large enough for David to stand on, and we watch David dangle there for a moment as he searches for his next handhold on the uneven bricks above.

Moving one limb at a time, David begins to scale the rough section of the wall, inching closer and closer to the open window. It is going to be a stretch, but he is going to make it. As worried as I am, I still feel a pulse of pride.

After what I am sure only takes five minutes but feels like an hour, David finally places his right hand on the edge of the windowsill. It takes a small leap of faith, but then he is pulling himself up into the window with both hands. The group cheers as he takes a seat in the corner of the window and looks down at us.

"Told ya I could do it," he says just a little cockily.

"Yeah yeah, you're amazing," Liss calls out sarcastically. "Now find a place to tie that rope so the rest of us can get up there, too."

"Wait, first tell us what you can see before you go in there," Adam corrects.

"Sure thing, boss-man." David turns his body in the window so that he can see inside. "It's not actually that dark. I mostly see more crumbled walls and walkways. The floor looks solid under the window. I'm gonna find a place to tie the rope."

"Be careful," Adam instructs.

As if on cue, a loud crash rings out from inside the tower, followed quickly by David's scream.

"David!" I shout as I rush forward, despite there being nothing I can do.

"David!" Michael repeats, looking desperately to the empty window.

"Oh fuck." Elisabeth stares at the tower with wide eyes. "What do we do?"

"We have to get inside, *now*." I turn to Adam, ready to spring to action.

"Liss, take Tsula and Nate and head back down the mountain. Riley, I need you to use that shapeshifting of yours to fly down and get a rescue party organized and meet the others halfway back up." Adam begins forming a plan.

"*'m okay*," I hear a voice call out weakly. *David?!*

"Did you hear that?" I ask the others, stepping toward the tower. The wolf suddenly barks on our left near the tower entrance. There must be enough small gaps in the rubble for David's voice to carry through. I rush over. "David, can you hear me?"

"I said I'm okay," the voice says louder.

"Are you hurt?" I ask the stupid question.

"Just a little banged up." He is sounding more like himself, at least.

"What happened?" It is Adam's turn. "Did the rope give out?"

"Oh no, the column I tied the rope around is rock solid. The floor right next to it, though..." He trails off before continuing. "Crumbled right under my feet. I grabbed the rope on the way down, which saved me from the worst of the fall, but I still slammed into the wall pretty hard."

"Anything broken? How does your head feel?" Corrine calls out, assessing David's injuries and no doubt still worried about his previous ones.

"Just some bruises," David answers. "Good news though: I think I found the source of the anti-magic field."

"Really? What is it?" Piper asks excitedly.

"A giant, creepily glowing crystal in the center of the tower," David responds flatly. "Seriously, what is with magic and all these fucking crystals? This is like the hundredth time it's come up."

"Well, I told you, magical energy acts a lot like light, and crystals are capable of refracting and diffusing light, and certain kinds of crystals—"

"Mike, focus," David chastises his twin. "You can give me the lesson later."

"Sorry." Michael sighs. "What color is it?"

"Kind of a smoky grey? Hard to tell with the whole glowing thing."

"Smoky grey? That sounds like reponiam," Piper confers with Michael.

"The stuff you guys need to get home?" Liss confirms. "That's good news, right?"

"No, if it's glowing like he said, then it's already storing..." Michael trails off, eyes growing large as he turns back toward the tower. "David, you didn't touch it, did you?"

"What? No," he replies, offended. "I'm not stupid enough to touch the giant glowing object sitting in a skeleton's lap."

"A skeleton?" Michael suddenly sounds very excited. "What does it look like? Can you tell how old it is? Is it an elf, gnome, or human?"

"I don't know, dude. It's a fucking skeleton. I mean, I guess it could be a human. I just assumed it was an elf because of all the..." There is a brief pause. "You can't see, but I just gestured to everything."

As angry as I might still be, knowing he feels well enough to joke makes me smile. "Are you able to climb back up to the window?"

"Yeah, shouldn't even really need the rope." *That is good news.* "So... How do I turn this thing off? Do I smash it?"

"*No!*" Michael immediately shouts. "We have *no* idea what kind of magic it's holding, destroying it would drop the field but also release whatever is making it glow."

"Okay, okay, not smashing the crystal." *At least he asked first.* "What's the plan, then?"

"If that is reponiam, and *also* the source of the anti-magic field..." Michael pauses and then shakes his head. "It doesn't make sense."

"What do you mean?" Liss asks for clarification.

"Well, at least in theory, the field would prevent the spell from activating as long as it was up but destroying the crystal would drop the field and release the magic anyway." Michael looks like he is still thinking and shakes his head. "The only thing that would really protect it from would be other spells being cast on the crystal. I just don't really get why someone would do that."

"It seems to be doing a good job of keeping us out right now," Liss grouses.

"Sure, but you can cast an anti-magic field on lots of things," Michael points out. "The fact that it's a crystal that is holding another spell makes me think something dangerous could be in there. We need to be careful and see if we can figure out what is inside before dropping the field."

"Can any of you climb the rope?" I hear a guffaw from inside the tower at Adam's question.

"Don't look at me," Piper tells the rest of us. "I'm still trying to get used to sleeping outside. I will not be climbing up *anything*, thank you very much."

"I might be able to?" Riley offers with uncertainty.

"What if I just moved it?" David's question has everyone looking at the blocked entrance.

"What do you mean?" Michael asks his twin to clarify.

"Well, we just need you guys to be able to use your magic to unblock the entrance, right? If the field is only a little bigger than the tower, couldn't I just like, move it away from the door?" That is sound logic. "It's kind of cramped down here, but there's a room a few floors up across from the main doorway. If I took it in there, then the field would move far enough away that you can do whatever mojo you need to get inside, right? That way no one else has to climb in through the window."

"That's...not a bad idea, David," Michael admits.

"Does it look safe enough to carry it up that high?" Adam asks next.

"Yeah, I think so, and we're gonna have to climb up anyway, right?" There is a brief pause. "Gods, I hope not all the way to the top though."

"Alright David, solid plan," Adam commends. "Go ahead and start moving. Just be careful. For real this time."

"Will do," I hear the faint sounds of rock moving against rock as he climbs over more rubble.

"You seriously need to be careful when you're holding that thing, David," Michael tells his brother sternly. "Do you remember what the interviewer from the institute said when we were younger? About your latent magic? That means you could accidentally activate the reponiam."

"I thought you said because of the field it wouldn't work?" David sounds annoyed at his brother's perceived doubletalk.

"It *shouldn't*, but I've never actually heard of someone doing this before, so just be fucking careful, okay?" I am not sure if I should take the bickering as a sign that they are making up or not.

"Alright, shit, being extra careful." I can hear David climbing toward the crystal again. "I'll even carry it with my shirt."

"Just carry it like a normal person." There is no verbal response to Michael's request, but I know David rolled his eyes.

We are waiting for a few minutes in silence, only the faint sounds of rock scraping over rock or loose stones falling coming from inside. I fight the urge to pace as I wait for any sort of update on David's progress. When I finally see a head poking out of the window on our right, I relax a little and point him out to the others.

"Just in case," David says as he drops the rope out the window to the ground, then continues his climb.

Not long after his brief appearance, I can feel the oppressive weight of the anti-magic field being lifted as my magic returns to me. The bond between me and the wolf thrums with energy as it falls back into place, and I can feel that she is happy to sense me again as well. Around me, the others mumble happily as they feel their own skills returning, and Michael is the first to step toward the tower.

"It worked, David!" He calls up through the rubble, unsure of if he can be heard or not. "Riley, you're probably the best choice for this."

The druid steps forward, stretching out his arms before holding his hands in front of him. I do not catch what he says, but afterward, his hands begin to glow a faint white. Pressing them against the crumbled stone, he begins pushing and molding it like it is made of clay. Even more malleable, as it only takes him maybe three minutes to finish carving out a narrow doorway allowing all of us to slip inside. I still have to crouch, but it is far more impressive than anything I could have done.

We enter into a large, circular room, feeling the effects of the anti-magic field return as we step back in its range. All around us, the floor is littered with the remains of broken columns and walkways. In the middle of the room is a particularly large pile, at the center of which skeletal remains can be seen. The rubble looks to be like some sort of bridge or walkway, no doubt from farther up the tower. I look up and see that the room seemingly extends...forever. There are stairs and bridges going in all directions, different doors and rooms jutting out at odd angles. My stomach suddenly drops out, and the full weight of what we will have to do comes crashing down.

"Well, there's our skeleton friend," Corrine comments as if it were the most normal thing in the world, stepping over and onto the rocks to get a closer look.

"Can you tell us anything about it?" Michael sounds as excited as he did when David first revealed its existence. "Like how old it is?"

"It's definitely an elf. You can tell from the slightly elongated skull." She climbs over more rubble and crouches down. "As far as how old it is, I can't give you an exact date, but it's much younger than a few thousand years, especially if it's been out in the open like this."

"Everyone, you gotta get up here." David's voice rings out from above us. "There's a ton of cool-looking stuff, and I don't know what *any* of it is."

"Alright, hold on. We're on our way," Adam calls back with a chuckle.

"Stay here and guard the entrance," I tell my wolf, doing my best to hide my fears but also allowing the others to go first. She pushes her head against my hand, attempting to calm the nervousness I know she can feel coming off me in waves.

The room is a little dark, the only light coming from open windows, but it is enough to see without aid for now. There is a large staircase, or at least the remains of one, to our left. It spirals around the walls of the room as it continues above us, its width dependent on how much of it has crumbled to the floor below. I hug the wall closely as we climb, watching my steps carefully but refusing to look down once we reach a certain height. As we circle around, we can feel the anti-magic field leave and return at various points, reminding me that we must make this climb unaided at the moment. Should any of us fall, there is nothing anyone could do about it.

"I'll be glad when that thing's gone and my magic's back so I can do this with a little more grace," Riley complains on my left as we shuffle across a particularly narrow piece of walkway.

"It will be much safer that way as well," I reply stiffly.

We step onto a landing, one with more room and that feels sturdier than the rail-thin section we just finished crossing. I take a moment to compose myself, thankful that no one is watching me as they look at how to traverse the path forward. Just as we start to climb again, a blood-curdling scream rings out from above. *DAVID!*

Chapter 14

I push past everyone, vaulting over a fallen column as I rush toward David's scream. Aside from rubble, my path is mostly clear, with the exception of another narrow section that would require hugging the wall again to cross. Cursing as I run—and deciding the ground on the opposite side looks solid enough—I leap across the gap instead, landing as lightly as I can before continuing my speedy climb.

When I approach the area where the scream originated, I notice a set of double doors ahead of me, slightly ajar. *He must be inside.* I grip the edge of the stone door and yank the rest of the way open, barreling my way inside to find David...standing there. Wearing an uncomfortable smile as he takes me in. I return his look, confused.

"Hey." He waves awkwardly. "I, uh, swear that was funnier when I did it in my head."

My face instantly sours, and I take a deep, angry breath.

"What's going on? What happened?" Michael's concerned voice rings out from behind us.

"He is fine," I grit out. "Just a *joke*, I suppose."

"Are you fucking kidding me?" Michael grits out just as angrily.

"I'm sorry?" David offers, guilt growing on his face.

I can only shake my head, stepping to the side to make room for the rest of the group to enter once they finish making it up the stairs. The room we are in seems to be a throne room of sorts, large and open with a raised platform at one end, two stone chairs at its center. A glowing crystal sits on the right throne, presumably the one David moved. No one attempts to say anything to him, though I believe it is only me and Michael who are actually angry. The mages, seeing the crystal, immediately move toward the throne to inspect it more closely.

"That is *huge*," Michael comments in awe at the crystal's size.

"What do you think is inside?" Nathaniel asks.

"No idea." Piper sways her hips a bit as she thinks. "Sometimes the color of the energy can offer a clue, but this is just white."

"Is there anything you can do to figure it out?" Elisabeth questions next. "What about your special sorcerer abilities?"

"Sadly, they function the same way as magic," Piper admits. "A spellcaster of significant power might be able to break through. That likely rules out any of us individually, but it couldn't hurt to try as a group."

"Yeah, it's worth a shot," Michael agrees.

"Anything the rest of us can do to help?" Adam asks on behalf of the other non-magical people in the group.

"No, thank you though." She shakes her head. "Riley, Tsula, Corrine, we are just going to attempt a simple identification spell."

"Alright, have at it." Adam steps back with Elisabeth, allowing the others to step forward and begin working.

I am not offended that she did not name me—my magical talents are almost insignificant compared to the others. Seeing that things are under control, I step outside of the room to clear my head. Across from me is another set of double doors, a flat walkway between them and the spiral staircase continuing up just past it. Curious, I make my way across when a sharp bark rings up from the center of the tower—the wolf is concerned after hearing the scream as well.

"Everything is alright," I call down to her, receiving a softer bark of acknowledgement in return.

I slowly open one of the doors to reveal a room almost as large as the throne room. The floor is covered with random stone and debris, the only real object being the tattered remains of an elaborate tapestry hanging limply from the far wall. It seems to have fallen under the same disenchantment issue as the other items found, only certain parts having survived the thousands of years of wear and tear. I can make out what look like green fields, or maybe mountains, and what could possibly be part of the tower, but it is not clear. To be honest, I am surprised to find something like this here at all. Even as destroyed as it is, I would expect someone should want to preserve it is a piece of their history. *Is travel to this place truly that taboo?*

"Hey." I turn to see David has followed me from the other room.

"Hello," I greet him flatly, then go back to examining the tapestry.

"I'm really sorry," he apologizes to my back. "I was just trying to lighten the mood, which I know nobody asked for. I completely forgot about your fear of heights."

"Funny enough, once I heard your scream, so did I." Despite the apology, him admitting to being inconsiderate does little to make me feel better.

"Really? That's... Wow. Thank you. Sorry, again." I can hear the guilt in his voice. "I know there's a lot we need to talk about..."

"You are right. There is." I sigh, finally turning to meet his eyes. "But now is probably not the best time."

Proving my point, Adam's head leans in through the doorway behind David.

"There you guys are." He enters the room fully. "Everything okay?"

"Yes, I noticed that these doors matched the room we entered." I nod to the open doors behind him. "I wanted to see if there was anything that might help while the others worked."

"Anything useful?" He looks around the room.

"Afraid not." I shrug, then point to the tapestry. "Only that."

"Ah." He looks at the tattered cloth, unimpressed. "Well, I think they're almost done trying whatever it was they were doing. Doesn't look like it's gonna work."

"What do we do if it doesn't work?" David asks as we both follow Adam out of the room.

"I'm gonna wait and hear what they think, first." Adam leads us across to the other room. "They're the experts."

Reentering the throne room, I see the spellcasters still gathered around the crystal, inspecting it. Some look as if they are attempting to cast something, but nothing is happening. I assume that means they are unable to overcome the field's effects. They break apart a short while later, looking disappointed.

"Damn," Piper grouses.

"Did you get anything at all?" Michael asks, hopeful.

"Nothing." Piper shakes her head.

"So, what should we do now?" Adam asks the group of spellcasters.

"We could just leave it and keep going up, I guess?" Michael offers.

"Problem." David holds up a hand, pointing a finger to the ceiling. "Half a floor up is that collapsed bridge Riley mentioned. He was right. We're not gonna be able to cross without magic."

"We could always take it back down to the ground floor?" Nathaniel suggests next.

"I am not sure that will be far enough," I counter. "Remember how the field extended outside of the tower's perimeter? We would need to take it outside."

"That's a lot of walking, and we already got a late start today. Not to mention that we'd just be moving the problem to a new location. Is there a way we could somehow safely set it off?" Like myself, Adam (and hopefully the rest of us) is feeling extra cautious after yesterday's monster attack.

"The crystal is pretty fragile. As long as someone is a good shot, we could all hide behind something at a distance while they fired an arrow," Michael explains. "But whatever's inside could be strong enough to take out part of the tower with it."

"Is that really the only way?" Liss asks. "Breaking the damn thing?"

"Why not chuck it out the window?" David asks.

The group collectively turns to look at David after his suggestion, silent.

"For some reason that feels...wrong?" Adam hesitates.

"Is it, though?" Liss counters. "If that thing has to blow up, better that it do it outside than in here, right? Not even just for safety. This place seems a lot more important than the homes out there."

"And that's assuming it even explodes," Piper adds. "The spell could be much, much less volatile than that."

"Wait, are we really gonna throw it out the window?" David clarifies, grinning.

"I guess so?" Adam scratches his head before turning to Tsula. "I feel like I should apologize that we're about to do this."

"It seems like a reasonable solution to me." She shrugs. "I won't tell you if you don't."

"So, who's got the strongest throwing arm?" David points his thumb at the crystal.

"Khazak?" Liss asks.

"I believe it would be me," I admit. There is a large open window just to our right. I step over to the crystal, feeling its weight and finding a good place to grab hold. It is much lighter than I would have expected. Even with its bulk and odd size, I should not have any trouble. "You just want me to throw it as far away from the tower as I can?"

"Yeah, pretty much." Adam nods.

"Alright." I nod as well, stepping away from the throne with the reponiam.

I take a few steps back, lining myself up as the others clear a path to the window. Making a few practice swings, I test the object's weight before I lock my eyes on the window, ready. Taking a few steps forward, I hurl the crystal through the window, sending it flying into the open air.

I do not bother tracking its descent to the ground; my companions are more than happy to do that for me, several of them rushing forward to peer out the window. I see the backs of their heads tilting down as they track its fall and very quickly feel my magic returning once more when the field is finally out of reach. When the crystal smashes against something in the distance, some of the others make sounds of disappointment, still staring at the ground.

"What happened?" I ask when they turn around.

"Nothing," David complains. "A small flash, a puff of smoke, and then nothing."

"What's up with that?" Liss asks, turning toward Michael and Piper.

"It could be a lot of things," Michael starts to explain, counting on his fingers. "I've never seen reponiam that old, so maybe it had just been so long that the spell returned to its basic magical energy state and dissipated. Or maybe the parameters of the spells no longer apply because the people or items it was supposed to target no longer exist. Or maybe it was set to only work during a certain time of day or in a certain place..."

"All that really matters now is that with it gone, we are back to our full strength." Piper takes a moment to stretch her arms out at her sides, her hands glowing a brief purple. Then she turns to her fellow mages. "Now that *that* is taken care of...featherfall?"

"Ooo, smart thinkin', Williams," Riley commends her.

"That's a great idea," Tsula adds, though I am still confused as to what they are talking about.

"What the hell is 'featherfall?'" David asks his twin. *Glad to see I am not the only one.*

"A spell that will be very, very useful as we climb this tower," Michael assures him, then turns to Riley. "Do you have enough feathers? I left my big bag of spell components back home."

"Aye, I should have us covered." Riley rummages through his own bag.

The druid's hand emerges clutching a handful of bird feathers. He holds them out for Tsula, Michael, and Piper, who in turn pass one to each of the rest of us. Once we are all holding one, the mages come to each of us individually to cast their spell, Piper standing in front of me.

"*Plumalapsus!*" She raises her hands up slowly from where they rest at her side, as if lifting the air around me, and then I do in fact find myself feeling lighter.

"What did you just do?" I hear David ask his brother.

"Try jumping," Michael replies. I turn to watch as David does so and see that his decent back to the ground is much slower.

"This is awesome!" My pup cheers as he touches the floor.

"Now if any more floors collapse, at least it won't be the fall that kills us," the wizard reasons.

I test things for myself, pleased when I get the same results. I would not say I have forgotten about my fear of height by any means, but this does help to put me a bit more at ease. If I, or anyone else falls, we will just float safely to the ground. *As long as there are no more anti-magic fields...*

"Alright, ready to start exploring for real?" Adam confirms with everyone after the spellcasters have finished.

"Yes, let's get moving," Liss quickly answers for everyone. "It's almost noon, and I don't want to be here all night. This place is only going to get creepier after dark."

We file out of the room and onto the walkway. After a brief moment for the others to inspect the tapestry room, we continue up the stairs and come face to face with our first obstacle: the broken bridge. There is no easy way across the chasm, the gap is far too large for any of us to jump on our own. But with the anti-magic field dropped, that opens up magical solutions.

Michael offers up a flying spell that he qualifies by explaining that is hard to control in tight spaces, Piper wants to try shapeshifting each of us into birds, and Nathaniel claims to know a spell that will simply, as he puts it, "make us jump really well." It should go without saying that all of these solutions make me uncomfortable, if not outright terrify me.

"Will ya pipe down and move outta the way?" Riley interrupts the three arguing arcane casters, standing next to a toppled column with a smirk. "I told ya I was gonna get a lotta use outta this spell today."

Rubbing his hands together, he begins to mold the stone of the column as he did when forming the entryway downstairs. It takes some time and is more nerve-wracking than I can handle—I spend most of the time staring blankly at the wall—but eventually Riley forms a solid, if not thin bridge across the chasm. We cross one at a time, as even with the featherfall spell lightening our weight, no one wants to take any chances. I go last, and it is only by staring straight ahead and mentally repeating the silent mantra of "you will not die if you fall" that I make it.

Following the bridge, the stairs continue to wind clockwise around the tower. The crumbling stone and lack of lighting lend themselves to the tower's already eerie atmosphere. Every so often, we come to another landing with a door that is sometimes blocked, sometimes not, all leading to rooms of varying sizes. It is easy to speculate on their uses based on the furniture that has survived. Parts of them at least, the parts that are made of solid stone: the room full of bed frames was likely a servant's quarters, and the one with desks some kind of office.

Sometimes the stairs lead us to rooms that jut out from the rest of the tower oddly, forcing us to enter to keep moving forward. These rooms function like a hallway with a door across from our entrance leading to the stairs that continue upward, and a door on either our left or right leading to another room. Statues line the walls, perhaps depicting elven royalty or their ancient gods. Several have crumbled to little more than piles of rubble. For a split second, I think I see one of them move, but it must have been a trick of the light.

The rooms these hanging hallways lead us to are much larger than the others we have entered, taking up the entire "ring" that makes up that floor of the tower. They also serve more obvious and specific purposes, like the library, which by now is little more than dozens, maybe even hundreds of empty bookshelves. Another appears to be an art gallery, filled with pedestals of worn-down statues and empty frames.

Eventually, we come to a hallway with two doors: the one on the left leads to a dining room, and the one on the right to a bridge that takes you to the kitchens. The rooms are connected at either end for easy travel between the two, likely used by servants—I cannot imagine having to cross that chasm with your arms laden with food trays.

The dining room is mostly intact with only a few of the long tables having collapsed. Stone candelabras sit at the center of each table, resembling gnarled hands, covered in cobwebs and missing several of their oddly shaped digits. The kitchens are in much worse shape, apparently having suffered a fire in its final days. Whatever remains of the ovens and counters are covered in blackened scorch marks with pieces of melted metal fused into some of the rock.

"Alright, let's break here for a minute. Someone check how high up we are," Adam makes the request to no one in particular, taking a seat at one of the dining room tables. We have spent nearly three hours now exploring the tower below us, so I am also curious.

"Looks like we're about halfway up," Liss informs us while sticking her head out of a window and looking up and down. "Maybe a little more than?"

"Good headway, I guess. Hopefully going down is much easier." Adam leans back in his chair and squirms as he tries to find a good sitting position. "This chair is *really* uncomfortable."

"I'm guessing that's because any padding they might have had has long since deteriorated." Tsula tells him, taking a seat of her own.

"Is there anything you can tell us about the elves that used to live here in the tower?" I decide to inquire. The rest of us have each begun to take our own seats, pulling out our lunch rations to refuel for the rest of the day.

"Not much. All of the information we have is from stories and anecdotes, and what little has been gleaned while exploring the ruins," Tsula informs with a frown. "I can tell you that the city was a monarchy, normally ruled by a king and a queen, but there was only a queen in the city's final years."

"A queen you say?" Piper leans forward with a smile. "Do tell more. I love hearing about women in positions of power."

"She was said to be a kind ruler and also a very powerful wizard," Tsula continues. "Some people speculate that *she* might have been the cause of the magical cataclysm, but there's no proof of that. I think people just like to make up a good story."

"A single woman, a queen, *and* a spellcaster? I think I would have liked to meet her," Piper concludes before returning to her meal.

"I am so sick of trail rations," Michael complains after a few more minutes of eating in silence.

"You get used to them," David assures his brother, taking a bite of jerky. "Or at least you start to figure out the stuff you hate less than others, so you know what to buy."

"Yeah, well, I hope I'm not stuck here long enough to get *too* used to them," Michael tells him with a cold stare, making David flinch and look away. *Dammit, now I feel bad for still being angry with him.*

Finished with our mediocre lunch (I feel like my father, actually wishing I could cook for everyone right now), we resume scaling the tower. A few times now, Riley has had to use his magic to clear a doorway or repair a broken path so we can continue forward. He has not shown any signs of tiring, but I hope he will be able to make it to the top. Or that we will find what we are looking for before we reach the top. My fear of heights has gotten slightly easier to handle, if only because I have no other choice.

We reach another four-way split a few floors above the dining room. Both directions lead to dark rooms, which we learn are the same room after entering and walking all the way around. What few windows this room had all seem to have collapsed or have been blocked, forcing us to light a few torches to save the humans from bumping into the furniture in the darkness.

"This must have been the guard barracks," I announce as the room is illuminated and the countless bunks come into view as well the weapon racks that line the walls.

"That's a lot of guards," Nathaniel comments, attempting to peer around the bend of the room to see how far down the beds go.

"They were protecting the queen." Elisabeth shrugs.

"I doubt we'll find anything useful, but it can't hurt to look." Adam walks toward one of the bunks, which has a stone chest at its feet, and opens it. "Empty."

Several of the beds have chests like the one Adam spotted, some already open or destroyed, but most are empty, so our search moves pretty quickly. Approximately halfway around the room, just past the door to the bridge, is another. I crouch down to open it, flipping back the lid to reveal another empty container, when I feel the hairs on the back of my neck stand straight up. Right after that, a very soft, very low moan echo from down the hall. *At least I think?* I stand, searching the room with my eyes and ears, trying to find the source.

"Did anyone else hear that?" I finally ask when my efforts turn up nothing.

"Hear what?" Adam asks, everyone else turning to hear my answer.

"Someone moaning, very faintly." Saying the words out loud makes me feel silly, especially when no one else seems to believe me.

"No, I don't think any of us heard anything." Adam looks around for confirmation, stopping on David with slight worry. *Am I hearing things the way he did?*

David, sensing the similarity as well, turns to his brother and the other spellcasters. "Can any of you detect anything magical in the room that might be causing it?"

Michael and Piper, both using their abilities, step forward to make such a check, their eyes glowing green and purple respectively as they scan the area. After looking at each other to confirm, they both shake their heads.

"Nope, nothing out of the ordinary." Michael shrugs.

"Just the occasional odd piece of enchanted clothing or furniture, I think," Piper offers more detail.

Suddenly, a strong gust of wind blows through the room, extinguishing both torches and causing several of our number to shriek in fear and surprise. There is a moment of panic as the room falls once more into darkness, most of us too afraid to move. I hear the familiar *flick* of a piece of flint being struck, the sparks illuminating Adam's torso as he attempts to relight a torch.

"What the hell was that?" Elisabeth asks as soon as everyone can see again.

"Don't look at me this time." Riley holds up both hands in innocence.

"It was probably whatever was causing the moaning Khazak heard." David is quick to connect the two.

"I'm still not sensing anything unusual." Piper shakes her head again. "It doesn't feel like a spell was cast."

"It was probably just a draft." Nathaniel does not sound very confident about his own theory. *Neither am I.*

"Ah yes, the draft that has been blowing through this room with no open windows and only two sets of doors," I deadpan.

"Let's just keep moving, everyone," Adam refocuses us.

With no evidence of anything happening, we finish searching the floor and move onto the next. The farther we ascend, the fewer windows I notice, and I understand why when I pass in front of one and the temperature of the air outside is bone chilling. This also has the added effect of making the tower grow darker the higher we go, and with the sun only a few hours away from setting, the atmosphere is going to shift drastically. When we are roughly three-quarters of the way to the top (at least according to Liss's very scientific calculations), we pass a landing with a door that makes Tsula stop and turn.

"H-hold on," Tsula calls for the rest of us as she steps toward it. "I think this might be the room where the conduit crystals would be kept."

The door is not as imposing as some of the others we have entered, but I do note some symbols carved onto the outside that appear to be in the shapes of crystals or diamonds. It takes a good shove to open, revealing a small room on the other side. There is not much to see aside from a window, a desk covered in some sort of complicated mechanism, and a pile of crystals.

"Yes!" Michael cheers as he moves toward the crystalline horde.

"Those are the conduit crystals?" Adam confirms as others move to join him.

"Yep!" Michael happily picks one up and moves to show it to the rest of us. "They're made of a special type of quartz that's been treated to resonate with the energy of the leylines. Another ancient elven craft we have been unable to duplicate. If you hold it at the right angle, you can see the runes etched into the crystal. Not even just the surface but actually *inside* the crystal."

While several of the group begin to pack a few crystals into their bags to take with us, I grab one to take a closer look. They are large, at least twelve centimeters around, and about the same in length. Weighty too—you could do some serious damage if you were to throw one at someone's head. They have a slight pinkish hue that is visible when light passes through, and just as Michael said, I can make out small symbols seemingly etched inside when it is held at a certain angle.

"Is this the machine?" David asks, examining the equipment on the desk. "The... What did you call it? Prism transferrer?"

"Prismatic transmitter," Piper corrects. "And yes, this is what the ancient elven cities used to communicate with each other. Well, not this one. This one's broken. Pákannon must have found a working one and moved it from this room."

It is hard to describe the transmitter, especially as it is broken. The base is rectangular with the side facing us sloped and covered with dozens of different buttons and dials. Above that is another rectangle with a crystal pyramid at its center. This crystal appears to be made of the same type of quartz, though it is cracked. Next to the pyramid are two circular slots about the same size as a conduit crystal. The entire object is set into the wall, or at least was, as there is a transmitter-shaped hole behind it.

"I'm surprised to see it so up high. See the black stone in the cracks here?" Piper bends over the desk and points into the hole. "Lodestone. It's used to store and move magical energy. It would have to go almost all the way down to the base of the tower to be close enough to connect with the leyline."

"Ley*lines*." It is Michael's turn to correct. "There were probably multiple that ran right under the tower."

"Why past tense?" Adam questions his choice of words.

"They're not really there anymore," the mage responds. "Leylines can sometimes shift over time, but it's more likely that the rending drained them, same as it did a lot of the other magic in the area."

"That's one thing down, but we still need the reponiam, right?" Liss confirms as we finish packing our crystals.

"Yep. So, we keep going up," Adam tells her as we turn to leave. "The storeroom will be near the top of the tower."

After exiting the crystal room, we reach another hanging hallway. This time, the bridge on the right splits into three, though one of them is broken. Each ends at a different landing with a set of double doors, all decorated with flowing, asymmetrical shapes along their edges and intricate looking script along the top. The set of doors on the inside of the hallway to the left appears larger than the others but otherwise look the same.

"Can you read what these say, Tsula?" I point above the door.

"No, sorry. It's Old Elvish." She shakes her head.

"Let us see what is inside then," I say before daring to open the doors and reveal a large bedroom to the group.

"We must have finally hit some of the royal's personal rooms," Piper comments after peeking inside.

"The other rooms are probably also bedrooms," Adam speculates. "Alright, there's only four so we'll split up. Liss, you, Khazak, and Tsula take this one. Riley, you fix the bridge to the broken one while the rest of us take care of the other two."

"Might just be easier to hop over and take look myself," the redhead offers.

"Go for it," the blonde agrees, leading the others out of the hallway as the three of us enter our assigned room.

The room is opulent to say the least with more surviving furniture than I have seen in most of the others. The large stone bed is covered with a canopy, a few scraps of dark blue fabric still hanging from the frame. In one corner is a wooden desk—or considering the mirror at its center, more likely a vanity—and in another the remains of a lounge chair, which has been hobbled, missing two of its legs. Along another wall are a set of wardrobes that are also made of wood, both in relatively good condition.

"I am surprised all of this is still here," I comment as I walk deeper into the room.

"This area of the tower must have been better protected than the rest." Tsula looks around the room with me. "With how big it is, it may have even been the queen's bedroom."

"I more meant that the city would leave all of these items here." I walk to the vanity and look in the mirror, cracked. "Not to use but for historical purposes."

"It would be kinda hard to drag some of this down and out of the tower, don't you think?" Liss points out.

"It's because of superstition," Tsula informs us with a tired look. "People in Pákannon think that the city, and the things in it, are cursed. So other than looters, everyone else is too afraid to bring anything outside the ruins. Except for when the mayor or elven council deem something 'necessary,' like the conduit crystals. Which seems kind of convenient if you ask me."

"You will hear no arguments on that from me." Since I have Tsula here, I should probably take the opportunity to ask her about the report. Although now that Michael is aware of David's death, I have to wonder if the continued secrecy is even needed. "Tsula, were you able to read through any more of the report?"

"Oh yes! I'm so sorry I haven't talked to either of you about it," she apologizes. "I'm just about through the section on myths. There are a *lot*, but Uncle Atsadi, Aunt Ahyoka, and the other archeologists did manage to decipher almost all of them."

"Were there any that seemed particularly relevant?" I do not need a rundown on each one, I hope.

"There were the ones the Harpe appears in—Perseus, Heracles, Cronus and others—the weapon is described and depicted *exactly* the same as David's sword. Relative to being carved onto a wall," she quickly tags on.

"So that may be an actual mythical weapon that David is carrying around?" I know we talked about it last time, but it still seems so far-fetched.

"David's carrying a what?" Liss rises from searching under the bed in surprise at our discussion.

"The third sword David has been carrying, the one that killed him," I clarify. "It appears that it may be an Olympian weapon of legend, wielded by heroes and even gods of the past."

"...David's carrying a *what*?" she repeats, *mostly* as a joke.

"It appeared in one more myth on the temple walls, one they couldn't identify," Tsula resumes telling me her findings. "It looked like it might be showing events taking place in the temple itself, some sort of sacrifice. Since it wasn't a myth any of them were familiar with, they made a lot of guesses. Uncle Atsadi thought it might be depicting what took place at the time of the temple's creation, but *I* think it could possibly be about what happened to David."

"You do?" That would be shocking to say the least. "Why?"

"The inscription on the basin. It's actually part of a longer inscription on this part of the wall." That does seem like more than just a coincidence. "I wish I could remember the full translation from memory. Something about oceans… Sorry, I knew I should have written it down."

"That is still good information to have." *That hopefully Nylan's father Atsadi will be able to clear up for us.* "Thank you again for all your reading, Tsula."

"I'll be able to tell you when we're back at camp. There's just one more section, and it looks like it might be the longest." *I am not sure if that is meant as a warning or not.* "It's where they go into detail on the theories on how the altar was meant to function. It looks like they even recorded the experiments they attempted."

"Maybe they will be able to shed some light on the method of David's resurrection." *Even Murbank and Redwish were shocked that it worked on David.* "I'll relay the information to David. Thank you again."

"I'll let you know as soon as I know more," she promises with a nod. "…I'm sorry that you and Michael don't seem to be getting along."

"Yes, I do not expect we will become pen pals after this," I respond with a chuckle. "But please do not let our interactions color your opinion of him." *We cannot always help who we are attracted to.*

Our discussion finished, I turn to face the rest of the room and begin searching. Elisabeth has already searched the bed and moved onto the corner with the lounge chair, and Tsula has turned her attention back to the vanity and its drawers, which really only leaves me with the wardrobes. Simple enough. Facing the wall, I decide to start on the left when I hear something rattling inside the wardrobe on the right.

"What was that?" Elisabeth asks before I have a chance.

We hear the rattle again, this time causing the wardrobe to shake.

"It's coming from inside." I point at the wardrobe in question.

"Maybe an animal got stuck? Like a rat?" Tsula offers hopefully.

"Sounds like a pretty big rat," Liss warns.

"There is only one way to find out." I steel myself as I approach the wardrobe.

I pull out my sword when it shakes a third time, both women taking positions behind me on either side. Slowly reaching out my hand, I wait for the noise to stop before quickly grabbing the handle and flinging the door open. I jump back as whatever is inside tries to tackle me, Tsula and Elisabeth both shrieking as it hits the ground. I draw my weapon back, ready to strike whatever just tried to attack me, when I see that it is...a dress mannequin. One that is perfectly still. *What in the spirit's name?* Seeing what frightened us so badly causes Liss to start laughing uncontrollably, just as the other seven members of our group rush in to see what the commotion is about.

"What happened?" Adam takes in Liss's laughing form.

"We heard something rustling in one of the closets." I point to the mannequin on the floor. "But when I opened it, that was all that fell out."

"Hearing things again?" Michael scoffs.

"I heard it too, actually," Tsula defends me. "All three of us did."

Michael looks confused, either by her answer or her defense of me, and joins the others in looking at the mannequin.

"That could not have been the source of the noise." I search the inside of the closet but find nothing, not even clothing. "We heard it *multiple* times. Even if it was this, something had to have been moving it."

Piper steps forward, her eyes already glowing as she searches the area for magic. "This is a lovely piece of vintage dressmaking, but other than the preservation enchantments on it and the other objects in the room, I'm not able to detect anything magical. Sorry." She gives me an apologetic look before looking back at the mannequin. "It's a pity. I would love to bring something like this back home with me."

"Don't be so sure. From what I hear, this stuff might be cursed," Elisabeth half-jokes, half-warns. Between what happened here and in the barracks below, I am starting to worry she may be right.

Chapter 15

After the excitement in the queen's alleged bedroom, all of the groups are sad to report the same thing: none have found anything. The other rooms, though smaller and slightly less opulent, had even fewer places to search. This feels especially disappointing given how high up we are, and how much more well preserved these rooms are compared to the others. I think some of us may be starting to doubt the existence of this fabled storeroom, and we are running out of tower to search.

Nonetheless, we advance up into the increasingly dark and so very high up citadel. For whatever reason, despite the quality of care that befell the bedrooms, the walkways in this part of the tower only get more dilapidated and perilous. Piper has assured me that the featherfall spell she cast will last long into the night, but that is doing little to quell my anxiety as I remember just how tall the tower looked from the outside, and just how high inside we are in relation to that.

Obstacles that should be trivial, like a gap between walkways small enough for a child to skip over, prove deadly. Michael, the last of us to make the jump, somehow manages to land on the *one* loose tile on the opposite bank, and though I am fast enough for my arm to reach out and steady him, I still find myself sending a silent plea for protection to the gods I barely remember to speak to once a year. *If High Priest Bhok could see me now... Sky-Father, if you can hear me, please watch over me and the others while we foolishly stumble our way through the upper atmosphere.*

"Thanks," Michael tells me after releasing his tight grip on my forearm, and I will give him credit for at least attempting to not sound begrudging.

"I think we're almost there. Or almost somewhere." From the front of the group, Adam points up. "Look."

Above us, the path continues to wind around the tower for another few floors, though without any further landings or doorways on the sides to enter. Instead, it ends just under the room's ceiling, in front of what else but of a pair of large, stone double doors. The kind we have seen indicate other rooms of importance. Wherever we are going, this is the only way forward.

Adam is the first to reach the doors, which open easily under his touch after he grips both handles. In fact, I cannot recall having issues opening any of the large, ornate doors. My stepfather Jarek would be fascinated by the craftsmanship.

The path leads up only another hundred meters or so, emptying into a room that appears to take up the entire width of the tower. The walls are lined with more statues, larger and more detailed than those we saw downstairs. The ceiling extends far above us, held up by six large columns, thicker than the trees we have back home. There are two square windows cut into the walls on either side of us, opening to the east and west, and on the opposite end of the room is a raised platform, at the top of which sits five chairs. Thrones.

"I thought the throne room was downstairs?" Elisabeth makes the observation as we walk into the room.

"They probably used that one for meeting with citizens and other day-to-day things," Tsula remarks as she steps toward the platform. "This would have been for more formal occasions."

"Makes sense," she accepts. "Why are there five though?"

"Children," I say offhandedly, examining the thrones for myself. They're of varying sizes, two being larger than the others. "The bedrooms we found downstairs. They must have been for the king and queen's three children."

"Didn't you say this palace was only ruled by a queen back before everything went all... ghost town?" David asks Tsula.

"As far as I know, it was." I do not want to think long on the implications of this information.

"So, is this it?" Nathaniel asks as he looks around the room. "I mean, we're at the top, right?"

"We're not at the top," Liss tells us, her head sticking out of one of the windows. "First, the tower had a pointed dome and the ceiling in here is flat, and second, I can see that the wall on the outside goes up higher than on the inside. There's definitely a room up there."

"That would check out with what Mayor Elajor said about the storeroom at the top of the tower," Adam confirms. "I guess he was being literal."

"Did he say how to get inside?" I ask next.

"He did not." Adam shakes his head.

"Of course not. We were able to find what *he* needed without any problems," I grumble. This entire venture has felt like running one long errand.

"There is something up there," Piper comments while squinting at the ceiling, her eyes glowing purple. "Something magical. I can't quite tell what from this distance."

"There has to be a way up," Michael adds, also looking at the ceiling.

"Like a secret passage or something?" David asks, only half serious.

"Not exactly, but maybe?" Michael responds, still looking up. "It's possible that they used magic to hide the entrance."

"Would you be able to detect something like that?" David asks next.

"Not if the magic was dispelled or drained." Michael shakes his head. "You'd just have a bunch of mechanisms that don't work anymore. *But*, if we knew what and where they were, we could try and reactivate them or at least get some idea of how to open the way."

"Riley, couldn't you use your melty-stone spell to brute force our way in?" Nathaniel asks the druid.

"Maybe. I'm not sure I have much juice left," he answers, joining his friends in examining the ceiling. "There's also the matter o' not knowin' what's up there. Could risk everything comin' down on us."

"There has to be another way up," I conclude. "I highly doubt the ancient elves were using 'brute force' to get upstairs, no matter how magically inclined they may have been."

"Mike and Khazak are both right," Adam voices a sentence I did not expect to hear. "Start looking for anything out of the ordinary."

We split up and begin searching different corners of the room. Some of us crouch down on the floor, closely examining the tiles, while others walk slowly around pillars, scouring every inch of their surface with our eyes. Riley has even transformed into a small bird and is attempting to survey the ceiling. It isn't long before the sun begins setting, and Piper and Michael are forced to create a set of magical lights from the stone weapons on some of the statues so we can continue working.

"I found something! I think," Tsula calls out excitedly, crouched down behind a pillar.

"What is it? What did you find?" Michael kneels down next to her.

"Right here." The elf girl points at a spot on the column. "If you look closely at this stone, you can see a groove, one that's too straight to be natural."

"She's right. There's something in this column," Michael confirms, his gaze turning to the floor and then Riley. "Riley, can you use the last of your magic to dig into the floor here?"

"Alright, ya sure? Cause I think this might be it for me today." He waits for Michael's nod of confirmation before kneeling down and using his magic on the spot indicated. As he pushes through the stone like it was sand, something black comes into view.

"I knew it!" Michael exclaims excitedly "Lodestone."

"Like we saw in the wall downstairs?" Elisabeth asks.

"Correct. Charged lodestone is used to power long-term enchantments," I tell her. Our coffee pot, for example, has a lodestone base that allows the device to function.

"The enchanted mechanism must be in the column." Piper joins Michael in examining the stone. "It might be possible to activate it ourselves, but with a lodestone that large, it's likely more complicated than a simple unlocking spell."

"What about recharging the stone?" Adam asks next.

"It's possible, but we would need some sort of conductor," Piper tells him. "Enchanters are the only spellcasters capable of charging objects without one."

"Let me guess: some kind of crystal?" David questions flatly.

"How ever did you guess?" The sorceress smiles wearily.

"Would one of the conduit crystals work?" Corrine suggests.

"The name makes it seem like they'd be perfect, but no." Michael enters the conversation, shaking his head. "They've already been fine-tuned for their specific task. They'd just burn out if we tried."

"What about that fancy scale you pulled off that snake's head, Liss?" Nathaniel asks his...girlfriend?

"Left it back at camp." She shakes her head. "Didn't think we'd need it for anything."

"Oh! Would this work?" The group looks over to see David pull the crystalline antler piece from his pocket.

"What's that?" Michael inquires, examining the crystal in David's hand.

"A piece of a crystal hart's antler." He holds it up. "Supposed to be magical as hell."

"Yeah, this should actually work." Michael takes the piece, holding it up in the light. "I'll go first. I'm pretty sure I've got more energy left than you do, Piper."

Michael kneels down next to the hole in the floor, placing the crystal onto the lodestone and then covering it with both hands. His hands begin to glow a dim green as he pushes the energy from his body into the stone. No words are spoken, but I can see the sheen of sweat starting on his forehead before long.

"Almost...got it..." he grunts out almost ten minutes later, still charging.

Suddenly, we hear what sounds like a loud click, and the column in front of us starts to rumble. As Michael and Tsula scramble back from their spot on the floor, the stones making up the column begin to shift, pushing out to form a makeshift spiral staircase. The stones around the column in the ceiling move as well, revealing the opening we have been looking for.

"I think we found it, everyone," Adam announces with a smile.

Even I find myself feeling a little excited, almost enough to look past the *additional set of stairs* I now have to climb. I tell myself it is fine. What is one more flight after however many we've taken to get up here? At least thirty... *Oh spirits, how high up are we?* I close my eyes for a minute and breathe, trying to calm myself. I also jump to verify that the feather-fall spell is still active, which helps.

For hopefully the final time, the group ascends the stairs, leaving me to bring up the rear. David has hung back, I believe with the intent of helping me, though the concern for my acrophobia feels a little late. The room we enter is dark, our lights still in the room below, so the first thing Adam does is light a torch. Looking around in the flickering light, I see the room is filled with different types of strange equipment, like some sort of laboratory. I see beakers and tubes used for potion making, magnifying glasses and even a telescope for stargazing, right below a recess in the slanted ceiling where it looks like the roof may open.

Piper uses a rusted candlestick to make us a more per-manent light, making the room much easier to search through and at least a little less creepy. Once my eyes have adjusted, I notice something odd tucked into one of the empty shelves near our entrance: a leather bag. I would hardly say it is in good shape, but it still seems much more modern than anything else we have found in the ruins.

"I found something," I call out as I carefully open the bag to peer inside, finding not much else but some ash and a book.

"This looks newer than the rest of the room," Tsula comments when she joins me.

"I was thinking the same thing." I pull out the journal, flipping it open and noting what seems to be Elvish written inside.

"It's a journal." Tsula reaches over and runs her finger down a page. "It's written in Elvish, but the way the person is talking makes it seem pretty old. May I?"

"By all means." I hand over the bag.

"I believe I have located the source of the magic I was detecting before." It is Piper's turn to call for attention, standing against the wall opposite the stairs and looking at some sort of metallic symbol embedded within the wall, like a seal or insignia.

"What is it?" Michael asks, examining it for himself.

"I'm not sure. I can't get a clear read." She rubs her hands over it. "I'm not even positive what kind of metal this is. Very reflective."

"Hey, haven't we seen this black powder before?" We turn our heads at Liss's voice, finding her examining the contents of a large table off to one side. As she stated, it appears to be covered in piles of some sort of black powder. No, it is *ash*—the remnants of a large amount of reponiam crystals.

"Oh no. Michael, is that—"

"Reponiam," Michael cuts Piper off, half in shock as they both rush toward the table. "All of it—gone. Burned up.

"Probably has been for years," Riley adds after joining his friends, sounding and looking equally dejected.

"There was never any here for us to find at all." Piper sounds frustrated as she speaks.

"We're... We're stuck here." Michael still seems like he's in shock. "We won't be home for a month."

"...*uuuuuuunnnnnnnhhhhhhh...*" Before anyone can say anything else, a low moan spreads through the room.

"*Would you fucking stop it with the ghost shit already?!*" Michael suddenly turns and yells at David. "This is fucking serious!"

"I... What are you talking about?" David is taken aback, confused by his brother's outburst.

"The moaning, the scream downstairs, that shit in the closet," Michael begins listing things I had not suspected David of doing at all. "I know you got Riley or someone else to blow wind through the barracks!"

"Mike, I swear I haven't done any of that," David defends himself, and I am inclined to believe him. "The only thing I did was scream downstairs, and I apologized for that."

"Cut the shit, David. I know you're——"

"*...uuuuuUUUUNNNNNNNHHHhhhh...*" The moaning grows even louder.

"David..." Michael warns.

"I told you——that's not me!" David defends himself. The others and I are looking around for the source when the magical light is snuffed out.

"Aaaahhh!" Someone——I think Piper——screams.

"Hold on," Adam says in the dark, and then I hear the familiar *flick* of flint being struck as he relights his torch. "There we——"

Adam cuts himself off, frozen like the rest of us as we stare at the ghostly figure now hovering in the center of the room. It is a person——or is at least shaped like one——a woman in a long white dress that seems to billow in the air. Her head is bent down, her long silvery hair flowing over her shoulders, the exposed skin of her arms as pale as the fabric of her dress. Her entire body seems to ripple almost ethereally, and when she finally lifts her head, her eyes are pure white, so bright they might be glowing.

And then she opens her mouth and releases one of the most agonizing screams I have ever heard.

Nearly all of us scream right back.

"GHOST!" Nathaniel shouts, everyone already clambering for the exit.

Ten people trying to squeeze through a small opening and rush down a thin staircase with no railing goes about as well as you think it would. We manage to get out of the room quickly, but none of us actually makes it down the stairs. Instead, everyone almost immediately loses their balance and falls off the side. The featherfall spell prevents any injuries but does not help any of us to land gracefully. Most of us have barely hit the ground when the specter passes down through the ceiling, passing through it like it was air. Several of us scramble backward as she floats to the center of the room, her gaze seemingly flicking from one of us to the next.

"*Salen nha ua shradi?*" Her mouth moves as she speaks, but it is as though her voice echoes from everywhere around us.

"What is she saying?" I ask aloud, though I doubt anyone else can understand her either.

"Why are we bothering to find out?" Liss quickly replies.

The spirit's face contorts into anger when she does not get the response she seeks, unleashing another scream, this one so loud that I am forced to cover my ears.

"*SALEN NHA UA SHRADI?!*" she repeats what I think is a question when she finishes screeching.

"Would you stop that!?" Several meters to my left, David picks up a loose stone and throws it at the wailing woman, which of course passes through her as if nothing were there.

That fact does not seem to matter all that much to her, her already angry face changing into one of pure rage, her ghostly white eyes locked onto David. As she rises into the air, her hands begin to glow, dark energy crackling around her. With another scream, she hurls a bolt of energy at David, forcing him to leap out of the way. Not content to miss, she fires another towards Piper, who is only pulled back in time by a quick-thinking Riley.

This starts a whole fresh wave of panic as everyone runs for cover. Whatever the ghost just attacked with left dark scorch marks in its wake, and none of us are eager to learn how taking a direct hit might feel. None of this matters to the spirit, who floats through a pillar above us to strike once more. Before we can react, she reaches out with one of her hands and swipes it down through my upper shoulder.

I roar in pain as the spectral claw rakes through my skin like a set of ice-cold daggers, but when I look, I can see no damage whatsoever to my skin. We try to defend ourselves as we flee to the stairs, throwing more rocks, and Liss even fires an arrow, but of course all the projectiles pass through her harmlessly. The mages have a bit more luck in attacking her as Piper and Michael fire off energy bolts of their own, though even after they strike her form, she is able to ignore any damage they may be causing.

She continues to chase us down, floating through the floor as she is not subject to the laws of gravity or any sort of normal physics. I watch as pieces of rubble along the path ahead begin to float, just before they come flying in our direction. We are forced to dodge more of her attacks as we run down the stairs, trying to remain conscious of the gigantic hole located perilously at the center of the tower. Below us, it would seem that my wolf companion has also sensed this supernatural disturbance, the distant sounds of her barking filtering upward.

"Okay, at this point we're just running around trying not to get hit by things," David complains as we rush downstairs. "What exactly is the plan here?"

"I don't know. None of us can touch her and she's shrugging off any of the magic being thrown her way," Adam replies, exasperated.

The woman lets out another shriek, forcing us to once again cover our ears as we reach a windowed landing.

"We cannot fight her. We have to get out of here," I state the obvious.

"Yeah, really looking forward to being chased by a ghost all the way back down the tower," Michael states something even more obvious, but I am not sure what other options we have.

"Hey, the featherfall spell works no matter how high up we are, right?" David asks his brother, looking toward a large open window just behind me.

"Yeah, why?" Michael asks, confused, but David is already turning to me.

"I hope you know I am really, *really*, sorry about this," he tells me, sounding sad.

"What are you talk—" And then he tackles me *out of the fucking window.*

"*AAAAAHHHHH!!!*" I scream as we go flying, my body clinging to David's as if that will somehow prevent either of us from falling to our deaths.

"I know. I know. It's okay. You're okay," he tries to reassure me, though I can barely hear him over the sound of my screaming. "I'm sorry. I am so, *so* sorry. I had to get us out of there."

I am in a full-blown panic. My only thoughts are of our impending doom when over David's shoulder I can see the others jumping out after us (some much more hesitant than others). That helps my brain finally catch up with the rest of my body, and I remember that we are not, in fact, falling to our deaths. That gets me to stop screaming, though my limbs still hold onto David tightly as we are *still falling*, just at a much slower rate. I can still see the woman's ghostly form in the open window, watching in silence as we float away.

I land flat on my back with a soft *thud*, unable to release my hold on David until my mind is able to register that I am back on solid ground. After releasing him, he helps me to stand, and as I take his hand, pain shoots through my shoulder where the ghost attacked me. At the same time, the wolf comes rushing out of the tower toward us, barking. She plants herself between me and the tower, turning to growl at it menacingly as the rest of the group lands. Dusting ourselves off, we look back at the tower only once before everyone rushes back to camp.

"Alright, let's start packing so we can get out of here," Michael says in a hurry, rushing toward his tent.

"Whoa, whoa, whoa," Adam tries to slow him down. "Hold on. We're not going anywhere tonight."

"You can't possibly expect us to *stay here*, Adam." Michael cannot seem to believe his friend.

"Not in the ruins, no, but it's not safe to travel through the mountains at night like this," he tries to reason with the frightened wizard. "We'll move outside into the vale for the night."

"So, you want us to camp out just *outside* the haunted city? Great." I am starting to think Michael may be even more dramatic than his twin.

"Haunted city is a bit of a stretch." Adam eyes his friend skeptically. "It doesn't even look like she followed us out of the tower. Maybe she can't."

"You don't know that!" Michael tells him angrily. "You don't know anything about fighting a ghost. None of us—"

"That wasn't a ghost," Corrine states plainly. "At least not a normal one."

"What do you mean?" I ask the cleric. She *would* know more about dealing with the undead than the rest of us.

"It's hard to explain..." She worries her lip as she thinks.

"Not to be a dick or anything," David interjects, "but could we maybe have this discussion after we've moved far away from the haunted tower?"

"Right. Okay, everyone grab your sleeping bags and anything else essential," Adam gives the order. "We'll come back for the rest in the morning."

We work quickly to grab our belongings from our tents, not even bothering to pack things away very carefully. When everyone starts to file up to the city's exit, I make sure to retrieve an item from David's tent before I leave. Moving back through the waterfall cave, we walk a short way into the clearing, finding a decent spot to build a new campfire.

"Now, what was it you were saying, Corrine?" I ask once we have finished setting up our makeshift camp.

"That she wasn't a ghost. Most ghosts aren't really 'ghosts,' not in the way we think of them." She sits on her bedroll as she starts to explain. "When a person dies, sometimes the trauma of what happened can cause the surrounding area to sort of... 'remember' the event as their spirit moves onto the astral plane. It's like a copy of the person at the time of their death. An echo."

"That definitely wasn't an echo," Liss comments, taking her own seat, and I do the same.

"No, it was not." I try to adjust my shoulder, which still feels as though it's been cut by a knife.

"Let me help." Seeing that I am in pain, Corrine stands in front of me and places one of her hands where my neck meets my shoulder. She uses her magic to soothe the pain of the invisible wound. "Sometimes, after an *extremely* traumatic death and when very powerful magic is involved, it's possible for a person's entire spirit to be ripped from their bodies. Those are 'real' ghosts—actual souls of the dead trapped on the material plane, capable of possessing people, or objects, even entire buildings. The more time they spend here without passing on, the more they start to forget who they were. Eventually they stop remembering that they were once a person at all, becoming more aggressive and taking on stronger, more monstrous forms. Wraiths."

"So, is that what she was—a wraith?" David asks, looking at the rest of the group around the fire. "Besides being the Woman in White from Tsula's ghost story. We all got that, right?"

"She was also *very* obviously the last Karthani queen," I tack on.

"I'm not sure," Corrine hesitates, shaking her head before continuing. "It was my first thought, but the way she used magic...the way she *spoke* to us. It doesn't add up to being a wraith, and she was much too powerful and *old* to be a regular ghost."

"I do not suppose anyone was able to catch exactly what she was saying to us?" I look around hopefully, my eyes stopping on Tsula, the only one of us potentially capable.

"I-It was Old Elvish," she answers nervously as all eyes turn to her. "A question, I think. I might have caught the word for 'family,' but I-I'm not sure. I think I know what she is, though."

I notice now that in her lap sits the journal we found at the top of the tower.

"This journal—it belonged an explorer named Galilahi." She tries to stand up a little straighter. "I think he might have been the skeleton we found. H-he was in the tower because of the spirit. I think he was trying to help her."

"What does it say?" I encourage her to continue.

"Well, in some of the early entries he writes about her makes it seem like he's investigated ghosts before. But as the entries go on, he starts to talk about how he 'learned what she truly is,' and was looking for a way to free her. I don't know the word he's using, but it was some sort of object, something that 'holds the splinter of a soul,' whatever that means."

"A soul-trap," Corrine says aloud, turn all eyes back in her direction. "It's called a soul-trap. You use them to bind a piece of a person's soul to this plane."

"Why would someone do that?" Nathaniel asks the next question.

"Because it keeps the rest of their soul from passing on." She looks uncomfortable as she continues. "By tying it to an object on the material plane, when their bodies die, instead of moving to the afterlife, their souls return to the soul-trap. Even if their spirit were somehow destroyed, they would eventually reform from the piece still in the trap."

"People use them to cheat death," Liss summarizes succinctly.

"Essentially." Corrine nods her head. "But you're only living half a life. We're our bodies as much as our souls. A body can't function without a soul, and souls aren't meant to exist on this plane without a body to be anchored to. Without a connection to the physical world, you would go insane. That's what creates wraiths."

"These people just choose to be a ghost forever, knowing that it will eventually make them crazy?" I have to agree with David. That sounds like a terrible bargain.

"Well, from what I've heard, they would usually have another body on hand to inhabit." She grimaces slightly as she says it.

"Where would someone get an extra... Oh *gross*." David makes a sound of disgust when he realizes the implications. "Just stockpiling dead bodies to inhabit later?"

"I don't know. I've never actually known someone to do it." She shakes her head. "But I have to imagine taking possession of a body that isn't yours would have its own issues, not to mention how you complete the ritual. You have to *cut off* a part of your soul."

"That sounds painful," Nathaniel snarks.

"How do you know so much about this stuff, Cor?" Adam is surprised by his teammate's knowledge of something so dark.

"Dealing with the undead must have been part of your training at this church you attended, correct?" I offer as that seems like the most logical answer to me.

"Yep, just a normal part of priest training," Corrine agrees a little too hastily. *Is no one in this group a good liar?*

"I think Galilahi found her soul-trap," Tsula continues to read as she speaks, forgetting enough about the audience as she actively calls for our attention. "He talks about finding a metal object. Some kind of crest?"

"That metal symbol on the wall, the one I was getting the strange magical readings from." Piper thinks aloud. "That must have been the soul-trap."

"Is that possible?" Adam questions Corrine.

"Soul-traps can look like anything," she all but confirms. "It would be something well-hidden and strong. The last thing you would want would be for someone else to find and destroy it."

"He thought that destroying it would free her spirit, but he wasn't able to even damage it because it was made out of... Dammit, he's using another word I'm not familiar with," Tsula begins to play with her braid while she concentrates. "It's some kind of special metal. Lightweight and extremely durable, unable to be damaged by most weaponry."

"Mithril," I reply without thinking. "It goes by many names, but from the description, it could be mithril."

"That sounds right and would definitely cause some problems," Adam agrees.

"It looks like after he failed to destroy it, he came up with a backup plan to…hold her somehow until he was able to come back and try again." She flips to what appears to be the last entry, the paper on the following page blank.

"He was going to trap her spirit in some kind of 'memory crystal,' and then make that crystal the focus of an anti-magic field."

"Memory crystal? Anti-magic field?" Michael asks for confirmation as a sense of dread settles over us all.

"Th-the crystal we broke. The large piece of reponiam." Tsula looks up, her eyes wide in surprise. "She was inside of it. We did this. We let her out."

"We don't know that." Michael shakes his head in denial.

"Would that even work? Trapping her like that?" David questions his twin.

"Yes," Piper answers when Michael does not. "At least I think so. Normally, if you tried to trap a ghost or any incorporeal magical creature in reponiam, they would just escape. They're already made of energy so it would be nothing to them. But if they were in an anti-magic field, they wouldn't have access to any of their abilities, wouldn't even be able to move on the astral plane—effectively trapping them. I can't believe I've never thought of it."

"Maybe because of the soul-trap, whatever caused all of the other elves to vanish didn't work the same on her," Riley joins in speculating. "Or maybe it changed somethin' about the magic that tied her soul to the object."

"Great, so we know where the ghost came from." Michael gets up and throws his hands to the night sky, sounding annoyed by the entire conversation. "Does it really matter? We're leaving first thing in the morning."

"We can't just leave her like this." Corrine stands.

"I mean, we can if she did this to herself," Liss reasons, agreeing at least partially with Michael.

"Even if she did, she clearly has no idea what's going on now. She deserves to be able to rest the same anyone else, even if we weren't the ones to release her," Corrine insists.

"What the hell are we supposed to do?" Michael shoots back. "We can't fight her."

"W-we finish what Galilahi started," Tsula states as she stands next to Corrine. "We just need to destroy the soul-trap, right?"

"That's half of it," Corrine responds. "After that, we would still need to send her soul to the afterlife."

"And how would we destroy the soul-trap?" Michael stares at both women incredulously, especially Tsula. "None of us are strong enough to damage a piece of mithril, not even with magic."

"That is not entirely true." Ignoring Michael's glare, I make eye contact with David who watches me reach into my satchel and pull out a worn-leather scabbard, the one containing the sword he has been too afraid to handle since his death, the one I made sure to take from his tent before we fled the ruins. He eyes it nervously as I walk toward him, holding out a hand to help him stand and nodding at the forest. "I think it is time we had that talk."

Chapter 16

"**Why did you bring that thing?**" David glares at the sword at my side before locking eyes with me.

"Really?" I ask flatly. "After discussing our need to destroy something near-indestructible, you want to know why I brought the magic sword that can cut through anything?"

David says nothing, narrowing his eyes and crossing his arms where he stands across from me in the dark forest, far enough away from the group to give us privacy. Moonlight streams in through the trees, the sound of crickets filling the night air. His eyes move to the worn leather scabbard I am holding, continuing to glare daggers at the weapon held within. It is that animosity that I intend to get to the bottom of.

"Why are you so afraid of the sword, David?" I ask directly.

"What?" His gaze whips back up to mine. "I'm not afraid of it."

"Then why haven't you touched it since the night in the temple ruins?" I continue my questioning.

"What are you talking about?" He looks at me like I am speaking nonsense. "I've touched it plenty of times."

"No, you have held it by the scabbard and strapped it to your back, but not once have you actually attempted to wield it," I point out.

"If you want to use it so bad, go ahead!" He throws his arms up in frustration.

"That is exactly what I was planning on doing," I tell him plainly, rolling my eyes and reaching for the blade's handle.

"No, wait—!" David's eyes grow in panic.

I cock an eyebrow at the display as I pull the sword from its sheath. David's panic recedes as fast as it appeared, but I am unsure as to where it came from. "The sword is powerful whether you wield it or not. What I want to know is why you are afraid of even holding it."

"Has it occurred to you that maybe I just don't want to use the same fucking sword that killed me?!" he snaps, frustrated.

"Of course it has, but I wouldn't actually know how you are feeling because you *won't talk to me about it!*" I snap back, angrier than I mean to sound.

"Maybe because I don't want to relive any of it! Maybe I just want to move on! Why do you even care so fucking much?!" He's practically yelling now. "Problem solved: you use the damn sword." All hopes of further discussion start to evaporate as he stomps away from me, and remembering Adam's advice, I try one last thing.

"I'm having them, too." Hearing my words, David stops in his tracks and turns around, confused. "Nightmares. I have been having them as well."

"What do you mean?" He steps closer, and I can see him fighting against the concern growing on his face.

"It doesn't happen every night, but multiple times now, I have dreamt about your death." All the heat from our conversation has evaporated. "I wake up in a panic each time.

My first instinct is always to look over and check that you are alright. That you are not…"

"Why didn't I ever notice?" He is starting to sound guilty.

"I always woke up before you did." I shrug, leaning back against a tree.

"How come you never said anything?" David leans against the same tree next to me.

"We were already dealing with a lot, and as your nightmares were more frequent and arguably worse, I did not want to bother you with mine," I state simply as I resheathe the sword.

"That's stupid." David shakes his head. "You wouldn't be bothering me. If something is keeping you up at night, you can always talk to me about it. I'd want to help you in any way I can."

"So, you agree that if someone were having terrible nightmares, talking about them might help them to feel better?" I allow some teasing to enter my tone as I wait for David's answer.

"That's not… I wasn't—" David cuts himself off with a frustrated growl, crossing his arms and pouting while I silently wait for him to continue. "It's always the same thing. The nightmares. Me, sword in hand, tearing through the cult members. I can still smell the blood, hear their screams echoing off the—" He cuts himself off again, waiting for a beat of silence before continuing. "I just want to forget everything that happened that night. Talking about it means reliving it and makes it that much harder for the memory to fade away."

"David, I do not think this is something you are going to be able to forget about, probably ever." I hold his right hand with my left and squeeze. "It is something we will likely both carry for the rest of our lives."

"When I was still training to be a knight, I knew that one day, I'd have to kill someone. It's just part of the job. But this..." He looks down at his hands, sounding lost. "I killed so many people, Khaz, all at once. People we knew, people that we worked with."

"Taking a life is never easy." I step into his space, putting a hand on shoulder. "But I am not sure I would want it to be."

"How many... How many people have *you* killed?" He hesitates to ask, perhaps only realizing that I might have experience in this area.

"Four," I answer honestly, hoping that my lower count does not detract from my point. "All while on duty, in defense of myself or someone else."

"What was it like? After the first time." He looks up at me for an answer.

"I remember the day vividly. I was only twenty, had barely been an officer for a year, not even assigned my own cases yet," I start to recount. "One morning, we received reports of a man in the marketplace acting erratically. By the time me and the other officers arrived, things had progressed into violence. We soon realized he was under the influence of graxim—you might know it as ragewort. When ingested, it dulls the body's pain receptors and increases aggression. Warriors often take it before large battles, but ingesting too much can send you into a berserker's rage. We found out later that, after having discovered his lover had been unfaithful, the man had downed nearly an entire bottle, intent on confronting the other man. Only he never made it that far."

"He was armed with an axe and had already taken down two other officers before charging toward me next," I continue with a sigh. "I can still remember shakily pulling out my sword as he came at me. We tried to get him to a healer in time, but his wounds were too severe... He bled out. Of course, no one blamed me; doing what I did I saved lives, but all I could think about was the look on the man's face after running him through with my sword."

"That sounds...awful." He moves closer, taking one of my hands. "How did you deal with it?"

"By talking about it with my friends, with my father, with coworkers. It helped me process my guilt and see that a lot of it was misplaced," I pull him in closer, wrapping my arms around his shoulder. "Taking a life is serious, and present company excluded, is not something that can generally be undone. But your situation David..." I pause, wanting to choose my words carefully. "This is not meant in any way to diminish what happened to you, or your feelings about it, but if you did not 'lose control' in the way you did, we would not be here right now. Not just us, but Nylan, Ragnar, Glasha, and countless others. Murbank and Redwish would not have ended their plans with us; who knows how many other people would have been killed in their quest for power? You saved many, many lives that night, David."

He seems to take my words into consideration as I hold him. "It doesn't feel that way. It feels like I'm being punished for something. Do you... Do you think they're connected?" He sounds entirely unsure of himself. "The nightmares. Are we both having them because of what happened? Are we... cursed or something?"

"No, David, I think we both just went through something extremely traumatic." This line of questioning is so bizarre it has me pulling back to look at him just to make sure I heard him correctly. David never struck me as superstitious, though I suppose we did meet a ghost today. "The nightmares are our mind's way of trying to process it. Honestly, we both should probably be speaking to a counselor of some sort, but seeing as that is not really an option at the moment, we will need to rely on each other and our friends."

The moment is broken when a twig snaps, both of us separating and wheeling around to find the source. A familiar coat of shaggy black fur slinks out from the foliage, the wolf coming to a stop at my feet and sitting up with a whine, concern evident in her bright yellow eyes as she looks between the two of us. With a chuckle, I kneel down and stroke my hand over her head, letting her know I am alright.

"What are *you* doing here, fuzzface?" David asks the canine.

"She was worried," I tell him as I continue to pet her fur. "She either overheard our conversation or felt my emotions through the bond. I think sneaking around is just what comes naturally to her. I am thinking of naming her Sona. Do you like that name?"

She tilts her head to the side, before barking in acceptance and wagging her tail.

"That means 'shadow' in Atasi, right?" I look at David with a surprised smile at the correct translation. "What? I can remember things." David crouches down to our level. "So, you guys really just had an instant connection? Is that what the magic does?"

"I am not sure if the magic creates the bond, so much as it becomes active once two compatible beings cross paths under the right circumstances." I give Sona one last scratch behind the ears before standing. "We can understand one another, even sense the way the other is feeling. Wolves are creatures known for their loyalty, but the trust between us will still have to be built up like any other relationship."

"...I'm sorry for not talking to you about my nightmares," he apologizes, standing up straight.

"Thank you." I reach for and squeeze his hand again. "Now, will you tell me why you are afraid of the sword?"

"I'm not—"

"David," I sigh.

"...What if I lose control again?" he asks me quietly.

"What do you mean?" I assume he is talking about the immediate aftermath of his resurrection.

"The last time I picked up that sword, I went on a rampage that killed almost a dozen people." He looks down as he says it. "What if it happens again? What if no one can stop me this time?"

"That is what you are worried about? You think touching the sword will...trigger something?" I realize too late that my tone sounds more condescending than I meant to.

"Okay, don't act like I'm being crazy." He is immediately defensive. "You were there; you saw how bad it was. Not one person stood a chance. What if I hurt someone?"

"I am sorry. That is not what I meant," I try to backtrack. "I am just not sure that is even what happened the first time. To me, you appeared to be in your...*enraged* state as soon as you woke up before you touched the sword."

"Right after that same sword stabbed me to death," he fires back. "We don't know how it works, but we do know that the sword is connected. So why risk it?"

"Your plan is to never touch the sword again?" I could not help my tone this time. "I do not think that is an acceptable solution."

"Too bad because it's the solution we're going with." *Oh, he is just begging for a spanking.*

"You might want to remember who you are speaking to, *pup*," I warn with a growl. "I think if I can survive being *tackled out of a godsdamned window*, you can risk touching the sword."

"It's not the same thing! You don't know what it was like!" he snaps. "To be inside your body but feel this force pushing you, filling you with so much anger that you want to tear through everyone and everything around you!"

"You are right, I do not know what that is like," I try to empathize, softening my voice. "But you cannot let this *object* control you like that. You are stronger than that. Stronger than *it*."

"You don't know that!" he counters, throwing his arms up.

"I know you would not hurt me." I step into his space, taking his hand again. "It is not true that no one could stop you last time. I stopped you. And, on the off chance that this 'transformation' does happen again, I will be right here to stop you once more."

I pull the Harpe from its scabbard with my free hand, holding it pommel-up in front of David. His right hand reaches for it tentatively, shaking when he stutters in hesitation. Below us, Sona makes a noise of confusion as she watches the display, and I give David's other hand another squeeze of encouragement. Taking a breath, he shakes his head, flexes his fingers, and then finally wraps them around the handle.

And nothing happens.

We both exhale, feeling more anxious than I anticipated. David releases my hand, holding the sword more confidently as he steps away. I watch him for a few moments as he goes through the motions of testing its weight, swinging it tentatively through the air.

"Do you feel any different?" I ask, wanting confirmation.

"No, I don't think so." He shakes his head.

"Good." I hold out the scabbard for him to take—the weapon is his after all.

"Thank you." He resheathes the sword in the worn leather before strapping it to his back, then turns to me with regret on his face. "I've been a complete ass the last few days. I'm sorry for yelling at you, and for being such a coward, and I'm especially sorry for how much of a *dick* my brother has been."

"That is a good start." I resume leaning against the tree. "For the record, you are not responsible for your brother's behavior—though I maintain that telling him about us would have saved us some trouble. We still have a lot we need to discuss, but I am afraid that we will need to wait until we have solved our ghost problem."

"Are... Are you mad about being tackled out the window?" He looks down at his feet.

"Believe it or not, I had actually managed to block it from my memory until a moment ago." I laugh, thinking back to the terrifying moment of falling out of the tower. "I will not say I *like* what you did, but I understand why you did it. It may have even helped some with my fears."

"So... Are we okay?" he asks very hesitantly.

"We are okay," I tell him with a smile, holding out my arms for him to step into. Sensing the emotions of the moment, Sona presses herself against our legs, her presence making me giggle as I come to a realization.

"What?" David asks, confused.

"I have two puppies now," I tell him with a childish grin.

David groans in mock disgust, pressing his forehead to my chest and laughing. "So bad."

"You love it." I kiss the top of his head.

"So, Sir," David starts after a moment of being held. "Are you sure there isn't anything I can do to start making things up to you?"

I pull back enough to look at his face because is he seriously propositioning me right now? He bites his lip, his hands coming to rest on the waist of my pants—but not seeking entry, yet. My first instinct is to say no and point out how any of our group, including his brother, could come upon us at any moment, just as Sona did. But it would be a shame to dissuade him from taking the initiative like this... Right?

"Sona, back to camp," I tell the wolf, feeling David's hands tighten in response. The wolf leaves with a gentle huff, and once she is far enough away, it is time for my pup to make good on his request. "On your knees."

Biting his lip, David silently sinks to the forest floor, finding a comfortable spot on the grass for his knees. His hands start to slowly work each of the buttons of my pants loose, spreading my fly. Reaching into my subligar, he wraps his fingers around the soft flesh of my cock, pulling it out above the fabric.

Leaning forward, he lowers his head so that he can wrap his lips around my (cock)head. Then, with a playful glint in his eye, he slowly takes the rest into the warm heat of his mouth until he's swallowed me all the way down to the base. He sucks me gently, my cock quickly expanding within the wet confines of his mouth until it has grown enough that he is forced to pull back in order to avoid gagging.

As tempting as it is to grab the back of his head and take out some of the frustrations of the past few days, now is not the best time. Even if he were not trying to hide things from his brother (and I am not still clear on where we stand with that), we have nothing to clean up with, and returning to camp with red eyes, swollen lips, and a drool covered face is not an option. So, David will just have to do most of the work himself.

Once I have grown to my full size, he slowly bobs up and down along the length a few times before pulling off completely. He leans forward, nosing and then lapping at my sack, making me shudder. He nuzzles into my crotch, inhaling my scent before sucking one of my balls into his mouth, rolling it around with his tongue. After repeating this on my other testicle, he pulls back, ready for my cock once more.

"I know this won't take long since it's been three days for us both," he tells me with a grin.

"Well, three days for you." He gives me a look of confusion as I pull him toward my waiting erection, halting any potential response. "But that is a story that will have to wait until later."

David half-heartedly glares as his gullet is once again gorged but is easily soothed by the gentle forward rocking of my hips, slowly feeding him more of my length. He quickly takes over for me and is soon happily servicing my prick like it is his favorite pastime. He is able to take me more than two-thirds of the way down without gagging, pulling back until his lips are just behind my head before swallowing me back down and repeating himself.

He works his mouth on my cock, engulfing more and more of me on each pass, slowly sinking farther down, centimeter by centimeter. On his next attempt, his nose presses against the dark wiry hair that calls my crotch home, and he holds himself there for a few seconds before finally pulling back and taking a deep breath. He returns to bobbing up and down on what he can easily manage before once again pushing all the way down again without gagging.

By the third time this happens, I find my hips humping forward against his face automatically, forcing myself even farther into his throat. This seems to be the reaction he was hoping for, as he hums (or gurgles) happily, his arms coming up to wrap around my thighs. The only sign he is in any distress at all are his watery eyes, which the darkness should hopefully conceal for anyone who looks too closely.

The heat of his mouth, the tightness of his throat, and the eagerness on display all work in concert to push me toward an orgasm. When my hips start to stutter from the rhythm the two of us have set, I know I am getting close, and once I can see the end on the horizon, all bets are off. Grabbing his head with both of my hands, I pump into it roughly not even a dozen times before I cum with a muffled shout, forcing him all the way down and exploding straight into his throat.

I release David's head, allowing him to pull back, finish swallowing, and take an actual breath. Still panting, he leans against my legs as he angles his head up, lapping my softening cock clean. After tucking myself away, I help him to his feet, pulling him to my chest as I lean back against the tree.

His arms come up to wrap around me as his head comes to rest in the crook of my neck. Once both our heart rates have calmed, he pushes back and tilts his face upward, meeting me halfway for a kiss. I can still feel some residual heat on his lips, and the taste of my spend lingers on his tongue. Deepening our kiss further, David starts rutting his own erection against my inner thigh, and I finally have the sense to pull us apart.

"Oh, does my puppy want some relief as well?" I ask, sliding a hand down his stomach toward his crotch.

"Yes, he would, Sir," he answers, looking up at me shyly and biting his still-swollen lip.

"Then you should have thought about that before you *yelled and cursed at me yesterday*." I grin evil as I squeeze his erection roughly—though not enough to actually hurt—through his pants, making him squirm and whimper in my hold. "In fact, you are not even allowed to *masturbate* until I allow it."

"What?! But, but—" I pull back, daring him to challenge me with a raised eyebrow. "...Fine. Yes, Sir. Can't blame me for trying."

"It was less the boldness and more the fact that you are not anticipating a nice long appointment with a certain cage in the near future." I push off the tree, looking for the direction of our makeshift camp.

"You brought that thing with you!?" He sounds shocked.

"Of course I did." I look at him like he has lost his mind. "Why would I not?"

"Because it's barbaric?" I am not sure if he even believes that.

"Well then, I suppose some of the stories your people tell about mine are true," I respond cheekily. "We should get back to camp before they start to worry or wonder."

"Yes, Sir." David steps up to my side, threading the fingers of our hand together briefly.

We walk through the dark forest, myself in the lead, until we can see the faint light of our makeshift campfire in the distance. We do not try to mask our steps, and when they hear us approach, all faces turn to us. They are gathered closely together, obviously discussing something.

"Everything okay?" Adam sits up as we rejoin them.

"Yeah, we're cool," David answers for us, taking a seat on the grass.

"Is everything alright here?" I ask as I join him.

"Yep, just coming up with a plan." Adam nods his head confidently. "Corrine was just explaining some basic info about ghosts to the rest of us."

"Like I was saying, she should be weaker during the daytime," our cleric explains. "Ghosts can't move in direct sunlight; it disrupts their metaphysical form. She won't have any problem moving around in the shadows, though."

Talking about light gives me an idea. "If light is one of their weaknesses, could we somehow weaponize the light spells the arcane spellcasters have been using?" I suggest.

"Afraid not," Piper responds reluctantly. "The light created by that spell isn't comparable to sunlight; it's more artificial."

"I might have a solution to that," Riley speaks up, holding up a finger. "Have a light spell of my own. It won't last as long, but it mimics the actual sun. Might do the trick."

"As long as it is the same as real sunlight, it should work." Corrine nods.

"Why can't she leave the tower?" David asks with his hands raised. "In Tsula's story, she was wandering all over the city, but she didn't chase us when we left."

"Spirits are normally bound to a specific location, but they can usually wander a decent distance from it." Corrine tries to think of an answer. "She might not be at her full strength yet."

"We still don't have a way of actually attacking her," Elisabeth points out next.

"Or destroying the thing she bound her soul to," Nathaniel adds.

"Yeah, I kept saying that all of this is pointless without a way to destroy the mithril soul-trap," Michael corrects him. "We *might* be able to do it with magic, but a spell that powerful would blow the roof off of the tower, probably before bringing the whole thing down."

"Don't worry about destroying that mithril thing." David pulls the Harpe's scabbard from his back and sets it across his lap. "I've got that covered."

"You're gonna do it with that?" Michael looks at the weapon skeptically.

"It's a lot more powerful than it looks." David pats the weapon's handle. "Trust me."

"Yeah, really full of trust for you right now," Michael mutters as he turns away.

"You sure it'll get the job done?" Adam questions, looking at the sword.

"Positive." David nods. "So, after I destroy that thing, what happens next? Her soul will be free, and she'll go up to elf heaven or something?"

"I wish it were that easy," Corrine tells him with a sad smile. "No, that will free the part of her soul that is bound to this plane, but she'll still have to leave it of her own accord, or more likely, we'll have to force her to. It's that or try to destroy her, which I'm not sure would be any easier."

"Is that possible? Destroying her?" I ask. I am afraid I only have rudimentary knowledge on matters pertaining to spirits.

"Yes, with enough magical firepower." She nods her head slowly. "It is a very violent way to end things though, one I'd prefer not to do. Her spirit wouldn't rest. She would just...cease to exist."

"But banishing her spirit, sending her to the afterlife, that is something you can do?" I ask her next. I know most divine casters possess some manner of skill related to dealing with the undead, but I yet to see anything of the sort from Corrine.

"Yes, I think so." She nods, hesitantly. "Banishing spirits to the afterlife is tricky, and I could *feel* her presence, feel how powerful she was. I don't think she will go easily."

"Just tell us what you need, and we'll be there to back you up," Adam tells her with a thumbs up.

"I should have everything. Let me check my bag to be sure." She takes a moment to rummage through her pack, looking for spell components.

"I'm glad everyone's feeling confident about all this, but I again feel the need to ask why we are doing this in the first place." Michael takes the temporary silence as an opportunity to argue his point again. "It's not our fault she's a ghost."

"No, but it is our fault that she's loose now," David counters his brother. "What if someone else tried to come up here? She'd be just as much a danger to them."

"Then let someone else deal with it." Michael rolls his eyes. "Someone a lot stronger who knows what they're doing."

"What if there isn't anyone else? Or what if *they* screw up and end up getting hurt?" David attempts to poke holes in his brother's argument. "Even if we *weren't* the ones to release her—which we definitely were—this woman's been trapped for thousands of years. What if she's in pain or something? Helping her is the right thing to do."

"We were literally just talking about the ways we'll be able to attack her," Michael points out, stubbornly. "How exactly is that helping?"

"Oh, come *on*. You know being able to defend ourselves is not the same as attacking her." Now David rolls his eyes.

"Look Mike, no one's going to force you to come with us, but I think you're the only one not on board with this," Adam tells him with a slight grimace. "If you want, you can wait here in the morning while the rest of us head back inside to take care of things."

"No, it's not that I don't want to help her. It's just..." He grumbles something to himself I do not quite catch, then huffs and looks away. "I'm just being cautious. It doesn't exactly seem like something very high on the list of priorities in this group."

"You can't spend your entire life worrying about being careful; you gotta take a risk now and again." David looks over at me, smiling as he speaks. "The rewards can be pretty great."

Chapter 17

"**<You seem quite taken with that boy, considering he is** *a criminal,>*" *Orlun, my father, comments as he cleans the grill.*

"*<He is not all that bad and has been a wonderful houseguest.>*" *I lie, not quite wanting to explain everything that has happened since David entered my home for the first time.*

"*<He seems to be pretty fond of you as well,>*" *Rurig, my other father says from my left, rinsing and drying the dishes when I finish washing them. We just finished having dinner, one that was in honor of my sister's return home for the first time in over a year. It was also David's first time meeting my family, and after the events of the past few days, I was understandably nervous at how it would go. Thankfully, other than some brief awkwardness at the start of the night and my sister's usual frustrating antics, I think it went well.*

"*<I am not so sure about that, Ruda,>*" *I try to downplay, not wanting to focus on the topic of my love life—one of the reasons I was hoping David would skip.* "*<Besides, he is only with me temporarily. I am sure he cannot wait until his friends are released so he can leave.>*"

"*<You know, I told myself that your father was only tempo-rary,>*" *he tells me slyly.* "*<And then we both said the same thing about Jarek.>*"

"*<Funny enough, I was thinking the same about the two of you,>*" *Jarek adds from behind us as he packs away the leftover food. He is the third of my "three fucking dads" as David put it before dinner.*

I smile at the conversation but keep my thoughts to myself. It is not that I doubt what they are saying—I am very attracted to David, and I know he is attracted to me or else he would not have been the one to propose our new "arrangement." But after everything we have gone through in the past week, the way we have treated each other, I cannot fathom that he would actually want to stay here any longer than he has to.

I was not entirely wrong after that first family dinner: David did not stay in V'rok'sh Tah'lj any longer than he had to. Neither did I. And I am happy to be wrong about the rest of my thoughts that evening. The man can be unbelievably frustrating at times, but the fact that we have been able to overcome so much turmoil in such a short time (and a lot of it from external sources) only reinforces that I made the right choice in following him. Even if I want to spend the next three days spanking his ass red.

It is early the next morning, the rest of the group just waking up after a night of fitful sleep. Our sleeping bags are arranged in a circle around the campfire, having abandoned our tents in the city. We worked in pairs during our watch shifts, not wanting to risk anything while out in the open. Trying to sleep while completely exposed to the elements can be difficult, and that was before the moaning started.

Things were fine until around four or five in the morning while Corrine and I were on duty. At first, I thought it was the wind, but as the howling sounds grew louder, it became apparent they were the doing of our ghostly friend in the tower. They continued until the sun finally began to rise, by which time neither myself nor Corrine were interested in trying for more sleep.

Once everyone is up, we pack up our temporary camp. We went over the plan for several times before sleeping last night, and though it is nothing overly complicated, I am sure everyone is focusing on their parts. The ruins are silent as we pass back through the waterfall cave, and we approach the tower with grim determination.

The first part of the plan is simply to get to the top unharmed, which may prove difficult depending on how active the tower's ghostly guest is at this hour. Corrine said that ghosts are less active during the daytime hours and are weak to direct sunlight. Our options are limited, but Riley has a spell that, while short lasting, is an effective facsimile of actual sunlight and should work as a good defense.

"Alright, let's buff up," Adam gives the order as we stand outside the tower's front entrance.

The mages of the group proceed to divvy up responsibilities, casting spells on themselves and then the rest of us. Everyone receives the featherfall spell as they did yesterday, and those of us who are physical fighters also have our strength and agility increased. With our equipment on and preparations out of the way, we enter the tower, where everything is as it was yesterday, dark and crumbling to pieces.

"Stay here. Guard the entrance." As much as I would like to bring Sona with me, she will be unable to navigate some of the tower's more perilous walkways.

<*Khazak friend stay safe.*> She presses into my hand when I stroke over her head.

There is nothing but silence above us, which is hopefully a good sign that our friend is doing...whatever it is ghosts do during the day. *Do spirits need to sleep?* We begin our ascent, moving as fast as we can without making noise or drawing attention. We make it past the lower throne room when Sona lets out a bark from down below, right before the doors slam shut. *She knows we are here.*

We make it up three floors before something else happens: a stray pebble hits my upper arm. *Where did that come from?* It happens again a second later to Piper, then

Elisabeth. Their trajectory is coming from the walkways on the opposite side of the tower, and when I look across, I see several stones levitating into the air. Including one the size of my fist.

"Run!" I shout, pulling my sword out just in time to use it to deflect the rock.

With our cover officially blown, we rush our way up the stairs. Now that her targets are no longer lined up, our invisible attacker decides to up the ante, and soon all manner of debris is being hurled our way. It becomes a mad dash to the top of the tower as we are forced to dodge and deflect everything she throws at us.

"Look out!" Adam uses his shield to block a stone flying toward Corrine.

"Fuck lady, would you cut it out already?!" David angrily requests after jumping out of the way of a chunk of the wall that was thrown his way. "We're trying to help you!"

"I don't think she knows or cares," Liss responds dryly, dodging her own projectile.

"Look, we're almost at the first hallway!" Michael exclaims happily. "We can hide in there."

"I don't think you can really hide from a ghost," Nate points out snidely.

"No, but there are probably fewer things inside for her to throw at us," I reason. *At least I hope.*

We make it through the hallway's doors and slam them behind us, which has the added effect of plunging the room into complete darkness. Before the ghost has the chance to make any appearances, Riley quickly casts his daylight spell with a shouted "*solas!*" A small yellow orb appears near the room's ceiling as the sound of things pelting the walls outside slowly dies down.

"Alright, we can break for a second, but we need to keep moving," Adam tells us as he examines the room.

I was correct. There is much less rubble in this room to be thrown at us. Not much in here at all except for four statues, all in relatively good condition. I lean back against the wall, closing my eyes for a moment to catch my breath. I hear what sounds like stone scraping over stone and open my eyes to see the statues moving of their own accord.

"Haunted statutes!" Michael cries as one of them, a sword-wielding elven warrior, approaches him.

Another of the statues dives toward Piper, who jumps back with a shriek, causing the stone figure to almost lose its balance when it misses. Seeing an opportunity, Adam barrels into it with his shield, sending it toppling to the ground and breaking its arms and torso into pieces. My first instinct is to reach for my sword, but steel is not going to do much against solid rock, so I take Adam's lead and attempt to grapple with one instead—and dammit, they are *strong*.

"How the hell are we supposed to fight these things?" Liss growls in frustration, likely for the same reasons.

"I got it!" David replies, and a second later the statue I am locking arms with is missing its lower half after he cleaves through it with the Harpe.

I toss the statue's upper body to the ground as David makes quick work of the two that are still ambulatory. His weapon slices through them like a hot knife through butter, their severed pieces falling harmlessly to the ground. Rescue complete, he sheaths the sword, grinning cockily as he stands over the statues' remains.

"What exactly is that thing made out of?" Nathaniel asks what most of the others are likely thinking.

"It—" David cuts himself off to look down at his leg, where one of the statues' arms is attempting to grab his ankle. "Aaahh! What the hell?!"

David quickly kicks the wriggling limb away. I can see now that several of the statue pieces are still moving, crawling toward us. *Spirits, that is disturbing.*

"Alright, break's over," Adam announces, deciding that our attempt at rest was futile.

Exiting the room on the other side, we continue the treacherous climb, once again dodging rocks and other objects that are flung in our direction. We sprint as fast we can toward the next hallway, not bothering to close the door as we will not be stopping. David takes point, rushing forward to cut through anymore stony soldiers that might be waiting for us.

This becomes our pattern as we move through the tower, one that we are able to keep up with, despite it getting more and more exhausting. The higher we go, the fewer open windows there are, which means less sunlight is able to enter. And the more shadows there are, the more frequent the attacks become.

Things come to a head when we're nearly at the top, the main throne room's double doors visible two floors above us. Up here, things are dark enough for the queen to finally make a personal appearance, flying out of the wall with an ear-piercing shriek. Riley barely reacts in time with another sunlight spell, banishing her form as she speeds toward us. That seems to buy us a moment of reprieve.

"I don't get it. Is she trying to keep us out because she knows what we're trying to do?" Adam asks from the front of the group as we rush up the stairs.

"Maybe. She might not want anyone here at all," Corrine speculates. "It's been so long that she's probably very confused. She might even think we're the ones responsible for all the destruction."

"What? Why?" David questions next.

"Memory is a tricky thing, especially when you don't have a body," Corrine answers. "Memories are stored in the brain, which is made of all these complex nerves and synapses... I don't think anyone fully understands how they work. Souls can retain memories, and spiritual beings like ghosts can obviously create forms that *look* like a body, but without the mental wiring of a real brain, memories are difficult to process. Old events can get mixed together, or parts of them forgotten, and new things are hard to retain. It's a very sad existence."

"You *really* know a lot about ghosts, Cor," Liss points out as we approach the doors.

"I...had a lot of time to read back at the church," Corrine replies somewhat hesitantly. "There wasn't much to do when I wasn't taking lessons or studying scripture."

"Well, it's kinda cool and also very useful," David tells her.

The stone doors slam shut as we approach. Undeterred, Riley steps forward and uses his magic to melt a hole right in their center, allowing us to walk right into the large, empty room. Wasting no more time, we put the rest of our plan in motion.

"David, Khazak, Riley, you're up." Adam points up, toward the lab and storeroom above us.

The second and third parts of our plan are to happen at the same time. While the three of us venture upstairs to retrieve the soul-trap, the others will be assisting Corrine in consecrating an area in the center of the room: a place where the undead will be unable to enter and one that should help Corrine connect better with her god and the afterlife. I can see them using what appears to be salt to draw a circle on the ground as we reach the top of the stairs.

"*Solas!*" Before we even enter, Riley throws up another daylight spell.

"Work quickly," I tell him while taking stock of the room.

"On it." David heads straight for the mithril crest on the wall, sword already in hand.

I hear the repeated *chink* of David's sword cutting into the stone as he attempts to hack it from the wall, stabbing with the point of his sword like it was a very strange pickaxe. Destroying it will release the fragment of the wailing woman's soul, but Corrine still needs the item to help with the rest of her ritual. Things in the room are quiet for now, but I have a feeling she is not going to like what we are doing.

On my left I hear the sounds of something clanging together, and I turn just in time to see the doors on an old cupboard fly open. The three of us are barely able to move out of the way as the objects inside—empty vials and random chunks of wood and rock—come flying at us. The glass shatters as it hits the opposite wall, scattering the shards in random directions.

"David..." I warn as I see more objects on the shelves vibrate.

"Got it!" David cheers as the mithril hits the floor with a *clang*.

"Down!" Riley shouts, all of us ducking under the second volley.

Before the spirit has a chance to launch a third attack, David quickly kneels up over the seal, sword in hand. He drives it down into the object, splitting it in two. There is a bright flash of light accompanied by a loud *pop*, and a second later, an otherworldly scream echoes through the formerly-dark and windowless room.

"She does not sound very happy," Riley understates.

"Downstairs, now," I order, looking to the exit.

All three of us run for the stairs, David taking care to grab the two pieces of mithril as we flee. I feel an object fly right over my head just as my feet hit the stairs. We do not even attempt to climb down, leaping from the top of the staircase and using the featherfall spell to land on the throne room's floor.

"Here you go." David quickly hands off the broken pieces to Corrine.

"Perfect. Thank you." Corrine takes them and moves to kneel at the center of the consecrated area. "Okay, I'm going to get started. Be careful not to break the circle."

The circle she speaks of is less than two meters in diameter and is formed entirely out of salt. The lines forming them are thin, and at various points around the inside edge of the circle are small symbols or runes. Though I understand the circle will offer up some protection, there is not much room inside. *Perhaps I should stock up on salt in town in the event we run into any more supernatural obstacles.*

"The ghost won't be able to pass through the barrier, but other things can, so protecting Cory is priority one," Adam tells us as we draw into a circle around the praying priestess, enacting the fourth part of our plan while she does the fifth—sending the ghost to the afterlife.

The statues around us come to life almost immediately as Corrine begins her spell, walking toward us in a slow gait. Despite their lack of speed, they are no less intimidating, outnumbering us almost three-to-one. Given their size and the materials they are made from, they are most likely stronger and undoubtedly more durable than we are. David is still the only one of us with a weapon even capable of damaging them.

He is the first to rush forward, trying to cut one of them off at the knees, literally. His size and quick movements work in his favor, enabling him to easily dodge the statue's slow attacks. On my left, Adam charges at another, holding his shield in front of him like a battering ram and throwing his full weight against it and toppling over. That may be my best bet for fighting as well, and though I cannot see her, the same likely holds true for Liss. I wish either of us carried a shield.

The mages have their own issues to deal with, some having more luck with their spells than others. Magic may be powerful, but stone is stone, and any spells strong enough to destroy solid rock also risks damaging the tower, which is already falling apart. I see the purple flames of an arcane missile striking a statue on my left while someone else uses a freezing spell on another on my right (one that does not seem to require the use of any frozen meat), but both only succeed in slowing down rather than stopping their opponent.

While I grapple with my own statue, I see Riley slipping in behind it, using his stone-melding spell to reduce the statue's legs, limbs, and then torso into formless boulders, barely able to wriggle on their own. As useful as the spell is, the fact that it requires hand-to-stone contact makes it difficult to use on his own. I work with him to repeat the process on a couple of others, but we are soon overwhelmed, and I still have not noticed any change from Corrine.

"Corrine, is it working?" I call out for confirmation, ducking under a stone warrior's arm.

"I-I'm trying but she's fighting me. She's...*really* strong." Her eyes are squeezed shut in concentration as she answers.

"Keep trying!" Adam encourages, not wanting to let her on to the fact that we seem to be losing.

No longer content with just her stone soldiers, our invisible specter resumes her old trick of throwing objects at us. Pieces of the wall, the floor, the ceiling—even parts of the statues that David has hacked off—all of it starts to fly through the air. While some are thrown through the room at our heads, much of the debris begins floating around the outer ring of the room, forming a vortex as they circle around faster and faster, making the wind howl.

"Look out!" I turn in time to see Adam leap in front of a disembodied head that was aimed directly at Corrine, knocking it away with his shield.

"David, go help Adam!" I order without a second thought, pleased to see my pup moving to obey. His sword and the other man's shield are the only effective defenses we have as far as deflecting projectiles, and it would only take one well-placed strike for Corrine to go down.

We continue to fight hard, but you would have to be blind to tell we are struggling. We have managed thus far to keep all of our assailants away from the center of the room, but we are losing ground. Holding back a statue, evenly matched in strength, I am beginning to lose hope when the sudden glow of a white light over my shoulder reinvigorates me—Corrine's spell. I manage to swiftly knock out a statue's feet from under it, toppling it and shattering one of its arms.

The ghost has noticed the spell as well, unleashing an ear-splitting screech of rage too painful to ignore. Attempting to recover while remaining out of my stony assailants' reach, I spot the transparent form of our ghost in the shadow of a pillar. I watch her hands begin to glow with dark energy as she raises them above her head, preparing to fire.

"Behind the pillar!" I try to warn.

"*Sol—!*" Riley turns to try and stop her in time, but before the druid can finish casting, one of the statues strikes him on the head, knocking him out.

"Riley!" Piper cries out, rushing toward his unconscious body and firing bolts of arcane energy at his attacker. Unfortunately, she does not see the queen's own bolts, which strike her in the back and send her to the floor next to Riley.

After the two of them fall, the tides turn more and more in the spirit's favor. On my right, I can hear Elisabeth struggling against one of the statue's holds, and behind me, Adam grunts each time he blocks another projectile. Michael is panting as he tries to sling more spells as are Tsula and Nathaniel. Even I get sloppy, allowing two of the stone warriors to each take me by an arm and slam my back into a pillar, pinning me. While I fight to free myself, David rushes toward me, sword ready to strike—

"*NIVEIA!*" A voice booms through the room before everything goes pitch-black.

I think I may have gone blind until I see the pale white form of the elven queen floating into view. No longer content for her minions to do the work, she is taking matters into her own hands, cloaking the room in a magical darkness to block the sunlight. As I continue to struggle against those pinning me down, I notice another faint glow, one that slowly grows brighter until I can make out the form of Corrine's sanctuary circle and the two women inside of it.

While Corrine kneels at the center in prayer, Tsula stands between her and the queen, her arms outstretched toward the magical wall of force she has summoned to protect them. Her breathing is labored, and sweat is gathering on her brow as she gives everything she has to maintain the defense, pushing back against the darkness. The ghost watches the two of them with silent curiosity—right before she fires another arcane bolt. Tsula grunts in pain when it hits the force wall.

"*Cin ha kokolen bereth dan amin, ua kalen?*" She seems to be speaking directly to Tsula.

"*U... Ua ma nala,*" the timid mage stutters out, her focus torn between the spirit and her spell. "*Uan ma...fir talen va.*"

"*Sal ha cin? Salen nha ua shradi? Salen nha napan?!*" The ghost queen's hand begins to once more glow with dark energy as she grows frustrated with a lack of answers.

Tsula can only stare at the woman in painful silence as though afraid of what she is going to say next. "*A-Alfheim.*"

At hearing that single word, the spirit is taken aback, only moments before her body gives a jerk before going still in the air. Her head turns upward as she starts to glow, and I see Corrine on the floor behind Tsula in the same pose, her necklace shining like a tiny star around her neck. The glowing continues until in a bright flash of light, the ghost is gone, and the darkness gone with her. Her magic gone, the debris circling the room comes crashing to the ground, and without the queen to give them life, most of the statues topple over on their own, frozen in poses that have them off balance.

Not the ones holding me down, of course. I push those off and onto the floor. One by one, each member of our group slowly picks themselves up, looking around the now quiet room, sunlight streaming in the open window once more.

"Did... Did we do it?" Riley is the first to speak, having awoken from his brief spell of unconsciousness.

"I think so," Corrine hesitantly confirms, standing and dusting off her robes.

"Woohoo!" David cheers, jumping up from his spot on the floor not far from me. As more cheers ring out in response, David closes the distance between us. Overcome by the rush of victory, I grab him by the shoulders, pull him against me, and kiss him.

"What the hell!" We are suddenly wrenched apart by an angry brown-haired wizard. "Get the fuck off of my brother!"

Just as I am about to let Michael know *exactly* what I think of him, David beats me to it.

"Alright, that's it," he growls, gritting his teeth and taking his brother roughly by the wrist, dragging him to the opposite side of the room. "We're fucking settling this."

Chapter 18

David

"**Will you let go of me already!**" Michael shakes his wrist loose from my grip.

"Will you stop being such a dick to my boyfriend?" I fire back, getting right in his face.

"I am not being a..." He pauses. "Boyfriend?"

"I mean, yeah, kinda. We haven't exactly named what we are, I guess." At least not with a word that doesn't imply ownership. "But we're...together."

"Hey David, we're gonna..." Adam calls from across the room, hooking his thumb behind him toward the stairs.

"We'll catch up." I wave them off, turning back to Mike.

"You guys wanna take the short way down?" I hear Liss ask everyone else.

"What the hell." I watch in surprise as Khazak shrugs and joins her in jumping out of the window. *Wow, David. You either fixed him or broke him.*

"I don't understand." He's looking between me and the others as they leave. "You're ... together? But you're not... David, you like *girls*."

"Yeah, turns out, not so much," I try to set the record straight. "Sit down." I gesture toward the steps leading up to the throne nearby.

"David, you've had a ton of girlfriends," my brother exaggerates as we both take a seat. "When there was a dance, you always had a date. You brought some of them home to meet mom and dad. I can even remember you competing with Dickhead Darryl for girls at parties. What—"

"I love him, Mike," I tell him bluntly. "I'm *in* love with him. And he loves me back."

"Wow," is his stunned response. "But how did you... What about all those girls?"

"It's hard to explain." Mike cocks his eye at my poor choice of words. "I'm not just saying that. I'm still figuring out a lot of it myself. It's not that I didn't like any of the girls I dated. I just didn't like them in the way I thought I did. The way I thought I was supposed to."

"...What?" *Yeah, I gotta figure out a better way to explain this.*

"Okay, it's like... Every time I would kiss one of those girls, do you know what I'd be thinking?" Michael shakes his head no. "'Does this feel good?' Because they never felt *right*. I thought maybe it was because I was doing something wrong or that I just needed to meet the right girl, but it never clicked."

"...I'm sorry," he finally says after a long silence. "I...had no idea that's what it was like for you. I didn't know—"

"It's okay. I didn't know either." I don't need my brother to apologize for not knowing something I was even more clueless about myself. "I just figured that was how things were and didn't think about them that much. Then I met Khazak. The first time he kissed me was like..." I bite my lip, trying not to grin stupidly as I think of how to describe the feeling I had the first time I felt the orc's lips on mine, sprawled on the arena floor.

"Yeah okay, I know that look." *You* really *don't*. "I am sorry, though. I can't say I know what it's like to kiss a girl and not feel anything."

"Yeah, someone went off to wizard school and got all cool," I tease, an old habit from when I'm tired of being the focus of attention. "Grew a mustache and started getting laid all the time."

"Shut up." He scoffs and hits me on the shoulder but doesn't deny it. "Wait, does this mean I lost my virginity before you did?"

"Okay, don't get cocky." I roll my eyes at the way his voice gets excited.

"I *knew* it! *I'm* the cool twin!" he declares with glee to the empty room.

"Trust me, I've caught up," I tell him flatly, daring him to compare info.

Michael just laughs and shakes his head. "Sorry. It's still hard to wrap my head around. I've always had this idea of who you were in my mind."

"I know it's weird. It was weird for me too." Much, *much* weirder, I might argue.

"How'd it happen?" For a second, I think he's still talking about sex. "Did you just wake up one day and realize?"

"It's a long story." Michael's expression quickly flips to annoyed. "That I'm gonna tell you!" *Most of it, at least.* "Khazak isn't a guide. We didn't hire him to take us anywhere. We met him when he...arrested us."

"*Arrested?* For what?" Mike's eyes go wide at the revelation.

"Trespassing. And then attacking him and the other rangers who were there to stop us," I answer sheepishly.

"*David.*" He crosses his arms.

"It wasn't my fault! It was Nate's. He started throwing fireballs before we had a chance to talk. Then they threw us in a cell. I tried to get us out using this...weird loophole in the city's laws, but it ended up only working for me." *Or not working, whatever.* "While the others were stuck in jail for two months, I stayed and worked with Khazak. We lived together like that until... Well, when I died."

"Yeah, that conversation's still coming, by the way," Michael warns. "So, in those two months you guys...?"

"We got close." *Gods, I hope he wasn't going to end that sentence with 'fucked.'* "It was easy to pretend it was nothing at first, but as the weeks went on, and we spent more and more time together, it was impossible to ignore my attraction to him. Things just kept...happening. Things I couldn't just pretend weren't there, and one day I had to sorta look at myself and say: 'David, you're gay.'" My own words give me pause. "You know, I think that might be the first time I've actually said that out loud."

"Wow," is all he manages to say, looking down at the floor. "Why didn't you just tell me all of this?"

"Because I was afraid of how you might react," I answer honestly. "That you'd...think there was something wrong with me. Maybe even hate me."

"David, you're my twin. I could never hate you. I just thought... We used to tell each other everything. Even when I left for the institute, we wrote to each other all the time, but you never mentioned any of this. Or that you were thinking about leaving the knight academy, and then one day you were just...gone."

"Mike... It wasn't like I didn't want to tell you. I didn't know what to say, and I wasn't even really aware of the 'gay' thing yet." *Saying the 'G' word is going to take some getting used to.* "You were off in another country, finding yourself and turning into a badass, and I was stuck in a tiny room above the barracks, spending every other weekend standing guard outside of some rich asshole's house while he threw a party for other rich assholes. I didn't want to bother you with my stupid bullshit. It's not like you could have helped me. I needed to figure out who I was, and I wasn't going to be able to do that there."

"You still could have told me you were leaving." His tone is more hurt than angry.

"Yeah. I could've," I admit, grabbing him lightly on the shoulder. "I'm sorry."

He turns around and hugs me instead. "I'm just glad you're alright."

"Yeah, me too." I wrap my arms around my twin. "Love you, Mikey."

"Love you too, D." We break apart. "So, what are you gonna tell Mom and Dad?"

"What? Nothing." I look at him like his head's been bitten off.

"*David.*" *Why does everyone always say my name like that!?*

"What would I even say? 'Hey Dad, sorry I ran off without saying anything. I just really hated the thought of following in your footsteps,'" I mock talking to our father. "'Oh, by the way, I'm gay now. Would you like to meet my orc boyfriend?' Yeah, that'll go over *great.*"

"Well not if you say it like an asshole." He rolls his eyes. "You don't know he'd react that badly."

"Seriously? You don't remember all the times Dad had something shitty to say about 'those queers?' Cause I do." It's not like it came up a lot, but it was enough to let me know what he thought about them, and for the longest time, I knew it was something I definitely didn't want to be.

"...Well, you don't have to tell them everything," he offers.

"I don't have to tell them *anything*," I counter. "That's the great thing about being twenty-two. Happy birthday, by the way."

"Yeah, happy birthday," he repeats with a chuckle. "I just... I guess I'm kinda bummed that you feel like you *can't* say anything. That you never felt like you could talk about any of it."

"It's okay," I reassure him. "I told you, I had to figure some stuff out on my own. A lot of stuff, actually."

"Yeah, but did you really have to die to do it?" *Ugh, I still have that entire mess to explain.* "Are you really okay?"

"What do you mean?" I tilt my head, confused.

"You *died*, David. Even if you came back, that's horrible." He looks at me with sad eyes. "You've got that scar, you've lost a ton of weight, and I can't even imagine how traumatic it must have been."

"Technically, I lost all the weight months ago. I spent like a month on a boat, dude, and they do *not* feed you well." I rub my sadly-flat stomach. "And I happen to think the scars look kinda cool." *Or at least I'm starting to. Not gonna touch that trauma thing with a ten-foot pole, though.* "I'm okay. Really."

"Alright. But you know... Tell me if you're not?" He bumps his shoulder against mine.

"I will, I promise." I bump him back.

"Can I ask you something that might be kinda weird?" He asks me, wearing an uncomfortable face.

"Since when has that ever stopped you?" I'm only half-joking, Mike was *constantly* asking me weird shit when he was doing his late-night magic studies in our shared bedroom.

"Shut up." He rolls eyes. "Alright, so... Who's the girl?"

"Huh?" The question has me confused. "Who's what girl?"

"No, between you and Khazak," he tries to clarify.

"What?" I'm even more confused now. "Neither of us? That's kind of the point. We're both guys."

"No, I mean when you guys... Who does the...?" *Oh my god, is he serious?*

"Do you *seriously* want me to answer that?" I challenge, praying he won't call my bluff.

"...No, no I do not." He shakes his head. "Okay, I understand everything you've told me so far, but I guess there is one thing that's still kind of bothering me."

"What is it?" I ask, wondering what else he could possibly be talking about.

"Well, if you're gay, and we're twins... Does that mean that I'm also...?" From the worried look on his face, I can tell he's being completely serious.

"I don't think it works like that." I can't decide if I should laugh or not. "Also, we're not even identical."

"You don't know *how* it works," he points out. "You didn't even figure it out yourself until you met Khazak. How am I supposed to know?"

"I dunno. Kiss a guy?" I only mean it as a joke, but I see Mike starting to actually consider it, and I realize I better change the subject. "Look, I'm sorry I left without saying anything. Now that you know what's going on, do you think you could apologize to Khazak for being such a dick?"

"Huh?" *Okay, he was thinking* way *too hard about kissing a guy.* "Oh, yeah. Of course. I'm sorry to you, too."

"Thanks." I bump our shoulders together. "You know, I really think you guys would get along. He's like, *really* smart, and you both think *I'm* awesome."

Mike just rolls his eyes, standing and offering me a hand up. "Let's get out of here."

"Are we good?" I mean we fixed the one problem, but there's plenty of others.

"For now," he tells me with a smile. "When we get back into town, you're going to tell me all about this dying bullshit, and then we can figure out what we're gonna do about Mom and Dad."

Pretty sure the answer to that second problem is still going to be a resounding "nothing," seeing as I am a grown-ass man who can make his own decisions, but I keep my mouth shut for now. We'll cross that bridge when we get to it. The two of us walk toward the window we saw everyone else exit through, only pausing briefly to look at each other and shrug before jumping out ourselves. We head straight for camp once we land, our friends already in the process of packing things up.

"Khazak," I call to the orc who is half in his tent. "Mike has something he'd like to say to you."

"I just wanted to apologize," Mike starts as soon as Khazak stands up. "David explained everything, but even if he hadn't... I'm still really sorry I've been acting like such an ass. I hope we can be friends." He holds out his hand.

"Thank you." Khazak takes the offered hand and shakes it. "I would like that."

"Thank you, too. Alright, I'm gonna go get packed so we can get outta here." Michael thumbs at his tent as he walks away. He passes by Nate, and I watch him pause, consider something, then turn and grab the other wizard by the face, kissing him right on the mouth. He pulls back, a disappointed look on his face as he shakes his head. "Nope, nothing."

"What—What the hell was that!?" Nate blurts out once the shock of the moment wears off, Mike already at his tent.

"I think I have the same question as Nathaniel," Khazak says to me as he watches the flustered mage with amusement.

"Testing a theory?" I offer with a shrug, before taking one of his hands. "I wanted to apologize, too. Do you think we could be alone in the tent for a minute?"

"Of course." He steps to the side, holding open the tent flap and then following me inside.

As soon as he's down on the bedroll, I leap on top of him, wrapping my arms around his torso. He doesn't say anything, content to stroke a hand along my back as he holds me. We don't have a lot of time; we need to get moving soon so it's not too dark by the time we get back to the city, but I just need a few minutes of this. Of us.

"So, I take it that talking to your brother went well?" Khazak is the first to break the silence.

"Yeah." I nod, turning my head to the side. "It took a little convincing, and I think he's still getting used to some of it, but I got him to understand."

"What exactly did you tell him?" He's asking so he knows if there are any new lies he needs to keep track of.

"The truth with a few details left out," I answer honestly. "He knows we were arrested, and that I got out before the others, he just doesn't know exactly *how*. I told him I worked with you, and that we got closer in the two months we lived together—which isn't a lie. I left out the whole... slavery thing, for obvious reasons. I was too worried about the *gay* thing to even consider that."

"Gay?" Khazak asks me, confused.

"Yeah, you know. Gay. Like us." I point back and forth between us as I explain. "When a guy likes another guy. Or when a girl likes a girl, I guess."

"Ah, *homosexual*." He shakes his head, sounding exasperated.

"Sure, but that's too wordy." I forget there's still a bit of a language barrier when it comes to slang.

"Why do humans from your part of the world insist on shortening *every* word?" He muses with a chuckle.

"We just like talking fast." *Or maybe we're just that impatient.* "When Mike told me he'd apologize, he also agreed to try and get along with you, so if he still treats you like shit, you have my permission to kick his butt."

"Well, I will endeavor to do the same," he responds with a chuckle.

"I also wanted to say 'm sorry again, too," I mumble against his chest. "For distancing myself from you, for acting like an asshole, for yelling at you. Everything."

"Thank you, pup." His hand rubs down my back again. "If I'm being honest, I started to wonder if you would ever talk to him at all. The longer it went on, the more I grew worried that you would never actually tell him about me. That you planned to keep me and our relationship secret."

I pull back at his revelation to meet his eyes. "I am so sorry. I never wanted to make you feel like that. That's not how I think of you. I love you, Khaz."

"I love you too, pup." He kisses the top of my head, then pulls back so I meet his eyes. "Would you like to start making it up to me?"

I know what that means. "Yes, Sir," I answer with a playful sigh.

"Then get those pants off," he orders, allowing me to climb off of him before he begins rummaging through his bag.

I quickly unbutton and shimmy off my pants, taking my underwear with them since I have a feeling I know what's coming first. Sure enough, when Khazak turns back around, I see the shining metal chastity cage sitting in his palm. Crooking a finger on his other hand, he beckons me over with a smirk.

I take a seat in front of him, my bottom half nude and my legs spread. Despite knowing what's coming (or probably because of it), my dick starts to chub up. Seeing this, Khazak moves quickly, sliding the base ring down my shaft and under my balls and quickly attaching the rest, using the cold metal in an attempt to slow my growing erection. It works, but as soon as he's finished locking the two pieces together, I can feel the cage squeezing me.

"I am starting to think you enjoy being punished, puppy," he teases me, wrapping a large green hand around my encased genitals and giving a light squeeze.

"No, Sir, it's just been three days since I've seen any sort of action. Unlike some *other* people in this tent." I know I'm taunting him, but I'm pretty sure I'm already not going to be sitting comfortably for a week, so what's another ten? "You still owe me a story."

"Which you will get once you have completed your punishment." He lets my snark slide or at least doesn't tell me whatever he's just decided to add. "But lucky for you, I think we have enough time to take care of that first issue."

"We do?" I notice now that the cage wasn't the only thing retrieved from the spacious satchel. He's also got my cleansing charm and a plug. "But everyone's right outside. And you just finished locking up my dick."

"If you're not interested..." He looks back to his bag.

"I didn't say that..." I bite my lip, thinking. "...What'd you have in mind, Sir?"

Khazak grins and puts an arm around my shoulder, pulling us both down and maneuvering us so that I'm on my back and he's on his side. Gripping my left thigh, he pulls it between his own and then pushes at my right, encouraging me to spread wide. Putting the charm on my stomach and letting it do its work, he grabs the bottle of oil, pulling the cork out with his teeth and dribbling some onto his fingers. Then, because his other arm is trapped behind me, I have to use my hands to help him recork it.

Moving his slick fingers under my caged cock, he swipes them along my hole, my body shuddering at the touch. He slowly rubs in a circle around my entrance, making me want to spread my legs even wider. In its cage, my cock tires to get hard, as much as it is able, pressing feebly against the metal that encases it. I surprise myself with a noise that is half-moan, half-sigh of relief when he finally pushes the first finger inside.

"Shh, do you want someone outside to hear us?" Khazak teasingly shushes right as he strokes a finger over my prostate.

I bury my face in his shoulder as he laughs, biting my lip and holding back the moan I want to let go. Thankfully, my Sir takes pity on me, pulling my head back and capturing my mouth in a kiss, swallowing down any noises that threaten to slip out. His tongue probes my mouth as his finger sinks in deeper and deeper until he reaches the final knuckle, giving me a moment to adjust before he pumps his finger in and out.

One finger soon becomes two, bringing with it the familiar burn from the added stretch. He starts to play with my hole, scissoring his fingers apart and twirling them around, growling low when I squirm each time. He runs the pads of his fingers rhythmically over my prostate before he begins a slow, steady pump, sliding them out past the second knuckle before pushing all the way back in.

As his movements pick up speed, he alters the angle of entry so that his fingers slide directly over that wonderful spot with each stroke. I quietly yelp in surprise the first time he does it, making him pull back with a smirk, allowing the both of us to see his handiwork (*heh*). As I watch and feel his thick green finger pumping between my legs faster and faster, a familiar pressure starts to grow in my lower body. My cock, still trying to get hard in the cage, has been leaking a steady stream of precum, dripping down onto Khazak's hand and fingers as he fucks me.

When he shows no signs of stopping, I start to realize exactly what he meant by "taking care" of me. He's had his fingers inside of me before, of course, but that's always just been a prelude to something *else* going into my butt. I mean, I remember guys in school bragging about fingering their girlfriends but... Is this what that's like? I whimper as a wave of humiliation washes over me, my body flushing red.

"Sir?" I ask, my voice breathy, my body tense.

"Come on, puppy. Almost there. I can feel it," he encourages me in an equally breathy whisper.

Those words combined with everything else are enough to send me over the edge, my whole body shuddering as I cum. Khazak finger-fucks me through it, pressing them both as deep as they will before slowly driving them in and out only a few inches at a time as my hole spasms on his fingers. My hands grip tightly to his shirt as I return to burying my face in the crook of his neck while I try to hold in my noises. When it's finally over, I lay there panting, sprawled out in a relaxed heap.

"Good boy," he praises me, kissing the top of my head. "But I think you can give me at least one more."

I make a sound of confusion, but he recaptures my mouth before I can voice anything further. His fingers, never having left my ass, start to move again, finding even less resistance now that he's worked me over once already. Knowing I have no chance of stopping him (and sure, not really wanting to, whatever), I decide to work *with* him this time, spreading myself wider and deepening our kiss, all in the name of getting me off again. I can feel his tusked-grin against my lips as he realizes my change in tactics, and it's only a few more seconds of pumping before I'm cumming again on my owner's fingers.

He growls into my mouth as the second orgasm rolls through my body, his fingers still pumping as my ring pulses around them. My left leg gets tense as my muscles spasm, Khazak quickly trapping it between his own as he holds me tightly. He slowly brings things to a stop as my body relaxes, breaking our liplock as he pulls his fingers from my hole.

Pulling his arm from behind my shoulder, he lays me back while I catch my breath.

Despite the two anal orgasms, my dick is still crying to be let out and get some attention of its own. *Sorry buddy, you'll have to wait a little longer.* I giggle in surprise when I feel Khazak wiping a towel over my hole. Just as I'm expecting the order to get dressed, I feel the pressure of something else against my hole, opening my eyes in time to see Khazak pressing into me the plug he pulled from his bag earlier. I completely forgot he even pulled it out. It's going to be fun packing up camp with this in, not to mention...

"Wait, you're gonna make me wear it while we climb down the mountain?" I ask when I realize what he must be thinking.

"Well, I was going to check in with you at lunch to see how you were handling it, but more or less," he answers me with a cocky smile. "Complaints?"

I think about voicing a few but decide to play it smart for once and shake my head. "No, Sir."

"Excellent. I am sure this trip back down is going to be *very* memorable." There's something about the way he says it, something in his smile, that makes me think there's more going on than just a plug in my ass, but I can't put my finger on what.

I know questions aren't going to get me any answers, so I continue to keep any complaints to myself as I join Khazak in redressing, eyeing the fresh red jock he has pulled from the satchel for me. I suppose I no longer need to worry about Mike waking up and seeing me in them.

"You know, I can't believe you just jumped out of the window the way you did," I comment as I pull it on with a grin, not realizing how much I had missed having Sir pick out my underwear. "Are you over your fear of heights now?"

"Oh no, that was an absolutely terrible decision. I blacked out almost immediately," he tells me in a voice that is both jokey and serious. "I woke up to Sona licking my face on the ground."

I try not to laugh as I finish pulling my pants on, but I know my face is giving it away. *This cage isn't coming off anytime soon.* Once I'm re-pantsed, the two of us exit the tent, myself much more carefully than Khazak. I know it's silly at this point. I'm pretty sure *everyone* knows by now, but I can't help but look around and see if anyone's staring at us, part of me still afraid they might realize what we were just doing in there alone. But other than a random smile when I catch Tsula's eyes, everyone's busy packing their bags and taking down their tents. Khazak's hand on my shoulder brings me back to the present, and together the two of us break down his tent—*our* tent.

It feels *really* good to be able to say that again.

Chapter 19

Khazak

I try to contain my pleased grin as David exits the tent ahead of me, stepping gingerly thanks to the plug in his ass. I pat the control stone in my pocket, coming up with all sorts of wicked ideas on how I can use it to torture my pup. I am going to leave him alone, for now; allowing him to get used to his current predicament will make the surprise that much better.

Outside, the others are still packing up camp with only a few of them sparing us a glance as they finish their work. With most of the tents already being broken down, David and I get to work on ours—spirits it feels good to say that again—and soon the only sign our group was ever even here are the remnants of our campfire. After double-checking that we have everything, we march up the valley and through the waterfall cave out of the ruins.

Things are slow at first, those of us who are still new to traveling like this needing a moment to get their bearings. We all pause hesitantly outside of the first cave's entrance, remembering our bear encounter. Riley and Sona end up taking the lead, the druid shapeshifting into a wolf form of his own so the two can sniff out any potential danger.

The trip through the cave is long, but thankfully uneventful, though I cannot decide for sure if the disappearance of our ursine foe is a good sign or bad.

After the long cave comes the still-perilous narrow cliff-side, and while my experiences in Karthani may have lessened my fears, crossing is still an uncomfortable matter. Even Sona has an easier time than me.

Once we are on the other side, I decide it is time to give my pup his surprise. Reaching stealthily into my pocket, I quickly tap the stone three times in succession, smirking when David's body jerks in surprise. He manages to hold back any sounds, but he looks around furtively—his expression reading "what the hell is happening" when he catches my eye. I shrug in response, pretending to focus on the road ahead.

From an outsider's perspective, everything appears perfectly normal. But for those of us with enhanced hearing, if you listen *very* carefully, you can hear the faintest buzzing sound coming from David's rear. At the moment that only means myself and Tsula, who I am sure will either not know what the sound is or be too embarrassed to say anything, allowing me the freedom to play with my puppy in secret.

As we continue to travel through the winding mountain road (which is much easier to navigate in this direction), I use the stone in my pocket to shake things up, so to speak. I increase the speed, then slow it down, changing it at odd intervals. I am impressed each time when David manages to maintain his composure, though the frustrated glares he keeps throwing in my direction are starting to give him away.

I keep this up until we reach a clearing and decide it is a good time to break for a late lunch. It is late in the afternoon, and we are a little over halfway to Pákannon. We still have plenty of walking ahead of us and should hopefully arrive only a few hours after sunset. As everyone unloads their bags so they can relax, I excuse myself to relieve my bladder behind a tree. When I am finished, I find Adam waiting for me.

"So, I'm not exactly sure why, but David's acting jumpy and keeps looking at you, while you keep staring at his ass," Adam tells me bluntly. "What's going on?"

"Ah, you noticed that, did you?" *Which means others may have as well... I may need to be more careful about things like this going forward.* "Did anyone else?"

"I don't think so." He shrugs, waiting for me to continue.

"Alright, well, at the moment David has a...toy inside of him," I choose my words carefully. "A magical toy, one that vibrates."

"A *what?*" His eyes go wide at my explanation. "How do you... Where did you even get something like that?"

"I have a friend in V'rok'sh Tah'lj who specializes in such objects." *I still need to write Brull a thank you letter.* "I am able to control it from a distance with this." I pull out the control stone.

"How does it work?" Adam has a curious smile on when he asks.

"Much more simply than you'd think." I gesture for him to follow me behind a large tree, where we can see David speaking with his brother. "You tap it three times to turn the object on or off." I demonstrate, and we watch as David appears to grow less, and then more tense. "And to increase or decrease the speed and intensity, you move your fingers over the surface like a clock's hands." We once again watch as David's posture changes based on my manipulation of the toy.

"Wow. That is amazing." Adam sounds genuinely enthused before turning coy. "Do you think I could give it a try?"

Intrigued that Adam is actively showing interest and seeking us out for things of this nature, I think about his request. While not part of my initial plan, I can already think of a few fun ways to use this to my advantage. "Yes, but I need you to wait to change anything until you see me talking with David alone."

"I can do that." Adam accepts the stone from me, sticking to our hiding spot while I exit and make my way over to the talking brother.

"Michael, would you mind if I spoke with David for a moment?" I ask the brown-haired twin as I approach.

"He's all yours," he answers with a smile, nodding at his brother before turning to rejoin the others and give us some privacy.

"How are you feeling, pup?" I ask once Michael is out of earshot, my voice low.

"I don't know *how* you're doing this, but I know you're doing it," he tells me through gritted teeth, right before his eyes go wide—Adam no doubt starting to play. "How—?!"

"I am afraid I have no idea what you could be referring to," I respond innocently. "I am simply standing here, talking to you."

"Evil toy... Evil orcs..." he mutters to himself, a look of realization passing over his face. "Brull made this, didn't he?"

"Good guess." I drop the facade. "In all seriousness, I did want to make sure you were still alright."

"Yes Sir, I'm fine," he answers, smiling as he drops some of his own dramatics. "Just slowly going insane because of this thing." Only some.

"Good. You can take it out after lunch," I tell him, tousling his hair before we return to our makeshift camp.

Adam returns just after we do, getting all of our attention before we start in on our trail rations. "Alright, I know we left in kind of a hurry, but I just really wanted to say that we did a really great job back there. Great teamwork from everyone, but I especially wanted to call out Corrine and Tsula. You ladies really pulled it together at the end."

A small amount of applause goes up as the two women blush.

"It was nothing really," Corrine starts to downplay. "If it wasn't for Tsula talking to the spirit, I'm not sure it would have even worked. I think it distracted her enough to allow my spell to get through her defenses."

"What did you say to her, anyway?" Liss asks Tsula, who still looks embarrassed at the attention. "Did she actually understand you?"

"W-well I wasn't certain, but I thought I kept hearing the words for 'family' and 'location.'" She toys with the hem of her dress while she talks. "My Old Elvish is rusty, but I tried to tell her that they were gone. That they had passed on."

"You said 'Alfheim,'" Michael points out. "Like the old ruined city in northern Scania?"

"Alfheim is one of the names used for the afterlife of the ancient elves. The city was actually named after it," she corrects him. "I tried to tell her that's where everyone was. I'm not sure if she understood me or not."

"Wasn't her family already dead by the time the magical cataclysm or whatever wiped her and everyone else out?" David asks. "Did she not remember what happened?"

"Her memory must have degraded so much by that point that the two events bled together," I offer up as an explanation. "Or perhaps she could not remember either event at all and just assumed they were related. Either way, whatever her reasons were for creating the soul-trap, I do not think spending centuries as the tower's resident ghost was a part of her plan. If what happened to the elves, the 'Great Rending,' was sudden and unexpected, she would have been caught off guard the same as everyone else.

Becoming the 'Woman in White' may have just been the unfortunate result of her magical soul-splitting."

Everyone is quietly looking at me as they slowly digest my theory, which I realize now may have been a bit much.

"He was basically a detective," David leans over to tell his brother.

"I can't say I fully understand why she wanted to split her soul, but I know what it's like to lose your whole family," Adam says thoughtfully, breaking the silence. "Without the right people around you to help you through it, I could see it pushing you to some pretty dark places."

The group spends the next half-hour resting and eating lunch, Adam and I taking the time to torment David. I allow Adam to go for the first fifteen minutes—passing the stone back and forth would be too obvious. It also adds to the fun of David looking me over furtively every time Adam changes one of the settings. David manages to keep most of his squirming to a minimum, but knowing that the plug is buzzing right against his prostate makes me smile each time he does.

After Adam stealthily returns the stone to my hand, I have to be more careful, only altering the plug's speed when I know David is not looking. I make a game out of it in my head, adjusting the plug just a little faster each time David takes a bite of jerky. By the time we are finished, sweat has broken out along his forehead, his hands in tight fists at his sides.

"*Evil!*" he repeats, whispering to me when I hand him my satchel so that he can go remove the plug I have finally turned off and return it to its confines.

Bellies mostly full, we set off for the last half of our return journey. Just as I thought, the skies are dark by the time we exit the final cave, where two guards stand to greet us (though not the same two from our trip inside). Only briefly surprised by our appearance, one of them proceeds to lead us back down the mountain, torch in hand.

As we approach the city's outskirts, I become more aware of Sona's presence, mostly because the guard keeps looking back at her. It is understandable; despite our connection she is still a wild animal, and a wolf running loose through town is going to make more than a few people nervous. A collar would do much to assuage their fears, but until I can find one, she will need to remain outside of town. Before we reach the city walls, I send her off into the forest with instructions to meet us outside of the north gate in two days' time.

Despite the late hour, the streets are bustling with people. While this would normally be odd (especially for an Ignisday), tomorrow is the Summer Solstice, a day that will no doubt be filled with festivals and feasts of all kinds. All around us we can see the city has been decorated, with sun motifs painted along walls and strings of brightly colored flowers hanging overhead.

As we near the Council House, a group of giggling children in paper sun masks rushes past us in the opposite direction. The inside of the building seems no less busy than the rest of the city. With preparations for the holiday in full swing, we are happy to be told that Mayor Elajor is still in and are led straight to his office.

"The intrepid heroes return!" he greets after looking up from the papers on his desk. "It is wonderful to see you have all made it back safely. Was your mission a success?"

"Only half of it," Adam answers. "We managed to find the conduit crystals, but there was no intact reponiam."

"Oh no, I'm so sorry." The empathy seems genuine, but it is always hard to tell with politicians. "Did you run into any other problems?"

"Do you want to hear about the ghost or the giant snake first?" David eagerly relays our issues, causing the mayor's eyes to widen.

"That is... The Woman in White? Really?" His tone isn't doubtful, just shocked.

"We found this journal that should corroborate most of what we said." Tsula shows him the journal in question, our gathered conduit crystals in a pile on the table behind them.

"I will make sure this gets into the hands of the city historians right away. I will also have a crew sent to clean up the snake corpse," he affirms. "Fighting an uktena, casting out a ghost, and you even managed to reopen the entrance to the white tower. This city owes you and your friends a great debt. Also, your mother is going to kill me."

"We accept the usual gold and silver as payment." I once more find myself agreeing with Nathaniel's comments.

"I am sorry, but if you knew entrance to the tower was blocked off, how did you know where we would find the conduit crystals?" I decide to ask the mayor something that has been nagging at me since I realized we would have to find our own way inside the tower. "And how did you acquire previous replacements?"

"I am not sure when the location of the communications room was first discovered, but it is my understanding that previously, spellcasters would be assigned to retrieve them and would simply," he imitates his hand leaping over something, "fly over the anti-magic field and into the tower."

"And you did not think to warn us about that before we left?" I raise an eyebrow at the strange omission.

"I do apologize. By the time I remembered, you had all already left." He gives me an apologetic smile, one I do not fully believe. "But I knew you were a resourceful group and would figure something out."

"Yes, how fortunate of us." I do not hide the annoyance in my tone.

"Now, let me see... Leotie, could you please make a note to send a group to clean up the uktena remains. I also think regular patrols of the ruins may be in order," the mayor begins spouting off orders to his secretary, who has been quietly observing everything from a corner in the back of the room. "Please also contact the Elven Council and the Historians Guild. In addition to this journal, now that the white tower is opened, I am sure they will be eager to explore."

"Err, sir?" Michael interrupts before he can give the woman more orders. "I believe you told us that once we retrieved the crystals, it would be possible to use the prismatic transmitter to—"

"Oh yes, of course! We must contact the Institute at once!" he exclaims, plucking one of the pink crystals from the table. "Please, follow me."

The mayor leads us through a side door in his office that opens to a small, nondescript room. The walls are bare and there is no furniture to speak of except for a small table in the center of the room on which sits the prismatic transmitter. It looks identical in shape to the one in the white tower, though this one has obviously been more well maintained.

"Leotie, please connect us with the Elven Institute in Kirinyaga." He hands over the crystal to the stout woman. "It shouldn't be too early over there."

"Right away, sir," she answers as she makes her way over to the device.

I watch as the woman inserts a conduit crystal into an empty slot on top of the device, opposite the slot which already has a crystal inserted. Between the two is a small crystal pyramid, this one not cracked. She adjusts the knobs and dials all over the transmitter's surface until it begins to emit a low hum as all three crystals start to glow, a beam of light shooting from the tip of the pyramid onto the far wall. What starts as a point of light spreads until a pink rectangle is being projected onto the wall. The inside of the rectangle is an erratic mess of rapidly moving lines until suddenly an image of a dark-skinned elf is staring back at us. He is not exactly in color; everything is a different shade of pink. I think we are looking at a still image until he suddenly moves, and I almost jump.

"*Nira ratha,*" the man greets us in Elvish, his voice echoing out of the transmitter. "*Naj pul si lakus sen?*"

"Good morning. This is Mayor Austenaco Elajor of Pákannon," he greets the projection. "I need to speak with the headmaster. I have information regarding two of your students who I believe may be missing."

The man on the other end is taken aback by the mayor's claims at first, but then he squints his eyes, scrutinizing our group. "Ms. Williams? Mr. Cerano?" His eyes go wide, and he nods. "I will be right back with the headmaster." The man stands from his seat and exits the room through a door in the back.

"That is so cool," David comments from my left. "How does it work?"

"The crystal on the left is capturing an image of this room and sending that across the planet via leylines while the crystal on the right receives the image being sent to us by their crystal," the mayor explains. "The device itself captures the sound and sends it along the same signal."

The technology is truly fascinating, but before we have a chance to ask more questions, the man from earlier returns with an elf woman in long, flowing robes—the Institute's headmaster. After pointing at the screen, the man allows her to take his previous seat, where she wastes no time in greeting Elajor.

"Austenaco, my friend. Congratulations on becoming mayor again." The woman smiles warmly as she gives a small bow of her head before her expression turns stern. "Now would you mind explaining to me how you came to be in possession of two of my missing students?"

"Thank you, Visola. It is good to see you," the mayor greets his apparent old friend. "I think they will be much more qualified to explain that themselves." He steps to the side, allowing Piper and Michael to step forward.

"Good morning, Headmaster Barmasai," Piper speaks while Michael can only awkwardly wave.

"Well, I am glad to see you are both *alive*, rather than imploded as we all thought." Her large face looks back and forth between them. "I trust your friend Mr. O'Connor is also there with you?"

"Yes ma'am, right here." The druid waves his hand from the back of the room.

"Excellent. Now, what exactly happened four nights ago?" She crosses her arms.

"Well, ma'am, turns out we were right about our teleportation theory!" Michael tries to give her the positive news first. "There was just a *slight* miscalculation in where we teleported to." A miscalculation we still do not have an answer for.

"If I were not able to verify that you were contacting me from across the globe, I'm not sure I would believe it." Her stern face softens slightly. "If what you are saying is true, then you two have made a groundbreaking discovery. Travel, transportation, this could change the very face of Terra."

"Thank you, ma'am," Piper ducks her head slightly, suddenly feeling bashful. "We will be more than happy to share our notes when we return."

"You two can *also* expect to face disciplinary action." The stern look is back. "We have rules and safety protocols in place for a reason, and you risked not only your own safety, but possibly that of everyone in the area. Between the bright lights and sounds of an explosion, I think you may have woken up half the school."

"Yes, ma'am," the wizard and sorcerer say in unison, their heads hanging.

"We are also going to need to send out letters to your parents letting them know that you are not, in fact, deceased." She sighs. "Those will be interesting to write."

"Oh gods..." Michael's hand comes up to cover his mouth.

"Why *haven't* you two returned yet?" She looks curiously at both students.

"The teleportation spell requires reponiam a regent. Because of the miscalculation and added distance, we burned through all that we had on us," Piper explains while Michael has a small crisis. "We are unable to find more in the area, but we thought perhaps we could share our notes over the transmitter, and then someone could gather the needed reponiam to come and retrieve us."

"I see. And how many pages of notes would this entail?" She looks skeptical at best.

"Eight or nine," Michael admits in his stupor.

"Well, even if your spell did *not* have a 'slight miscalculation,' given the potential for any number of things to go wrong in such a complicated and volatile spell, that is not something we will be risking," she tells them pointedly. "I am afraid you two will be responsible for finding your own way home."

"Yes, ma'am," Piper accepts for them both. "By our current estimates, that may take us as long as three weeks."

"That is unfortunate, but we shall await your arrival." She gives them both a confident smile. "Mr. O'Connor, was there anyone you would like us to contact on your behalf?"

"Thank ya, but no ma'am," the redhead declines. "Already sent off a letter myself."

"Very well. Then I wish you and your companions safe travels, and we shall see you in three weeks." Her large eyes scan around the room once before settling on the mayor. "Austenaco, I trust you have been taking good care of my students while they are in your care?"

"Of course, dear, only the best," he boasts confidently, despite not having anything to do with our accommodations. "Perhaps once they work out the kinks in this teleportation business, you can drop by for a visit. We could get dinner, like old times." I mentally roll my eyes at the flirting.

"We'll see, Naco. *Nabaya*." I see the headmasters hand reach out toward the transmitter, turning another dial.

"*Nabaya*," the mayor repeats as he does the same, the pink light dimming and the image fading into nothingness. He turns around to face us. "I think that went well."

Both mages are too shell shocked to respond, so Adam steps in. "Thank you for helping our friends contact the Institute, sir."

"It was the least I could do. In fact, given all you've done and gone through, and how much of a journey you have ahead of you, I think a reward is in order." The mayor manages to perk some of our spirits up as he leads us from the room. "I'll work out the details and have it delivered to the inn in the morning. I've taken the liberty of paying for your rooms for the next two nights. I know you all have to get moving, but I do hope you'll stay for the festival tomorrow."

"Wow, sir, that's very generous," Adam continues to speak for the group. "We'd be happy to stay for the Solstice. We could use a day off after all of that."

"I am sure you could." He gives Adam a polite chuckle. "Now, if you will excuse me, there are a few last-minute preparations that still need to be made. I will see you all tomorrow."

We say our goodbyes and exit the office, making our way toward the inn.

"Anyone else get the weird feeling that Elajor knew more than he was letting on?" Liss is the first to voice her skepticism.

"You think he planned all this or something?" Nathaniel asks her.

"No, not exactly." She thinks on how to word what she means.

"I do not think he is aware of the dangers we would face, the snake or the ghost," I start to answer myself. "But there was never any reponiam for us to find, and that he knew."

"*That's* the vibe I got," Liss confirms with me.

"I wouldn't put it past him," Tsula tells us with a sigh. "I really need to get home. My parents are already going to freak out when they hear about everything that happened. Will I see you all tomorrow at the festival? There's a big lunchtime feast that happens in the town square."

"I love food. We will definitely see you tomorrow, Tsula," David confirms with a smile and nod.

"The last few days have been...wonderful, terrifying, fun..." She plays with her braid. "I just wanted to say thank you for bringing me along. Even with all the danger, I'm glad I did this."

"We're glad you came, too," Michael tells her, waving as she leaves for her own home.

With Tsula's exit, the rest of us trudge our way through town until the Sleeping Willow Inn is visible in the distance. After verifying that our accommodations are ready, we all order a small dinner and quickly retire to our rooms. There's only a brief moment of confusion when Michael realizes David will be bunking with me instead of himself.

As soon as he has his armor off, David flops face first onto the bed, groaning in pleasure at the soft fabric underneath him.

"Do not get too comfortable," I warn him with a chuckle. "Would you like to take care of the rest of your punishment now? That way we can fully enjoy the celebrations tomorrow."

"Enjoy them with a sore ass, you mean," he grumbles, sitting up. "Okay, I swear I'm not trying to get out of it, but how are you going to punish me without anyone else hearing? I know I just revealed everything to my brother but having him hear me get spanked is not something I'm ready to let happen."

Rather than answer verbally, I cast the sound dampening spell I normally use when hunting, bringing my hands together and then pushing them outward. As the shushing sound I make becomes inaudible, I cross my arms and cock my head, silently asking David if this is suitable enough. Narrowing his eyes and huffing, he nonetheless stands and removes his pants, and I quickly follow suit.

Grinning, mostly to myself, I take a seat on the edge of the bed and pull David over my lap. He squirms as he finds a comfortable position, the cool metal of his cage pressing against my inner thigh. Once he is in place, he moves his hands to the small of his back, where he knows it is easiest for me to hold them should it come to that.

I take a moment to admire the pale, unblemished, and slightly fuzzy skin of his ass. Squeezing it briefly, I draw my hand back and bring it down swiftly on his right cheek. The flesh ripples under my hand, David's body gives a slight jerk, but nothing more than a soft *paff* can be heard. I repeat this on his left cheek and continue alternating back and forth, slowly warming him up.

This would normally be the part where I would give David a lecture about why he was being punished, but the silencing spell makes that somewhat difficult. In addition to the numerous little snipes and jabs that have accumulated, the main reason I am spanking him is the way he spoke to me in the river that day during the argument with his brother. I have had more than enough time to cool off since then.

You should never punish someone while you are still angry with them. You need to be in control of your emotions; otherwise, you risk them bleeding into your actions. You could strike someone harder than intended or miss important signals that you need to stop. You are more prone to making rash decisions, and could do things you'll come to regret long after you are forgiven for them; so many different things could go wrong. I do not have a particular number in mind, as part of this is also to help rebalance our relationship after spending such a long time out of sync. We will both know when I am finished.

Once we reach around fifteen, I start to feel a slight sting with each smack as the flesh under my hand heats up. Stopping to give us both a brief break, I run my hand over the warm skin, loving the contrast between the shades of pink and my own green. Shaking any remaining sting from my hand, I resume my work, looking to turn that pink into more of a red.

As the spanking continues, I admire the jiggle and bounce of David's cheeks with each strike. The rest of his body has remained mostly still, aside from the occasional twitch of his hands. It is honestly a pity that we have to do this silently; I love hearing my pup's whimpers and whines. We will have to do something about that next time. Underneath him, my erection tents the front of my underwear, occasionally pressing into David's stomach.

After a few more minutes of this, I feel David's body relax on my lap. I look up toward his head, turned to the side and facing me, where his eyes are growing watery. *There we are.* That is what I was looking for: acceptance. I did not expect it to take us long to get there and am happy to stop things here. I move his hands, allowing him to lay more comfortably as I stroke mine along his back.

Moving backward onto the bed, I pull David with me until we are both laying down, him on his stomach half atop my chest. As his heart rate evens out, I reach into my bag, pulling out a handkerchief I use to wipe his face. I hold him a short while longer until I feel the pull of the bathroom calling me and I reluctantly wriggle out from underneath him to relieve my bladder.

When I turn around, the sight of David's red ass greeting me starts to pull my mind in a different direction. Especially when he lays on his stomach the way he does, one leg pulled up, spreading his cheeks and offering a peek at the tight hole within. A hole that itself is still slightly distended from having worn a plug most of the day. The sound dampening spell *is* still active, and it would be a pity to let it go to waste...

I stop to rummage through my bag again, retrieving my bottle of oil. Climbing back onto the bed and straddling David's straight leg, he looks back at me in confusion until he sees the object in my hand. Smiling and giving me a quick nod of approval, he turns onto his side and grabs himself under his thigh to hike his leg up even more, happy to grant me more access.

I slick my cock with oil, swiping my wet fingers along his crack until I find his hole, enjoying the way he tenses before pushing back against me, encouraging me to slip inside. Feeling that he's still adequately stretched, I grab his right cheek with one hand while I take aim with my cock in the other.

Thanks to the plug, I find very little resistance as I sink all the way inside. Pressing tightly against his ass, his skin feels hot against mine. Pulling back, I look down and watch as the thick green rod that is my cock slips out from between his red cheeks, disappearing once more as I press forward. The only things missing are all the breathless gasps and moans my pup usually makes—damned spell.

I squeeze the flesh in my hand, unable to help myself from giving it a few more light spanks. After the general lack of sex the last few days, I do not imagine this is going to take me very long. Especially when I think back to our brief time in the tent just before leaving. The tightness of David's hole around my fingers, the way they slid in and out of his slick hole, the feeling of them squeezing, pulsing, trying to push them out as he came on them. How have I never fingered David like that before? I will be remedying that going forward.

The memory of the tent, and the sight of my cock continuously driving in and out of his well-spanked ass, are more than enough to get me across the finish line. I push in as much as I can, forcing David farther up the bed as he takes every centimeter of the prick inside of him. I have to use my hand to catch myself on the wall as I fall forward when I finally unload, exploding deep inside the tightness of his hole.

Collapsing onto the bed and my pup, I roll us onto our sides while keeping us connected, pressing my chest to David's back and wrapping an arm around his chest. Once I can think straight again, I dismiss my silencing spell, allowing sound to filter back into the room, though the only noise audible is our breathing. We lay there, enjoying the warmth until the sweat finally cools, and we feel more sticky than sexy.

"That was...different," David tells me as I wipe him down with a wet cloth. "It was weird not being able to hear you. Or the long lecture I'm sure you wanted to give me."

"I was thinking the same thing. And my lectures are not that long." I pinch his ass in retaliation. "I should have done this before I cast the spell, but I do want to make sure you understand what you were being punished for."

"Wasn't it for acting like an ass the past few days?" he asks, looking at me over his shoulder.

"More or less," I chuckle as I climb back onto the bed. "I suppose I'm more referring to what you were *not* being punished for—not telling me about your nightmares and not telling your brother about our relationship."

"I'm *not* being punished for those things?" David looks at me confused as he lays on my chest.

"No." I shake my head. "You are being punished for how you acted during those moments, but while I did not *like* that you would not talk to me about those issues, it is not something I can force you to do. You had to decide to tell me on your own. Does that make sense?"

"Kinda." He frowns slightly as he thinks. "You weren't mad that I was afraid to talk about or deal with that stuff as you were mad at me for being an asshole *because* I wouldn't talk about or deal with it."

"Correct. Maybe next time, you can try that instead of avoiding your issues and save us both some trouble." I run my hand through his sweaty hair, laughing to myself at the way it looks slicked back. *Haircuts before we leave.*

"But then what reasons would you have to spank me, Sir?" he taunts, sticking his tongue out.

"Somehow, I think I will survive." I shake my head, leaning over to turn out the lantern.

"Easy for you to say—you're not the one going to sleep with his cock in a cage," David complains half-heartedly as he settles against my chest. "I don't know about you, Sir, but after the last few days, this puppy could use some pampering."

"I am sure he could." I kiss the top of his head.

"So, with my punishment over, are you gonna tell me about whatever happened with Adam?" my pup asks plainly, all cards on the table.

"I suppose you *have* earned it," I tease as I pull him back against my chest. "Three nights ago, the first night Adam and I shared a tent, I woke up to find him already awake. After some discussion, the night ended with a brief session of mutual masturbation."

"You jerked each other off?" he tries to clarify.

"No, we pleasured ourselves—we just talked and watched each other during," I answer, thinking back to that night.

"...What happened? What was it like?" My pup's curious mind gets the best of him.

"Well, I am happy to inform you that Adam is in possession of a nice-looking cock," I tell David, comparing their respective crotches. "More than adequate in its size. He also shot a respectable load of cum all over his stomach."

"Lucky him," David responds dryly, before his expression softens. "I love you, Khaz. I really, really, *really* love you. Sorry that things have been so crappy lately because of me."

"I love you too, David," I tell him honestly, allowing his words to sink in. "...Khaz? Is that what you're going to refer to me now?"

The human rolls his eyes at my response. "Oh come on. It's just you and me. I can't call you that even when we're alone?"

"Well, I *suppose* I don't mind the nickname, even if it is not my name," I complain before sighing.

"You act like I haven't heard you using contractions the last few days." He looks at me with mock-cockiness before pointing to himself and nodding. "Yeah, that's right—I know what contractions are."

I cannot help but laugh, the joke catching me completely off guard.

"You are only proving that you lot are rubbing off on me in all the wrong ways," I complain without any bite, kissing and nuzzling David as we wind down, thoughts of pampered pups filling my dreams as we slip off into sleep.

Chapter 20

"It really is beautiful," David tells me. "At least when you ignore the rotting snake carcass."

"It is," I agree with a chuckle. "Though I think the dead snake has some appeal."

We are sitting together on a grassy mountainside, overlooking the Ruins of Karthani. The sun is rising into the clear sky over the valley below. I can hear birds in the trees around us, wind rustling the branches, even a river in the distance. It all paints a wonderful picture.

One that is not real. This is a dream. I cannot tell you how I know; I just do. Still, I am not going to allow that to spoil a quiet moment like this for me. I reach for my dream-David, wrapping my arm around his shoulders and pulling him to my side.

"This was the kind of place I wanted to see when I left home," he tells me. "Secluded, magical. Somewhere secret you can escape to."

"I wish our visit could have been under better circumstances," I respond.

"Do you think we'll ever get to have times like this back in the real world?" he asks me next, calling out his own dream existence. "Quiet ones, where we're not being chased by someone or something that wants to kill us?"

"I certainly hope so," I answer, kissing him gently as we watch the sunrise.

I wake early in the morning, the first rays of sunlight streaming in through our room's window. I feel relaxed, my mind and chest filled with none of the usual anxiety that I've come to expect from a night of dreaming. Judging from the way David is still asleep soundly beside me, I would venture that he has had a nightmare-free night himself. Too awake to return to sleep, I lay there holding him, enjoying the feel of his slow, steady heartbeat when I rest my hand over his chest.

I do get up eventually, the need to stretch my legs and use the bathroom becoming too much to ignore. After carefully extracting and relieving myself, I take in David's sleeping form on the bed and remember his comment last night about pampering. He's not off the hook for everything—that cage is staying on for at least a few more days—but he could use a little bit of a break, at least when it comes to sleep.

After checking the room's clock for the time, I sit down quietly at the table in the room. Pulling out some papers, ink, and a pen from my bag, I set to work writing three letters home: one to my family, one to Brull, and one to Ragnar and Nylan. I update everyone on our progress, or lack thereof, in varying degrees of detail (more for Brull, Ragnar, and Nylan, and less for my family) about our travels and adventures so far. I include a thank you in Brull to him and his lady companion, and I might also include a section complaining about wanting to throttle a certain pup's equally bratty twin brother in Brull and Ragnar's if only because I feel the other dominants would understand.

After I'm satisfied with the letters, I take another look at the clock, the hour just before nine. Everyone else should be waking up now or soon if they are not already. As we have nothing important on the schedule for today, I am content to let David doze a little longer. It will give me time for the next part of the "puppy pampering plan."

Throwing on some clothes, I grab my bag and quietly exit the room, making my way downstairs. I move toward the kitchen, placing my bag on the counter while I wave for the cook's attention. It takes a little bribing (namely of a few rashers for himself), but I get the man to agree to fry up the bacon I've been saving, which I whisk upstairs back to our room, along with two mugs of coffee.

My hands full, opening the door is no easy task, though I am at least able to close it behind me with my foot. The sound of it clicking shut and perhaps the familiar smell of breakfasts past cause David to finally stir on the bed. Lifting up slightly on his hands, he makes to turn over, wincing and stuttering in his movements when his rump makes contact with the mattress. Before he can complain, he notices what I am carrying with me and immediately perks up.

"You made the bacon?" he asks excitedly.

"The cook did, but I helped by bribing him," I answer with a grin as I set it down on the nightstand along with the coffee.

"Where'd you learn to carry things like that?" He is referring to the way I hold the mugs and plate without dropping or spilling anything.

"I worked in my father's restaurant as a teenager," I confess, crawling back onto the bed next to David and sitting up against the headboard and reaching for the coffee.

"What was that like?" He settles comfortably against my side, accepting the offered mug.

"Stressful. I have never in my life experienced people more entitled or rude. Over *food*." I shake my head at the memories. "I quit before I took my journey with Ayla, applied to the rangers as soon as I returned, and never looked back."

"I didn't really work when I was younger, just went to school." He sips his coffee as he thinks. "The whole knight-in-training thing is the closest I've had to a real job."

"What would you call yourself now?" I reach to the plate for a piece of bacon.

"I dunno. An adventurer? Explorer? Maybe a treasure hunter? Never really gave it much thought." He opens his mouth as I bring the piece of bacon in close, biting into it with a moan. "You're the *best*, Sir."

I soak up the praise as I finish off the other half of the bacon strip. We spend the morning like that, tucked into the bed and each other as we devour the pile of bacon. Though I try my best, crumbs and grease inevitably end up on our sheets, and I will need to remember to leave a few coins on the table for the person responsible for washing them. It is more than worth it when I have a happy pup snuggled against my side, belly full. *That reminds me—I should pick up something for Sona before we leave.*

A knock on our door draws our attention. "Hey, you guys up? We're headed down for breakfast," Adam's voice calls out from the other side.

"We ate already. We'll meet up with you all afterwards," David answers for us both. As he settles back on the bed, his eyes fall on the table and the ink and paper I have left out. "What's that?"

"I was writing letters home, letting my family know we arrived safely," I tell him.

"So, you left out the parts with the deadly snake and evil ghost?" he asks pointedly.

"...Well not in the one to Ragnar and Nylan," I admit.

"That reminds me. Can I use some of that?" He sits up straight, pointing to my writing supplies.

"Of course. Who are you going to write to?" *His parents?*

"I made a deal with Nylan," is the only answer I get as he crawls over me and off the bed, once again hissing when he makes to sit in the wooden chair.

Amused, I watch as my pup puts pen to paper and begins no doubt writing out his own version of the past few days' events. By the time he has finished, I am freshly showered, having run downstairs to fill both sets of buckets while my pup worked. Getting dressed while he showers himself, I gather all four letters together and place them in my bag. The post office will likely be closed today, but we can stop by before we leave Terraday morning. They will have envelopes and seals.

Once my pup is dressed (with a fresh blue jockstrap underneath his clothes), I open our door a crack, signaling to the others that we are decent. It is only a few minutes before we have our first visitor, Michael timidly rapping his fingers against the door, opening it farther.

"Come in," I tell him as David moves to sit next to me on the bed, freeing the chair for his brother.

"Morning," he greets us, taking the empty seat.

"Morning," David repeats.

"Good morning," I follow.

"So, the mayor left us a pretty sizable reward. Over 200 gold." *That is a lot.* "I think we were all gonna head out and check out the festivities soon, but first I wanted to know if we could finally talk about the whole..."

"Dying thing?" David finishes.

"You make it sound like it's nothing." The brown-haired twin shakes his head.

"It's just still kinda hard for me to believe." David sighs, leaning forward. "It happened about two-and-a-half weeks ago. Although I guess everything really started two months before that, when we were arrested."

"Is that how you're connected to this, Khazak?" Michael asks me directly.

"Khazak didn't have anything to do with my death," David quickly corrects his brother. "He was there because we were captured together. He probably would have been killed right after me if it had stuck."

"Sorry, I didn't mean like that," he apologizes.

"It is alright." I did not sense any animosity in the question, for once. "What I believe David meant was that the location he was killed was the same location I arrested him in."

"Yeah. The Temple of Zeus." David nods his head. "The weird stuff started before he arrested us, before he even got there. There was this magical altar, and a sound coming from it that only I could hear. But in the confusion of everything that happened after, I didn't think about it again for months."

"That's when I was working with Khazak." David clasps his hand on my thigh. "Things started happening in town. Robberies, assaults, and then eventually...a bombing. They hurt people, Mike. And we didn't figure out what they really had planned, how it was all connected, until the night I died."

"We had been in the forest on patrol that night," David continues his explanation. "We weren't even supposed to be out there actually. We were covering for some friends of ours when our camp was attacked. We thought they were looking for the two of us and barely escaped, but then I walked us right into a trap."

"You had no way of knowing what they had planned," I attempt to reassure him. "We were completely outnumbered."

"They caught us, and that's when we found out they were actually looking for our friends," David moves on to the next part of the tale. "They tried really hard to get the information out of us. Worked us over real good, but when that wasn't working, they threatened Khazak's life, and I broke down and told them. Our friends were captured not long after that."

"David, I think you did what any of us would in that situation." I am happy to hear Michael also attempt to console his twin.

"I'm not saying I blame myself. It's just..." David stops, shaking his head once before continuing. "There's a lot more. That altar with the noise I kept hearing? It was a sacrificial altar. They were planning on sacrificing our friends."

"These people weren't just criminals. They were a cult," I step in, giving David a moment to compose himself. "They were our friends, even people we worked with. And they were being led by a man who wielded a lot of power and influence in my city's government. The bombing had been a distraction, and their real target that night was David's sword. It was originally discovered in the same temple and was apparently connected to the sacrificial ritual. Much later, after all the dust had settled, I found a message from the city's historians detailing the sword as the main item missing from the vault. It had been stolen the night of the bombing, and one of my deputies, who was a member of the cult, had hidden the message from me to hide their goals."

"Because the temple had been built by ancient elves, the cult thought that the sacrifice required elf blood." David finds his voice. "Our friends, Nylan and Ragnar, who are both half-elf, were who they were really after. The cult leader had selected Nylan specifically because of some of some really fucked up personal reasons. He's Tsula's cousin, by the way. They pulled him up onto the altar, the sword was in the guy's hand. They were going to kill him. I had to do something."

"So, what did you do?" Michael presses for more.

"What I do best. Screw things up. Just, for other people this time." I frown at David's choice of words but allow him to go on. "We caused a distraction, and then I ran up to the altar and tackled the guy holding Nylan. He managed to run away in all the confusion, but before I even realized it..." David mimes stabbing himself in the chest.

"The cult leader killed you?" Michael requests clarification.

"His flunky, actually. Or his partner? I'm not really sure what their relationship was. The guy wasn't who he said he was and caused us a whole bunch of other problems outside of this," David grouses and shakes his head. "It was weird, you know? Maybe it was the shock, but it didn't really hurt. I didn't even realize what had happened until I looked down and saw the sword sticking out of my chest." Maybe it is because of Michael's presence, but this is the most I have ever heard David talk about his death, and I remain silent so that he will continue. "Then it was like everything slowed down. I *knew* I was dying and that there was nothing I could do about it. I couldn't breathe. I could barely stand up. Everything got cold, and dark, and then..." David pauses, worrying his lip like he is lost in thought.

"What happened?" Michael asks quietly.

"The next thing I can remember is waking up," David continues after some hesitation. "Only it wasn't just me. It was like I was filled with all this anger. All I could feel was rage. I wanted to hurt these people, make them pay. And I knew stuff, too. Like about the sword, what it's called, how to use it. That it was...mine."

"You also spoke in a language I'm certain is foreign to both of us," I remind him.

"I did?" He looks at me in surprise, evidently not remembering that part. "A lot of that night is a blur. I started fighting, I was faster, stronger, but I... I hurt a lot of people,

Mike. I don't even really remember how it stopped. One minute I was fighting, and the next I was staring at Khazak, right before everything went black again."

"He was unconscious for four days," I finish the story. "We brought him to a healer, but they were unable to find anything wrong with him physically, only the scars on his chest and back. We could not determine anything, magical or otherwise, about how he was resurrected."

"Yeah, they gave me a clean bill of health when I woke up, but that's all we knew." David shrugs.

Michael stands from his chair to hug his brother. "I'm just glad you're alright."

"Yeah, me too," David returns his twin's hug.

"So, if you were in the same place for months before this, why couldn't my scrying spells find you?" Michael asks, retaking his seat.

"My city is...hidden from the general public," I answer. "There are powerful wards in place against scrying and spells that would reveal our location."

"A hidden city? Really?" Michael's eyes widen. "I guess at least that makes sense. So, what are you doing now? Why did you come here?"

"The group of researchers who first inspected the ruins came from Pákannon," I start to fill Michael in, happy to have any additional assistance on this we can get. "They wrote a report detailing their findings, and we came to get a copy for ourselves. Unfortunately, it is in Elvish, so Tsula has actually been helping us to translate it the past few days."

"Nylan's mom and dad are the ones who led the team inspecting the ruins—so, Tsula's aunt and uncle," David tells him next. "Some of the people on the team are dead now, and none of them live here anymore, so our next stop is to head north to..."

"Manamequohi," I finish his sentence.

"That place," David says as he points at me. "That's where Nylan's dad lives now, and if anyone knows more about the temple, it's him."

"What about his mom?" Michael questions next.

"She died twenty years ago," David answers somberly. "The cult leader was involved. It's part of why he 'picked' Nylan to sacrifice first."

"Sounds like a real piece of shit," Michael declares. "It's a good thing you stopped him."

"Yeah. He's...dead now," David responds hesitantly.

"But that other guy's still out there, right? The one who actually killed you?" He waits for David to nod. "Good, then there's still someone who's ass I get to kick." He crosses his arms. "There's one thing I still don't understand. What was the cult trying to accomplish? What was the ritual supposed to do?"

"In exchange for the sacrifice, they expected to receive some sort of *gifts* from the gods, I think perhaps similar to the increased speed and strength David mentioned. His resurrection was a surprise to all of them—they did not anticipate that it would be the person sacrificed that would be gifted." I still remember Redwish muttering a shocked *"impossible"* just before he fled. "The final section of the report detailed theories about the purpose and method of the ritual, but last we spoke, Tsula was still reading through it."

"She's really been helping you guys out, huh?" Michael smiles when he talks about the girl he obviously has a crush on.

"She has been very insightful and an invaluable resource." I nod my head. "Part of the report details the various Olympian myths inscribed on the temple's walls. The archaeologists were able to pinpoint all of them except for one—one that Tsula theorized may in fact be about David and the events that happened in the temple."

"She does?" both men say in unison, intrigued by that information.

"There's more," I continue to relay information David was not able to hear himself two days ago. "If the report is to be believed, then the sword David is carrying is not just any magical sword, but a weapon of legend. I am not even sure it was forged on Terra."

"The Harpe," David drops the weapon's name.

"Wait, the *Harpe*?" Michael's eyes widen. "Like from the old stories Yaya used to tell us?"

"Weird, right?" David confirms with his brother. "I thought about Grandma Yaya, too."

"No, David, just Yaya." Michael looks at his brother incredulously. "You...do know we're a quarter Olympian on mom's side, right?"

"Uhhh..." David draws a blank. "...Yes?"

"Yaya wasn't her name. It's an Olympian nickname that *means* Grandma," Michael explains in the face of his brother's obvious lie. "Mom's maiden name was Theodopoulos."

"Oh," David states blankly.

"That's why she used to tell us all those stories. They were from when she was a little girl." Michael shakes his head. "She was born in Olympia and lived there until she was a teenager when her family moved to Roma Alba. When she got older, she met and married our grandfather, but she was pregnant with Mom right when things started to get really bad there politically. They wanted to leave, but Yaya was the only one to make it out. Our grandfather—she called him Papou when she would talk to us about him—died getting her on the boat to Lutheria."

"Wow." David and I are both stunned by the depth of the story. "How come you know all of this and I don't?" *Alright, maybe just me.*

"I dunno. I listen when people are talking?" Michael cocks an eyebrow at his less-attentive brother.

David narrows his eyes at the dig. "Alright, smartass. Then what are you saying?"

"I dunno." Michael shrugs. "I wanna look at the report and talk to Tsula first, but it's a pretty weird coincidence."

One more strange occurrence to add to the ever-growing pile of mystery that is David, though it at least feels like we are getting closer to solving it. "I suppose it is a good thing we are all traveling to the same place so that now you are also able to help us." I try to lighten the mood.

"What were you guys originally looking for, anyway?" Michael asks David next. "In the temple, when you were arrested."

"We'd gotten a lead that there was something powerful there, some kind of artifact or something." David something. "I guess we found it. Or at least I did."

"Don't worry, D. We'll figure it out," Michael assures his brother. "Alright, I'm pretty sure everyone's waiting for us, so I'm gonna go grab my stuff. Meet you guys downstairs?"

"Yeah, we'll be right down," David tells his brother as he stands.

"Wait." As he turns to leave, Michael pauses, sniffing the air before his eyes land on the empty, grease-covered plate that once held our breakfast. "Where'd you guys get *bacon*?"

"That was all Khazak." David pats his belly with a satisfied grin.

"I want bacon," Michael whines, exactly like his brother.

"Then go find your own bacon-carrying orc," David taunts as he closes the door behind him. As soon as we are alone, he jumps back on the bed, flat on his back. With a chuckle, I join him.

"I think that went pretty well." It was certainly the most pleasant conversation I have had with the man.

"Yeah, there was a lot less yelling or talking about Mom and Dad than I expected," David agrees.

"I was curious about something." I turn my head toward his, taking the opportunity to probe my pup for some personal info. "His nickname for you. 'D?' Just the letter?"

"Oh, yeah, that," he says with a soft laugh, before biting his lip. "Alright, I'll tell you where it came from, but you have to promise not to say anything to anyone, okay?"

"I promise." Now I am even more curious.

"Okay, so when we were *really* little, like just starting school, Mike had a lisp. A really bad one," David starts to tell me. "He couldn't say his 'f's or 'v's, so 'David' would become 'Dawid.' Sometimes, other kids would hear him and make fun of him, and it would make him so sad. It just made me angry. So, one day I told him that he could just call me 'D.' And then I punched Darryl in his stupid six-year-old face."

"That is a sweet story, even with the child face punching." I cannot help the smile on my face, imagining the two of them as children, David rushing in to protect his brother from bullies.

"Thanks." He smiles, giving me a quick peck on the lips. "But seriously, you can't say anything. He still gets really embarrassed about it."

"My lips are sealed." I push myself up and off the bed, offering him a hand to help him stand. "Shall we join our friends?"

After putting on our footwear and grabbing my satchel, we leave our room and head down the stairs to find most of our group sitting and waiting. Once everyone has been gathered, we exit the inn, walking out into a bright, sunny day. It is late in the morning, just before 11, so we still have a couple of hours before the lunch feast is to take place.

We wander the town streets together, taking in the sights. The decorations are out in full force as are the citizens, dressed in bright blues and yellows. There are booths set up with small games of chance or skill for children—things like a walnut and shell game and a small archery range. Other booths are serving fruit juices and small fried confectionary treats shaped like—you guessed it—the sun. People are enjoying themselves all around us.

Once it is nearly time, we make our way toward the town square. The bonfire is burning as brightly as always, but all around the rest of the square and leading down the road toward the Council House are dozens of long tables, many already laden with food. No one is eating yet, and many covered trays are still being brought to other tables, but you can smell the oncoming feast.

Tsula and her family spot us, calling us over and asking us to sit with them. Her mother and father are just as pleasant as I remember them, and the girl herself is in bright spirits, especially when Michael begins to talk her ear off regarding the report. I make a note to speak with her myself regarding the final portion before the evening's festivities begin.

When the tables are all filled and seats finally taken—including by the people who have been working the festival—Mayor Elajor steps onto a small stage that has been set up in front of the Council House. He speaks to the gathered crowd, though it is in Pákagi so I do not catch much of it. His cadence makes it sounds like a prepared speech, one that makes the people around us nod and smile politely. Then toward the end, he gestures in our table's direction, causing many people to turn and look, a few even clapping.

"He just told them about sending us to Karthani and fighting the uktena," Tsula translates. "He wants to plan numerous expeditions to explore the ruins now that they are 'safe.'"

"Something he is taking full credit for, I'm sure," I say with a wry smile.

"At least we got paid," Liss adds.

After the mayor wraps up his speech, the feast can finally begin. Our tables are covered in trays and platters filled with all sorts of foods. There are roasted ears of corn, potato stew, and a salad made with mushrooms and wild greens. As delicious as those things sound, I am far more interested in the meats: turkey, grilled trout, and a venison roast.

As we eat our fill, our neighbors around us begin to talk to one another. As Tsula explains, one of the traditions of this festival is for people to share stories of their travels and experiences over the past year, a fitting topic for our group. Though the language barrier is an issue for most of us, my companions and I share what we can about our journey so far: the humans traveling across the ocean, our hike here from the south, even some of our adventure in Karthani. Noting that the mayor did not seem to mention it, and remembering Tsula's comments about the town being superstitious, I make sure to leave out any details concerning our ghostly encounter.

A few hours later, after the meal has ended and we have finished assisting with the cleanup, we walk around the city once more, letting the food settle in our stomachs. We retire to the inn after that, resting and chatting in the common area, conserving our energy for the night's activities. There are a lot of people here doing the same thing, and I even see the two strange men from the dining room, though they don't appear to be as jovial as the rest of the crowd. They've at least changed out of their strange black uniforms.

"Tsula," I turn in my chair, facing the shy elf girl who came back to the inn with us. "Were you able to finish reading the report?"

"Yes, I was," she tells me with a nod of her head. "It wasn't as useful as I would have hoped. They were able to determine a few things, like that the spells on the altar connected our plane to the astral plane with the sword acting as a component. They ran a lot of tests, but almost all of them came back inconclusive. They did learn that altar would react to blood, but with the small amounts they tried, nothing happened. Then the rest of the section is just a lot of theories. Some of them wanted to try testing with animal sacrifices—because obviously they didn't want to sacrifice any *people*—but most of the researchers weren't willing to do that. And I don't blame them. That seems pretty cruel."

"They may not have done it, but I know others did," I say with an unhappy sigh. "The cult leaders... I know they sacrificed a human before, and I would venture a guess that they probably tried an orc, and maybe others, as well."

"That's...awful," Michael comments from his spot next to Tsula. "What is wrong with people?"

"I wish I could tell you, bro." David shakes his head.

"Oh! The inscription!" Tsula says with sudden realization already rifling through her bag. "I never told you the full thing. I wrote it down somewhere."

"Inscription?" David looks at me with the question.

"The inscription on the basin was only part of a larger piece of text found on the wall," I explain. "It might be connected to you, in fact."

"Really?" David looks to Tsula, who finally pulls a piece of paper from her bag in triumph.

"Here we are!" She straightens it out. "When the Fates are blind and the gates are closed, only blood spilled in sacrifice can restore the strength of the gods. Oceans will split where the caged abyss bleeds and goat will fight eagle as the wolves' maws grow wide."

She puts down the paper as we all stare at her in stunned silence. I am…not sure what to make of that.

"What?" Neither is David, apparently.

"'Blood spilled in sacrifice?' That's gotta be about you, right?" Michael asks his twin.

"How would I know?" David responds, crossing his arms. "Lots of people get sacrificed."

"Do lots of them also come back from the dead?" Michael rolls his eyes.

"We are just trying to understand this, David." I try a less sarcastic approach.

"Can we talk about this later? Please?" He pleads with both of us. "We're supposed to be having fun today."

"Alright, fine, we can talk about it later," Michael says with a sigh. "I want to read through it myself anyway."

After some lighter conversation and with our bellies still full, David and I go upstairs to take a nap—something he calls a "food coma"—waking up not long before sunset. After freshening up, we find our friends and rejoin the festival outside. After the extremely large lunch we had, we settle on some simple cart food for dinner—you really cannot go wrong with meat on a stick.

The nighttime festivities are more along the lines of what I am used to, some of it even reminding me of the annual *Uzu'gor* festival back home, though with fewer people in revealing clothing or public sex. There are stages with bands set up at various parts of the city, booths and bars selling alcohol outdoors, and lots of people dancing. Taking a cue from my best friend Ragnar, I make David wait until I get at least two drinks in me before I acquiesce to his request to dance together.

Adequately inebriated, I join David on the dancefloor feeling far less self-conscious than I normally would. Maybe it is the alcohol, or maybe it is the knowledge that I will likely never see most of these people again, but I am able to let go and enjoy myself. All around us, our friends seem to do the same. Adam and Riley both seem fairly popular with some of the local women, Liss and Nate find a dark corner to sneak off to, and at one point I even see Corrine and Tsula dancing together, cheeks flushed red from alcohol.

David is certainly having no issues letting go—though he also misses the strange looks I catch his brother giving us on occasion when we make eye contact. I do not think much of it, not until later when David is off relieving himself and I am at the bar getting us both a refill of the fermented grape-and-apricot flavored drink we have been enjoying.

"Hey, sorry for all the weird looks." I turn my head to see Michael at my side. "I'm just not used to seeing him dance with a guy. Or like...*that*."

As the night has progressed, David's dancing has gotten progressively more...wanton. Pushing his ass back against me, grinding our crotches together, rarely taking his hands—and sometimes his mouth—off of me. I assume that is what Michael is referring to. "Apology accepted. Do not take this personally, but I think that the alcohol may have caused him to forget that his relative might be watching him."

"Yeah, once he starts drinking the fucks he gives usually go right out the window," he jokes, sounding slightly tipsy himself. "So. He told me he loves you."

"Oh." The information makes me smile without thinking. "Well, that is nice to hear. I love him, too."

"Good." Michael smiles. "I think this is the part where I'm supposed to threaten you bodily harm or something if you hurt him? I don't know. I've never done this before."

"I am not sure he would agree with the necessity, but I understand the sentiment," I tell him with a laugh. "I promise I intend to take good care of your brother."

"That's good to hear," he says with a nod. "Alright, so seeing as I'm really not interested in seeing David try to fuck you on the dancefloor, Tsula and I were going to walk around, maybe find another place to dance for a bit. See you guys back at the inn?"

"You two enjoy yourselves. We will see you later." It is very tempting to send him off with some sort of comment about using a contraception spell, but I want this man to like me. I watch as he walks off with Tsula, the two disappearing into the crowd. I turn back to the bar and finally get our two refills, and just as I am about to look for David, I notice Adam sidling up to the bar himself.

"Hey, you guys having fun?" he asks me as he leans over to get the bartender's attention.

"Oh yes, quite a lot." I take a sip of one of the drinks in my hands. "Seems like you are having a decent amount yourself."

"Yeah, nice girls," he tells me with a chuckle and a nod. "Most of them still live with their parents though, so I don't think we'll be doing much more than dancing tonight. Which is fine. You know, don't wanna get a reputation around here if we ever have to come back."

"Well, that is too bad." *For those girls that is.* I put down one of the drinks and reach into my pocket, putting another plan in motion. "Perhaps later, if David and I happen to find you in our room, we might be able to do something about that." I slide our room key across the bar toward Adam. I think that all three of us could stand to blow off some steam tonight, as David would say.

He ponders it for a moment, amused, before picking it up. "I'll make sure you see me leave," he tells me with a wink as he slides it into his own pocket.

I raise my glass to him in a silent toast, leaving him to get his drink and me to find my pup. I spot David on the dance-floor sandwiched between Piper and Corrine, the latter of whom is dancing far more provocatively than I would have thought possible. Happily taking one of the drinks, I join him in dancing with the two girls and then with each other. It is about forty-five minutes later when I notice Adam on the edge of the dancefloor, giving me a nod when we make eye-contact before slinking off in the direction of the inn. I decide to give the man a ten-minute head start before we follow.

"Puppy," I growl low in his ear, grinding my already engorged member against his ass. "With everyone out here dancing, how would you like to go back to our room?"

David responds by pushing back against me, turning his head and pulling me in for a kiss. I growl again, biting at his lips as he tries to suck my tongue into his mouth. *Question answered.* Without a second thought to those around us, we leave the dancefloor hand-in-hand, practically sprinting toward the inn. As we stumble our way up the stairs, my pup is so in the moment that he does not notice the door is already unlocked.

"There you are. I was starting to wonder if you guys were standing me up," the blonde tells us as we enter the room, standing from his seat on the bed.

"Adam? What are you doing here?" David is under-standably surprised by Adam's presence.

"Well, I was kinda striking out with the girls on the dancefloor, so your...*owner* here offered me your services instead," he responds with just a hint of cockiness as he closes the distance to David, who is blushing furiously at his words.

"I—I—" he stammers.

"David, hey." Adam's expression sobers. "First and foremost, you're my friend. My best friend. If you don't want to do this, if it's too weird, then just say the word and we stop. I'll head back to my room, and we can pretend this never happened."

A series of emotions passes over my pup's face—confusion, understanding, lust—before finally settling on determination. Wordlessly, he sinks to his knees in front of his friend.

"You know that wasn't a challenge, right?" Adam gives him a questioning look.

"I would save your breath on that one," I interject. If there was anyone who could turn sex into a competition, it would be David.

"So, are we doing this..." There's a brief pause before David finishes. "...sir?"

"That's gonna take some getting used to," Adam says with a shake of his head. "Alright, how *do* we do this?"

"What, you need help figuring out how to take it out or something?" David snarks from his spot floor, and I am too amused to correct him.

"Is he usually this mouthy?" Adam asks me.

"There's a pretty easy way to fix that, you know." David wiggles his eyebrows, and I cannot help myself, snorting a laugh at my pup's joke.

Adam only rolls his eyes while wearing an annoyed smile, hands already moving to undo the front of his pants. Reaching in through his open fly, he pulls out his cock, already hard from a night of dancing with attractive women, and probably some anticipation over this. Eye-level with it, David reaches a tentative hand toward the appendage as it twitches in the air.

"You were right, Sir," David tells me as he wraps his fingers around it. "He does have a nice-looking dick."

"Thank you?" Adam accepts the compliment unsurely.

"My pleasure," I respond, stepping up to Adam's side and fishing out my own erection.

After stroking him a few more times, David finally leans forward, opening his mouth and wrapping his lips around Adam's shaft. The blonde reacts with a sharp intake of breath before relaxing as David takes more of him in. Seeing me move closer, David reaches one hand in my direction blindly. Grasping his wrist, I guide him to his target, allowing him to stroke me in rhythm to the movements of his mouth on Adam.

As he is swallowed, I watch Adam's face for reactions, seeing a mixture of surprise and pleasure. I suppose hearing or talking about having sex with your best friend is different from actually participating. He makes no attempt to end things, though. David is harder to read, with his mouth stuffed and eyes half-closed. If he was feeling any nerves after Adam's appearance, I suspect they have been buried by his libido, which will only be made stronger the longer he is in chastity.

Satisfied with Adam for now, David pulls off him completely and turns his head toward me. I let out a content sigh as the warm heat surrounds me, my pup easily taking in half my length. His hand covers and strokes the remaining half while he does the same with his other hand on Adam, whose eyes are locked onto my erection as it disappears into David's mouth. I have always enjoyed being watched during sex, and this provides me an opportunity to show Adam how to properly use a boy like David.

"Do not be afraid to get rough with him," I tell the blonde as I move one hand to the back of David's head, who looks up at me questioningly. "He can handle quite a bit."

To demonstrate, I grip David by the hair and pull him all the way down my erection. His eyes go wide as his throat is filled, but he does not fight me, only his gag reflex. Adam watches in fascination, his own cock twitching. I fuck David's face for a few moments with the full length of my dick until his eyes start to water. Then I let him pull off with a *pop*, face red as he catches his breath.

"Wow. Can I try?" Adam asks me now that my pup's mouth is free.

"By all means." I bow slightly, gesturing to David.

David looks like he wants to respond to my given permission, but Adam is already hauling him toward his cock. Adam pushes his way into the open mouth, not stopping until David's nose is buried in the forest of golden hair covering his crotch. Taking a cue from me, Adam fucks his face, starting slow but picking up speed as he grows more confident. This is not meant as a criticism, but as he has a slightly shorter and thinner cock, it is easier for David to handle.

We pass David back and forth like this for a few minutes, giving him time to breathe but not speak as we plunder his oral orifice. As he flips back and forth, the two of us still standing subconsciously move closer to each other until I feel Adam brushing against me. Looking over, I catch his eyes, heavy with desire, and I am sure mine match. Tentatively wrapping my arm around his shoulder, I bring us closer together, inching our faces toward each other.

Our lips meet in a kiss that is all tongue and teeth, a low growl escaping my throat. Unlike David, Adam is an aggressive kisser like myself, something I should have anticipated. Our kiss becomes a small fight for dominance—one I have to be cautious about because between my tusks and naturally sharper canines, I could do some real damage without intending to. Our lips and teeth continue to clash as our erections are sucked and stroked until we break, faces and lips flushed.

"Okay, that was fucking hot," David says breathlessly, stroking us both as he looks up.

Arm still around him, I give Adam an amused smile, while he looks back with a cocky grin as David resumes his back-and-forth oral ministrations. With less aggressive input from either of us, he is able to work at his own pace, no less eager but a lot less red-faced. As happy as I am to share my pup's mouth, he has many other talents (and another hole) that I would like to make use of.

"So," I turn to Adam as David switches from my prick to his. "Would you like to fuck him?"

Hearing my question, David pauses, watching Adam for an answer while his mouth is still full of almost half of the other man's cock.

"I've never actually fucked another guy before," he admits. "But I think I'd like to."

"David, strip," I order with a pleased smile.

David stands to obey, unbuttoning the top few buttons on his shirt before pulling it over his head and laying it over the back of the room's chair. Adam and I start to undress ourselves as he works. Still turned around, his hands move to his belt and pants, unbuckling and opening them before shoving them down to his ankles. As he bends over to pull his pants off his feet, the blonde man takes notice of his recently spanked rump.

"What happened to your ass?" he asks David bluntly.

"Uh..." David straightens out, the rest of his body turning as red as his ass while he thinks of a way to explain.

"Yes David, what *did* happen to your ass?" I cannot help myself.

"...Remember when I yelled at Khazak in the river?" David grumbles while Adam nods yes. "It's because of that."

"He *spanked* you?" Adam does not hold back the small laugh that escapes with his question.

David narrows his eyes in challenge. "You wanna fuck me or not?"

"Alright, sorry. Just remind me not to piss you off, Khazak." Adam puts both his hands in the air before his eyes go down to David's jockstrap. "Interesting underwear. You gonna take 'em off? Kinda weird that you're the only one still wearing something."

"I mean with the open back, I don't really need to..." He tries to play it off, not wanting to reveal what is underneath.

Too bad for him that I do not share that sentiment. "Take off your underwear, David."

David gives me a half-glare until, with a huff, he hooks both of his thumbs in his jockstrap and pulls it down, revealing his locked-up cock underneath. He is hard, or at least is trying to be, visibly straining against the cage. Precum has gathered near the head, and I am sure it won't be long before he's dripping a steady stream.

"What is *that*?" Adam asks, eyes wide.

"A chastity cage," I respond. "After the calm and constructive conversation we had in the river, I felt he needed a reminder beyond the spanking."

"Does it hurt?" Adam asks David, eyes never leaving the cage.

"It can get a little uncomfortable, but no, not really," David answers with a sigh.

"David, why don't you get on the bed?" I instruct him while I go to my bag for our needed supplies—lubricant and the cleansing charm.

"How do you..." David stands near the bed, unsure of how he should be positioning himself.

"Maybe we can try on your back to start?" Adam offers.

With a nod, David sits on the bed before lying flat on his back. I move over to press the charm to his lower stomach so it can work its magic. Once that is finished, I lift both of his legs, exposing the hole that Adam will be entering for the first time. I open the bottle of oil, nodding for Adam to move closer while I dribble some onto my fingers, encouraging him to do the same.

"The charm cleaned him out, but we still ended to make sure he's adequately stretched," I explain to the first-time fucker, at least of men.

I push a slick finger into David's hole, hearing him groan as the ring of muscle is forced to expand. After fucking him with it for a few moments, I pull out so that Adam can try for himself. His face is locked onto David's, watching his expressions as he is opened up. After a bit I encourage Adam to add a second, and then even a third, each new digit pulling even more pleasurable noises from David.

"So open, but it still feels tight..." the blond comments absentmindedly as he removes his fingers.

Adam uses the oil one more time, slicking it over his erection with his fist. I move onto the bed near David's head, helping to hold back his legs as he is dragged toward the edge. Once everyone is ready and in position, Adam steps between David's legs, eyes locked on the tight hole in front of him. Cock still in hand, he inches forward, pushing the head against David's hole until the muscle gives way to the pressure and it pops in.

David's legs twitch slightly as he is penetrated, both his hands at his sides on the bed. Still watching his face for any discomfort, Adam presses the rest of the way inside, not stopping until his golden pubic hair is brushing against the black of my pup's. He grips the backs of David's thighs for purchase, pushing them down and back with his weight. For a man who has not done this before, I am impressed with his self-control. Many would have started pounding away by now.

"Are you alright?" Adam asks his best friend, who he is now fully inside of.

"Oh yeah." David sighs happily. "That's nice."

Nodding to himself, Adam starts to slowly pull back about halfway before slowly pushing back in. He fucks David with slow, tentative strokes, watching carefully for reactions. Gradually, he picks up speed, though I must admit it feels almost achingly slow to watch. While contemplating, I feel a hand on my crotch, looking down to see one of David's hands wrapping around me and squeezing gently.

"You can go faster, if you want," David informs Adam.

"I just wanted to make sure I wasn't going to hurt you or anything," he answers honestly.

"No offense dude, but if I can handle this thing," David wiggles my erection for emphasis, "then I can handle what you're packin'."

I see the challenge cross over Adam's face before David has even closed his mouth. Without saying a word, his grip on David's thighs tightens as he starts to snap his hips quicker. David bites his lip as a whimper escapes. Maybe I was wrong about him being the one to turn sex into a contest. *These two really are best friends.*

As Adam fucks him more confidently, David strokes my cock, turning his head to try and take it in his mouth. I move around the bed on my knees so I'm facing him, allowing me to push my cock inside with his head laid sideways. I cannot go terribly deep at this angle, but its more than enough to shallowly fuck the first seven or eight centimeters of my length between his lips.

Stuffed at both ends, David is now at the mercy of his two tops. While I enjoy the wet heat of his mouth, Adam fucks him with stronger and faster thrusts, the slap of their skins meeting echoing through the room. David's moans are muffled by my cock, but there is no doubt that he is enjoying himself. I watch Adam's wet prick disappear into his hole over and over, David's toes starting to curl from pleasure. *He is getting close.* It only takes a few more strokes for the orgasm to hit, David groaning loudly around me.

"Whoa, what just happened?" Adam stops moving, looking down confused. "It was like he started tightening up and then pushed out all of a sudden."

"That was an orgasm. A prostate orgasm," I start to say, looking down at my pup. "One of the reasons I suspect David does not actually mind the cage that much." He can only look up at me, innocently batting his eyes.

"So, he just came?" Adam clarifies.

"Essentially, though as you can see, without actual cum." I point out David's relatively clean crotch. "He will have several more before the night is over."

Adam seems to accept my explanation, nodding to himself as he resumes his fuck. I will have to explain more about those orgasms later. Perhaps he will even want to experience one for himself... I shake away the thought, not wanting to get ahead of myself seeing as we only just got the man in our bed. While David continues dealing with two cocks, I lean over his body to Adam, capturing his mouth in another hungry kiss.

"Fuck, I think I'm gonna cum," Adam announces a minute later when he breaks our liplock.

I watch the man's face screw up in concentration as he fucks David even harder. His eyes are closed, blonde hair matted to his forehead. His body is covered in a sheen of sweat, some of it dripping down the muscles of his chest and over his stomach. The smell of sex has filled the room, and David is moaning almost continuously.

Finally, with a loud grunt, Adam hits his peak, slamming his cock all the way home, almost doubled over David's body. The muscles of his stomach twitch as he unloads, his hips continuing to move and jerk with each shot, arms flexing as he holds David in place. I almost wish I was behind him because I bet his ass looks amazing right now as well.

"Wow," is all he manages to say, pulling out on unsteady legs. David whimpers at the loss and allows Adam to set his feet down on the floor.

"I had the same thoughts after our first time," I joke, ready to swap places.

While Adam takes a seat on the bed next to David, I pull my cock from his mouth and shuffle off the bed. Grabbing the oil, I lubricate my cock quickly before stepping between David's legs. Lifting them once more, I stroke my cock a few times as I inspect my target: David's hole. Puffy and red from use, a trickle of white dribbles down his rim, Adam's load already starting to leak out. *Only one way to fix that.* Pressing my cock against his entrance, I lean my weight forward and push inside.

Fuck, that is a nice feeling. Not just tight and warm, but with an added layer of slickness from Adam's seed. I lazily pump my hips in and out, just enjoying the sensations. The last time we did something like this was David's birthday, when I had a number of our friends over to celebrate just like this. I never would have guessed that our team leader would have wanted to be on the guest list.

Satisfied with his slippery hole, I start to fuck David faster, loving the way the pink ring swallows up my thick green club. He's already opened up, and I love seeing the way his hole grips me when I pull out, as if it did not want me to leave. I press right back in, watching my length disappear once more. Adam is looking intensely at the same thing, eyes full of curiosity and still hooded by lust, despite his recent orgasm. As David starts to moan once more, I feel his hole start to twitch, and I know he is close to another orgasm himself.

"Again?" Adam asks when David's body starts to convulse once more as he moans into the open air.

"Not the last, either," I point out as I continue pumping my hips.

I bring my hand down, stroking it against David's face, who is looking back up at me with hungry eyes. He takes hold of my hand, bringing my thumb to his mouth and sucking it inside, while his other hand clutches the bedsheet tightly as he whimpers in time with the pumping of my hips. He's nearly crossed over that line, the one where his hole starts to cum almost uncontrollably. I fuck David with deep, long strokes as I feel things building once more, pushing all the way in and holding myself in place when he cums again.

Needing a change of positions, I pull out and quickly flip David over, manhandling him onto his hands and knees. Stepping up behind him, I push back into his ass, eliciting a loud groan in response. Adam kneels up on the bed so he can get a better view of me turning out David's hole. As I fuck faster and harder, he moves one hand to David's ass, holding him open while my cock further plumbs his depths.

I can feel that I'm getting close myself, David's hole working to milk me just as it did Adam. The blonde moves up the bed, inserting his once more growing cock into David's waiting mouth. Filled in both holes by two tops for the second time tonight, David can do little else but what we want, which I have a feeling is exactly how *he* wants it. Looking at his lips wrapped around Adam and his ass around my cock, I finally reach my limit.

I slam forward with a growl, my grip on David's hips tight enough to leave bruises. I feel my prick pulse with each volley of cum I shoot inside of him, adding my load to

Adam's and pushing both of them even deeper. I look down as I hold him against me, David's bright red ass pressed tightly to my green thighs. Finally finished and thoroughly exerted, I let out a groan, still lodged firmly in my pup's hole.

"So," David tries to speak as though he is not completely out of breath, one hand still on Adam's nearly-rock hard prick. "You guys up for round two?"

"Clean bill of health!" David cheers as we exit the healer's office. "See? Told you there was nothing to worry about."

"I'm just glad we have actual confirmation of that now," Corrine responds with an amused tone.

It is Terraday, the day after the Summer Solstice and the first day of Cancea. The activities between myself, David, and Adam lasted late into the night, both of us using David in all manner of positions until he and I were thoroughly "drained," and he returned to his own room. We probably allowed things to go later than they should have given everything we needed to do today.

It is late in the morning, nearly noon, but we have accomplished a lot. Shortly after breakfast, our group of nine split up to take care of our various needs around the city. With our reward from the mayor, new supplies have been purchased, weapons and armor repaired, clothes washed, and hair has been cut. David and I stopped by the post office to send out our letters shortly before bringing him here with Corrine to the healer's office.

Finished with the healer, the three of us head for the bonfire in the center of town where we are due to meet back up with the others. When we arrive, I spot Adam and Liss sitting on a bench with Riley and Piper on another. Michael, however, is walking around and seems to be actively looking for someone. Someone who is not any of us, as when we make eye contact, he continues looking.

"Hey everyone." David greets them with a wave. "Are we almost ready to go? We still waiting on something?"

"Tsula," Adam answers. "She wanted to say goodbye to everyone."

"She told me last night that she'd meet us here at noon," Michael explains, still looking around.

"Oh yeah? You guys spend a lot of time together last night?" David nudges his brother with his elbow, wiggling his eyebrows.

"Not like *that*." Michael rolls his eyes. "She's a nice girl. We spent most of the night talking about the report. *You're welcome*, by the way." He hands the report in question over to David.

"It is almost noon now," I point out.

"We can wait another ten or fifteen minutes, but then we really gotta get going," Adam tells Michael.

"There she is!" Piper announces as she stands.

Looking in that direction she points, I can see Tsula heading toward us. Rushing, actually. She is carrying a large bag over one shoulder and a smaller one over the other. She looks exhausted, stressed, or both. When she finally reaches us, she is completely out of breath, needing a moment to compose herself before she actually speaks.

"So glad I made it in time. I was sure I would miss you," she says, still breathing heavily.

"Right on time," Michael tells her with a smile. "We were just getting ready to leave."

"That's something I was hoping to talk to you about." She starts to play with her braid nervously as she speaks. "The last few days have been some of the craziest of my life. The Spires activating, nearly getting eaten by the uktena, fighting and then freeing a *real* ghost. I've spent my entire life in this city, always too worried about what might be out there to venture very far from home. But...I don't think I'm afraid anymore. I know we just met, and I don't have even half of the experience the rest of you do, but I was wondering if it would be okay if I joined you on your journey to Manamequohi? Maybe even after if you'll have me?"

"Wow," Adam comments. "Are you sure? For all the excitement of the last couple of days, life on the road comes with a lot of downtime and walking. It can be downright boring at times."

"And it is a life that not all of those present have chosen willingly," Piper adds dryly.

"I'm positive." Tsula nods. "The downtime will give me time to read." She pats the bag at her side.

"Alright." Adam looks around at the rest of the group. "Should we vote?"

"We did not vote when I joined," I point out.

"No, you just negotiated for my ass," David mumbles too low for anyone else to hear.

"Didn't vote on the three of us joining either," Michael adds.

"Well alright then." Adam turns back to Tsula. "Looks like you're in."

"Yay!" she cheers. "Thank you so much. I promise you won't be disappointed."

"I don't think there was ever any doubt about that," Michael tells her with a soft smile.

"Welcome to the team," David tells her, a murmur of agreement spreading through the rest of us.

"Oh, I forgot to mention!" She lifts the bag in her hand. "My mother made lunch for us, sandwiches again, so we can eat on the road."

"Oh thank goodness," Piper declares. "Anything that will put off having to eat those bloody trail rations for a little longer."

Now officially a group of ten, we make our way out of the city, headed toward the northern gate. We exit without any issues, waving at the gate guards as we pass through. Once we are far enough from the city walls, I whistle loudly into the forest. Moments later, a familiar looking mass of black fur comes trotting out of the brush.

"There you are." I kneel down, stroking a hand through Sona's fur as she happily bounds up to me.

<Hello friend Khazak.> she "says" as she licks likes my face.

"Hey fuzzface," David greets her, amused.

"I have something for you," I tell the wolf as I reach into my satchel, pulling out a piece of roasted venison from yesterday's feast that I snuck into my bag. She takes it from my hand, chewing and swallowing before barking happily.

"Already spoiling your new pup, eh?" Riley teases, though he has no idea just how much I like to spoil my puppies.

"Aww, we're both new to the group, aren't we, girl?" Tsula bends over, hands on her knees as she speaks. I must say, it is nice to see the rest of the group being so welcoming to both Sona and Tsula.

"Now that we've got everyone back with us, we should get going," Adam informs us. "Manamequohi is a three-week hike from here."

"Are we going straight there?" Liss asks next.

"No, there are a few small villages and settlements we'll be able to stop at along the way. The biggest looks to be a halfling town called 'Rakatune' about ten-days north of here," Adam tells her with a shake of his head. "We'll stop, restock, and rest before we move on."

"Sounds like a plan, boss-man," David rhymes. "Let's go!"

Once more in agreement, our team moves into our traveling formation and starts on our journey north. It is hard to believe that days ago there were only six of us, and now we have almost doubled. More people mean more defenses when traveling in the open like this, but it can also lead to more interpersonal dramas, as me, David, and his brother can attest to.

While I think on how our group's dynamics may affect things, I feel something brushing against my hand, looking down just in time to see David take my hand in his. Looking into his green eyes, I feel him squeeze my hand as he smiles warmly, and it is like all my worries and concerns melt away. At least until he does the next thing I have to punish him for.

⬸━━━━━━━━━━━━━➤

Khazak, David, and the rest of their friends
will return in Steel & Thunder Book 4!

About the Author

Dominic N. Ashen is an author and avid reader with a heavy focus on gay BDSM-themed erotica. After spending his youth in search of books with characters who were more like himself—queer ones, specifically—he decided to start creating some of his own. His stories star queer protagonists, most often gay and bisexual men, and feature heavy themes of dominance, submission, and all sorts of kinks. Dominic loves the fantasy, sci-fi, and horror genres with a penchant for writing longer stories where he is able to weave in the sex and kink right alongside the plot.

https://www.dominicashen.com/

https://www.patreon.com/dominicashen

https://twitter.com/DomNAshen

https://www.facebook.com/dom.n.ashen

https://www.instagram.com/dom.n.ashen

4 Horsemen Publications

More from Dominic N. Ashen

Steel & Thunder
Storms & Sacrifice
& More to Come!

LGBT Erotica

Dominic N. Ashen
Steel & Thunder
Storms & Sacrifice
My Three Orc Dads: a Novella

Eskay Kabba
Hidden Love
Not So Hidden

Grayson Ace
How I Got Here
First Year Out of the Closet
You're Only a Top?
You're Only a Bottom?
I Think I'm a Serial Swiper

Lookin in All the Wrong Places
What Makes Me a Whore?
A Breach in Confidentiality
Back Door Pass
My European Adventure
An Unexpected Affair
Finding True Love

Leo Sparx
Before Alexander
Claiming Alexander
Taming Alexander
Saving Alexander
The Case of Armando

Erotica

Ali Whippe
Office Hours
Tutoring Center
Athletics
Extra Credit
Financial Aid
Bound for Release
Fetish Circuit
Now You See Him

Sexual Playground
Swingers

Chastity Veldt
Molly in Milwaukee
Irene in Indianapolis
Lydia in Louisville
Natasha in Nashville
Alyssa in Atlanta

4HORSEMENPUBLICATIONS.COM